Praise for these other novels by *New York Times* bestselling author Allison Brennan

"If you haven't been reading Brennan's truly exceptional Lucy Kincaid/Sean Rogan series, then you have been missing out . . . In this mind-blowing installment, Brennan also gives readers a fascinating look into the mindset of her epic villains. A chilling thrill-fest from beginning to end."

—*RT Book Reviews* (4½ stars, Top Pick!) on *No Good Deed*

"Allison Brennan reaches new heights in *Poisonous*, and this smart, sophisticated entry in the Maxine Revere series raises her to the level of Lisa Gardner and Harlan Coben." —*Providence Journal*

"A fast-paced, suspenseful read with interesting characters and sinister twists that keep you turning the pages for more." —Karin Slaughter

"Allison Brennan's *Poisonous* has it all . . . A twisty and compelling read." —Lisa Unger

"Don't miss Max Revere's roller-coaster new thriller. Talk about grit and courage, Max never gives up."

—Catherine Coulter on *Compulsion*

"Packs in the thrills as investigative reporter Max confronts new murders and old family secrets in a suspense novel guaranteed to keep you up late at night!" —Lisa Gardner on *Notorious*

"Amazing . . . The interconnectivity of Brennan's books allows her ensemble of characters to evolve, adding a rich flavor to the intense suspense."

—*RT Book Reviews* (4½ stars, Top Pick!) on *Best Laid Plans*

"Gut-wrenching and chilling, this is a story you won't soon forget!"

—*RT Book Reviews* (4½ stars) on *Dead Heat*

"All the excitement and suspense I have come to expect from Allison Brennan." —*Fresh Fiction* on *Stolen*

"Once again Brennan weaves a complex tale of murder, vengeance, and treachery filled with knife-edged tension and clever twists. The Lucy Kincaid/Sean Rogan novels just keep getting better!"

—*RT Book Reviews* (4½ stars, Top Pick!) on *Stalked*

Also by Allison Brennan

Shattered
Make Them Pay
The Lost Girls
Poisonous
No Good Deed
Best Laid Plans
Compulsion
Dead Heat
Notorious
Cold Snap
Stolen
Stalked
Silenced
If I Should Die
Kiss Me, Kill Me
Love Me to Death
Carnal Sin
Original Sin
Cutting Edge
Fatal Secrets
Sudden Death
Playing Dead
Tempting Evil
Killing Fear
Fear No Evil
See No Evil
Speak No Evil
The Kill
The Hunt
The Prey

"Brennan throws a lot of story lines into the air and juggles them like a master. The mystery proves to be both compelling and complex . . . [A] chilling and twisty romantic suspense gem."

—Associated Press on *Silenced*

"The evolution of Lucy Kincaid from former victim to instinctive and talented agent continues in Brennan's new heart-stopping thriller . . . From first to last, this story grabs hold and never lets go."

—*RT Book Reviews* (Top Pick!) on *Silenced*

"Explosive suspense ratchets up with every turn of the page . . . will leave people clamoring for more stories of Max Revere. I know I will be!"

—James Rollins on *Notorious*

"Brennan introduces readers to a new and fascinating heroine worth rooting for. She's an investigative reporter who's not afraid to kick butt, climb a tree, or go to jail in pursuit of her story. She's savvy and smart and takes no prisoners. Buckle up and brace yourself for Maxine Revere." —Sandra Brown on *Notorious*

BREAKING POINT

Allison Brennan

St. Martin's Paperbacks

This is a work of fiction. All of the characters, organizations, and events portrayed in this novel are either products of the author's imagination or are used fictitiously.

BREAKING POINT

For information address St. Martin's Press, 175 Fifth Avenue, New York, NY 10010.

ISBN: 978-1-250-16444-5

Our books may be purchased in bulk for promotional, educational, or business use. Please contact your local bookseller or the Macmillan Corporate and Premium Sales Department at 1-800-221-7945, ext. 5442, or by e-mail at MacmillanSpecialMarkets@macmillan.com.

Printed in the United States of America

St. Martin's Paperbacks edition / February 2018

St. Martin's Paperbacks are published by St. Martin's Press, 175 Fifth Avenue, New York, NY 10010.

10 9 8 7 6 5 4 3 2 1

PROLOGUE

Eighteen Years Ago

Bella Caruso stared at her reflection in the cracked mirror, doubting for a moment that she was actually *here.* Was this what an out-of-body experience felt like? She knew, intellectually, that she was standing in the cramped bathroom. But she felt nothing. Not the cold, broken tile on her bare feet. Not the pain in her throat. Not the familiar soreness between her legs. Not the warm blood dripping from the knife in her hands.

Then numbness took over and Bella froze, unable to think. Her mind was somewhere else. The only way she had survived the last year

thirteen months, one week, three days

was by shutting everything out. Blocking the pain, the humiliation, the anger. Forgetting her past, living each day beginning-to-end, burying the hope that she might be able to escape.

Until tonight.

The john would have killed her.

She had no choice.

it was him or you, him or you, him or you

Her bruised neck would prove her story. That he had

tried to strangle her while he had sex with her. Sergio would have to believe her.

Tommy set you up. He hates you and wanted you to suffer.

Slowly, the reality of her fate broke through the numbness. She would be dead by dawn if Sergio found out she had killed the john, no matter what he had done to her. Whores were a dime a dozen. She was just one whore in the stable, and if one whore could kill a john, the others might get ideas.

you're not a whore, you had no choice

Run away. The idea that there might be help somewhere had long ago been beaten out of her. Run away and disappear. She'd been stealing a little bit here and there, keeping the bills rolled tight in a loose panel of the house she lived in. Lived in? She didn't live in the house. She was kept prisoner there between the parties. Parties? That's what Sergio called them. "Get ready for a party, baby." Forced prostitution. The drinking. The drugs. It was the life.

Bella hated the drugs. She'd gotten really good at faking a high, really good at faking everything in her life, waiting for her opportunity . . . They thought they'd broken her because she'd humiliated herself, done things she'd never thought she would do, but she kept a tiny ember burning inside, waiting for the moment when she could run. Run fast and keep running.

But hope had been extinguished. Died with that john she knew only by the name Clark.

She had to run, even though Sergio would hunt her down like an animal. He would find her. He'd moved her and the others from city to city to keep them on edge, to prevent them from learning the area, the people, making friends. Pick up a few new girls, sell a few others, and move on. Los Angeles first, then Las Vegas, then Reno, now San Francisco.

Did he know when he moved her to San Francisco that they were now less than two hours from where she'd grown up? She didn't know what she would find in Sacramento, but she was closer to regaining the hope she'd lost, as she thought about her grandmother. She could walk there. How long would it take her? It was a hundred miles. She could walk ten miles a day, maybe more. If she had food and water, she could walk more. She knew people in Sacramento, people who would help her.

Or a phone. Find a phone and call her brother's best friend. Her brother didn't even know what had happened to her. He was probably on a ship somewhere protecting the country from foreign enemies. He was a hero. He saved people.

Not you.

He didn't know. He couldn't know that their father had given her away.

Bella washed her hands in water that smelled foul. She jumped at a sudden pounding on the bedroom door.

"Wrap up the party, we leave in fifteen."

She had to fake it. Fake that everything was okay. Get to the house, grab her stash, and sneak out through the second story window just before dawn, when everyone slept soundest.

She washed off the blood and slid into the short dress she'd been forced to wear. She looked at the dead man's watch. Almost four in the morning. She considered running now, but she looked like what she was: a hooker. They were in a small beach house on the north end of the city. She could swim, but it was February and the icy water might kill her before she could reach shore.

No matter what had happened to her since her father sold her into slavery, she had never wanted to kill herself. Other girls had. Other girls had succeeded. But Bella would not give into the pain. She would never break. *Never.*

So the Bay was out. She could run through the streets, the alleys, hide in the shadows of night. It might work. The police were out of the question. She didn't trust the police. How many had she been forced to screw? Too many. That also meant no hospitals. They would call the police. A fire department, maybe. But would they listen to her? Believe her? Would they call the police or her mother? The second time she'd escaped and called her mom from a stolen cell phone, her mother had betrayed her. Sergio had tracked her down and beaten her.

Bella didn't trust anyone.

The only person she trusted was her brother, but he was thousands of miles away, and she had no idea how to reach him.

She knew how to live on her own, on the streets, take care of herself.

Sergio's men might shoot her in the back. If she didn't die from a bullet, they'd take her to be tortured by that bastard.

Or, worse, hand her over to Tommy. Sergio ran a business. Bella could sometimes reason with him. Manipulate him—if she was very careful. But Tommy was vicious. He enjoyed causing pain. Especially to her. He had almost broken her for good. She let him believe that he had.

She didn't want to die, but right now running was her only chance of survival, slim though it was.

She still had the knife.

Gunfire erupted downstairs. The screams of girls cut through the bullets.

Bella had been in the middle of a gun battle once before, when Sergio's operation had been attacked by a rival organization in Las Vegas. Three of her friends—if that's what she could call the girls who hooked with her—had been killed. Bella had been one of the lucky ones.

Or unlucky, depending on how she looked at it.

There was no place to hide. Even the bathroom had no door. The bed was a mattress on the floor. Clark's blood had seeped into the stained bedding.

There was a door leading to the hall. Bella clutched the knife to her chest. It had been Clark's knife—a pocket-knife with a four-inch blade. She just wanted to make him stop. Not fucking her—that was her job, that's what she had to do to survive—but hurting her. She hadn't wanted to die.

She stood to the side of the door, right next to the hinges. She could only see shadows and darkness. Maybe, just maybe, they wouldn't see her when they opened the door. Maybe she could escape.

A gun went off right outside of her hiding place and a body collapsed with a grunt. The door opened.

She held her breath, her right hand tight around the knife handle.

you're going to die tonight

No, not tonight. She would kill again if she had to, but this was her best chance of escape. To finally be free.

She saw a hand with a gun before she saw the man.

She brought the knife up. If she died, he would die. Small victory, but it would be something.

The man stepped through the door and turned to her. He wore all black, head to toe, and she could only see his eyes.

His eyes changed focus. Just a small change, but she froze. She couldn't move. His eyes were green. Dark emerald green. Like hers.

"Bella."

He spoke in a whisper. But she knew.

"JT?" Her voice was raw; she didn't know if he'd heard her.

"I have her," he said. She looked around and didn't know who he was talking to. Then she saw an earpiece and cord going down behind his ear and under his shirt. "I'm coming out. Cover us."

He took the knife from her hand. Instead of dropping it, he pocketed it. "You're safe, Bella."

"Sergio—he'll hunt you down. He'll kill you. He never gives up."

"Sergio is dead," JT said. "He'll never hurt you again. But we have to go before the police get here."

She followed her brother. She was free.

She would never be a prisoner again.

CHAPTER ONE

Present Day-Monday

Bella Caruso had often found herself in prickly and dangerous situations where she faced impossible choices. Every time, she handled the situation to the best of her ability. Sometimes her skill and training had saved her, and sometimes luck kicked in. Usually a combination of both.

It appeared that her luck had run out, and the thousands of hours of training would do her no good. In the end, she was going to have to rely solely on her instincts.

Even then, she might end up dead.

She'd been roused from sleep—such as it was—by a pounding on her motel room door.

"Doc, get up, we have a situation."

It was Damien, Hirsch's enforcer.

She slid jeans over the boxer shorts she slept in and opened the door. It was barely dawn. Even though they were in Arizona, the early spring morning brought chills to her skin.

Damien slipped inside, shut the door. "We're pulling up stakes. The 10th Street house was compromised last night."

"What happened?"

She knew what had happened because she'd set the plan in motion, but she had to protect her cover. That was always the hardest part of this job. Not only did she stay far away from the house, but she had a solid alibi if Hirsch looked. She'd been playing poker in an illegal gambling hall downtown. Her gambling "problem" was one of the two reasons Hirsch knew she wasn't a cop. Illegal gambling was also the best way for her to keep in contact with her partner.

"Just get your black bag, you're going to need it."

Her heart raced. Declan had confirmed that he'd taken the two girls to the hospital, and that he'd gotten word to Laura. The hospital was the safest place for them until they could be put into protective custody. But it worried her that Roger hadn't made contact—with either her or Declan. *Especially* since he was supposed to extract *three* girls.

"I need to pack. It'll only take two minutes."

"We'll get what you need when we settle. Now, Doc."

She picked up the medical bag that had become her tether. "I need my shoes and jacket at least," she said.

He nodded. "Thirty seconds. The boss ain't happy."

Bella had worked months to gain the trust of these people. She'd saved some of their miserable lives, earned their respect—at least as much respect as any of them could give a woman. But she had no doubt that if they knew why she was here, they would kill her.

Bella put the bag on her bed, quickly slipped on her tennis shoes, and stuffed a page torn from a Bible under the filthy mattress. She didn't have time to write a note, but Declan would know what the verses meant.

Trouble.

She pulled a sweatshirt over her head, slipped a switchblade into the front pocket of her jeans, grabbed her last two water bottles and put them in her medical bag along with a clean shirt, and followed Damien out to his car.

She wasn't part of the inner circle and she never would be. That was okay—her cover was solid, but there were some things she couldn't do, and she didn't want to go too far. She'd crossed the line, but not too far over—nothing that she couldn't justify to save the life of an innocent. But sometimes it depended how the op ended, and right now she was worried everything had gone south.

She'd figured out Martin Hirsch pretty quickly—he hated women. Many of the men who worked for Hirsch were abusers, rapists, and had no respect for females, but they came at their jobs as a way to exercise their he-man dominance. They didn't hate women, they simply used them because they didn't respect or like anyone. Whores were a business, and they were just doing a job.

It had taken Bella months before she got her foot in the door. It had gotten to the point where Hirsch needed her—and relied on her—and he hated that. If he could find someone—preferably a man—to replace her he would, but he was a businessman first. She kept his girls healthy and working. She extracted bullets from his men when they crossed the wrong people, and she'd once saved Damien's life. That had been one of the hardest things she'd done. Not only because she wasn't a real doctor, but because Damien was a killer.

Damien glanced at his watch as he drove fast—but not too fast—through the shithole Bella had called home for the last four weeks. He went the long way to the freeway—the only reason was to avoid driving by the 10th Street house where nine girls had been living. There were three houses in Phoenix, all on Hirsch's circuit, but 10th Street was the newest. The girls in all three houses were prostitutes. Some came into the business because they felt they had no other options, some were forced into the business by boyfriends or family. And some were bought and sold like property, taken far from anyplace they might have known.

Bella knew exactly how they suffered.

In Phoenix, two of the houses were well established and Bella didn't trust any of those girls not to betray her, so she hadn't even attempted to extract them. It saddened her, because some were underage, but at sixteen and seventeen, they'd been seasoned and put out by Hirsch and men like him for years. They were broken and put back together the wrong way. They'd turn on Bella for a new dress or bubble bath or just another fix.

Bella wanted to kill Hirsch so badly she could taste it, the thirst for vengeance oozing from her pores. But she was patient and she wouldn't make a move before she found Hope. She wouldn't kill him unless she had to. She wasn't an assassin and she wasn't a vigilante.

But deep inside, in a dark spot where she didn't like to look too carefully, she wished that Hirsch would make the wrong move so Bella could justify putting a bullet in his head.

Or in his gut so she could watch him bleed out. A small suffering for how he tortured the girls and women he turned out.

Hirsch was a supplier. He ran a human pipeline and procured and moved "merchandise"—in this case women, girls, and sometimes boys—for the purposes of the multibillion-dollar sex trade. He'd been buying up small, independent trucking companies throughout the southwest to the Louisiana border to make it easier to move his products and launder his money. Bella had been collecting evidence on his operation for the last year, and she suspected if she turned everything over to the FBI they might be able to make a solid case against him.

Might was the operative word. But even if they could

shut down Hirsch, Bella knew there was someone bigger and badder than him—which was saying something. And she had no idea who he was, where he was located, or exactly what his role was.

Besides, calling in the feds too early wouldn't help her find Hope. The people Hirsch supplied would go to ground, disappear, and likely kill anyone connected to the man, should he end up in prison.

Hope first—then Bella would share her intel. Maybe by then she'd know who was holding Hirsch's leash.

The 10th Street house was newly established, run as a temporary way station. The girls had been brought from Los Angeles, though they had originally come from all over the country. These girls Bella had the best chance of saving. They hadn't chosen this life, some new and some clearly underage. Girls who wanted to walk away but deep fear rooted them in the life. Fear of being caught, fear of hunger, fear of being alone, fear of going back home. Hirsch and his people played on that fear to keep them in line, and it worked.

It worked very, very well, as Bella had learned firsthand many years ago.

As soon as Damien turned onto the freeway heading east, he tossed her a black cotton hood. "You know the drill, Doc."

"I thought we were beyond this shit."

"Boss's orders. We lost two girls last night, no taking chances." Even Damien wouldn't have put a bag over her head, except on orders. "Climb in the back, put on the hood, and just veg, Doc. Everything is fucked and I don't want you to get hurt."

It almost sounded like he cared. Damien didn't care about anyone—but he didn't hate anyone, either. He just did what he was told.

Bella climbed in the back of the SUV and put the bag over her head. She had a suspicion that she knew where they were going, but she couldn't let on that she had figured out how Hirsch transported his girls across state lines. She was alive because she kept her mouth shut.

She went along with it because she really had no choice. Damien would put a bullet in her rather than let her walk away. She hoped that she'd gained his trust enough that he would hesitate if ordered to kill her, and his hesitation would be enough time for her to get the upper hand, but she couldn't be certain. She still had a job to do.

If she died today, at least she'd saved two girls from a horrific fate. Two girls who now had a real future ahead of them. But she needed to find Hope.

She believed Hope was still alive. She *wanted* to believe. Fifteen months ago Hope had been sold by her stepfather to one of Hirsch's operatives. Three months later, a video surfaced through one of Bella's contacts, and that was what had prompted Bella's foray into the deep dark. But fifteen months was a lifetime when you were thirteen. Fifteen months could break even the strongest of girls. Just last week Hope had turned fourteen . . . was she already gone? Lost to the violence? Despair? Or worse, turned. Too many girls broke and accepted—even embraced—their fate. Those girls posed the greatest risk to Bella and anyone she tried to save because they could turn on a dime. It had taken Bella years of working with underage sex slaves to know who could be saved, and who was already lost.

She didn't focus on the lost. She couldn't and still do her job. But this time, she had to believe she could still save Hope.

Hirsch had multiple locations throughout southern California because his key to survival was to spread his assets around. Each group had a supervisor, as Hirsch called them. He preferred that term to some of the cruder slang used by traditional pimps. They were jailers as far as Bella was concerned. Some were worse than others, but they all did their job because Hirsch picked his men—and women—well. Yet if one cell was taken out, Hirsch had two dozen other permanent relocations spread along his pipeline. He'd been operating like this for years, he knew the ins and outs of the business, he had a sixth sense about when to move or cut his losses with one operation, and Bella was certain he had one or more cops on his payroll.

If she ever found a cop who had taken money at the expense of these girls, she would take him down hard.

Initially, Hirsch's operation was focused in the southwest, no farther east than Phoenix. But after getting inside Hirsch's operation, she realized he'd started to expand. Her organization initially believed he was the number one guy, and maybe he had been for a while, but at some point between Hirsch landing on their radar and when Bella infiltrated the group, he'd aligned himself with a far more powerful broker on the East Coast known only by the letter "Z."

The information she'd put together was thin, even after months of deep cover. But it was clear that Hirsch was using his growing trucking network to create a larger organization from the Pacific to the Atlantic, and that this Z was instrumental to the process.

Less than ten minutes after he merged onto the freeway, Damien exited and kept going straight. Count of fifteen. Turn right. *Three, two, one.* Right again. *Five, four, three, two, one.* Left. One minute. The SUV stopped.

She was right, they were at Hirsch's trucking company.

Damien spoke to someone, then a rolling door went up and Damien drove in. A minute later, the door closed and Damien shut off the ignition. "Stay put," he told her.

She did as he said and listened. At first, she only heard people moving around, muffled voices, a few girls complaining. A cry when one of the girls complained too much.

Bella's fists tightened.

Bella had started her undercover operation a year ago, almost to the day, once she had connected Hope to Hirsch. It took a few months, but she'd gotten in and now—after seven months working deep undercover—her total rescues equaled five.

Five out of hundreds.

Stop. If you save one it's enough. One is worth the sacrifice.

She repeated her mantra. Breathed deeply. Focus on survival. The search for Hope was not over. Bella had looked at the weary, fear-strained faces of Hope's maternal grandparents and knew that, dead or alive, she had to give them answers.

And for herself, exact justice on those who hurt the innocent.

Damien was talking to someone next to the driver's door. Bella didn't recognize the other voice.

"Where?" Damien was saying.

The guy mumbled. Bella made out "Seventeen North."

"And we're sure he's a cop?"

"Yep. The boss wants the Doc."

Bella's heart skipped a beat. Had she been compromised?

"You sure you can handle the move?"

"I got it." He mumbled something else, then walked away.

Damien got back into the car. He backed up and out. "Change of plans," he said.

"What's going on? Can I take off this damn hood?"

"Sorry."

That was it. *Sorry.* What did that mean? Sorry that he was going to have to kill her? Sorry that she couldn't take off the hood? Sorry that there was a change in plans? Information had been Bella's weapon, and now she had none.

"We're sure he's a cop?"

They had ID'd Roger. Had they figured out that Bella was working with him? She didn't think so. She'd never been seen with him. She and Roger had met years ago, but once she went deep cover, they communicated only through Declan. Declan had his own cover, and she'd been seen with him at poker tables. But by necessity, last night they had kept the extraction team small and Declan had to get the girls to safety. Had they traced Declan to Roger? Figured out their communication channel?

She didn't see it. Damien wouldn't have been so nice when he picked her up at the motel if he knew the truth. And if Declan had been compromised, he would have warned her.

Unless he was dead.

She couldn't lose her cool. She didn't know what Hirsch knew, but she had to believe that Damien wouldn't be this nice if he thought she was working with the cops. She had to stick it out—there were more lives at stake than hers.

Damien drove thirty, thirty-five minutes. By the turns and elevation it felt like they were heading to the hills north of Scottsdale. Though she had the hood on, light was coming in through the passenger side. East, because it was early morning. Hirsch had a warehouse outside Cave Creek where he kept an extra fleet of trucks. That had to be where they were heading.

One of Hirsch's moving companies had gotten her hooked up with Hirsch in the first place. She'd created a solid fake identity—Doctor Isabella Carter, who'd lost her license for malpractice. She used an informant to get in with the company in order to set up an illegal mobile clinic. She'd patched up more than a dozen gang bangers before Hirsch used her for one of his men who'd been attacked by a wired john. The john was dead, the gang banger sliced pretty bad. Then she patched up a bullet wound, no questions asked. Then another. Then getting antibiotics on the black market. Fifth time was the charm and she was offered a "real" job with Hirsch, seven months ago. Keeping his girls clean and healthy. Patching up his men. Being *his* doctor, not working for anyone else. No more mobile clinic.

She'd made sure Hirsch "learned" that she had a gambling problem, that she needed the money and she didn't care much how she got it. She made it clear from the get-go that she had no scruples but wouldn't kill anyone. When one of Hirsch's men had skimmed off the top, he'd handed her a gun and told her to take care of it.

"I'm a doctor," she'd told him. "I don't care what the fuck you do to this asshole, but I'm not pulling the trigger. You have a problem with it, I can walk. Go back to being my own boss."

She'd had to establish early on that she wasn't scared of him, that she would do what was necessary to feed her gambling habit, but she was a doctor first, and she saved lives, didn't take them. He seemed to be okay with that.

He'd shot the thief in the arm and told her to patch him up.

"Julio," Hirsch had said, "the next bullet goes through that pea-sized brain of yours."

Dr. Carter was the deepest, longest cover she'd ever had. She had advanced EMT training from when she was a cop, and on-the-job experience, but that was nothing compared to the crash course a doctor friend of Simon's had given her. She had to improvise more often than not. But since she'd ostensibly lost her license for malpractice, they didn't expect a brain surgeon.

Damien stopped the SUV and got out. A second later, the rear door opened and he said, "Let me help you out, Doc."

"This is fucked," she said.

"Sorry."

He sounded sorry. Considering that Damien was likely a clinical sociopath, she took that as a sign that he actually liked her. As much as a remorseless killer could like anyone.

Her legs wobbled a bit—she exaggerated her discomfort—and Damien grabbed her and helped her walk.

"I got it," she said.

Damien didn't take off the hood at first. He led her from the SUV into a warehouse. It was late March, but the temperature was rising with the sun. It'd top ninety today.

"We're climbing up," Damien said and helped her into the back of a moving truck.

She smelled blood.

As soon as she was inside, Damien jumped in next to her. One of the other men closed the trailer doors and locked them in. It was being locked in that bothered Bella more than the hood over her head.

There was no escape. And someone here was dying or already dead. The scent of blood filled her nostrils and she almost gagged.

The truck started to move and Damien took off her hood.

She blinked under the artificial light. A small generator hummed, providing both light and air conditioning.

A man was bleeding on the floor of the nearly empty container. His skin was pale and clammy. He was dying.

Roger, I'm so very sorry.

Officer Roger Beck had been her contact in Phoenix. A cop who helped her group on his own time because Bella's work wasn't sanctioned by any law enforcement agency. They had a few of these people, good men and women who didn't always support the rule of law when it benefitted the criminals over the victims, the hunters over the hunted.

Bella looked from Roger to Martin Hirsch who had braced himself in the corner as the truck gained speed. They were heading north. Toward Flagstaff. Where Hirsch had a private airstrip.

"This cop broke into *my* house and stole *my* merchandise." Hirsch scowled at Roger. "I want to know who the fucking traitor is. Stabilize him, Carter, so I can interrogate him."

"I—I'm not a surgeon." Bella knelt next to Roger and looked him over. He stared at her, his eyes unfocused. "He's dying. I . . . I can't fix this!" Roger had been shot three times, twice in the gut and once in the leg.

What had happened? Two girls escaped because Bella told them to be in the kitchen. There was supposed to be a third, but Bella knew the timing had to be perfect. Roger was supposed to grab them, take them into protective custody. He should never have been caught. How had they escaped and Roger been captured?

"I don't care if he dies as long as I get the information I want!" Hirsch slapped her.

She had to stay in character. If she broke now, he'd kill her and she'd never find Hope.

She jumped up and glared at him. "Do not touch me."

His nostrils flared. "Do your job," he ordered.

She gave him a long stare. Showed no fear. Never show fear. Without taking her eyes from Hirsch, she snapped her fingers. "Damien." She pointed to her medical bag.

Damien cleared his throat and slid over her bag.

She finally turned her gaze from Hirsch and knelt next to Roger. She wished she could do or say something to alleviate his pain. She opened her bag and looked for gauze. "I have to stop the bleeding," she said.

"I need him talking."

"He can't talk if he bleeds to death."

Roger grabbed her wrist so tight she yelped. Not so much in pain but surprise at his strength when he was so clearly suffering. "I. Won't. Talk."

He caught her eye. It was just for a split second, but she understood that he would die to save her.

She didn't want him dead, Roger or anyone else. But if she didn't save these girls, who would? They were lost to a system that had failed them. Roger and the others understood that. That's why Simon only recruited cops who didn't have families. Most had no siblings, no spouses, no offspring. Their work was dangerous and attachments made everyone vulnerable.

Roger was no exception.

"If you want him to talk, I have to stop the bleeding," Bella said again, quietly, firmly.

"Do it."

Hirsch didn't take his eyes off her.

Bella tore open Roger's shirt and winced. His intestines were visible in the mess that had been his abdomen. If he was at a hospital right now, Bella didn't think that he would make it.

"He's going into shock," she said. She didn't know for certain, but it sounded good. Roger was shaking, pale and clammy. Those were signs of shock.

She pulled out sheets of gauze and pressed them on his stomach. Blood seeped through immediately.

"I can't stop the bleeding."

"Sew him up! I need him talking."

"Ask your questions now because he's dying and I'm not God!"

Hirsch growled. Bella had never heard a human growl like Hirsch, who sounded so much like a wild animal that she expected him to pounce on her and rip open her neck with his teeth.

"Who told you about the house?" Hirsch demanded.

"Fuck. You."

"Give me a name or every one of those girls will be dead before nightfall." Hirsch put a glove on his hand and pressed his thumb into the wound on Roger's leg. Roger screamed.

"Who are you working with? Tell me." He pressed again. Then he looked at Bella. "Do something! Make him tell me!"

What did he think she could do, shoot him up with truth serum?

"Adrenaline might buy you time."

"Do it."

Bella hated herself. This could hurt Roger, and then he would certainly die.

But if she did nothing, he still wouldn't survive. Even if she blew her cover, was able to kill Hirsch and Damien with the switchblade she had, she would never be able to get Roger to a hospital in time.

Not to mention they were locked in the back of a moving truck.

She pulled out a vial of adrenaline, extracted the appropriate amount, and injected it into Roger. With the amount of pain he was in from the gunshot wounds, he didn't feel the prick. Almost immediately he convulsed. His breathing grew rapid.

"Cop, tell Mr. Hirsch what he wants to know and I'll make death quick."

Hirsch scowled at her. "He should suffer."

"Do you want answers or do you want to torture him?"

"Both."

"You have minutes. He's as good as dead."

Roger thrashed as the adrenaline pulsed through his system.

"Do it, tell him. Tell him!" Bella was shouting. She needed to control herself, but this situation was beyond control. Even Damien was surprised by her outburst. She was normally calm, cool, and collected.

"Christina. C-C-Christina Garrett."

Bella held her breath. It took Hirsch a minute to process the name.

"The ginger whore?" he said.

"I saw her. There's a-a-a sheet on her, I recognized her. Missing person. Followed." His breathing was erratic and he closed his eyes. His body shook and he groaned. Bella applied more pressure on his gut to see if she could stop the bleeding. Though she wore gloves, her arms and sleeves were red with blood.

"You recognized her? Just like that?" Hirsch didn't buy it, but he would. He would have to, or Bella was at risk.

"I . . . I work missing persons." That was true. If Hirsch followed up, he'd know that Roger had been assigned to the missing persons task force. "Good face. Good eye."

"He's fading."

"Inject him again! I don't believe him!"

"He said he followed her!" Bella shouted back. "It was just your bad luck."

Hirsch wanted to hit her again, she could see it in his half-crazy eyes.

But he was only half crazy. The other half of Martin Hirsch was a cold-blooded sex trafficker, a businessman. That was the side that won.

"You saw her on the street and followed her," Hirsch repeated.

"T-two days ago. Couldn't g-g-get a task force together. F-fuck. Fucking. B-bureaucracy." He groaned again.

"So you walked into *my* house and took her? Took what isn't yours?"

Roger convulsed, then lost consciousness.

Hirsch was thinking. He picked up his radio. "Where are we now?"

The driver responded, "Seventeen north approaching Black Canyon City."

"Next exit, go east two miles. There'll be a road south, turn. We have some garbage to toss."

There was nothing Bella could do to save Roger. Every cell in her body ached with pain, regret, rage.

She hated Martin Hirsch and barely resisted the urge to kill him right now. But even if she could, if she could kill him and Damien without being mortally wounded, the driver and bodyguard up front would find her in the back with three dead men.

And she would never save anyone else or find Hope. Roger Beck would have died in vain. His death had to mean something. It had to!

She felt for his pulse.

Nothing.

"He's gone," she said.

"We're changing protocols," Hirsch said. "I'm taking the plane to El Paso. Damien, you and Dr. Carter clean up this mess and drive out to meet me. Phoenix is off the table until I can confirm there isn't a breech in our security."

"Yes, boss," Damien said.

El Paso. She knew they were expanding east, but El Paso was a big jump. How far had they gotten?

The truck stopped. Behind them was a black limo.

Hirsch and his two men climbed into the back without another word, leaving Damien and Bella with the truck and Roger's dead body.

Damien showed no emotion as he dragged Roger's body to the ditch. He searched him.

He pulled out his wallet, looked inside, pocketed the cash, and tossed the wallet into the ditch. "Nice knife," he said when he pulled it out of Beck's sock. He kept that as well.

Bella wanted to gut Damien with it. She fingered the switchblade in her pocket. She could kill Damien now and leave. She'd blow her cover but she would be safe.

And Roger would have died for nothing.

"What's this?" Damien pulled out a folded piece of paper. It was the missing persons flyer for Christina Garrett. "Huh. He wasn't lying."

Roger had more than saved her cover, he'd protected her—even in his death.

"I told Hirsch early on not to let his people grab girls off the street," Bella said. "It is sloppy."

"Almost got yourself killed," he said. "Mr. Hirsch doesn't like women telling him what to do."

"And I don't want to go to prison. *A cop*, Damien. This is fucked and you damn well know it."

Damien looked marginally worried, but it passed. He wasn't an idiot, but he had no emotions. He didn't get angry or sad or happy or worried. Not for long. It was like his genes were poorly wired and nothing got to him. *Nothing*. He didn't even take pleasure in screwing the girls, and Hirsch always gave him "pick of the litter" as he called it.

Disgusting.

"Help me roll him over," Damien said.

The ravine wasn't a long drop, but it might take days before someone found him. And chances were, predators would do serious damage to his body before a person came across him. They were on a little used road, south of the county landfill.

But Bella didn't know when she'd be able to make contact with Simon, this might be her only chance. She couldn't contact Declan, on the chance that he'd been compromised. She didn't think so—Roger would have given her a sign, *something*. Hirsch would have mentioned a partner. But because there was a slim chance, she would only reach out to Simon until she knew for certain that Declan still had a solid cover. If Declan found her note—and she had no doubt that he would—he'd know she was in trouble.

Bella and Damien pushed Roger's body over the edge.

I'm so sorry, Roger. You didn't deserve any of this. I'll kill him. I'll find Hope and kill Hirsch. Forgive me.

"Let's start cleaning up," Damien said.

New location meant change in protocol. She had to dump her burner phone because if Damien found it on her, he would grow more suspicious.

"I need to pee," she said.

He waved over to a grove of trees.

"I'll start bleaching the truck," he said.

He might not fully trust her, but he didn't think she was working against them. If anything, he'd believe she was out for herself.

She peed behind a tree just in case Damien was watching. She took the slim burner phone she'd stashed in her bra, under her breasts, and sent a single text message.

She turned off the phone and buried it in case Damien came looking, then went back to the truck to help him clean up Roger's blood. Thirty minutes later they headed back to Scottsdale and ditched the truck at one of Hirsch's facilities.

Damien said, "Look, Doc, I like you, okay? But you've

got to back off of the boss. Don't get in his face like that, it really pisses him off. I'd be upset if I had to whack you, got it?"

She nodded and considered herself lucky.

She was alive.

And so was Christina Garrett.

CHAPTER TWO

Tuesday

Declan Cross spotted Laura Dixon as soon as she stepped out of the Phoenix Sky Harbor airport. "I got her," he told Adam Dixon, Laura's husband, over the phone. The last hour of conversation with Adam and Bella's brother JT Caruso had been uncomfortable, to say the least. "I'll fill her in."

"Do you have someone on the hospital?" Adam asked.

He was irritated that Adam even asked. "Yes. I'll call you when I learn more."

He ended the call before Adam could make him feel more like shit than he already did. He stopped the rented black Town Car as close to Laura Dixon as he could. She was an attractive middle-aged woman who dressed conservatively and had an air of peace wherever she went. Even now, when everything was going to hell, Laura remained calm.

He got out and called out, "Laura."

As soon as Laura recognized him, she smiled widely. She hugged him tight, and he kissed both her checks. "It's been too long," he said, emotion choking his voice. Three years. Ever since Adam gave Bella the ultimatum and she walked away.

At one time Adam and Bella had been very close. Adam was the father figure Bella sorely needed, and Bella was the daughter Adam and Laura could never have. After her brother JT rescued young Bella out of a forced prostitution ring, she came to live with the Dixons because JT didn't know how to help her. Hell, Declan couldn't blame him—though he knew that Bella had been hurt, that she thought her brother somehow thought less of her. Declan told her nothing was further from the truth, but it still bothered her.

"It has been far too long," Laura agreed. "I saw Adam's text message that you were picking me up when I got off the plane. Is Bella okay?"

"I don't know," he admitted. He wouldn't lie to Laura. He took her overnight bag from her shoulder and put it in the backseat, then opened the passenger door for her.

"You don't know where she is?"

"Get in, we'll talk."

Laura sat down and brought her hand to the small gold cross she never took off. Declan shut the door and took a moment to control his emotions.

Three years ago, Declan had walked away from his two closest friends when he went with Bella to work for Simon Egan, a multimillionaire who had made it his personal mission to rescue underage girls from sex trafficking. At the time, he thought it was the right thing to do. He was tired of the rules that Genesis Road, the organization Adam and Laura ran, insisted on following. Rules that none of the bastards who trafficked in people ever followed. Declan had been swept up by Egan's charisma as well as the need to keep an eye out for Bella. After all, she was JT's sister, and JT was his brother in every way except blood.

But as he and Bella had gone deeper down the rabbit hole with Egan, Declan realized the guy was borderline crazy. Bella didn't see it. Not because she was an idiot, but because she was a bit crazy too when it came to stopping predators like Martin Hirsch.

But being a bit crazy was not being stupid. Bella might put herself on the line, but she was the smartest field operative he knew. Now she needed help.

Declan got back into the car when he spotted a cop start toward him, circling his finger in a gesture to move along. He pulled away from the curb, uncertain how to tell Laura. It was one thing to explain to Adam and JT about Bella's undercover activities, but Laura was different.

"I knew as soon as I got the call yesterday that Bella had rescued the girls," Laura said. "But she didn't call me. Even though our relationship has been strained, she always calls me with information."

"I would have called you, but I didn't have an opportunity." Adam wouldn't shelter Laura and Declan couldn't, either. "A local cop, Roger Beck, and I rescued the girls early Monday morning. I knew immediately there was a situation when only two girls came out without Roger. There was supposed to be three. I took them to the hospital, made sure they knew to call you and talk to no one else, and then went back to find Roger." He paused. "I didn't want to leave him in the first place but the girls were in danger. And now Roger is dead."

Laura squeezed his arm. "I'm so sorry about Roger."

Declan felt the peace Laura shared, and while he was still angry and worried, he breathed a bit easier. Laura had that way about her, that even in the middle of chaos, everything would turn out all right.

"I got back to the house, not even an hour later, but it had already been cleaned out. There was blood inside, no body. I couldn't risk Bella's cover, so went around to Hirsch's other houses to see if there was any activity. They were moving some of the girls. I traced them to a warehouse, but couldn't find Roger. By the time I got to Bella's crib, she was gone." He took a folded paper from his right breast pocket and handed it to Laura. "She left that."

Laura looked at the torn Bible page. "The first book of Samuel. A code?"

Declan quoted from memory:

"And David inquired of the Lord, 'Shall I pursue this raiding party? Will I overtake them?' 'Pursue them,' he answered. 'You will certainly overtake them and succeed in the rescue.' "

Declan glanced at her. "It means she's in trouble, I need to find her. I must have just missed her. By the time I got back to her motel, she was gone."

"When? Yesterday? And you waited until today to call for help?"

The slight accusation in her voice made Declan feel guiltier. He shouldn't have waited twenty-four hours, but he didn't think Hirsch could move his operation that fast.

"I thought I'd found her, wasted half the day following one of Hirsch's trucks, but Bella wasn't inside. I backtracked when I got a message from Simon that she'd contacted him, gave him the location of Roger's body and said she was going dark."

Declan merged onto the freeway and navigated through the late commuter traffic. He glanced over at Laura. A small frown marred her unadorned face.

"What happened to Roger?" she asked.

"Tortured and murdered. My guess is he was shot at the house and they kept him alive long enough to get information out of him. But he didn't talk."

"How do you know?" Laura asked.

"Because Bella's body wasn't with his!" Declan said sharply. He took a deep breath. "I'm sorry, Laura. I fucked up. Worse, Simon thinks her message to him about going dark supersedes her message to me about extracting her from the operation, so he's not doing shit." He paused, then mumbled, "Sorry."

Adam and Laura didn't swear. Declan wasn't a big believer in religion, but his mother was devout, and so were the Dixons. Declan had the utmost respect for Adam and Laura, and he tried to live up to their standards. But he'd never quite felt like he had, even after he left the Navy and started working for them. It's how he met Bella, then a cop in Seattle. It's how he learned about the multibillion-dollar worldwide sex-trafficking business and the innocent young girls who were forced into it. How his former commanding officer could remain calm in the face of such evil, Declan didn't know.

"Who is Martin Hirsch?" Laura asked. "I don't recognize the name."

"You work primarily overseas, so I'm not surprised. Hirsch runs the pipeline along the I-10 corridor. Originally, he ran the circuit between L.A., Las Vegas, and Phoenix, but in the year Bella's been undercover they've expanded into Texas, and we believe their goal is to run the entire southern network."

"A year?"

Laura knew just as well as he did that a year undercover was soul-breaking work.

"How did Bella get in?" she asked.

Declan didn't say anything.

"Do we have a trust issue?"

"Of course not." He just knew Laura wouldn't like it, and he couldn't figure out a way to sugarcoat the situation.

"You know I don't approve of Bella's work with Simon, but I need to know what I'm getting into, Declan."

Her voice was firm. She didn't need to raise it to make her point.

"The only thing you're going to do is get those two girls to Seattle and keep them safe. Adam already started the ball rolling when I filled him in this morning."

"What are you not telling me? I will call Adam, but I want you to tell me."

"I didn't just speak to Adam this morning. I called JT."

That had been the fucking hardest call he'd made in a long, long time.

"JT? You talked to him?"

He glanced at her. "Bella and JT may not have spoken for the last three years, but I didn't cut off all ties."

"I didn't know."

"I didn't tell Bella. Look—I'm not trying to justify what we've done. We did what we did and saved dozens of young girls over the last three years. JT didn't trust Egan, but he and Adam built a brick wall and told Bella to stand down. You and I both know Bella isn't going to stand down, especially when she can do something."

Laura sighed and rubbed her eyes. "This has been difficult for everyone. Adam and Bella were both right—and both wrong."

"And both stubborn." He hesitated, then added, "Bella was hurt when JT sided with Adam and not her. And she drew her line in the sand. I told JT he was being an ass, but both Carusos are stubborn."

Declan had two years' service in the Navy when JT Caruso enlisted, and they both served under Adam's command. They were Navy SEALs—bonded for life. Declan could no more turn his back on JT than he could turn his back on an innocent child suffering under the hand of evil.

"JT trusted me to have Bella's back, and for three years I did. Until yesterday. I finally got information out of Simon, but I had to promise him I would locate her, not extract her."

"She's in danger. You know it!" Laura didn't lose her temper often, and she might as well have slapped Declan.

"Laura, I told Simon what he wanted to hear because he's the one Bella will contact when she can, and I need any information he has. My role has always been to back Bella up—but by necessity I have to stay in the background to best protect her. I promise you, as soon as I can, I will pull her out. This has gone on way too long, but the only way it works is if I stay inside Egan's operation. JT concurs, but he's going to light a fire under Egan anyway. We'll see what happens."

"You didn't tell me how she infiltrated a major trafficking organization."

"She went in as a doctor who lost her license. Isabella Carter. Simon set up a brilliant identity, we were playing the long game."

"What for?"

"To find a missing girl sold by her stepfather into Hirsch's network. Hope Anderson. She's been missing for fifteen months, but we had evidence that she was alive and created the undercover plan."

"More than a year?"

"We knew it'd take time."

"This isn't going to end well," Laura said. "Bella has never been so deep for so long. With a sex trafficker? What has she had to do to prove herself?"

"Laura—I have her back." Until now. Declan would never forgive himself for this fuckup. What had happened? Why had she left? Did they threaten her? If she'd known that Roger had been shot, she would never have disappeared. He hoped.

Because the one niggle of doubt in the back of Declan's mind was that Bella had become obsessed with finding Hope, to the point where she might not be thinking like the decorated cop she had been, but thinking like the vigilante Simon wanted her to be.

"You didn't answer my question."

"I'm not going to." Laura didn't need to know details, but Declan couldn't lie to her. Bella had straddled the line. Hell, they'd both stepped across a couple of times, but desperate times and all that.

Laura was tense, and Declan couldn't blame her. "What did JT say?"

"He's talking to Kane Rogan and they're putting together a plan, starting with getting information out of Simon." Declan navigated the exit ramp and after a series of quick turns pulled into the unloading zone at the hospital. He put the car in park, but didn't turn off the ignition. "Laura, do what you do best. Make those girls feel safe. Everything Bella has done is to save girls like Christina and Ashley. They might have information about where Hirsch was moving the girls. If anyone can get anything out of them, it's you. I'm going to find her, Laura. I promise."

CHAPTER THREE

"They couldn't just disappear," Damien was saying over the phone. Bella pretended to be half asleep on the couch of the crap-hole house in the middle of nowhere. She suspected they were on the outskirts of El Paso, on the Texas/New Mexico/Mexico border. "The boss isn't going to take *I don't know* as an answer."

Bella didn't know who Damien was talking to, but she suspected a police informant. Hirsch had them everywhere; often their best source of information was a disgruntled cop or civilian employee who liked the money that came from sex trafficking or was being blackmailed because he used prostitutes.

Damien listened and then said, "Check every fucking hospital, got it? They're probably under fake names. Check Jane Does. Bring them back or kill them. No loose ends."

By this point, Declan would have protection on the girls. For a while she'd been worried that he, too, had been caught by Hirsch's people, but after listening to Damien for the last twenty-four hours, she relaxed. Declan was safe. He'd get her message and find a way to extract her.

Except Bella wasn't certain she wanted to be pulled anymore. Leaving the Samuel Bible passage had been a knee-jerk reaction born out of deeply ingrained survival skills. She almost wished she hadn't. *Almost.* She was worried, but only because her backup was two states away and had no idea where she was. After what happened to Roger she was more angry than scared for herself, and sent Simon the message instead of Declan because she wanted retribution. She wanted to take Hirsch down hard. And she wanted to find Hope.

Right now, she was safe, but how long would it last?

Hirsch was angry, but he wasn't as angry as Bella had expected him to be. That bothered her. She'd known Phoenix was a temporary landing spot. He was checking on his business, then planned to continue moving the underage girls east. But she didn't know what his end game was—other than expanding his organization and merging it with the mysterious "Z." She had no idea who his partner was. Simon had run Z when she first heard the name, but nothing popped. *Nothing.* An alias of an alias? A new player? Or someone so entrenched in the business that he knew how to keep a very low profile?

Damien ended his call, sat next to Bella, and closed his eyes.

She wanted to slit his throat. Instead she said, "What's going on?"

"No one can do their fucking job right," he muttered.

"I need my own place."

"We're not staying. Just a few days here."

"There's a card room I want to try out. You should come with me. We both need to decompress."

He turned his head to look at her. His expression was impossible to read. What would it be like to have no emotions? No feelings about anything? Sometimes, Bella looked at Damien and wished she could be without empathy, without feeling, without regret.

"Last time I went with you I lost a thousand bucks."

"What else are you going to do with your money?

And besides, the other night I made five large. It was a good night."

"For some people, maybe," he grumbled.

The front door opened and Desiree and her main goon walked in. Desiree called him Thad. Bella called him Bam-Bam—he was dumb as a statue but liked to pound things, including people.

"Whatcha lookin' at, bitch?"

Bella glared at her. "Nothing worth looking at."

"Knock it off," Damien said.

Desiree hated everyone, but mostly she hated Bella. Fine by her, she didn't need to make friends with the old hooker. Desiree had been a bottom bitch from the age of fourteen until her pimp was picked up in a major sting operation in Los Angeles. She took his stable of girls and broke out—rare, and Bella would have admired her if she wasn't as cruel and violent as Hirsch himself. Desiree ran her girls with an iron fist, and Bam-Bam was her muscle.

Bella hadn't been privy to the agreement between Hirsch and Desiree, but based on what Damien had said and Desiree's attitude, the merging of Desiree's girls with Hirsch was less a mutual decision and more a threat from Hirsch.

Join me or I'll kill you.

Generally, an operation that was marginally successful like Desiree's was an asset to a man like Hirsch. First, he could expand his network. Second, if shit happened, Hirsch had a fall guy—or gal. Plus, Desiree had a long history of keeping her girls working hard and under the radar. Until Hirsch, however, Desiree only worked traditional prostitution. When she was arrested, she got out with time served. Bella had run her sheet—the longest she'd spent in prison was three months, and only because she'd been caught with heroin.

Desiree wasn't happy about the arrangement because

she hadn't wanted to leave L.A. She knew the score there. But like with prostitutes, Hirsch understood that when you took someone out of their comfort zone, they became dependent. He promised her the world—for Desiree, that was money—but so far he hadn't delivered. And he never would. It was a game to him, and once Desiree had lost her foothold in L.A. because she was halfway across the country, Hirsch would own her.

Hirsch had to have a reason—he did nothing without a reason—but Bella hadn't been able to figure out what benefit Desiree was to him. One of the few times Bella and Declan had talked face to face since she'd been deep undercover, they'd discussed it—and Declan suspected Hirsch wanted her territory more than he wanted her working for him. Simon was working on finding more info because it would help build whatever case they turned over to the feds.

Unfortunately, Desiree had begun to grow more suspicious of Hirsch and his motives, and she took her frustration out on the girls. She berated them, threatened them, abused them. Though she'd probably never been a nice person, she seemed to take pleasure in hurting others. Bam-Bam was happy to oblige. While Hirsch detested women, Bam-Bam enjoyed taking what he wanted, when he wanted. Bella couldn't wait to take him down.

Damien said, "We have business and then we're leaving. Both of you take a chill pill."

Bella's ears perked up. She'd thought they were just hanging to make sure the trouble in Phoenix didn't follow them. But business meant this was a planned move. Had they sped up the expansion because of Roger? Or was this a new deal?

Desiree glared at Bella then stomped upstairs, Bam-Bam on her heels.

"I don't trust her," Bella said.

"I don't care," Damien said.

Bella knew that Damien didn't trust Desiree either, though not for the same reasons as Bella. The only real argument she'd heard between Damien and Hirsch was a month ago, the night before they left L.A., when Hirsch told Damien that Desiree was coming east with them. Damien wanted to leave her in charge of the L.A. operation. Hirsch insisted she would be valuable in the expansion. When Hirsch shut Damien down, the enforcer went out with Bella, got wasted, and ranted. Damien didn't rant long, and even drunk he had enough self-control not to give away the store, but Bella had picked up her best intel that evening. That's when she learned about Hirsch's plan to set up operations at every major city along the I-10. That his partner Z was bankrolling the expansion because he had taken over a huge network on the east coast and needed Hirsch's trucking network not only to move girls, but to launder his money.

"We had a good thing going, you know? Big enough to make real money, small enough to stay under the radar."

Damien had been nostalgic, almost sad, about leaving. Bella had filed that tidbit away; now was the time to bring it up again.

"Damien, I've told you I'm game for just about anything, but going to prison is not an option. Hirsch had a great setup in L.A. and it worked, you know?"

He nodded and shrugged at the same time, the only concession she would get that he agreed with her.

She continued, hoping he'd talk. "We all made money. For the last four weeks everything has been up in the air, he killed a fucking *cop*, and that's going to bring down the heat faster than the desert sun."

"Shut. Up."

It was his tone more than his words that had her zipping it. Okay, she pushed too hard, but his tone confirmed that *something* was going on that she didn't know about.

She stomped off—an act, really, because she didn't want to leave the living room. Hirsch would be back soon, and she could pick up on a lot of things just by hanging around. She needed to contact Declan. He would be worried because of the Bible message that was their code for extraction. She wanted to tell him she was alive, that they were moving east, and confirm that they had found Roger's body. The cop deserved a proper burial.

She went into the bathroom and closed the door. Took a deep breath and looked into the cracked mirror. The house was old, falling apart around them. Flashes of the past hit her, harder than she expected, and she took another deep breath. Air in; hold ten seconds. Air out; hold ten seconds. Repeat as needed.

The last direct contact she'd had with Simon was right before Hirsch moved a group of his girls from L.A. to Phoenix. Simon had ventured into a card room, sat next to her. They played for an hour in silence then met up in the ladies' room, where they crammed into a stall. Cover, in case anyone walked in. Bella would never have sex with Simon, and she'd never have sex in a public bathroom, but she'd do anything to protect her cover and didn't give a shit what people thought.

She wanted out. She had contacts and outs in L.A. She knew the people, the ropes. Phoenix? She had no one. She would be without backup, except for Declan.

"Declan is the best and the brightest," Simon had told her. The tone was a bit derisive, which was odd. Declan was proud of his military service, and half the men and women who worked with Simon were former soldiers.

"I trust him with my life, but he'll have to stay hidden. Here, he has his own cover. There's no reason for

him to go to Phoenix. We can't let any of Hirsch's people see him, which puts both of us at risk."

"If you're getting too nervous, I'll have you extracted. You can walk away tomorrow. We'll find another way to track Hope."

"You don't sound optimistic."

"We're close."

"It's been over a year since she disappeared, and ten months since the last video was posted. I want to believe, but—hell." She didn't want to give up on Hope. She couldn't. Her brother had never given up on her, and she was in the life for just as long. If she could survive, if she was unbreakable, Hope could be too.

"We've never had anyone so deep before," Simon said. "Your information is gold. We've shut down operations on the periphery. Dozens of girls saved as a result. And because of you, two girls were rescued from a brothel in Long Beach. Both fifteen, both runaways. You picked them well."

"I have another one—Christina. She's terrified, but I can convince her to walk."

"Tonight?"

"I don't think so—she's attached to another girl, has become her protector." Bella knew how that was. She'd had a protector once. An older girl who taught her the ropes and helped her stay under the radar. Julie had saved her life.

And Bella had gotten her killed. She'd never forgive herself. She'd forgiven herself for nearly everything from her past, because being sold to Sergio to be prostituted in order to clear her father's debt was not her fault. Surviving in the business wasn't her fault. There were two kinds of girls. Those who would do anything to survive, and those who died.

But Julie . . . Julie was her savior. Bella had never given in until . . . until Sergio had Julie killed.

Simon looked Bella in the eye, their faces only inches apart. He whispered, "When she's ready to go, I'll get them both out. If you can convince her to leave when you reach Phoenix, Roger Beck is there—he'll do it."

"Okay," she said, though she was nervous. More nervous than she'd ever been undercover. "I'll stay."

Bella stared at her reflection, calmer now. She'd saved those two girls in L.A., she'd saved Trinity when the poor girl was about to be gang raped in order to break her, and she'd saved Ashley and Christina. They were only five girls after months of work . . . but they were five girls. Five young women who now had a future. Five women who had a chance to grow up. To *live.*

She had to focus on the good, not the bad. Not Savannah Egan whom she couldn't save in time. Not Julie, who had died because Bella had nearly escaped all those years ago.

She had to focus on Hope Anderson—that Bella could find her, that she could be saved. No matter how long it took. No matter how far she had to travel. The life of one innocent girl was worth it.

It had to be.

CHAPTER FOUR

Laura Dixon took a few moments to compose herself in the ladies' room Tuesday night.

It had been a long, difficult day.

As if her husband could sense her disquiet, her phone rang and caller ID revealed Adam. Her heart, for that moment, lifted and she answered.

"Hello, sweetheart." She sat on a small bench outside the stalls. There was no one else around; it was late and after regular visiting hours.

"You're tired."

"I'm fine."

"I took care of the legal paperwork. As soon as their doctor releases them, you can bring both of them to Seattle."

Christina's mother had arrived late that afternoon, and at first she'd resisted Laura's suggestion that her daughter come to Seattle for a few weeks—or longer—to receive specialized counseling and live in a safe environment until she was ready to integrate back into her life. But after talking to Christina, then meeting with the doctor and Laura, Ms. Garrett agreed. It was a relief, because Laura knew Ashley would feel safer if Christina—who had clearly been her protector for quite some time—was with her.

Adam continued. "How are the girls?"

"Christina is a fighter. She'll be okay." *Like Bella*, but Laura didn't say that. Adam was angry and heartbroken over the choices Bella had made. Laura was sad—but she understood in a way even more than Adam, who was the most forgiving and understanding man Laura had ever known, why Bella had made the choices she did. There was nothing Laura wanted more than to bring peace to the two people she loved most, and the only way that would happen would be if they could forgive each other.

"Ashley," Laura continued, "has far more problems. Her doctor—" Laura took a deep breath.

"It's okay, honey. I'm here."

"She's been abused since she was little." According to the doctor, Ashley had never lived a life free of violence. "A history of broken bones that didn't heal right," Laura said, "including a skull fracture that the doctor believes is six to seven years old. The amount of pain her little body has endured in her thirteen years—she's a survivor, but she's in constant pain. There's a cracked rib, recent, that the doctor is watching closely because it's putting pressure on her liver. She may need surgery. She's scarred—old cigarette burns all over her b-back." Her voice cracked and she closed her eyes. Laura had worked with abused girls all of her adult life, but had never become desensitized. Each child she rescued—and every child she couldn't—she ached for. She'd learned to compartmentalize.

But with Adam, she could let her shields down, just for a moment. Because he understood.

"They're safe now."

"I'll feel better when they're at the house. I'm hoping for tomorrow, but I suspect Thursday."

"Did the police agree to put a guard on their door?"

"Yes, and Declan brought in two men, former military."

"I know. I just spoke with him."

Adam's voice had grown hard. "He has always had Bella's back, you know that, Adam."

"Until now."

"Don't do that to him. He's torn up about what happened, and he's turning over every rock to find her."

"JT is now involved, with the full resources of Rogan-Caruso-Kincaid. Declan told JT that Bella wanted an extraction a full month ago, when she was in L.A., and Simon talked her out of it. I never trusted him, and now a cop is dead and Bella is missing."

"She saved these two girls," Laura reminded him.

"At what cost? Declan said she disappeared sometime between three and six Monday morning. Over thirty-six hours and no contact other than one text message she sent to Simon about where to find that poor cop's dead body. We don't know what she's doing, where she is, or if she's even alive. How far has she gone? She's already passed the point of no return."

"She's not. Have faith."

"I've tried. The good Lord knows I've tried. She's going to get herself killed, Laura. I—I don't want to go to her funeral."

She heard the tears in her husband's voice, and she ached for him.

"I'll never give up on her, Adam. I know you won't, either."

"You're my life, sweetheart. I will worry about you until you're home. Bella—I can't anymore. My fear for her is so great it hurts."

And that was the crux of Adam's pain. He feared for Bella's life—and for her soul. That she would reach the point of no return and never come home.

"I know, Adam. I fear for her as well, but I have hope.

Bella is the strongest person I have ever met, other than you. I love you. I'll call you as soon as I know when the girls can leave with me."

She ended the call and took a deep breath.

As soon as she left the bathroom, she saw Declan Cross walking toward her. He didn't look like he'd had much sleep in the last two days.

"I have a lead, I have to go," he said. "I just wanted you to know that my men will stay here watching the girls, and when you leave the hospital, one of them will escort you to your hotel. Don't argue with me, I promised Adam you'd be safe."

"I wasn't going to argue," she said. "You know where she is?"

"Hirsch's right hand was spotted in Las Cruces last night."

"New Mexico?"

"Right on the I-10 corridor. They're moving east, and Bella must be with them. I talked to JT and he's on his way to have a conversation with Simon, get more information out of him."

"Be careful, Declan." She hugged him tightly, whispered a prayer. She had to believe that God would be watching out for Bella, and for Declan.

Otherwise, she'd curl into a ball and cry.

CHAPTER FIVE

JT Caruso shot a glance at his partner Jack Kincaid, who was driving the borrowed SUV toward Simon Egan's compound in Montecito, the exclusive community outside Santa Barbara. They'd flown in on Jack's plane, landing fifteen minutes ago as the sun was setting.

"Don't say it," Jack said. "I got your back."

"Egan isn't a threat."

"That's not what I meant."

In the seven years that Jack had been a partner at Rogan Caruso Kincaid Protective Services, he'd more than proven himself. He'd married one of JT's closest friends, and Little Rogan—Sean—had married Jack's sister. But Jack hadn't been with them from the beginning. Only Kane Rogan knew the truth about JT, his family, and his failures.

His many failures.

Kane Rogan, who had founded the original Rogan Caruso Protective Services with JT nearly two decades ago, was in Texas and had been the first call JT made after he got off the phone with Declan Cross late last night. Kane would learn everything that could be learned, use every resource, call in any and all favors, to locate Bella. JT didn't trust that Simon Egan would tell him the truth, but if he lied, JT would beat him to within an inch of his life.

Which was why Kane had told JT to bring Jack, to make sure JT didn't cross the line. Where Bella was concerned, JT saw red. His sister was his Achilles' heel, and Kane knew it. Simon Egan was the bastard who enabled her.

Still. Jack had faced his own crucible. He too had killed to protect his family. If Kane couldn't be here, there was no one else JT wanted by his side other than Jack.

Simon Egan lived behind gates. JT had considered breaking into the compound, but decided to try it the easy way first. Egan wasn't a military strategist, nor would he shoot first. He liked to think of himself as a noble do-gooder, so talking was always his first method for conflict avoidance.

But nothing Egan said or did, short of giving JT the exact location of his sister, would avoid conflict.

The gate opened as soon as they approached.

"Bastard," JT mumbled. "When he ignored Adam's calls, he knew I'd be coming. What the hell does he get out of playing this game?"

"Time," Jack said.

Jack was right. Time to find out what happened to Bella during an unsanctioned private undercover operation that left one cop dead and Bella in the wind.

Jack drove up the long drive and stopped immediately in front of steps that led to a mansion. JT had been here only once, when he tried to convince Bella to reconsider her decision to work with Egan. That had been three years ago.

He hadn't spoken to Bella since. He regretted it. If he'd kept tabs on her, he would know where she was. He could have prevented her from following Egan too far down the rabbit hole. Egan had nothing to lose—and

Bella *thought* she had nothing to lose. Together they were dangerous.

Egan's group was similar to RCK in some ways—they hired mostly former military and law enforcement and strictly vetted their staff—but there the similarities ended. Egan focused on one thing: rescuing underage girls from the sex trade. Noble in many ways—if Egan hadn't severely and repeatedly crossed the line, JT could have worked with him.

But Egan was lost, and he'd brought Bella along for the ride.

Simon Egan himself opened the door before JT even knocked. He nodded, glanced at Jack. "Kincaid, right?"

Jack didn't respond.

JT said, "Where is Bella?"

"It's complicated."

It took all of JT's willpower not to deck Egan.

"Come in," he said and opened the door wider. Two plainclothes guards stood at strategic points in the entry. Egan nodded to them, and they walked away. Unseen, but certainly following JT's every move. "I'm trusting we can have a civil conversation," Egan said.

"Are you going to lie to me?"

"My office." Simon walked down the wide hall toward the back of the mansion and opened a set of double doors. His office was stately, looking out on the backyard through six two-story-tall windows, three on either side of his desk. Lights illuminated the dusk, revealing well-manicured lawns, a swimming pool, and many trees affording shade and privacy. The office doubled as a war room with maps and tables for meetings, multiple chairs, a white board with numbers that would take JT time to decipher. Doors on either side of the office led to other rooms.

Simon had made his money during the dotcom boom more than twenty years ago. Once, he and JT had been friends. Simon had hired Rogan-Caruso—long before Jack came on board—twice. Once to solve a corporate espionage case, and once as protection for him and his board when they traveled to Hong Kong for a critical meeting. Simon sold his company years ago for a fortune, and retired to Montecito with his daughter after his wife died of breast cancer. She'd only been thirty-six.

Once, JT had sympathy for the man. Losing his wife and raising a young daughter was difficult, no matter how much money one had. Egan consulted from time to time with other up-and-coming businesses, but mostly he became a recluse. He was eccentric and brilliant and had built a castle for his daughter.

Like many teenagers, Savannah thought the castle had a moat, and she rebelled. One of her rebellions went south real quick. The boy she was dating was not so much a boy as a young man prone to criminal acts. He stole a yacht and ended up being caught by Mexican authorities off their coast. He and Savannah were put in prison, and Simon paid to get Savannah out—but not the kid. Savannah was furious, went back to try to buy her boyfriend's freedom, and was again arrested—only this time, Simon couldn't get to her.

Simon didn't call JT for help, at least at first. And a bad situation turned ten times worse.

By the time Genesis Road, Laura and Adam's organization, had found Savannah in a brothel, she was addicted to heroin and half out of her mind. They brought her home. Simon did everything in his power to help his daughter, but in the end, Savannah killed herself and Simon found her body.

He'd never stopped blaming himself. And, in many ways, he blamed Laura and Bella, who had negotiated for Savannah's release. Too little, too late, he'd once said in a rage.

Simon created a vigilante group to rescue underage girls from forced prostitution. JT knew that Simon used Bella's guilt that she couldn't save his daughter against her. Twisted it into some sort of justification for vigilante justice. Bella was ripe for the picking, and Simon knew it.

JT would never forgive him.

"Explain," JT demanded. "Where Bella is, what she's been doing, why she's impersonating a doctor."

"Sit down, JT. Jack. Please."

JT didn't budge. Jack stood just inside the door. Whether he was protecting JT from Simon's men outside, or Simon from JT, he wasn't certain.

"Bella is fine," Simon said. "I can assure you."

"Call her right now, have her tell me that herself."

"That would put her in danger. She's deep cover, as you know."

"As I found out last night. No bullshit, Simon. Tell me exactly what's going on."

"If you sit down, I'll explain. We used to be friends, JT. Please, sit."

JT didn't want to give him the satisfaction, but he sat across from Simon's desk. Jack remained standing by the door. Simon sat across from JT. He had a tablet on his clear desk. He typed a command, then turned the tablet to face JT.

"Bella sent this Monday morning."

JT read the message twice, burned it into his memory.

Going dark, dumping phone. 2 girls out, RB didn't make it. Think we're heading east, don't know how far. Will make contact soonest. Alert Dec.

"Where is she?" JT asked again.

"She's fine, she'll reach out as soon as it's safe."

JT slammed his fist on Simon's desk. "You haven't heard from her in over thirty-six hours! She's *not* safe. You don't know if she's been compromised or killed.

Don't you have a handler on her? Doesn't she have back-up?"

JT knew she did—and knew who it was—but after talking with Declan, they agreed that Simon shouldn't know they were already working together. If Simon shut Declan out of the information loop, Bella would be in even greater danger.

Simon bristled. "I have a man in Phoenix who Bella trusts. He's working on tracking the group. He knows what he's doing. You trust him too."

JT waited a good five seconds before he said, "Cross."

Simon nodded. "One of your own."

"He burned that bridge three years ago when he went to work with you."

"That was your bridge to burn, not his or Bella's. I'm sorry about how everything turned out, but Bella is a grown woman who can make her own decisions."

It was all JT could do not to leap over Simon's desk and choke him. Instead, he said through clenched teeth, "I want everything you have on what Bella has been doing undercover. She's been under for *months*. Moving from city to city with these people."

Simon didn't react.

"A cop was murdered and you think this is okay?"

"You know me better—"

"That's right, I do. And you are so twisted up inside that you will justify anything."

When Simon remained silent, JT said, "You either work with me to find her, or I will find her on my own. Do not doubt that I can."

"You'll risk the lives of hundreds of innocent girls. Can you live with yourself?"

JT stood and started to walk out.

"JT, wait."

He turned to face him.

"Martin Hirsch is the number two guy in the largest

human trafficking organization in the southwest. He has more than two dozen cells—houses with ten to twelve girls—spread all over Los Angeles, Tijuana, Phoenix, Juarez, El Paso . . . and he's growing. We were brought in to locate Hope Anderson who was sold by her stepfather fifteen months ago. One of Bella's contacts said Hirsch lost his doctor, so we created a perfect false identification. She has a passport, license, social, full history as Isabella Carter. A doctor who lost her license because of a malpractice situation. We planted court documents if they looked that far. It took her months, but she was finally brought into the organization. She's already directly rescued five girls—five girls who have a future because Bella was there. Indirectly, she's saved hundreds. But we haven't found Hope, and she's at great risk. We don't know who's in charge. Hirsch is number two."

"Why aren't the police investigating him?"

"He's wily. No hard evidence. No one will speak out against him. His inner circle is extremely small—he trusts very few people. That Bella could get so close is a miracle, and I'm not going to blow it."

"She's in danger!" JT wanted to throw the code at Simon—that Bella had asked Declan to extract her—but then Simon would know that Declan was talking to JT and cut him out of all future information. Declan was the only conduit to Simon at this point.

"She knows what she's doing, JT. She has a lead on the guy in charge, but until we get eyes on him, we can't do shit. Our intel—which Bella has worked painstakingly to get—tells us that Hirsch and his partner are trying to establish a major operation in a port city. We don't know where. We're thinking either Galveston or Shreveport, possibly New Orleans. With everything that's happened to the cartels and the human trafficking operation in Texas over the last year, there's no clear group in charge."

JT's instincts hummed. Kane had been instrumental in shutting down several trafficking organizations in Texas and northern Mexico, largely because RCK's mission collided with cases Jack's sister Lucy had worked in the FBI. Working together, law enforcement with RCK, they'd stopped a lot of bad people.

But there was always someone ready to take their place.

"I assure you," Simon continued, "Bella sent that message—and she's safe. She's the smartest operative I've ever worked with—I shouldn't have to tell you that. She's in deep because that's the only way we can find Hope and shut Hirsch down."

"You mean kill him."

Egan didn't say anything.

JT couldn't very well judge Egan for taking out a human trafficker who bought and sold girls like property. But the game was dangerous for all involved, including the girls being prostituted, and Bella was in the middle of it.

"Where is my sister?"

"You read the message. She'll call me when she can. My team in Phoenix is tracking her. I promise to call you when I hear from her."

Team? By *team* Simon meant one person. Declan had already told JT that he was the only operative on the ground with Bella.

"Do that," JT said. "And one more thing: tell her to call *me*."

"I don't think that would be wise."

"Because you think I can convince her to stand down."

"Because you will put her at risk."

"That's bullshit."

"Right now, she's gathering information because she's a trusted part of Hirsch's operation. As soon as we get a location on Hope and rescue her, we'll pull the plug—Bella will walk with as many girls as she can. We had a huge success last year in Nevada. I'm certain you heard about it."

JT had. But Bella hadn't been the one in deep cover—she'd been the handler, tracking her partner, making decisions with all the intel her partner developed. Now? Bella was in deep, too deep, for too long.

"Undercover work is dangerous," JT said. "And the longer an operative stays deep, the more dangerous—and difficult—the work is. What did she have to do to prove herself? These people aren't going to sit back and let her take the moral high ground on anything. Bella is going to have to live with the consequences of her actions—as if she doesn't have enough to deal with."

"You've never given her enough credit, JT. You still see her as the wounded dove you rescued. She's a warrior, and she always has been."

He'd never seen Bella as a wounded bird. She had always been a fighter—it was the fight that was tearing her apart. He'd been so proud of her when she joined the Seattle PD. Her skills, her strong sense of honor, of justice, of right and wrong. She'd made a great cop. The structure of the police department and the rules they had to live by tempered her vigilante streak. She'd needed the rules, she needed to believe in something more than her own vendetta.

And then Simon Egan came along and shattered everything that JT and the Dixons had built in Bella.

"I want to see any message she sends," JT said. "You have my private number. I want the message, and I want to know exactly where she is. If you lie to me, if you bullshit me, I will find her myself."

"I promise, as soon as I hear from her, I'll contact you," Egan said.

He was relieved, and that made JT even more suspicious.

"If I don't hear from you within the next twenty-four hours, I'm going in."

Egan bristled. "We are so close to locating Hope—"

"But you don't know where she is, and you don't know where Bella is, so from where I'm sitting, you know shit."

JT rose from his seat and walked out. Jack followed. As soon as they reached the car, Jack said, "You don't believe him."

"He knows more than he's saying—I think he knows where Hirsch was heading when Bella went dark. Declan said he's on his way to Las Cruces, but that's too small to be the final destination. He has to be going to El Paso or San Antonio or Houston. A major city with a lot more places to hide out than Las Cruces. He also didn't tell us everything."

"Like about this 'Z' Declan Cross mentioned as being the possible leader. He specifically said that they *didn't* know who was running things."

"He would argue that he doesn't know who 'Z' really is, but it's just semantics. He didn't want us to have that information."

"It also confirms that Cross is on our side."

"Cross is on Bella's side, I have never doubted that, but that doesn't mean *our* side." JT paused. "I also think Simon's worried. He's good, but he has a tell. We're going to find Bella—but we need help."

"Anything."

JT glanced behind him as Jack pulled out of Simon's compound. "You caught the intel about Texas."

"I did."

"Lucy might have information that will help."

"Because she recently took down the Flores human trafficking pipeline."

"That, and because she understands better than most how those people operate—and who might be taking over."

"You don't need my permission."

"I don't have to tell you how dangerous this is—even for an FBI agent."

"Lucy can take care of herself. And she has Sean. Make the call."

JT called Kane, filled him in on what Simon said.

"You want me to reach out to Lucy," Kane said.

"You read my mind. Can you stay close to her for awhile? In case there's some blowback?"

"Of course." He hung up.

Jack pulled into the private airstrip outside Santa Barbara. "Are we heading to Texas?"

JT didn't know where to go next. He called Declan.

"You were right," JT said. "Simon didn't tell us about the extraction note."

"Bastard. Is he onto us?"

"No. I cursed you." JT almost laughed. While he hadn't been happy with Bella's decision to join Simon's group, he had been relieved when Declan did—and quietly promised JT that he would take care of her. What Simon didn't understand about Navy SEALs is that when you served in the same platoon, when you lived and breathed the same mission for years, you didn't let disagreements affect your loyalty.

But Simon was loyal to no one.

"I just left Phoenix. I'll be in Las Cruces in the middle of the night then pound the pavement. You on your way?"

"Laura said the girls didn't have any information about where Hirsch might be headed. I want to talk to them before Laura takes them to Seattle."

"You know how she gets—she's very protective."

"They know more than they think they do."

"Kid gloves."

"You don't have to tell me. Let me know what you find in Las Cruces—and if Bella reaches out."

"Roger that."

CHAPTER SIX

Wednesday

FBI Special Agent Lucy Kincaid opened the last cold case file on the table.

She hated that she kept looking at her watch, waiting for the lunch hour to arrive, but she was almost done with this unnecessary and time-consuming project.

For two months she'd pored over every cold case in the San Antonio office, verifying information, calling witnesses and victims to update their contact information and ask if they had anything to add, anything that might help agents take another look. She'd organized cases of agents who'd left the bureau, updating the information and sorting through those with only dead ends. Lucy forwarded all cases where the statute of limitations had expired to the head analyst to close. The work was time consuming, boring, and thankless.

Yes, the work should be done, but it could easily be completed by an analyst or civilian employee. As a sworn agent, she was stuck at a desk—well, the smallest conference room because of the plethora of files—and tasked with a tedious chore. It wasn't that she thought it was beneath her, but there were only eight sworn agents in her squad and everyone was overworked. Except her—because her boss wouldn't assign her a case.

She had *every* cold case file in front of her, not just the Violent Crimes squad. Most were computerized, but one of her tasks was to verify information in the computer with the hard copies. Every discrepancy she noted and every fact she verified, then wrote up a one-page report for the field agent and gave the file back to them. Cases of agents no longer in the office were compiled and sent to the current supervisor of the appropriate unit: cybercrimes got cybercrime cold cases, white collar crimes got white collar cases, and so forth. Most of the cases were duds, no chance of being solved with the information they had or could reasonably obtain.

Some of the conversations she'd had were heartbreaking—like the grandmother who was the lone surviving family member of a college boy who'd died under suspicious circumstances at a local university. There was no new information on the case, and Lucy felt distinctly uncomfortable, as if by calling she'd given the elderly woman false hope.

The children, now grown, who'd become orphans after their parents had gone missing while on vacation in Mexico.

The husband who'd remarried after his wife was the fourth of five victims of a serial killer who preyed on young redheaded women throughout the large state of Texas—an investigation that encompassed three FBI offices, more than ten years ago—then nothing. The agent in charge of the investigation was long gone from the FBI, and there was no new information or victims. Conventional wisdom was that the killer had gone to prison for another crime. The husband broke down during their call.

However, Lucy admitted to her husband Sean that some of the case files she'd analyzed were helpful to her as an agent. Absorbing the thought process of other agents was a valuable learning tool. The way they approached witnesses or victims, the questions they'd asked, things they'd seen—or things that were clearly missing—all helped her become a better agent herself. But she felt underutilized. She'd always been someone who learned best by doing, not reading.

The last case she had in front of her seemed boring on the surface—insurance fraud. She made the calls, but none of the phone numbers for the three witnesses were working. Odd. Or maybe not—the case was six years old. She made note of the addresses—someone would need to verify the information.

Done.

The last thing she had to do was write up a final report for her boss, Rachel Vaughn. She'd kept meticulous notes, and when she was tired of making calls had input the info into the database. She'd be done this afternoon. She smiled in relief and let out a deep breath. Done, done, done!

Maybe Rachel would send her into the field with a real case, something interesting. She'd take anything at this point.

She put the last file in the unassigned box. This agent had been transferred to another office—Chicago or New York or Boston. One of the big offices. Whoever Rachel assigned the case would have a clear plan, so Lucy felt she'd done the job required of her. She didn't want her boss to have any complaints about the quality of her work.

She went back to her desk to grab her purse. She planned to meet Nate for lunch. Nate Dunning, a fellow agent as well as a friend, wasn't any happier about her long assignment than she was. Lucy wondered if Nate's skepticism about Vaughn was because of how Lucy was treated or something more.

"Hey, Kincaid."

She glanced up. Jason Lopez was a new agent. Not a rookie—he'd most recently come from the Phoenix FBI office. He'd worked with Rachel in the past. He started here in San Antonio last month, when Ryan's transfer to the Austin Resident Agency went through. Ryan wanted to be closer to his two young sons, so it was a good move for him. He'd be the Supervisory Special Agent within a year because the current SSA of the Austin office was retiring. Lucy missed him, but she was happy for him.

Like Ryan, Jason was bilingual, a huge benefit when working in a culturally diverse community like San Antonio. But like Rachel, the jury was out on him. Lucy had the odd and uncomfortable sensation that he watched her too closely.

"Hi."

"Noon. Right on time."

"Excuse me?"

"You leave for lunch every day at noon. Just saying."

"Four hours straight of reading files, I need the break." Why was she justifying herself to him? Better yet, why was he keeping tabs on her? She looked at her watch. 12:20. But she didn't correct him.

"Not judging," he said.

"I'll be back in an hour."

"I haven't eaten, care if I join you?"

"I'm meeting my husband. Maybe next time." She didn't know why she'd lied to him, except that she didn't want him to know she was meeting Nate downtown, out of the way so they could have privacy. She didn't want her days in the doghouse to rub off on her colleague.

"Right. The newlyweds."

She and Sean had been married for five months.

Maybe they were still considered newlyweds, but why comment?

Maybe she was reading too much into the conversation. She smiled. "See you at one-twenty."

She walked out. Why was she so irritated?

She knew why. It was a culmination of everything that had happened over the last five months.

After she and Sean married at the end of October, they'd gone on a much needed two-week honeymoon. Rachel started her assignment during that time, and when Lucy returned she felt like she was playing catch up. Two new agents also started during those weeks—replacing agents that had left previously, one into forced retirement and one who went on disability after being injured in the line of duty.

From the beginning, Lucy felt like she had something to prove—she worked long hours, made sure she did everything asked of her, and did it well. But, Rachel found fault with everything she did.

"I know you were on vacation when I started, so let me explain how I like reports to be written . . .

"I know you're a newlywed and your mind is not focused on work, so I'll let this error slide this time . . .

"You put in too many hours, Lucy. There is no need to work weekends unless you're on call. Burnout is a problem with some agents, I don't want it to happen to you.

And then January happened, and she had lied to her boss about being sick in order to go to San Diego and investigate the cold case murder of her nephew, Justin. Her boss found out and a bad situation became ten times worse. That's when she was assigned the cold case files to review and update. And the criticisms continued.

"Honestly, Lucy, you leave at five every day . . . some of your colleagues are beginning to question your commitment to this squad.

"I need a weekly report on your progress, Lucy. And no more going out into the field to verify information—leave that to the agents of record, okay?"

When she'd commented that she was only going out when the agent of record had left the office, Rachel said, "*Separate those cases and give them to the SSA of the division. If there's something time-critical, bring it to my attention.*"

Lucy could handle the verbal criticism, she figured she needed to atone for her sin of lying to her boss. But ever since Ryan left and Jason arrived, he'd been watching her all the time, walking into the conference room for no apparent reason, sometimes following her out to her car when she left, ostensibly just to chat. But it was never about anything substantive. It was enough to drive her crazy.

She saw someone sitting in the passenger seat of her car as she approached. Her hand immediately went for her gun until she recognized the man.

Sean's brother, Kane.

She slid into the driver's seat. "I don't want to ask how you got past security."

"Maybe you should."

"You could have called."

"I haven't been waiting long. Going home?"

"I'm meeting Nate for lunch."

"I'll join you."

Her curiosity piqued. "Okay."

"I need a favor," Kane said.

"Do you want me to cancel Nate?"

"No."

Nothing more. Kane didn't talk much, but Lucy had gotten used to it. She headed toward the Mexican restaurant she and Nate liked.

Having her brother-in-law around was comforting. He and Sean had a rocky patch before the wedding, but they'd mended fences. She was thrilled that Kane had settled in Texas. He lived a few hours south, outside Hidalgo, in a house once owned by her brother Jack. Jack had given the property to RCK. With three Rogans and two Kincaids working full-time for RCK, it had become the family business.

Lucy glanced at Kane. "Why do I think you knew that I was meeting Nate?"

He winked.

Lucy wasn't going to speculate why—Kane was still almost as mysterious as when she first met him.

Ten minutes later, Lucy parked and they walked into the restaurant. It was one of Lucy's favorite places, since it reminded her of her mom's cooking. It was the spices—the slight Cuban flair, more authentic than the popular Tex-Mex fare.

Nate was already at the restaurant munching on chips and salsa. "Sorry I'm late," Lucy said, sitting across from Nate.

"You brought company." Nate fist bumped Kane. "Sean coming?"

"No," Lucy said. "Jason wanted to join me for lunch; I told him I was meeting Sean to get him off my back."

"Who?" Kane asked.

"New agent," Nate said.

"Background?"

"I thought RCK vetted the San Antonio staff after the Rollins escape."

"One-time assignment."

"Rachel Vaughn brought him in from Phoenix."

RCK had vetted Rachel—Lucy was privy to their report. Which made working for her under these conditions doubly odd. Rachel was a solid agent with more than a decade of experience. She'd been ranked in the top ten percent of her class at Quantico, born and raised in Los Angeles, graduated with a dual degree in criminal justice and business economics from UCLA, worked three years for a Wall Street company in New York, then got her masters in Criminal Justice from Syracuse. Did her two rookie years in white collar crimes in San Francisco, then transferred to the Phoenix office and into the violent crimes unit. Three years ago she was promoted to SSA and put in charge of the Tucson Resident Agency, where she had one of the highest clearance rates among all RAs in the country.

Brad Donnelly, the Assistant Special Agent in Charge of the local DEA office and a good friend of Lucy's, had known Rachel professionally when he'd been in Phoenix, though they weren't close. When he first heard she was coming in, he was optimistic—she had a reputation for running an efficient office that cleared cases. Her staff liked her. And so far, everyone on the violent crimes squad seemed to work well with Rachel. Everyone except Lucy.

Brad had the best insight. He'd come over for dinner one night and Lucy spilled her frustrations.

Brad said, "Lucy, you're a smart, independent woman. Rachel is the same. Two strong-willed women working together can cause friction."

"Kenzie and Marie don't seem to have any problems." Kenzie had been with the unit since before Lucy, and Marie had come on board at the end of Noah's run, right before Lucy's wedding. "Neither of them are wimps."

Brad laughed. "Kenzie definitely kicks ass, but her years in the military have her working well in a leadership structure and taking direction without question. I don't know Marie, but she's only two years out of Quantico. New town, new colleagues, no waves. And wasn't she a lawyer?"

"Prosecutor for ten years in Portland."

"So she's doing something completely different. And

truthfully, Lucy—you're unique. You're a threat to some people who like the status quo. Give Rachel time to warm up. She will."

Lucy hoped Brad was right. Because of his insight, Lucy did everything Rachel told her to do, and did it well. But she was still relegated to a desk, and she couldn't seem to impress her boss with anything.

After the waitress took their orders, Lucy said, "Enough about work. I assume your visit today isn't all pleasure."

Kane replied, "We have a situation. JT's sister Bella is missing. She went dark while working deep undercover for a group that rescues sex slaves. No contact for more than forty-eight hours. Normally JT wouldn't panic, but this situation is more volatile than most. A cop was killed after helping Bella rescue two girls, and she asked her handler for an extraction, but no one has been able to find her. JT thinks she may have been compromised, or will be compromised because her partner doesn't know where she is. Apparently, no one does."

Lucy had never met JT's sister. She didn't know much about her other than she'd been a vice cop in Seattle for twelve years before quitting to work for a private organization that located missing persons, specifically runaways and minors sold into the US sex industry. She'd always wanted to meet the woman, but Sean said JT and Bella had had a falling out and it was a sensitive subject, so she didn't push.

"What can I do?"

Kane slid over a piece of paper. Lucy opened it.

Martin Hirsch.

"He's the number two guy, or partnered with someone known by the alias 'Z.' No known address, description, nada. I'm looking into it, but so far RCK contacts are stumped. Hirsch has a key associate named Damien. We need everything the FBI has on Hirsch, and if possible an ID on any known associates named Damien. He was most recently in Los Angeles, moved to Phoenix four weeks ago, and is suspected to be in Las Cruces or West Texas—someplace along the I-10 corridor is our guess. El Paso, San Antonio are the two cities that popped as possible."

"Because there's a void," Lucy said.

"Exactly. In addition to running him, you more than anyone know the players—those in jail, those who are out, those aligning with a new boss."

"Not only me," she said.

"You're not letting Rachel get into your head, are you?" Nate snapped.

"No—that's not what I meant. But there's someone else who might have information." She glanced at Kane.

"Marisol."

She nodded. "Marisol *and* Siobhan."

Marisol de la Cruz had been trafficked for two years, forced into prostitution with her younger sister. When they got pregnant, the organization that imprisoned them sold their babies on the black market. Kane's girlfriend Siobhan Walsh had uncovered information that ultimately led to the demise of the criminal enterprise. *That* criminal enterprise. There was always someone else willing to step up and take over.

"I should have thought of it."

"You did." Lucy knew Kane, they thought things through the same way. "If you don't want to drag them into it, I understand."

"You're right. I didn't want to ask them, especially now." Marisol's sister had given birth to twins late last year and Marisol had been reunited with her two-year-old son. It was a bittersweet and emotional time for everyone. "But I'll talk to Siobhan this afternoon and see what she knows."

"At a minimum, she and Marisol will be able to put

together a list of locations and underlings who might be approached by Hirsch. It will give us a good starting point."

Nate cleared his throat, his eyes skirting toward the door.

Jason Lopez walked in with Kenzie Malone.

Impossible. No, not impossible. *The jerk.*

"He followed me," Lucy said.

Kane immediately tensed beside her.

Jason and Kenzie spotted them and approached. "Kincaid, Dunning. You must be Sean."

Kane looked Jason in the eye and didn't say a word.

Lucy said, "This is my brother-in-law, Kane." She glanced at Kenzie. She seemed as surprised as Lucy that they'd met up here. Lucy often came here—Ryan Quiroz had introduced her to the place when they first started working together on a joint task force and it had become a favorite place of hers and Sean's—but it was far enough from headquarters that she couldn't remember ever seeing someone else from work.

Was he waiting for an invitation to join them? She hoped not.

Fortunately, their food arrived at that moment, and Kenzie said, "We'll let you eat. See you later."

Lucy watched them sit four booths down. They wouldn't be able to hear their conversation—not in this place—but she still didn't feel comfortable with the knowledge that Jason Lopez had followed her.

Kane asked, "Sean said you were getting shit about what happened in San Diego."

"It's fine," she said. She didn't want any more conflict in her workplace. And while Kane might mean well, she didn't want anyone else to fight her battles. She'd made Sean promise not to involve himself.

"It's bullshit," Nate said.

She gave Nate a look and mouthed, *You're not helping.*

He ignored her.

"I'll take care of it," she said. She had to do something, but she had to put all that aside for now. Finding JT's sister would be a welcome diversion from the drudgery that her job had become.

"Anything else I need to know about Hirsch or Bella?" Lucy asked as she spooned extra hot salsa onto her tostada.

"JT and Jack are in Phoenix. JT wants to talk to the two young girls Bella rescued. They may have information on where Hirsch is headed or details about his plan. They'll have more intel after that." He paused, glanced over to where Kenzie and Jason were sitting. They seemed to be involved in their own conversation. Quietly, Kane said, "A Phoenix cop who helped Bella and her partner rescue the girls is dead. We don't know how he was captured, but he was shot and tortured, then his body dumped in a remote area outside Scottsdale. He was working off-book."

Lucy's stomach tightened. "Do you think he gave up Bella?"

"No way to know, but her partner thinks not. We need a handle on the situation, locate her, then JT will make the call as to whether we extract her." He looked from Lucy to Nate. "That won't be a government op."

"JT has been there for Sean and me every time we've needed him," Lucy said. "Anything you need, I'm with you."

CHAPTER SEVEN

When Lucy returned to the office, it was quiet. She ran Martin Hirsch in the criminal database. Two records popped up from New York. The first: a rape conviction at the age of nineteen—he served three of a six-month sentence. Three months for rape. Lucy didn't know the details, but it seemed slack. He must have had a good lawyer because he wasn't required to register as a sex offender, and the charge was listed as a misdemeanor.

Then, three years after he got out, he was arrested in a joint FBI/NYPD/DEA drug sting. Possession with intent, again pled down to a misdemeanor, and served one year on an eighteen-month sentence.

She made note of his lawyer—Gretchen Barton. Same lawyer both times. After Lucy's work on the black market baby case, she realized that some lawyers were far less scrupulous than others—and much harder to pin a crime on.

Nothing on Hirsch in twenty years. He served his time, lived in Brooklyn during his probation, then left the state. She searched other databases. She couldn't access tax records without a warrant, but she learned his permanent residence was in Las Vegas. He was in his early forties, but there were no current photos. She downloaded his mugshot and emailed it to her personal account. Tonight, she'd play around with age enhancement software and see if they could get something more current from that.

She sent all the information to Kane from her personal account—RCK could dig deeper into Hirsch's personal life than she legally could without a warrant. Most likely, Kane had asked Sean to run a full background on Hirsch. The only thing Sean couldn't access were criminal records, unless they were in a public court document. So she put the information she had aside and called her good friend Suzanne Madeaux, the FBI liaison to the NYPD. Suzanne had been in her wedding, and Lucy trusted her to keep her request confidential.

"If it isn't Mrs. Rogan," Suzanne said. "I haven't heard from you since your wedding—except for the very nice thank-you note."

"Trying to get caught up. We have a new SSA."

"I heard."

"Oh?"

"Nothing bad or good, just info. You're okay though, aren't you?"

"I think so." Lucy glanced around. No one was at their desks. Everyone had real cases to work, not the grunt cold case review Rachel had assigned her. Still, she kept her voice low. "My new boss doesn't like me. She's given me crap work and for the last two months I haven't been out in the field. Most recently I've been updating contact information on witnesses and victims for all cold case files."

"Shit. I'd hang myself. Still, you *are* a rookie and Violent Crimes doesn't have the same resources as other squads."

Lucy wished it was just because she was a rookie, but she suspected it was directly related to her investigation into Justin's murder. "I keep telling myself that. I have a personal favor to ask."

"Shoot."

"A low-level drug dealer named Martin Hirsch was arrested twenty years ago in Manhattan. Did six months for possession with intent. Prior to that he pled out a rape case and did three months. Left New York after his probation and moved west to Las Vegas. He's a person of interest in a sex trafficking case."

"I thought you weren't in the field."

"I'm not. This isn't an active investigation. Just gathering information."

"Gotcha. What else do you have on him?"

Lucy read off his Social Security number, last known address. "He was taken down in a joint task force sting. Before your time—before Joe's time—but maybe Joe can find out more about him. I'd really love to know how a two-bit dealer rises to running a major sex trafficking organization."

"Cream rises to the top," Suzanne said sarcastically. "I'll dig around. Known associates, see how the bust happened. Joe's old partner retired a couple years ago, but he used to work Vice. He might have some intel."

"I appreciate it. If any of the players he ran with then have connections out of state—particularly in the southwest. California, Arizona, Nevada, Texas."

"I'll see what I can get on the QT."

"Thanks."

"Don't be a stranger. When are you and Sean coming to visit?"

"I don't think I'll have any vacation time for the next ten years."

"That bad?"

"Maybe." She was about to say goodbye when she remembered that Jason Lopez had spent his two rookie years in New York. "Rachel just brought in a new agent. He has seven years in, last five in Phoenix, but spent his rookie years in New York."

"Hmm. We have a gazillion agents in this building, and seven years ago I was in counterterrorism."

"He was in violent crimes, that's all I know."

"That's easy—I know all those guys. Is he giving you shit?"

"I don't know."

Suzanne laughed. "Evasive."

"Rachel Vaughn brought him in, he followed me to lunch."

"Followed?"

"I was meeting someone off the beaten path. I don't know how else he would have found the place if he didn't follow me. And he was acting odd when I was in the office. I can't explain it—I just have this sense he's been watching me. I want to know if he's spying on me for Rachel, or if there's another reason."

"Either way, that's fucked. Watch yourself."

"Ten-four." Lucy hung up and went back to the conference room. She finished up her report and sent it to Rachel, along with a list of follow-ups she planned on starting tomorrow—people she couldn't reach but hadn't confirmed that they'd moved or died. While on the one hand, she'd hated every minute she had to work on this project; now that it was done she felt a sense of accomplishment. She'd also streamlined the process so next time, there was a sheet of everyone she spoke to, verified, who moved, and the like. It would go much faster.

If it ever had to be done again.

She hated watching the clock, but she had an hour before five. She pulled out the notes she'd made on the cases where she hadn't been able to reach anyone involved and reviewed them, then wrote out a strategy for tomorrow's follow-ups. She was actually excited to get back out in the field, even though it would be grunt work. Grunt work outside the office was better than riding a desk. If she timed everything right with traffic and expected length of interviews, she could complete the entire project by Friday afternoon.

She hadn't seen Kenzie or Jason since lunch—she hadn't seen Nate, either, and wondered if he had gone off with Kane. Nate had been in the Army, like Jack, and had the same edge that her brother and brother-in-law shared.

"Lucy," Rachel called from her office. "A word."

Lucy stepped into the threshold.

"Close the door."

This wasn't going to be good.

Lucy shut the door and sat down. Rachel was forty, attractive even though she wore her hair and make-up quite severely. Her dark blond hair was pulled into a sleek ponytail, not a hair out of place. She dressed impeccably in a pant suit and white blouse.

"Is there something wrong with my report?" she asked.

"I haven't read it yet. Why were you running Martin Hirsch?"

Lucy blanked. How did Rachel know she'd run Hirsch? No way would Suzanne have tipped her off. She hadn't talked to anyone else. She'd run the name through . . .

The criminal database. She had to put in her badge number and a case number, which she'd created just for this purpose. That wasn't unusual. Agents did it all the time. Noah told her how to do it when she was still a training agent in the DC office, before she even went to Quantico. She didn't think twice.

Maybe she should have.

"His name came up."

"You have no active investigations. You created a case without approval."

"Just informative at this time—"

Rachel interrupted. "Why did you run his name?

Does it have something to do with your brother-in-law paying you a visit?"

Lucy fumed. Jason had reported to Rachel about Kane? Why?

"I had lunch with my brother-in-law, I don't see how that's relevant."

"If you're using government resources to assist a private contractor in a private investigation without approval, that's a breach of protocol and possibly a violation of the law." She stared at Lucy. Did she want Lucy to dig herself into a hole? Did she want Lucy to justify herself? Apologize?

Lucy kept her mouth shut.

Rachel spoke first. "Based on your record last year, you regularly put in ten- to twelve-hour days, closed dozens of cases, and had several letters of commendation from San Antonio PD, the DEA, and your former supervisor. This year, you run out when the clock strikes five. You put in your minimal time, and now you're running a name through the criminal database for a case that doesn't exist. Do you know what that tells me? When you're working with your friends, you're willing to go above and beyond. But when someone gives you an assignment you don't like, you drag your heels and do the bare minimum to get by. The FBI is not all glamour. Most of our work *is* grunt work, paper work, building and closing cases."

"I've spent the last two months reviewing every cold case file going back twenty years. I made over one thousand phone calls, sent hundreds of letters, and verified every address, name, and phone number in more than two hundred cases."

"So because I gave you paperwork you don't like, that justifies breaking the rules and running Hirsch for your brother-in-law?"

Lucy didn't know what to say. She didn't want to put

Bella in jeopardy, or RCK's relationship with the FBI. She would have to take the consequences. She always had before—only this time, it burned because she hadn't done anything wrong.

"Hirsch's name came up in an investigation that left a cop dead in Phoenix. I was doing a favor, yes, but it was for a legitimate reason."

Her eyes clouded, just for a second. Rachel knew something about it.

"Is this related to the Roger Beck homicide?"

Lucy hadn't heard the name of the dead cop, but she nodded.

"That's out of our jurisdiction. Send me what you found out and I'll pass it along to my former office. And that's the end of this, Lucy. This isn't your case. You don't work for your brother-in-law or your husband. If you can't separate the two, then we'll have a problem."

"Ma'am, there is no problem," Lucy said.

"I certainly hope not." Lucy rose and Rachel said, "I'm not done."

Lucy sat back in the chair.

"My strength is asset management," Rachel said. "I've made changes in this unit in order to maximize our limited resources. Violent Crimes has gotten the short end of the stick since 9/11, and that's not going to change in the foreseeable future. I've read every case file you've worked—as well as every case file for the last two years of everyone else in this unit. My predecessor, Noah Armstrong, was here temporarily after the Nicole Rollins fiasco. While he did an exemplary job at cleaning house—a necessity considering the circumstances—he wasn't a manager. He spent nearly as much time in the field as his staff.

"I want to send you back out into the field. Your skill set is unique and could be an asset to our unit. Unfortunately, your loyalties are divided and that's a problem for me. I can't have you running around doing your own thing, using FBI resources to run criminals for your husband's private business—their connection as a private government contractor notwithstanding. There is a process to use civilian consultants and you need to follow it. Your fellow agents are skeptical and concerned. I don't appreciate being kept in the dark about operations that were undertaken by this office, or that several files have been redacted by national headquarters. All files that *you* are connected to."

Lucy wanted to justify everything she'd done, but she didn't. She hadn't redacted anything—that was the decision of her superiors. She'd always played by the rules until she realized that sometimes, rules didn't work. She would stand up for what she'd done because in the end, right or wrong, lives were saved.

"When I say that I've gone over your cases, I mean I've gone over every word of every report you've written and the ones your colleagues have written that involve you. On the one hand, I want to sing your praises—Armstrong's report into the black market baby operation you, Agent Dunning, and Armstrong shut down in September showed me that you're not only smart on your feet, you are levelheaded in the field. You saved numerous lives, including the baby of a dying woman. I called the doctor who treated the infant because I thought that Armstrong may have exaggerated; I learned instead that he toned down your heroics.

"And then," Rachel continued, "I saw a series of vague and partially redacted reports a month later about the recovery of another infant from Mexico. Considering how complete and detailed Armstrong's reports were about the initial investigation—and how completely vague and ultimately misleading his reports were a month later, I realized that the private government contractor that had gone to Mexico to recover an infant was most likely your husband's business partners. It's clear that the FBI can't operate across borders without jumping through numerous hoops that take time and money, so I wouldn't be surprised if they quickly asked for private assistance. Nothing illegal about it that I can tell. Maybe the government didn't ask. Maybe you did. Still, nothing *overtly* illegal."

"I don't understand what you're trying to say," Lucy said, choosing her words carefully. "RCK has a long history of rescuing American hostages."

"As well as accepting bounties on fugitives and the like." That comment was said with venom that Lucy didn't have an opportunity to analyze before Rachel continued. "They have quite a checkered history. However, what is not okay is for a federal agent to travel to Mexico and retrieve an infant then lie about it on official reports. And honestly? That's what I think you did."

"I didn't go to Mexico to rescue baby Joshua." That was the truth. But if that's what Rachel thought happened, Lucy was relieved.

If she knew the whole truth, there would be far more problems for Lucy and for RCK.

"I'm not a fool, Agent Kincaid. I know how this business works. I understand that you have friends in high places. You earned this spot and graduated high in your class at Quantico across the board. That can't be faked. Your master's degree in criminal psychology is an asset, and your ability to apply your experience and education in the field has been exemplary. You're a certified forensic pathologist, you've been certified in underwater search and rescue, and you have a unique criminology background that is a big help in the field. At the same time, I know that your mistakes have all been erased."

Lucy hated confrontation, and she didn't know what to say now. Rachel first commends her then criticizes her? Shares her theory about Lucy going down to Mexico—as inaccurate as her theory is. Yet mistakes? What mistakes? Yes—there had been situations that had been glossed over or redacted because of the people involved. Or the places Lucy had to go. She wouldn't risk her friends, family, or colleagues by exposing them when everything they'd done was to save human lives. But *mistakes?* No. She wouldn't own up to mistakes. Because how could it be a mistake when someone lived who would have died had she done nothing?

Rachel nodded, as if she'd seen something in Lucy's expression that Lucy was pretty certain she'd hidden well. "I'm telling you right now, Lucy: you don't have a free pass with me. You will not work any unsanctioned investigations. For the remainder of your time as a rookie, you will not be working on any joint task force because I would not be your direct supervisor. You have friends in the DEA—and the new assistant agent in charge, Brad Donnelly? I understand he's a personal friend of yours. I know Brad from his time in Phoenix, and he's a maverick. He will look the other way, and I suspect he has many times—likely because you and he operate in much the same way. He's requested you twice in as many months to liaison on different DEA cases, and I declined. Because I can't control your actions, and he will sugarcoat any transgressions. Probably encourage them.

"I cannot let you operate as you have been for the last year. It damages morale and creates problems in this office and with sister agencies. If your fellow agents can't trust you, you have a problem. I hope to rectify that quickly. You will answer to me anytime you overstep, and I expect a complete and honest answer. Do you understand?"

"Yes, ma'am." Lucy was surprised she could say anything. This was the most that Rachel had said to her since Rachel came on board nearly five months ago.

"Think about what I've said. You have the potential to be a great agent. Before I came here, when I first got the jackets on all the staff, I was intrigued by you and excited to meet you. I thought we had the foundation of a terrific team and I was thrilled to get this position. Then I read your reports, talked to your colleagues, heard about those last two cases. I grew concerned. And not three months after I started you lied to me about why you went to San Diego. You put yourself in the middle of a cold case investigation, lied about it, and got away with it."

"That's not how it happened."

"You don't see how difficult this is for me, do you? I would have fired you—or at least had you written up and facing OPR. Then I get a call from the ASAC in San Diego about how you negotiated a tense hostage situation and saved the lives of two federal agents and a young boy and his family, and she wanted to put a commendation in your file. That's when I realized we have a huge problem. I won't tolerate a maverick like Brad Donnelly. It may have worked for him, but trust me when I tell you it doesn't usually end so well."

Lucy didn't say anything. After months, she finally understood Rachel Vaughn. She almost couldn't blame her—other than her theory about the infant Joshua, nothing she said was inaccurate.

But she couldn't very well tell her new boss that she had in fact been in Mexico, nor why she'd been down there.

"Am I dismissed?" Lucy asked.

Rachel stared at her. "I'm assigning Agent Lopez to work with you to follow up on the cold case verifications."

Of course she was. Because Jason was her spy, and he had already ratted Lucy out about who she was having lunch with.

"I'm looking forward to it." Lucy commended herself that she could keep her emotions under such tight control when she'd rarely found herself this angry—and this worried—all at once.

She left Rachel's office, grabbed her bag, and walked out of the building.

CHAPTER EIGHT

Lucy went straight home after meeting with her boss. Meeting? She wouldn't call it that. She didn't know what to call the conversation. Part lecture, part praise, but all antagonistic.

She wasn't surprised to see Nate's truck parked in front of her house. She pulled into the garage and the door lumbered closed behind her. She stayed in her car, took a long, deep breath.

Rachel was right about so many things. Lucy had taken so much for granted. She'd been given a lot of autonomy when she worked on the joint task force with Brad Donnelly, and then when Noah was here to clean up the office after corrupt DEA Agent Nicole Rollins and her criminal enterprise was taken down, he trusted her and gave her the freedom to run her investigations the way she saw fit.

But he'd also warned her that she hadn't chosen the easy path. That because of her associations some people may not trust her as he did. But largely, her issues with her squad started a year ago, when she went to Mexico to help rescue Brad Donnelly and a group of boys who'd been used as mules for a drug cartel. That one act had ignited a chain of events that resulted in one of their own—and favored—agents, Barry Crawford, being kidnapped, tortured, and nearly killed. Barry would never be the same, and the way people looked at her—Lucy realized now that they blamed her.

The garage side door opened and Lucy jumped. Sean stepped out, opened her car door.

"I heard you drive in ten minutes ago."

"Thinking," she said.

He took her hand and pulled her up. Kissed her. "What's wrong?"

"I'll tell you later—we have company."

"Nate and Kane can wait." He searched her eyes. "Luce, talk to me."

Sean was her rock. She had to share with someone, or this anxiety would fester deep inside. "Rachel finally explained what her issue is with me. And she's right."

"I'm sure that's not true."

"At least I understand her."

"What did she say?"

"Essentially, she was impressed with my cases, especially the black market baby investigation."

"As she should be." He put his arms around her waist and kissed her.

"But I'm a maverick, like Brad Donnelly. My colleagues don't trust me, half my files are redacted, and I lied to her about going to San Diego in January."

"Yet you saved a little boy's life."

"She pointed that out, but that doesn't justify my actions. And she's right—it doesn't. Everything she said is true, except." She shouldn't say anything. She slipped out of Sean's arms because this was all harder to talk about than she'd thought.

"What." It wasn't a question.

Lucy bit her lip."She thinks I went to Mexico in October specifically to bring back Baby Joshua."

Sean tensed, and she knew she shouldn't have told him now. Later, when they were alone, in bed, when they were relaxed and remembered that no matter what happened in the past or could happen in the future, they had each other now.

"You were taken to Mexico against your will, and that is none of her fucking business."

"Sean—"

"There is no record of you being there. None. Even the Navy SEALs files are classified. Rick made sure of it. Everyone is on the same page."

"She got that part wrong—but honestly? If I knew that Baby Joshua was down there, and if I thought that I was the only one who could safely bring him back by using RCK or any other resource at my disposal, I would have done it. We both know that. So while Joshua may have not been the reason I was there, it *could* have been."

"Why does she even care about that? Baby Joshua had been ripped from his dead mother's womb and sold on the black market. The people who had him didn't deserve him, nor would they have been able to keep him safe considering they were working with some very dangerous people. So what if you went down there?"

"Sean—a federal agent is prohibited from working across borders. It's a matter of trust. She doesn't trust me. Maybe that's why she was pushing on the baby. I don't know."

"Stop, Lucy. Everything you've done from the day we landed in San Antonio may have crossed a few lines, but you did them for the right reasons. You have to stop second guessing yourself on everything you do."

"I'm not."

"Yes you are. You're letting Rachel get inside your head and make you feel guilty for things you should be proud of. I'm not being naïve, Luce, I know there are a lot of gray areas in this business. I know you wouldn't have done anything differently. Would you?"

She shook her head. "We've both done things for the greater good, but at what cost?"

"It's a price you and I have always been willing to pay; don't let Rachel Vaughn change that."

"She's monitoring all my activities. She knew that I ran a search on Martin Hirsch and asked why. I was vague and she called me on it. She also knew that I had lunch with Kane and made a point of saying I had to stay out of this, that it's not a San Antonio investigation."

"How the hell did she know you had lunch with Kane?"

"My guess? The new agent, the one from her old office, told her. He saw us in the restaurant."

"Kane told me he followed you."

"I didn't know—I'm usually good at picking up a tail."

"Then you're out of this. We'll do this with RCK only."

"I *want* to do this." She's been thinking about it all the way home, weighing the pros and cons, and in the end she realized she was a valuable asset. Kane was right—she knew many of the players, but more importantly, she understood the human trafficking business. For the last six months she'd been tracking the babies sold on the black market and had learned far more than she'd ever wanted about the buying and selling of human beings.

"You sure?"

"JT has always been there for us. *Always.* He's never asked for anything in return. Now his sister's missing. I'm not turning my back on him. Kane is right. I know the players, I understand the business of sex trafficking. There *is* a void, and before Ryan left we were putting together a list of potential players. We destroyed one major network, but there are always more people looking to cash in. I've been looking for Mona Hill."

"*What*? Why?"

Mona Hill had run a group of prostitutes in San Antonio until she disappeared early last summer. Some in the FBI thought she was dead; Lucy didn't. If she was dead they would know, because at the time Tobias—Nicole Rollins's front man—would have wanted to make an example of her. This was long before their network was destroyed. Ryan had tracked her to Houston. Now, Lucy had no idea where she was, but she *would* find her.

"Mona Hill knows the sex business better than anyone, but there was never a hint of her trafficking. Every girl who worked for her was of age and willing. I think she can help if properly motivated." She paused, looked up at him. "Do you think I'm wrong?"

"No—I just don't know that she will help, or that she'll be easy to find."

"Well, she's not easy to find. I haven't yet, but admittedly it hasn't been on the top of my to-do list." She took his hand, kissed his palm. "Don't say anything to Kane or Nate about Rachel, okay? I thought about this while driving home, and I'm going to help JT. Bella could be in serious trouble. I'll just have to do it quietly and on my own time."

They walked into the kitchen. Kane was typing a text message on his flip phone—he still hadn't converted to a smart phone. Nate was drinking a beer at the large center counter where they often ate.

Bandit was at Kane's feet, but as soon as Sean walked in, he ran to his master as if he'd been gone for hours instead of ten minutes. Sean scratched the Golden Retriever, then Bandit went to Lucy for the same greeting.

"Oh, I know who's your favorite," Lucy said, bending down to kiss Bandit on the top of the head. "I'm second fiddle."

They had adopted the young dog while on their honeymoon, after Bandit's owner was murdered. The dog had been happy and loved, but not trained. Over the last five months, Sean had Bandit obeying most every command. Bandit listened to Lucy, but worshipped Sean. Sean had started taking Bandit with him when he went out, and was getting him trained as a search and rescue dog, not only because it was a valuable skill but so he could bring him anywhere as a service dog. There was a sense of peace and purpose that had fallen over Sean when they brought Bandit home with them. Sean had even bought a new car—a Jeep Wrangler with extra-durable seats, unlike the buttery leather seats in his custom Mustang—so Bandit's nails wouldn't destroy them.

Lucy dropped her purse on the desk in the kitchen and sat next to Kane. "After I sent the information about Hirsch to you, I called Suzanne Madeaux in the New York office. You met her at the wedding."

Kane nodded.

"She's going to talk to NYPD and find out who his connections were, if there's any chatter about him. I also asked her to find out who he bunked with in prison. He was in for two short stints. But he's been completely under the radar for twenty years."

"JT and Jack are heading to El Paso in the morning," Kane said. "One of the girls Bella rescued overheard something about El Paso, and Declan Cross also heard a rumor they were heading there. I called in favors and there's chatter that something's going down, people are antsy."

"Who's Declan Cross?"

"He served in the SEALs with JT and Rick, stayed longer than all of us. When he got out, he went to work for Adam and Laura Dixon, the people I told you run

Genesis Road, a group that rescues sex slaves, primarily outside the U.S. Now he and Bella work for Simon Egan."

"How's he involved?"

"He was supposed to be backup, but Bella slipped away when he wasn't looking."

Lucy frowned. "He screwed up?"

Kane shrugged. "JT's giving him the benefit of the doubt, and so far he's been more help than hindrance, but a lot of shit has gone down over the years, and I don't know how far I would trust him."

Sean said, "Simon Egan runs a group like Genesis Road, only they focus in the States."

Kane grunted. "Don't say that to the Dixons."

"I feel like I stepped into the middle of something," Lucy said.

"Egan's a former dotcom millionaire turned PI." He said it with disdain, a tone Lucy rarely heard from the even-tempered Kane. "Questionable practices."

"Sounds like a mess," Nate said.

"When Bella was forced out of Seattle PD—that's another long story—she went to work for Egan. I get it—she was frustrated with the system and the rules she had to follow, rules that ultimately benefited the predators more than the victims. JT didn't—she's his little sister, and with her history, he wants to protect her. He wanted her to work with Genesis. It's run by JT and Rick's former CO, Adam Dixon. Dix is a few years older, resigned his commission to run Genesis with his wife, Laura. After JT and I rescued Bella, she went to live with them."

Lucy blinked. "Backup. Rescued Bella? When?"

Kane hesitated a moment. "It's really JT's story to tell, but he still doesn't like to talk about it."

"Does it pertain to what's happening now?"

Kane nodded solemnly. "JT's dad was a career criminal. His mother was a drug addict. That's why JT spent so much time at our house, Sean, he had to get away. Bella is ten years younger, lived with her grandmother most of the time because their mother would go on binges and disappear for weeks. Grandma Sue." Kane got a wistful look on his face. "She baked the best pies on the planet. I miss them."

He glanced at Sean, then faced Lucy. "JT enlisted in the Navy, I went Marines, but we always kept in touch. JT planned on making the Navy his career. I kept re-upping because I didn't know what else to do, and I was a good soldier. Six years in, JT found out that his father had been out of prison for nearly a year and back with his mother. Grandma Sue became ill, they took Bella from her. JT didn't even know his father was out of prison, until he got word from Grandma Sue's lawyer that she'd died. He went back for the funeral and Bella was gone. It took us weeks to learn that their father sold her into prostitution to pay off a debt to some asshole. Their father didn't like Bella's mouth—basically, Bella challenged him and when beating her didn't work and she ran away, he found her and got rid of two of his problems—Bella and his debt.

"JT needed my help to find her, so I didn't re-enlist. It took us months to track her down. She was moved from city to city in forced prostitution for thirteen months before we rescued her. She was fifteen by that time, and JT didn't know how to help her. She was angry, bitter, guilty, and terrified. Dix and Laura took her in. What can you do when someone is trafficked for over a year? The prick who had her moved them around so they'd never be comfortable in one place. There were cops on their payroll, so the girls didn't trust law enforcement. And even then, most just wanted to escape—but they had no home to go to. Stayed voluntarily? I don't know—but when you think you have no other options, or you're broken to the point you lose all free will, staying was de facto the only choice. Bella was bought and sold, but I suspect she felt like she should have found a way to escape. It took years before she understood the psychology of torture and threats, and how it impacted her as a young teen."

"I had no idea," Lucy said. But she understood what Bella had gone through. Lucy's own ordeal was short-lived, but the guilt and fear had stayed with her for a long time. *If only* she'd fought harder, *if only* she had been smarter . . .

"JT doesn't talk about it," Kane said. "He has his own guilt over not being around when his bastard dad got out of prison. But they had something—a connection—and growing up with Dix and Laura helped. Then, a couple years ago, JT and Bella had a blowout about her working for Egan, before you and Sean hooked up."

Lucy absorbed everything Kane said. She had known JT had a sister, but she didn't know anything about her. What she must have endured . . . that she'd gotten out and made something of herself was remarkable.

"That was JT on the phone when you walked in. I had some information from Siobhan he needed to know. She and Marisol have been putting together a list of potential locations in west Texas where Hirsch might be holed up. Mostly border towns, but we're going with the El Paso lead. Plus JT said Hirsch uses moving truck companies. He thinks he owns several independent companies all along the I-10 corridor, though Declan only knows of one by name. JT is sending us the information."

Sean rubbed Lucy's neck. "I'll run the company Declan knows against similar companies and see if I can find a pattern and other connections, then we can check them out."

"Focus on any company that's been sold within the last month," Kane said. "JT thinks there might have been a new transaction. The girls were moved from L.A. to Phoenix in newly painted trucks. He also wants to know if you were able to break Bella's cover."

Sean didn't say anything for a beat.

"Sean?"

"Yes, I broke it. I don't believe the average person can, however."

"It's that good?"

"On the surface it's outstanding. There were falsified news reports that were uploaded into archives, a court transcript that I was able to download that looks clean. A driver's license with a history—great fake IDs. I mean, they're not fake—they're the real deal, they created a real person on paper. She has a Social Security number and false employment data with a hospital in Los Angeles."

"That's elaborate. And illegal," Lucy said.

"The clincher is I don't know if the documents physically exist—other than her driver's license. I would have to go to L.A. and try to pull the court case. If it's actually there, they had to have bought someone off to insert it in the archives. At that point the only thing that would tip her hand was if someone went to the judge of record."

"I don't see these people hanging out at a courthouse pulling docs," Nate said.

"No—and that's a good thing," Sean said. "Because nothing is foolproof."

"So if her cover gets blown, it's not because of the setup," Kane said.

"Correct."

"How'd you break it?" Lucy asked.

"They set up a solid background on her, but they either didn't think to or they couldn't hack into the small medical school she ostensibly graduated from. They forged a degree, and created a fake article about her graduation, but there's no record at the college itself of Isabella Carter attending, let alone graduating."

Sean handed out more beers, then sat back down. "It shouldn't take me long to find the trucking company he bought. We'll check it out tomorrow."

"Actually, you and I will be in El Paso tomorrow, unless we confirm that Hirsch isn't there," Kane said. "Where JT goes, we go. They'll need back up." He glanced at Nate. "You can help Lucy with the truck company and monitoring the local prostitution rings?"

Nate nodded.

"You're looking for someone ripe for a takeover," Lucy said. "Honestly, they all are. Lots of infighting, no one clearly in charge. Our best bet is to read in Tia Mancini. She's with SAPD and I trust her. Plus, she knows the local sex business better than anyone."

"Is she back full time?" Kane asked.

Last May Tia had been shot and nearly killed when a criminal organization targeted Lucy for assassination. "She started full-time active duty the week we returned from Colorado. She's doing good."

"I'm glad. Read her in as much as necessary, but we're protecting Bella's cover. That's need to know."

"Of course."

"If we're in El Paso and Hirsch slips away, San Antonio is going to be his next stop. While ultimately it's JT's decision about whether we extract Bella, if you locate her and she's in immediate danger, don't wait for permission."

Nate left and Kane was bunking out in the pool house. Bandit was in his dog bed in the corner of the master bedroom. Finally, Sean had Lucy alone.

"We need to talk about something," Sean said. He'd hoped this day wouldn't come. Kane had told him last year he needed to tell Lucy the truth about Mona Hill, but Sean hadn't. He should have known that everything would come around full circle.

"I knew something was bothering you all night. It's my boss, isn't it? I can handle what's going on at work, but I'm not turning my back on JT or his sister."

"That's not it." Sean was worried about Lucy's job security, but only because losing her badge would hit her a lot harder than she thought. He took her hands and sat down on the end of their bed. He kissed them. "It's about Mona Hill."

"I'm listening."

"I know where she is."

Her brows dipped in. She looked confused, not worried. "You found her that fast?"

"I've always known where she is."

Lucy didn't say anything. Sean searched her eyes. She was still confused, and now a bit worried, a little suspicious. But she would listen, and he prayed she understood.

"Last year after you told me that Mona Hill knew about your past, I dug into hers. I more than dug—I learned everything about her. She was born Ramona Jefferson to a drug addict mother who prostituted her at a young age. Mona had a younger half-sister who, when the mother went to prison, was in and out of foster care. Eventually she landed in a decent place, changed her name, and managed to make a life for herself. Has a son, is now a teacher, her kid plays baseball, neither of them have been in any trouble. Mona has been supporting her through a blind trust. She falsified death records in another state so that her sister believed she'd been killed in an accident and left her the trust. The trust was supported through Mona's prostitution ring.

"Mona Hill isn't a nice person, but I believed her when she said she didn't realize what she was getting into when she helped Nicole Rollins's criminal enterprise. She thought it was a straight-up sex and blackmail scheme. Do you remember when Ryan and Nate apprehended Elise at Mona's place?" Elise was Nicole's younger half-sister and she'd been part of the organization that had fingers in drug running, gun running, and human trafficking. Elise was a pure sociopath, and one of Sean's greatest fears was that she'd someday get out of prison. Because of her young age, many people thought she'd been used and manipulated. Sean and Lucy knew the truth: she was a cold-blooded killer who should never be free again.

"I remember," Lucy said quietly.

"Remember, I was there—I'd tracked Elise through the GPS in her phone. Mona was her driver. I convinced Mona to run and leave Elise behind. Not because I thought that they'd escape—they'd have been caught eventually—but because I crossed a few lines and didn't want Mona to expose me."

"What lines?"

"I destroyed all her computer files and videos."

"Why?"

He was about to answer, but then he saw that Lucy realized the truth.

"She had a video of me. When I was raped."

He nodded. "She was going to sell it to Nicole's people. I should have told you then, but I didn't know how. I let Mona go, didn't tell Ryan and Nate that I saw her."

"Oh, Sean."

"Don't be angry with me. I mean, yell at me if you have to, but please forgive me. I love you, Lucy—I couldn't bear for you to be hurt. That was a dark time for you—after we rescued the boys, you were having nightmares, the drug cartel had put a target on your back. Mona isn't a saint, but I understand her. I wouldn't go so far to say that everything she did she did for her sister, but I would say she wanted her sister and nephew to have a chance at a good future, far from the life that their mother had."

"And you know where she is. Right now."

Sean couldn't tell if Lucy was angry or upset. Her voice was even, calm.

"Yes. It took me awhile, but I needed to know because if she ever went back on her word to cut ties with Nicole's organization—this was before we shut them down—I had to know where she was."

"Is she back in the business?"

He nodded. "It's the only way she knows how to make money. But to her credit, she's cleaned up her act a bit. She runs a high-end escort service in Houston and Dallas. Half legit. Changed her name to Odette, which was her middle name. Just Odette. Rarely goes out in public—I told her we shut down everything, but she's paranoid someone from her past will catch up with her. She swore to me she wouldn't go back to blackmail."

"Yet she's still prostituting women."

"More or less. I'm not saying it's right—but she doesn't force anyone. She hires only adults, both men and women. No minors, no drugs. She'll talk to me."

"Why?"

"Because I gave her a second chance. Last summer, when I found her again, we had a face-to-face. I told her I would be watching and if she crossed the line I would nail her. She hasn't."

"Sean."

"Tell me you understand. Please. I should have told you earlier, but back then—everything was a mess. And her name has never come up until now."

"I understand, Sean—I just wish you'd told me."

He was relieved, though he wasn't certain if Lucy was really okay. "I wanted to—but with everything that was going on, it just didn't seem like a good time to rehash this."

"I'm glad you told me now. I need to talk to her."

"I'll do it, Lucy."

"*I* need to."

"Is this about trust? You know I'll tell you everything—"

"It's not about trust. I trust you, but I need to read her myself. I hope *you* understand."

He did. He didn't like when Lucy went to confront the darkness, but he understood why she had to.

"I'll give you everything I have on her."

"Does she know who you are?"

"She didn't then; she does now."

"Okay."

"Luce—are we okay?"

She touched his face. "Yes."

He sighed in relief. "I love you so much, Lucy."

She kissed him, then smiled. "I know."

CHAPTER NINE

There were times in one's life when a hard decision needed to be made, and now was one of those times.

Bella was alone in the shit hole of a house with sixteen prostitutes Hirsch had brought with him from L.A. and Phoenix. Four were underage.

She could walk with the four girls, though she wasn't positive they would willingly go. Only one—Sara—had been with them since Los Angeles. But Sara was cold—colder than nearly anyone Bella had met in a long time. She was sixteen and Bella suspected she'd been prostituting herself since thirteen—or younger. She'd learned some of Sara's story—her father was in prison, her mother was dead, she'd run away from foster care multiple times until either they stopped looking or she got better at disappearing. She had recruited several girls into the business without qualms. The only thing Bella didn't know was how she hooked up with Hirsch's operation. There was more to the story, but Bella didn't want to ask. She could fill in some details from her own experience, and those details weren't painting a pretty picture.

She was beginning to suspect Sara had been the one who squealed on Christina and Ashley, resulting in Roger's murder. On the one hand, Bella had sympathy for the girl—at least, the girl she used to be and the woman she could have become. But if Sara had gone down the path of least resistance and joined Hirsch, Bella couldn't say word one to her about walking. She'd expose Bella in a heartbeat.

The other three girls were from Phoenix, and they were newish to the business and in the middle of being seasoned. They weren't one hundred percent reliable, so kept on a short leash. Scared to stay, but more scared to leave. Two had been runaways turning tricks on the street, and the third was quiet. Madison. She might have been sold or picked up somewhere, but she was fresh meat, according to Desiree.

Madison might not have been turned out yet. What if she was a special order? Bella didn't know how she could protect her. She could take the three of them, the two runaways and Madison, with only Desiree's goon keeping an eye on the place. He was big and tough, but he was stupid, and Bella was anything but stupid. Except that they were in the middle of nowhere, she didn't have a vehicle, and she didn't have a safe place to take them.

Three girls, break cover, and leave. Call in the cavalry and go home.

Home. What home? Adam had told her if she worked for Simon Egan that she no longer had a home. And while she could stay at Simon's indefinitely, she couldn't bear to look him in the face and admit that she'd failed.

I couldn't do it. I couldn't stick it out. I didn't find Hope. I think she's dead.

No!

Hope wasn't dead, she'd been sold or traded, Bella was almost positive . . . but there was that niggle of doubt that her belief that Hope was alive was only wishful thinking. Desperate thinking. But, the only way

Bella could find her or know for certain what had happened to her would be to stick it out. And if she were dead . . . *if* . . . then didn't her grandparents deserve the truth? Hope was why Bella had gone this deep in the first place. But her mission had become bigger than one girl.

Bella wanted to shut down Hirsch's entire network. She wanted to identify his partner Z and take him out as well. Their goal, which they were fast making a reality, was to run transportation of the sex trade coast to coast, control the entire southern pipeline. The southern route was the most crucial because there was more open space, less weather issues, more places to hide, more ports. Hirsch already owned more than a dozen small trucking companies, and that gave him a legitimate avenue to launder money and move his human product.

It was a big plan, a real criminal vision, and Hirsch wasn't the only one playing it. Bella needed to get eyes on his elusive boss. There was no record of the alias "Z" in any criminal database, and even Simon's wealth and reach hadn't identified him.

Bella had to stay. She had to identify Z and take that information to the authorities. Because while she would rescue any girl for Simon, she wasn't going to be his assassin. She wasn't going to risk her freedom.

She'd been a prisoner for more than a year;

thirteen months one week three days

and she wasn't going to be anyone's prisoner again. She would disappear before she went to jail.

Be brave. Survive.

Long dead Julie was the strongest person Bella had ever known. She'd protected all of them, which Bella hadn't known at the time. If she could turn back the clock she would never have run that night. She would never have thought she knew anything. Because she hadn't. She'd known shit and her actions had cost her her only friend, her protector, her soul.

Nineteen Years Ago

Bella limped up the stairs of the house she would never call home. Tears streamed down her face, she hated herself and hated the men who had hurt her. She had tried to run, just walk away after they were done. She'd thought Sergio's men were gone; they weren't. They were waiting.

Tommy hit her. "Don't even think of it, Blondie." He chuckled.

Her second week in captivity, Tommy had dyed her dark blonde hair—dirty blonde for a dirty whore, he'd said—to platinum, a cheap blonde.

"Makes you look younger, you'll bring in more money."

She hated him. She hated herself.

Julie was sitting on the bed they shared in a small room. Two double beds—mattresses on the floor—for the four girls. Julie had been there the longest. She was seventeen and in charge of the girls in this room. She took care of them.

Tommy pushed her through the doorway. "Julie! Tell Blondie that if she tries to run again, she won't like the consequences. And neither will you."

He closed the door. Bella grimaced because she hurt. She hurt everywhere.

Julie got up. "Take a shower, you'll feel better."

"I can't do this anymore."

Julie made her look her in the eye. "Yes, you can. You don't want to die."

"Maybe I do."

"No you don't," Julie said, her voice firm, harsher than Bella had heard her before. "You can survive. It's not so bad once you block it out. I make up stories in my head. A fantastic fantasy world of witches and demons and goblins and reapers. I go back there and punish the wicked. Someday I'm going to write them down. Someday I'm going to make money with my stories. They are so real to me. This isn't forever. When we're too old to work, they'll let us go."

Bella didn't believe it, but Julie did—and Julie almost made Bella believe.

"Make up your own world, sweetheart. The beach. Surfing tall waves, the cool water refreshing you. Or a cabin in the middle of the woods where you hear nothing but the birds chirping and the rustle of leaves."

Bella stared at her. "How?" she whispered.

"Remember that they've paid for your body, but your body isn't important. They'll never have your mind. They can't unless you let them. You will survive. You will be strong. I see it in you."

"For how long?"

"However long it takes."

"Takes for what?"

Julie didn't have an answer. Was she waiting for the police to stop Sergio and Tommy? Was she waiting for an opportunity to escape? Waiting to get "too old" however old that was? Julie had more freedom than anyone else here, why didn't she just disappear? There'd been at least three times in the last month when Julie was alone in the house. Why didn't she run away?

But Bella didn't ask her why. She should have, but she didn't.

She took her shower, a long, cold shower. Well, lukewarm because the water never got cold and never got hot. She didn't care.

I don't care. I don't care about anything.

She couldn't care because her life was no longer her own. She tried to tell herself that, tried to believe it, but the rage grew inside.

Tiffany has pills. You can take them. Drink vodka. Go to sleep. Sleep forever . . .

She opened her eyes and stared at her reflection. Dried her bruised skin with the small towel she shared with the others. She didn't want to die, but she feared the longer she was forced to have sex with strangers, the more she wanted to make it stop. How could she disappear in her mind? How could she play along but not really be there?

Julie had told her it would get easier, but after three months it hadn't. It hadn't made anything easier, and the idea that she would be doing this for the rest of her life, until one of the johns or Tommy or Sergio killed her, sent her into a deep despair.

If she could get home, to her grandmother, they would go to the police. They would have to protect her. She could find her brother. She didn't know where he was stationed, he was someplace on the other side of the world, but he would come, wouldn't he? He'd once told her if she ever needed him, to just call.

Just call.

And if he didn't answer, she'd go to the Rogan house because Kane Rogan was his best friend and they were good people. A real family and they would protect her.

But she didn't know who to call to find Kane, she didn't know how to reach him, she didn't remember where the Rogans lived, she couldn't go home to her mother, and she wanted to kill her father.

And it hurt. It *hurt* to think like this, to feel like that there was no way out.

Feel? Feel what? There is no fucking way out. No. Way. Out. Escape or die. Your choice.

And deep down, when she escaped, when she was free, she knew exactly what she would do.

Vengeance was sweet. It stopped her from wanting to end her own life. It would be much better to die while taking out those who hurt her the most.

She waited until everyone was asleep. And then a little longer. She slipped out from under the thin blanket, knowing Julie wouldn't wake up because she had taken a downer. Uppers and downers. To get by. To make things better. She had no emotions, no real feelings, and Bella envied her. If she didn't feel then she couldn't hurt.

Bella didn't take the pills, not unless they forced her to. It would be too easy to become an addict, to depend on the pills to survive. To give in to Tommy and Sergio because she needed the pills. Almost all the girls had some level of addiction, and Tommy especially used it to control them.

And it worked.

She drank because sometimes she had to—and she could fake being high. Because she had to.

Do what you have to to survive, Bella, Julie had often told her.

To survive she had to escape.

She slipped out of the house. Not easy because there was always a goon around. But tonight's goon was watching a rerun of a basketball game and not paying attention. She was quiet. Very quiet.

And then she was out. On the street. Free.

It was cold, but she didn't care. The first breath of freedom was intoxicating. It was motivating. She ran in her socks because she didn't have shoes—the tall heels they made her wear would have encumbered her. She almost laughed, but that would make her crazy, right?

Maybe she was crazy. But if she could get to the

police station or a fire station or a hospital she would be safe.

At first she ran because she was free, but she was soon forced to slow down. She was weak and sore and had no idea where she was. She didn't see anyone. They were in a mixed-use area, industrial buildings and crumbling apartment buildings and vacant lots. An occasional car passed and she would hide. What if they were looking for her?

They'd kill her. She didn't want to die.

Hide. Hide. Hide. Run, run, run!

Hide and run. Run and hide. The longer she was out, the more desperate she became because she didn't see a police car or a fire station or a hospital. Should she knock on a door? Then there were no more houses. No apartments. She didn't know where she was, she couldn't read the street signs because all the lights were burned out. Or broken.

A car turned down the street and she looked for a place to hide. It wasn't light yet, she didn't know what time it was—shouldn't the sun be coming up? It felt like she'd been walking for hours, but the sun wasn't even on the horizon.

There was no place to hide.

She turned and ran down a long narrow road, big warehouse buildings on both sides. The street was sloped, such a steep slope that she couldn't run at all. Her socks had holes in them, her feet hurt, she thought they were bleeding.

A spotlight illuminated everything in front of her, except her shadow.

"Stop. This is the police."

She stopped. The police! He would help her.

She turned around.

The car stopped right in front of her. The door opened.

A man got out. He wore a uniform and had a gun and she was shaking and she didn't know why.

"Help me?" she said. Whispered. Her voice was raw. She was out of breath.

"What's your name?"

"Bella."

"Bella what?"

"B-B-Bella Caruso. I was taken—I'm from Sacramento. I just want to go home."

"You ran away?"

"No—someone kidnapped me from Sacramento, made me—made me come here. I escaped. Please help me?"

It was a question, because there was something about this man that made her nervous.

She took a step backward.

"Don't move," he said.

She turned to run.

He ran after her. He was faster, stronger, and he caught her.

"Please don't hurt me," she cried.

"I'm not going to hurt you. Come with me."

She wanted to believe him.

But she didn't.

She woke up hours later, sore from a beating she only half remembered. Julie was there next to her, putting ice on her head. Julie had been crying.

Bella had never seen Julie cry.

As soon as Bella opened her eyes, Julie got up.

"Don't go," Bella said.

Julie ignored her. She went downstairs. A long time later, Sergio came up the stairs. He pushed open the door. "Get up," he said.

She slowly got to her feet, unsteady. She didn't think anything was broken, but every muscle hurt.

Sergio grabbed her and pulled her out of the room. Bella cried as her sore head hit the door jamb.

Sergio hauled her downstairs and outside. It was dark again. Had she been unconscious all day?

He pushed her into his van. Julie was already there.

She had been alone in the car. She could have run. She could have escaped!

Sergio and Tommy drove on the same streets Bella had been running through last night. Julia took her hand. She whispered, "Be brave."

"They're going to kill us."

"No," Julie said.

Bella didn't believe her. They were going to kill them. Or worse, let others hurt them. There were some things worse than death.

Julie leaned over and whispered, "You will survive. You're stronger than me, Bella. I knew you were stronger the day you walked in."

Julie took the rough men, Julie stood up for her, Julie had nursed her injuries whenever Bella was hurt. She held her when she cried and she had kept her hope alive.

Hope that it would get better.

They pulled next to an empty field and stopped the car. Tommy grabbed Bella and held her close. "Watch and learn, Blondie," he whispered in her ear.

Sergio ordered Julie to get out. She walked ahead of them. Tommy forced Bella to follow.

They were going to kill them. Leave their bodies in the middle of this disgusting garbage-filled field.

No one would know who she was. She would be a nobody. She would be nothing.

I don't want to die!

She screamed and Tommy slapped his hand over her mouth. "Watch," he said and held Bella tight against him.

"Make sure she watches," Sergio said.

"With pleasure." Tommy held her chin up.

Sergio turned back to Julie. "On your knees."

Julie got on her knees.

"Look at me," Sergio ordered her.

Julie looked at him. "I'm sorry," she said.

Sergio took out a gun and shot her in the face.

Bella screamed. She kicked and fought Tommy but she had no strength and crumpled onto the filthy ground, sobbing. Tommy wasn't tall, but he was strong. He yanked her up, held her tightly against him, his chest pressed against her back. He covered her mouth with his hand and said in her ear, "She's dead because of you. If anyone else tries to walk out, you will join her. Do you understand me?"

She shook her head, tried to break free. She smelled Julie's blood. Felt drops of blood and brain on her skin. Julie was dead. Dead!

Sergio said, "I liked Julie and I didn't want her to suffer. She died quickly. You? I don't like you, Bitch. Tommy hates you. You will suffer. I will make sure of it. Do you understand me?"

Then it sank in. Julie hadn't escaped because others would die, and Julie knew it. She stayed to protect them.

Julie was killed because Bella ran.

She stopped fighting, slumped against Tommy. She had no choice.

Be brave, Bella. Survive.

She would escape. Someday, somehow, she would be free. Even if she had to kill Sergio to do it.

CHAPTER TEN

Thursday

"Wake up, Doc."

Bam-Bam kicked the back of the couch as he walked in from the back of the house.

Bella hadn't been sleeping, but she opened her eyes halfway. "It's fucking one in the morning."

"They're back."

He sounded nervous. Bam-Bam was too stupid to get nervous, so Desiree must have given him a heads-up.

Desiree stomped in first, followed by two goons, then Hirsch. Damien wasn't there.

"He's not going to do it," Desiree said.

"Shut the fuck up," Hirsch said. "I've had it to here with you."

"I warned you," Desiree pushed.

The way Hirsch looked at her, Bella was certain he would kill her. Maybe not now, not tonight, but the woman had signed her death warrant and she didn't even know it.

"Make sure your girls are ready and know the score."

Desiree ranted as she stormed upstairs in the sprawling, remote ranch on the edge of town. A ranch where

Hirsch could kill everyone and their rotting corpses wouldn't be found for weeks. If ever.

"Where's Damien?" Bella asked.

Hirsch stared at her. "Why do you care? Are you fucking him?"

"Are you?" she countered.

He scowled.

"He left with you, he's not back," Bella said. "This whole situation is fucked. Yeah, I'm worried. I've already pulled one bullet out of his ass."

"He's working." Hirsch turned to his muscle and told them to watch the house, then he left.

He never slept where the girls slept. Why had he come out here in the first place? Because something had happened to Damien? To check on them? To leave protection?

She didn't know why she was worried about Damien. He was a criminal, a brute on many levels. But unlike Hirsch, he wasn't unnecessarily cruel. He did his job, nothing more or less. She'd met people like Damien before, both criminals and cops. They were predictable. He was loyal to Hirsch, but he was also pragmatic. Had he walked?

No, Bella didn't think he would ever leave Hirsch. She didn't know his history, but something Damien had said when she first met him had her thinking he would never walk away. She could respect his loyalty, but she also feared it. No matter how good she'd been at staying on Damien's good side, he would kill her if Hirsch ordered it.

Bella checked on the girls. "Go to sleep," she told them. She walked from room to room. Did a head count. One girl was missing. Who?

Penny.

Her heart twisted. She hadn't seen Penny since

Phoenix, but while they were watching television earlier, Madison had asked Sara where Penny was and it came out that she'd been in a different truck than the others.

Bella's first thought was that she'd been sold. Traded for something. Or sent to someone who had the time and inclination to break her. Or they'd tortured and killed her because they thought she knew who helped Christina and Ashley escape.

She was supposed to run.

Christina had promised not to say a word to anyone, but what if she slipped? What if . . .

Stop. Penny doesn't know about you.

Bella went to the refrigerator—which barely kept anything cold—and pulled out a semi-chilled beer. She opened it and drank half. She had to regain her focus. Come up with a plan. If the shit was flying, she could move the three girls. They were outside El Paso. She had no contacts here, at least none that she trusted one hundred percent. But Declan was waiting for her call. He could be here in half a day. He knew the plan was taking them east, he might already be on his way. Maybe he was already here.

She sat down and might have been dozing—she never really slept these days—when the back door opened. Damien came in. His head was bloodied and he walked immediately to the refrigerator for a beer. When he opened and drained a bottle, she saw his fists were bloodied and bruised as well.

She got up. "Let me get my bag."

"I'm fine."

He pushed her back into the chair, then sat down across from her.

"Tell me the other guy's worse."

He didn't say anything.

"Let me clean you up, D. That cut is deep. It could get infected."

He nodded once.

She was staying in the small room off the kitchen and grabbed her medical bag from the end of her bed. Cleaning cuts was easy—it's something she'd been doing since she was a kid, when her mother would get knocked around by whatever lowlife prick she was dealing for. In silence, she cleaned the wound, extracting a small piece of green glass in the process. She had questions—lots of questions—but kept her mouth shut.

He needed stitches, but he refused, so she taped the wound closed as best she could, then cleaned up her mess. She filled a bowl with ice and water and said, "Soak your hands or you're going to be doubly sore tomorrow."

He put his right hand into the bowl and scowled. Damien was good at keeping his pain in check.

"Are you hurt anywhere else?" she asked.

"It's fine," he mumbled.

"You're not going to do Hirsch any good if you have a broken rib or cracked skull."

He shifted, seemed to assess himself. "I'm good," he said, more confident. "Sore," he admitted. "Nothing broken."

"What happened?"

He didn't answer. Instead, he nodded toward the refrigerator. She retrieved another two beers, opened them, and handed one to Damien.

They drank in silence. Damien wouldn't talk if he didn't want to, and any more questions on her part might rouse suspicion. But she had to know.

"Where's Penny? She's not upstairs. The girls said she came out with them, but—"

"Don't worry about Penny."

"But—"

He glared at her. Sore subject. "Shut up."

She tossed her empty beer bottle in the trash and said, "I'm going to bed."

She walked into her room and shut the door. Immediately, she pulled Damien's cell phone from her pocket. She sent Declan and Simon a message, deleted it, and took a deep breath.

She came out of her room. Damien was still sitting in the same spot.

"I need my bag," she said. "I don't trust Desiree or Bam Bam not to steal my shit." She turned to Damien. "Are you sure you're okay, buddy?" she asked.

He looked at her—finally. He might have a concussion, she realized. His eyes weren't quite right. She'd had a concussion before, it was no fun.

She opened her bag. "Let me look—"

He grabbed her wrist and squeezed. His hand was freezing from the ice water it had been soaking in. "Watch your back, Doc."

What could that mean? What the fuck was going on? Did he know she'd lifted his phone? She was good—really good—at picking pockets. One of the few skills she'd picked up from her year on the streets.

"Thanks," she mumbled. She patted him on the shoulder, slipped his phone back into his jacket pocket, picked up her medical bag, and went to her bedroom.

Shit was going down and she feared she'd be caught in the crossfire.

"It's Declan," JT told Jack. They were in a dive motel in El Paso after landing a few hours ago. JT couldn't sleep even though it was three in the morning, and answered his cell phone on the second ring. "Caruso."

"Bella sent Simon and me a message."

Relief flooded through JT. His sister was alive. "And?"

"She's outside El Paso. Said something is going down, but her cover is still good. She asked me to keep a low profile."

"Shit, Declan! She's in trouble, and you know it."

Declan didn't say anything.

"What?" JT pushed. "Am I wrong?"

"Yes and no. Look—I want to get her out. But if I go in too early, and we lose any chance of finding Hope, she'll never forgive me."

"But she'll be alive."

"Hirsch is a sick bastard, but he's a businessman first. And his network is far bigger than we knew going into this. If we can take him out and identify Z, we can deal a severe blow to the entire human trafficking circuit. It'll take them months—maybe years—to recover."

"Bella has been in deep for too long, and you know it."

"You're here, right?"

"Yes."

"Let's meet for breakfast and talk about this."

"Kane and Sean Rogan are coming."

"Good."

JT hoped Declan was serious about that.

"I'm going to keep a low profile, but I have a few people I can talk to. I'll find out where she is at a minimum. You trust me, right?"

JT wanted to. He'd known Declan his entire adult life. They'd fought side-by-side. He was as much a brother to him as Adam Dixon or Matt Elliott or Rick Stockton. But they didn't always see eye-to-eye. He appreciated that Declan had Bella's back for the three years they had worked for Simon, but he'd hoped Declan could have talked Bella out of it.

"Yes," he said.

"You had to think?"

"Damn, Dec, this is my sister. I'm not going to fail her again."

"You've never failed her, JT. I'll call you in a few hours. Get some sleep."

JT rubbed his eyes.

"We should have stocked up on supplies," Jack said.

"Kane's bringing extra firepower," JT said.

"I have a bad feeling."

So did JT.

Jack continued. "Tell me it's none of my business. But why haven't you called in Stockton?"

The FBI Assistant Director Rick Stockton was JT's closest friend, other than Kane. They'd met in boot camp—Rick had gone in as an officer-in-training after four years in college, and JT was a scrawny eighteen-year-old kid who still had growing to do. But when you're put together in a unit and face a common enemy, bonds are forged that are never severed. Rick had saved RCK many times because of his position. He used to run the laboratory at Quantico but was promoted to assistant director a few years ago. Having one of your closest friends as the number two person in the FBI had its benefits.

"I talked to him after I spoke to Laura the other night. He's waiting for my call—but we need something solid so he can send his people in with actionable evidence. He'll be here in a heartbeat, but he can't send in an FBI team without knowing the score."

"Understood," Jack said. "At least we have Lucy and Nate."

JT glanced at him. "Not really."

"What does that mean?"

"They're working on their own time. If Armstrong was still in San Antonio we wouldn't have an issue, but Vaughn is by-the-book. She's not going to let them run with an unsanctioned op."

"They have no backup?"

"She's your sister, I get it—believe me—but Dunning is solid."

"Agreed," Jack said, though he didn't sound happy about it. "But we need Stockton sooner rather than later. What about reaching out to Lucy's friend from the DEA. We cleared him last year."

"Donnelly? He worked out of Arizona for a time, but he was never assigned to El Paso."

"JT."

JT glanced over at Jack. At first he couldn't read his expression, then he realized that Jack was thinking bigger than he was. "Shit, you're right. Donnelly will know who we can trust."

JT called Kane, not surprised that he answered at three in the morning. "Buddy, can you reach out to Donnelly? We need a contact in El Paso—someone with deep ties and one hundred percent trustworthy."

"On it."

CHAPTER ELEVEN

Lucy woke up at 6:30 and Sean wasn't in bed. She must have been exhausted, because she hadn't even heard him get up. She pulled on sweatpants and went downstairs. Kane was drinking coffee and Sean was making breakfast.

"You've been a good influence on Sean," Kane said with a wink.

She kissed Sean on the shoulder and poured herself coffee. "I'm still trying to lose the ten pounds I gained on our honeymoon."

"You're perfect," Sean said. "Eat. Kane and I are flying to El Paso, so I won't be here when you get home tonight." He put plates of eggs, sausage, and fruit in front of first Lucy then Kane.

Lucy asked, "You found Bella?"

"She made contact with her partner confirming that she was in El Paso, which we'd already figured out based on JT and Jack's investigation. We don't have a location, but sources say there's something going down among local criminal elements, and we think Hirsch is involved. Nothing solid, but we need people on the ground." Kane sipped his coffee. "Siobhan also reached out to some contacts and rumor is a new player is making noise and the local thugs aren't happy."

"Why El Paso? Because it's on the I-10 corridor?"

Sean sat down with his own food. "Border town, widespread corruption, easy to stay under the radar."

"It's temporary," Kane said.

"Why?" Sean asked.

"L.A. has a much bigger market. Why is he leaving L.A. for El Paso? It makes no sense. That tells me he has a bigger plan in the works. We don't know shit because Simon Egan told us shit, but my guess is they're taking over smaller markets to merge them into a bigger network, where they can more easily move their products—girls, drugs, weapons, whatever they want. It fits with our intel that Hirsch is buying up small trucking companies, and with Declan confirming that they're moving girls from west to east. Did you get anywhere with that, Sean?"

"I've put together a list of all trucking companies within twenty miles of I-10 from L.A. to Jacksonville. I've weeded out the large national companies, but we're still looking at an extensive list. I considered that he'd want independents, so divided the list between independent trucking companies and small chains. Commercial sales are trackable, but not necessarily up-to-date. And I don't have the name he's buying under. It's not his own. He would likely have a shell corp, nothing that would connect to him or whoever he's working with. But since we know he's moving into Texas, I'm focusing in-state."

"He's been doing this for awhile, correct?" Lucy asked.

"Bella's been undercover for a year," Kane said. "She got in through one of his trucking companies."

"Is there a way to sort the data by sale date? If he started on the west coast and is now moving east, wouldn't it make sense that the first companies he purchased are in California? Then we can look at a pattern and maybe identify the shell company that way."

Sean nodded. "It's possible. The problem is that every state reports the data differently, so I need to match up the fields. I only have the raw data. I'll let Kane fly and work on sorting the data manually."

"Sean will send you a list of locals for you and Nate to follow up," Kane said. "But do it incognito—no cop persona."

"Got it." Lucy cleared her plate and rinsed it. "When will you be back?"

"Hopefully tomorrow," Sean said. "I'll call when I can."

"Be careful, both of you," Lucy said. "I need to get ready for work."

Sean followed her upstairs. "You okay with all this?"

"Of course."

"I contacted Mona Hill. She's going to call you today to set up a meet. I told her neutral territory. I don't think she's going to do anything, but bring backup."

"Why are you worried?"

"I'm not."

She raised an eyebrow. "You sound worried."

He sat down on the bed and pulled her down next to him. "First, I always worry, but that's par for the course. But Kane's worried, and that freaks me out. Kane is always cool as a cucumber."

"He's worried about JT, and this undercover operation of Bella's is dangerous."

"Partly. It's like when you were missing last fall—he almost benched me because I couldn't focus. So Kane's concerned about JT's judgment regarding his sister, but I think he's more worried about Bella and how deep she's gotten. He cares a lot about both her and JT. Undercover work is difficult, but undercover work when you're not a cop? She has no backup. If anything happens to her—JT will lose it. Kane isn't concerned about the repercussions with Hirsch and his people. But Simon Egan has a lot of friends—powerful people who help him behind the scenes. We can't go to war with him."

"You mean war figuratively."

"If anything happens to Bella, it will get bloody, and a battle between Egan and RCK is going to force high-level people to take sides. It'll be a mess. That's what Kane is trying to prevent. He reached out to Brad Donnelly—Donnelly said the SSA in the El Paso DEA is solid, so he's getting us a sit-down with her. We need someone local to work with. Just wanted to let you know in case something leaks—I don't want it coming back to bite you."

"I'll be fine. Just keep my head down and do the job. If Kane's watching JT's back, you need to have his."

"I do." He kissed her. "Be careful with Mona."

"I can take care of Mona Hill."

"Don't let her get under your skin. She's good at that."

Sean kissed Lucy again and left.

Bella was up early. Hell, she hadn't slept more than a couple hours a night in months. She made a pot of coffee in the stained coffeepot and stared at it, waiting for it to brew. The beat-up house they were in was bank owned—a torn, faded foreclosure sign was nailed to the door—but it was dated three years ago, and if there had been a For Sale sign posted anywhere, it was long gone. The house had once been a meth lab—remnants of the tools of that disgusting drug trade were littered throughout the place. But they either had been arrested or OD'd because they hadn't been here in months, based on the layers of dust and grime.

They'd only been here a couple days, since they bailed out of Phoenix, but Bella was antsy and the longer she was out of contact with people, the more depressed she got.

Where was Penny?

Where had Hirsch sent two of Desiree's girls last night?

Why did Damien seem depressed?

Was Hope alive?

Laura had once called Bella the "most optimistic pessimist" on the planet. Bella believed Hope was alive because she needed to believe in order to keep her cover, especially as the weeks turned into months and being a part of this life was eating her up inside. Now . . . she was beginning to doubt Hope had survived her ordeal. Fifteen months in this life . . . no matter how strong you were, fifteen months was enough to break anyone, especially a young girl.

Bella had almost broken so many times. If JT hadn't saved her when he did, she would be dead by now. Laura, who had the patience of a saint, had never wavered from her belief that Bella would have survived. That Bella was somehow special.

She wasn't. She was no more special than Hope or Christina or Penny.

Voices outside jolted her out of her trance. The coffee had finished brewing, she must have been standing here for ten minutes or more just feeling sorry for herself.

Who was outside this early?

She looked out the window. Desiree and Bam-Bam were standing by a car talking in hushed voices. Desiree never woke up before noon—it wasn't even seven in the morning—she must be as on edge as Bella. She almost laughed that she had something in common with the bitch of a madam. But while Desiree was a violent predator, she was street smart. She thought something was awry, and that confirmed Bella's suspicions.

Bella poured herself a mug of coffee and walked out the side door, where they couldn't see her, and hugged the side of the house until their voices were audible. It took her a few seconds to catch on. Desiree was upset, and Bam-Bam was trying to calm her down.

"Don't tell me they'll be back, Thad! He took two of *my* girls, not *his*. Diaz took them without paying a fucking red cent!"

"Shh."

Two girls . . . the girls that she was pissed off about last night? The freebies?

"Don't shush me. We need to go back to L.A. This is fucked."

"We made a deal."

"I'm losing control."

"Look, let's just go with the flow, okay? We're tapping into a shitload of money."

"And losing everything. He's not right in the head."

Another thing Desiree and Bella agreed with.

They exchanged a few words that Bella couldn't make out, but then Desiree became agitated again and her voice rose.

"Look what he did to that whiny white bitch."

Bella froze. Desiree had always called Penny the whiny white bitch. What had Hirsch done with Penny? She'd come to El Paso, according to the other girls, but no one had seen her at the house. Had he sold her? To Diaz? To someone else?

"None of our girls are going to die," Bam-Bam said. "That little whore brought it on herself."

Penny was dead? No, no that couldn't be.

"I have a contact in San Antonio. Someone who can give Hirsch a run for his money," Desiree said. "We bail there, I'll get us protection until we're clear."

"I dunno."

"I do."

Bella could barely focus on Desiree's plan of switching sides. Penny was dead. It had to be because Christina and Ashley escaped. Had Penny been caught? Is that how Roger died? Or had something else happened after Roger went back inside for Penny?

Anger, fear, and deep, deep sorrow coursed through her veins and she went back inside the house. She had to risk exposure—she needed to get out of here. If Penny was dead, Hope was certainly dead, and Bella had been a fool to think otherwise. A total idiot.

She went into the room Desiree and Bam-Bam were sharing. It reeked of sex and liquor. She grabbed a phone, she didn't know whose, and slipped back outside, toward the barn.

She kept her eye on the house through one of the broken slats and dialed Simon's direct line. She didn't care that it was five in the morning in California.

Simon hadn't been sleeping. He answered on the first ring. Like her, sleep was the enemy for Simon Egan.

"It's Bella."

"Thank God. Are you okay?"

"I need to get out."

He didn't say anything.

"Simon—did you hear me?"

"Is your cover blown?"

"No."

"What happened? After the text last night you said you wanted to stay. What's going on with you?"

She realized that she'd changed her mind on a daily basis since Monday morning when Damien came for her. Leave, stay, leave. Of course he would think she was losing it. Maybe she was.

"They killed Penny. Roger's dead, and now Penny—

the girl who was supposed to leave with Christina and Ashley—is dead, too."

"I'm sorry."

"I don't think Hope's alive. I'm here to find Hope, and I don't think I can."

"Do you have proof that she's dead?"

"No, but—"

"Bella, we knew this would be a long-term assignment. I'll get you out, if you *really* want to leave. But we still have Hope's videos."

"They're nearly a year old!"

"Another group surfaced. We've dated them three to six months ago."

"Why didn't you tell me?"

"We just learned of them. We're working on finding more. She's out there, you know it in your gut."

Bella didn't know if she could trust her gut anymore.

"Something big is going down with this guy Diaz that Hirsch is trying to negotiate with. Desiree is worried that Hirsch is giving her girls away."

"That's not our concern. You're there to find Hope and safely extract girls like Christina and Ashley."

"I know." She stared through the slat in the barn. Desiree and Bam-Bam were still talking, but it had lost the intensity of their earlier conversation. Planning. Plotting. Up to no good.

"You knew this wasn't going to be an easy job. Are you in for the long haul? Are you up for it?"

Was she? Could she keep doing this? She was losing her humanity. When Damien Drake—a sociopathic brute—was her only friend, and she actually felt *safer* with him than with anyone else, she knew she was tumbling off the edge, the avalanche of bad decisions and deep cover lies weighing her down.

"Yes," she said. What else could she do? If Hope was

really alive, and she bailed now, she would never forgive herself. She'd never backed down before when things got hard. Why now? Because of one dead girl? She'd seen the dead before. She'd buried the dead. She had to block it out. Block it out until she slept.

If she ever slept soundly again.

"Good," Simon said. He sounded relieved. "Thank you, Bella. We couldn't do this without you."

"I think their next stop is San Antonio. A few things I overheard—and I suspect Desiree is going to bail. It's not going to end well for her."

"He's moving fast. Give it two, three more weeks. If we're no closer to finding Hope, we'll turn everything over to the authorities."

Though he said the words like he meant them, she didn't believe him. Simon didn't like giving anything to the authorities.

"Do you have any physical proof?" Simon asked.

"Some." It was nearly impossible for her to document anything. "I've given Declan names, photos, a few high-profile johns the cops can flip. And my word—I can't keep a journal, but I've given notes to Declan when I've seen him. We have Christina and Ashley. Christina will testify—I'm pretty certain of that. I have three more I think will walk."

"Not now—it's too risky after Phoenix."

"One of them is suicidal, I'm worried about her. In San Antonio—if Desiree makes a scene or gives me the opportunity, I'm going to slip them out. Send Declan there—I'll handle El Paso."

"Are you sure?"

No, she wasn't sure about anything anymore.

From her hiding spot, she saw Damien step outside. He stared at Desiree and Bam-Bam. He didn't look happy.

"I have to go." She ended the call, then wiped the history from the phone. She'd have to slip it down the back of the couch when no one was looking.

It wasn't like she hadn't been to this rodeo before.

CHAPTER TWELVE

As Lucy rode shotgun in the FBI sedan with her partner for the day, Jason Lopez, she had moved from angry to worried then back to angry. It wasn't fair to either of them that their boss had Jason following her and reporting back. That didn't instill support among agents, especially when Lucy had to depend on Jason to watch her back. It wasn't fair to Jason to put him in the position of being a spy.

She remained silent most of the morning as they confirmed information from the cold case files. For three hours they'd gone from place to place to make contact with witnesses and victims and update information. They only found one of the dozen people they tried to speak with, an elderly woman with no family who had been moved to a nursing home. She had her faculties, but didn't have anything to add to her statement, and her doctor informed Lucy that she was probably not going to live until the end of the year.

At lunch, she was melancholy. The woman may never live to find out who killed her grandson. While murder was not generally an FBI case, they'd been assisting the San Antonio PD because the murder happened on a college campus and there was evidence of a larger crime—but nothing had panned out at the time, and it went cold.

She didn't want to eat with Jason, but they didn't have much of a choice. They were an hour south of the office and still had a list of people to locate and speak with.

"You're quiet," Jason said. They were eating at a food truck off Interstate 37 near Three Rivers. It was a pleasant afternoon, and if she were here with Nate or Ryan or Kenzie or frankly almost anyone else, she would have enjoyed the break and cool breeze.

"I have nothing to say," she said.

"Ouch."

"Okay, how about this—why did you follow me to lunch yesterday and then report back to Rachel who I was eating with?"

At first she thought he was going to lie to her. That would have angered her even more. He bit into his taco, chewed, swallowed, sipped water.

"She asked me to."

"So she's having you follow me. You did a good job. I didn't know I had a tail." Her tone was far less complimentary than her words.

"Don't shoot the messenger."

"You're not the messenger. Don't do it again."

"I can't promise that. Look, I'm sorry. I don't like this anymore than you do. Rachel is a good agent. I think you're a good agent."

"How would you even know considering I've worked zero cases in the last two months?"

"People talk."

"Why is she having you follow me?"

"I don't know—and it's not all the time. If I had to guess, I think she's still ticked off about San Diego."

"You know about that?"

"Well, yeah. Who doesn't know? Besides, I just got

here a month ago. Someone mentioned something, I dug around, talked to people, read the file. It was great work. But—well—Rachel doesn't like mavericks, and she's labeled you such."

"So she said yesterday."

There was more to it than that—there had to be. Two months in the doghouse. But it wasn't just the last two months. Before San Diego, Rachel had been hypercritical of her work as well.

"You talked to her about it?" He sounded surprised.

"She knew about my lunch with Kane—which she got from you—and has been monitoring everything I do. She believes things that aren't true and I don't know what to say to fix it. So I'm just going to leave it alone."

"You mean about the baby in Mexico."

She didn't respond to that question. "Don't dig around into my life, Lopez. All you really need to know about me is that I'm a good agent and I will always have your back. What bothers me most is that I don't know if you'll have mine."

That surprised him. "Of course I do."

She wanted to believe him, but she didn't know much about him. She didn't want to feel this way about anyone she worked with.

"I want to give you the benefit of the doubt," she said.

"But you don't."

"My own boss is having me followed during my lunch break. That doesn't say a lot about her, or about her trust in me. It was *lunch*."

"Why'd you tell me you were having lunch with your husband?"

"Because I didn't want to have lunch with you."

"Double ouch." But he didn't seem too bothered by her admission. Either he truly wasn't concerned about what she thought of him, or he had a great poker face.

"You wanted honest."

"Fair enough."

He seemed to be waiting for more, his body language practically screaming *I'm just pretending not to be interested, but I really want you to spill everything.* But Lucy had no intention of sharing anything personal with him. She *was* angry about being followed, and she was frustrated that Rachel had put her colleague in this position. She realized she'd have to take it up with her boss directly if they were ever going to get beyond this.

Her phone rang. The number was blocked. "Kincaid," she answered. She had legally changed her name to Rogan and used her maiden name as her middle name, but for work she still used Kincaid. It was easier that way.

"I heard you want to talk to me."

Mona Hill. Or Ramona Jefferson. Or Odette. Or whatever she wanted to be called today.

"Yes," she said.

"Neutral territory, I was told."

"Name a time and place."

"I have business in Austin tonight. I'll text you the address. A public coffee shop. Nine p.m."

Mona hung up.

Lucy ended the call and ignored Jason's curious expression. She sent Sean a message that she'd heard from their "friend in Houston" then sent Nate a message asking if he was available this evening for a road trip. He responded immediately that he'd be at her place at six.

Lucy finished her lunch and tossed her garbage in a receptacle. Jason followed her, then they went back to the car. "For what it's worth," he said when he turned on the ignition, "I told Rachel it was a bad idea to follow you."

"Oh, in that case, all is forgiven," she said sarcastically. "Let's just get this done, okay?"

Jason started driving and Lucy typed the address of the next witness into her GPS. The eight-year-old case had been fairly straightforward, though it had never been solved. It was a felony hit and run, and the only reason that the FBI had been involved was because the victim had been a federal judge. The witness said that a large SUV—gold, late model, possibly a Cadillac Escalade or something that looked like it—had hit the judge's car going at least forty miles an hour. The witness said the SUV was driving erratically, and the judge tried to get over but didn't have time. At the last minute, the SUV swerved to try to avoid the car, but ended up sideswiping it and sent the car over the embankment. The judge later died of his injuries.

The FBI took lead, and all the evidence from the scene supported the lone witness. But they were never able to find the drunk driver. They searched for the vehicle and came up dry.

"Where are we going?" Jason prompted.

"The address isn't coming up. Hold on."

She flipped through her notes to see if she'd written the address down wrong. No, everything was correct. She called Zach Charles, the squad analyst, and asked him to check the original file. A minute later he said, "That's the address the case agent had."

"Thanks, Zach. Maybe she transposed the numbers. Can you run this Theresa Clark? Her name and last known address and number are in that file. Maybe she moved or got married or is on record for something else."

"Will do."

She ended the call.

"Back to the office?"

"No, let's see what's on that block."

Jason shrugged, but drove the twenty minutes to the street the witness claimed she lived on. The address was on the 6400 block, but the street ended at the 5000 block.

"What if it should be 4650 instead of 6450?" Lucy mused.

Jason drove down to address number 4650. The address was a duplex—4650A and 4650B.

"You want to talk to the people?"

"We're here," Lucy said.

The residents knew nothing about a Theresa Clark and none recalled the hit-and-run that ended the life of the federal judge. When they finally pulled themselves away, Lucy looked up the press articles about the case. There was very little. Judge Redmond had been a consistent and fair judge, no one had complaints about him, and there was no evidence that the hit and run had been intentional. All the markers pointed to drunk driver, though Lucy didn't remember seeing any crime scene photos in the file. The written report confirmed that the tire marks supported the witness statement. There had been no follow-up with the witness because there had been no vehicle or suspect located.

But no one really dug deep into the judge's life to see if the hit-and-run wasn't as it appeared on paper, and now that they knew the witness had lied about her address—unless there was an error in the original paperwork—Lucy was becoming suspicious.

"What are you thinking?" Jason asked.

"Unless the agent of record made a mistake when inputting this information into the database, the witness lied."

"That's a leap, isn't it?"

"It's easy to verify. We need to talk to the agent, look at her original notes, see if maybe the address was input wrong, verify the phone number. Check with Clark's employer at the time—she worked for a real estate company. But there was no follow-up with her employer because there was no reason to contact her again. Now there is. And maybe Zach will be able to track her down, though with only her name, age and a fake address it might not be that easy. We should definitely review all the physical evidence again, talk to Judge Redmond's family, his colleagues. Maybe they'll have a recollection, though after eight years there probably wouldn't be anything."

"We need to figure out what happened in the reports at a minimum," Jason said, "but I don't know what benefit there would be rehashing all this with the judge's family."

"If there is a logical explanation, then no, of course not, but without an answer? There's something . . . odd about all of this."

They arrived back at FBI headquarters late that afternoon. Lucy followed up with Zach—he had no updates, only confirmed that the information Lucy had was what was originally entered into the files, both digital and written. Lucy wrote up the report of the entire day and sent it to Rachel, along with a plan on the judge's case.

Not ten minutes later, Rachel called Lucy and Jason into her office. "Judge Redmond—what's this about a missing witness?"

Jason said, "The address in our records doesn't exist. We checked on other addresses in case there was a transposed number, but dead end."

"That seems to be a waste of time," Rachel said. "Did you call Zach?"

"Yes," Lucy said, "he was pulling the original files and notes to verify it had been input correctly. But we were already in the neighborhood."

Rachel flipped through papers. "This is a hit and run. Seems unrealistic that the witness was lying, but it makes sense to track her down and get the right information. Jason, locate the witness, get her current information. Contact the agent of record in her new office—she's out of Louisiana now—get any recollections from her, look at her personal notes. Review the file in detail, see if there is something missing, send the forensics report to Quantico, make sure our people didn't miss anything with the analysis. If necessary, look at the background on Judge Redmond, maybe something odd is there that the original agent missed. Use Kenzie on this," Rachel said.

Jason opened his mouth and then closed it. "Okay," he mumbled.

Lucy's jaw tightened. Kenzie? Kenzie was a good agent, but this was Lucy's case. She'd had nothing to work on for two months and she had already familiarized herself with this case, far more than Jason. This should have been hers.

Rachel turned to Lucy. "Do you have a problem, Agent Kincaid?"

She had a lot of problems, but anything she said would get her in bigger trouble.

"No, ma'am."

"Dismissed."

Lucy walked out. She went to her desk. 5:10. She was out of here.

Jason approached her. "Hey, I'm sorry about that."

Lucy ignored him. She shut down her computer.

"Really, Lucy," he said. "I would have been happy to work this case with you."

Lucy turned to face him. "You lied to me."

"No—I explained—"

"At lunch you told me that you had my back."

"She should have given it to you. I agree. But—"

She brushed past him and walked out of the office. She didn't care that everyone was watching her. She didn't care that Rachel knew that she'd gotten to Lucy. This should have been Lucy's case. There was no reason

offered a major promotion to run the training program at Quantico—rare and prestigious for a young agent like herself, barely forty—but she declined because, according to Donnelly, she wanted to finish what she started.

So while Sean didn't think Murphy would betray them, he wanted to dig deeper. But he wasn't going to let Jack go into this situation blind. JT trusted Declan Cross because they'd been in the Navy together, but he was still not one of them, as far as Sean was concerned, and Jack was family.

"There's nothing out here," Jack said in his earpiece. "Cross, are you certain about this?"

It was muffled, but Sean heard Declan answer in the affirmative, that his source was trustworthy.

Sean typed one-handed on his tablet. It lagged a bit, but then popped up. "There are several parcels of privately owned land, mostly multi-acre spreads. To the east are a couple thousand acres owned by the federal government. Only three of the parcels to the west and north have structures. The road ends—though there's definitely backroad activity. ATVs, most likely. We can get through that way, if necessary, and have sufficient cover."

"How can you tell that?"

"I downloaded the most recent satellite data of the area."

Jack grunted—or laughed, Sean couldn't tell.

Sean clicked through. "The northern most property was foreclosed on a couple years back, no recent sales."

Jack repeated that information to Declan. Then said to Sean, "Okay, we'll go in from the south, you pass us and go in from the north. Do not approach until I give the order."

"Roger that."

Sean passed the nearly invisible entrance to the Double Q Ranch and sped up. One of the benefits of desert driving, at least here, was the terrain—because they'd come off a wetter than average winter with no recent rain, the ground was packed, making it much easier to drive on. But there were cacti and rocks he needed to avoid, so he had to slow down.

"Sean, we're in position," Jack said in his earpiece. "We're one hundred yards south of the main structure. There are no vehicles in sight, but proceed with caution."

"I'm two minutes from position." Sean sped up as much as he dared, turned onto a dry creek bed and followed it to a spot directly north of the house. Then he turned and slowly drove to a crumbling rail-fence that had seen better days long ago.

He slipped on his backpack—Kane had laid down the law about being prepared when he first trained Sean, and he'd reiterated it this morning.

"This is the desert. Water, ammo, knife, emergency kit at all times."

Sean looked around him. A large lizard scurried from rock to rock. Prickly pear cactus grew everywhere, and the purple Texas sage bloomed. He walked through a broken section of the fence and ran low toward the house until he had it in view.

"I'm in position," Sean told Jack. "I have a visual on the house."

"Activity?"

"Negative."

Sean scanned for possible vantage points. A decrepit barn provided the best cover, though he'd have to run through an open area to reach it.

"I'm heading to the barn," Sean said.

He made it without incident. He took a look inside—several of the panels were completely gone. A rusting tractor with weeds growing out of it, moldy hay, and stacks of rotting wood littered the place. Jars filled with dark liquid that Sean didn't even want to go near lined one wall.

He walked around the edge of the barn until he could see the house. "I'm in place," he said over the com.

"Hold your position, cover us."

As Sean watched, Jack and Declan came in low and fast from the south. They stopped up against the house. Sean didn't see any activity on the perimeter. The house felt empty.

"No movement," Sean said.

Declan and Jack took opposite sides of the house, then met at the door. "Clear," Jack said.

Sean came out of the barn and ran up to the door. "We need to search the place," Jack said, "but my guess is they cleaned it out. If there's no one here, they're not coming back."

"Bella sent me two messages this morning," Declan said. "First, that she wanted out and to wait for her signal. Then fifteen minutes later said plans had changed. It's Simon fucking with her head."

"Why didn't you tell JT earlier?" Jack said.

"Because when it comes to Bella, JT doesn't think clearly. I know he's your partner—hell, we served together, I *know* him. He is one of the best soldiers I fought with, but Bella is his sister."

Everyone had a blind spot.

"Why Simon?"

"Because she called him. If she'd talked to me, I would have pulled her. But Simon has a way of convincing the smartest operatives to do dangerous things. And he knows exactly what strings to pull with Bella."

"Finding this girl, Hope," Jack said.

"Yes—that's what he's holding over her—but I think his game is far bigger. He's not talking to me anymore. He might suspect I'm working with you. You cannot underestimate his reach or paranoia."

Sean was sick and tired of hearing about Simon Egan. The guy was brilliant, but as far as Sean was concerned, he'd lost his edge when he put people at risk. Even trained operatives who knew the score like Bella Caruso.

"She's not going to leave until she finds Hope," Sean said.

"Or gets herself killed," Jack said.

Declan rubbed both hands over his face. "If I found her before she talked to Simon, she'd be safe right now."

Jack glanced at Sean. "Search the house, see what you can learn."

Sean went inside while Jack and Declan kept watch outside.

The place was a dive. Though it had been foreclosed on by the bank, it was clear it had been used on and off by any number of people. Faded, torn, mismatched couches lined the large living room. A lopsided dining table with a couple chairs was littered with cigarette butts, papers, and beer bottles. There was power to the house—whether the bank kept it on or someone spliced into the network, Sean wasn't certain. He checked the refrigerator. A few water bottles, some beers, that was it. The garbage was fresh—and there was a bundle of bloody gauze near the top.

Sean dumped the garbage in the sink, but there was nothing else of interest.

A room off the kitchen was surprisingly clean compared to the rest of the house. Someone had been living in here, though it had once been a large pantry. There was room only for a bed, which had been made with linens that were relatively new. A few strands of blonde hair were on the pillow. Bella?

He searched under the linens and mattress but didn't find a note or any clue to her whereabouts. There were shelves that had once held canned and boxed goods, but they were mostly empty. A couple rolls of towels, cleaning supplies that were nearly empty.

Bella had only had a general idea where she was and Declan's contacts had narrowed it down to this abandoned property. If Bella had told Declan to extract her, why hadn't she left him a message? Was she caught off guard? Why had she changed her mind in the first place? When did they leave? Sean had encountered no one on the road leading out here—fifteen minutes straight through the desert to this place, off the highway. They didn't *just* miss them. They must have left at least an hour ago.

Sean walked through the house. There were several mattresses on the floor of a large room downstairs, and several rooms upstairs. The bathrooms were functional but dirty. Odds and ends of clothing were tossed around, small containers of shampoo and conditioner, the sinks stained with make-up. He couldn't tell how many people had been here recently, it could have been a few up to twenty. More if they were crammed in, which was certainly possible.

There were no backpacks, luggage, anything to indicate that someone was returning.

In the back bedroom he found a disgusting bowl of cigarette butts and ashes. Three matchbooks, all partly used, from an El Paso bar. He grabbed one.

"Jack, all clear," he said through the com. "No personal effects. No computers, phones, notes, weapons. Found matchbooks from an El Paso bar, however. Recent signs of smoking."

"Come on out."

Sean stepped out on the porch. "My sources are antsy about something going down tonight," Declan said. "I need to make contact with Bella face-to-face and find out exactly what's going on."

"*We* will make contact," Jack said.

"I know this business better than any of you. Look—I've already blown my job. Simon isn't an idiot—he knows that while I may have been working with him, it was only because of Bella. And now that Bella is in trouble, he knows where my loyalties lie. But remember this: I've been working with Bella for three years, and Genesis Road years before, and understand the ins and outs of sex trafficking better than any of you."

"I agree," Jack said, "but you were in Los Angeles and Phoenix, and if just one of Hirsch's people saw you with Bella there, they're going to peg you for a cop if they see you here. You need to keep a low profile."

"Then we're at a standstill," Declan said.

"No, we're not." Jack held up the matchbook that Sean had retrieved from the house. "I have a plan."

"Sorry I'm late, boys."

Supervisory Special Agent Gianna Murphy wore jeans, two guns in a shoulder holster over a light grey T-shirt, and a loose fitting jacket. Her long dark hair was braided tightly down her back, and sharp high cheekbones and a strong jaw hinted at Native American ancestry.

She'd set up a meeting at a bar. JT was skeptical, but she said, "The owner is retired Army and a buddy of mine. There won't be any trouble."

She slid into the seat next to JT. They were in a corner booth where all of them could see the front door, and Kane had eyes on the back door.

JT introduced himself and Kane. "Donnelly vouches for you," JT said. "RCK doesn't have a contact here, and we have a situation. I don't know who we can trust."

"Brad is a good man. Was my husband's best friend. Brad said Kane Rogan here risked his life to save him, so that makes you both family, as far as I'm concerned. Whatever you tell me is off the record, I got it. If I can't help, I'll tell you so."

The bartender walked over with a bottle of something JT didn't recognize—a local brewery, perhaps.

"Two more?" he asked JT and Kane.

Kane nodded. JT hadn't even finished his first beer, but it had grown warm.

"Did Brad explain what we do?"

"Private security. Hostage rescue. That sort of thing. Both ex-military."

"There's a civilian working undercover in a sex trafficking organization and she's gone dark."

"Civilian?"

"Former cop. Works for a private organization that locates underage prostitutes and extracts them from the business."

"Hmm."

Interest or suspicion? JT couldn't tell. He continued. "She contacted her partner and we learned that she was in El Paso—could still be here—but they bailed from the house they'd holed up in since Monday. However, we know something big is going down, possibly tonight. We think a turf battle, but we don't have confirmation." Kane was staring at JT. "What?" JT said.

Kane didn't say anything. He didn't have to. It was his look—and JT knew what he had to do.

"Full disclosure," JT said. "The undercover is my sister. I need to find her—she is good at this, damn good at undercover work, but she's been in for so long—let's just say I'm worried. She asked to be pulled from the assignment, then rescinded the request—but we're skeptical. At a minimum, we need to make contact and ensure that she's safe."

Gianna nodded. "What do you need?"

"Information."

"Ask."

"Martin Hirsch is the suspect in question. He's been running prostitution rings in southern California and Arizona for a long time, and is in the midst of an expansion east, either creating or taking over the pipeline along the I-10 corridor. We believe he's the number two guy or has a partner, but we don't have an identity on the other man—just goes by the initial 'Z.' We don't have the hierarchy nailed down. What we do know is that the expansion started last year, possibly because of the shake-up in Texas. The DEA took out a major drug transportation ring, followed by the FBI knocking out a key source of sex slaves into the U.S. from Mexico. There've been some turf wars, but no one has emerged as a leader."

"I'm aware of the operations, mostly through Brad's task force. They definitely left a void. But in our regional meeting, Brad said he had a handle on the situation, as much as we can."

"I'm sure he does, but sex trafficking—though it uses similar networks for transportation as the drug business—is still a different business that the DEA isn't equipped to handle."

"Agreed."

"My sister went undercover because her firm was hired to find a girl who was sold to Hirsch." JT had begun to doubt Simon's story—who had hired him? JT suspected Simon was bankrolling the entire operation. "She's successfully extracted several underage girls who were forced into prostitution, but hasn't found Hope Anderson. In Phoenix, a cop who helped was killed, by Hirsch or one of his men, but Bella is still entrenched."

"Where are they holed up?"

"They were at a spread north of here, abandoned ranch."

"Lots of space up there," Gianna said. "If they've gone, what do you need from me?"

"Names. People in the business. I know you're DEA, but Donnelly said you keep your finger on the pulse of every crime and criminal in El Paso."

She nodded. "True." She pulled out a notepad and started writing as she spoke. "The drug trade deals more with forced labor than sex slaves, but same principle. With the big guns being taken out last year, there've been a whole bunch of small time dealers trying to expand their businesses. Which is ultimately a good thing—don't get me wrong—but some of these lowlifes are violent, some are just stupid. Weeding through the idiots takes time and resources, and after the shake-up in the DEA, I have half an office of new agents. I stand by every single one of them, they're solid, but most are either rookies or new to the territory." She tore off a sheet of paper and handed it to JT. "Those are the three big players in town. They're into everything. The first two will traffic people. The third probably not, but sometimes you don't know. The third guy is focused on distribution. I wrote down a list of their known hangouts, but the first address is going to be the most likely place you'll find any of them."

"This is good—thank you."

"Now, I gotta ask you—what's your plan?"

"Observe at this point. I'm only going to extract Bella if she's in immediate danger, but I need to know she's alive." His voice cracked. He didn't realize how emotional he was about his sister. He handed the list to Kane.

Gianna nodded. "If you need backup, call me. I wrote my cell number down. I'll bring reinforcements. I ask for one thing in return." She noticed their faces and laughed. "Don't look so worried. I simply want your intel. You learn anything that can help me nail any of these bastards, pass it along. Even if it's not drug related—we have a new police chief and he's a hard-ass, but damn, I love his can-do attitude. We've worked real well together. Not all his cops are solid, however, so we have some problems. Nothing we can't handle."

"That we can do."

She looked like she was going to leave, then she said, "If you are able to rescue any of those girls, call me. I'll take care of them."

"Thank you."

"I'll make a few discreet calls, let you know if I hear anything about sex trafficking, new players, a turf war. I have your number."

"Thanks for your help."

"Obliged," she said, tipped an invisible hat and walked out.

Kane said, "That went well. Look here." He pointed to one of the names on the list. Milo Feliciano. "He works at a trucking company."

"Now we know where to start."

CHAPTER FOURTEEN

Lucy was glad Nate didn't talk much on the drive to Austin. She didn't want to explain her bad mood, and she was still fuming over Jason Lopez. She supposed she should be angrier with Rachel, but Jason was her colleague, her partner, and he hadn't stood up for her.

And she was sad. Working with Ryan and Nate had been symbiotic. She and Kenzie had become friends, or so she thought. The friendship was thin, she realized, after Kenzie blamed her for the attack on fellow agent Barry Crawford. And she'd *thought* that her partnership with Barry had been solid after a rocky beginning—then she learned that he didn't trust her. Not her skills—but *her.* He'd told her former supervisor that, essentially, she took unnecessary risks and would burn out quickly.

Had Rachel seen that letter from Barry? Lucy didn't know. Noah had—and he'd implied that he'd taken care of it. But by that did he mean he'd destroyed it? Buried it? Sealed it? Had Barry talked to Rachel one-on-one? Lucy had wanted to talk to him after everything, make sure that he was okay, but he'd shut everyone out and moved to Austin to be closer to his family. The guilt she felt over what happened—even though she'd had many sleepless nights thinking about all the other ways she could have done things, none of which would have turned out any different—was still there. Smaller, more manageable, but still present.

"We have time," Nate said. "Let's check out Ryan's new place."

"I don't want to drop in unannounced," Lucy said.

Nate snorted. "He told me to come over anytime. Trust me."

Ryan had a small house in an older neighborhood of Austin with tree-lined streets and wide sidewalks. It was a charming, quiet community that reminded Lucy of large groups of kids trick-or-treating or playing soccer in the middle of the street. Ryan was in the middle of a major renovation project—half the house was painted and roof tiles were stacked on a partly finished roof.

"He got it on the cheap because it was falling apart," Nate confided.

"Have you been here before?"

"Once, when he was looking at buying it. He moved in three weeks ago."

"It's very cute."

"Cute. For a cop. Yeah, you tell him that."

Nate rang the bell. It was a classic chime. There was a crash, several expletives, then the door opened. Ryan stood there in paint-splattered fatigues and a white T-shirt. "Lucy! Come in!" He seemed genuinely happy to see them. "Beer?"

"Can't," Nate said.

"Work?"

"Of sorts."

Ryan helped himself to a beer, and tossed water bottles toward Nate and Lucy. "I'm glad you came by. I'm going to have a barbecue when I get the backyard fixed up, but the roof was a huge expense and it had to be done first. It's the only thing I'm not doing myself."

"I love this place," Lucy said.

"I'll give you the quick tour—just watch your step."

The house was two bedrooms, two baths with a sunroom that had been turned into a man cave for Ryan and his two young sons. Video games, movies, large screen television. The backyard was surprisingly large—narrow and deep—with a peanut-shaped pool, crumbling patio, and lots of shade trees. "The pool is actually in good shape," Ryan said. "But I'm going to put in a deck. I can do the deck myself, but I can't pour concrete, so in the end it'll be cheaper."

"When you're ready for the hard labor, call me up," Nate said. "I'll drag the Rogan brothers with me, you'll get this done in a weekend."

"I'm holding you to that."

They chatted about Ryan's kids and the fact that his ex-wife had been cool about the move, the Austin office and what Ryan was working on, and Sean and Lucy's wedding. Lucy enjoyed catching up, though her heart wasn't in it. She missed working with Ryan. They had had a comfortable partnership.

"Still in the doghouse, Lucy?"

Ryan had only left the San Antonio office last month. He knew how frustrated she'd been working at the desk.

"No sign of getting out anytime soon."

Nate looked surprised. "You finished that god-awful project. Didn't you and Lopez uncover something odd in one of the case files?"

"Yep, and Rachel won't give me the case. I'm still riding a desk."

"It's tough now, but stick it out," Ryan said. "Keep your head down. You can transfer at the end of the year if it doesn't get better."

"I've thought of it," Lucy admitted, "but Sean and I really love San Antonio. We don't want to leave. We love our house, Kane isn't far, we have friends. I don't want to start over. It's my battle, I'll figure it out."

"Do you guys need help with this 'sort of' work

thing?" Ryan asked. "I'm getting ready to call it a night. There's only so much wrestling I can do with the damn plumbing. I'm thinking I might have to hire someone for that, too. This place is becoming a money pit."

"I know how much you paid for it," Nate said. "You got a steal."

"I'm not complaining."

"Much," Nate said with a cough.

"Seriously, I wouldn't mind getting out for a few hours."

"It's something for RCK," Lucy said. "I don't want to get you stuck in the middle."

"We got it," Nate said. "But thanks for the offer."

"You need anything, call."

They said good-bye and left. "So that's why you were sitting there fuming the entire drive up," Nate said. "You could have told me."

"I guess I just enjoyed feeling sorry for myself." She took a deep breath. No more. She had to deal with Rachel, with Jason, and stop the worry and self-reprisal. "I want things to go back to the way they were, and they can't. I'll be fine."

She would be, too. She had Sean, she had friends, she had a solid record—the bullshit coming from her current supervisor notwithstanding.

"I think it's fucked. I didn't like her asking questions of everyone, but nothing made me suspicious that she had it out for you. I really think you just pissed her off because you didn't tell her why you went to San Diego and she had to hear about it from someone else. Everything else is just window dressing. Excuses. But this RCK operation could bite you in the ass."

"I'm already prepared for it," Lucy said. "You know, I understand her position. She feels like she has no control over me and she needs to put her foot down hard now."

"It's more than that—it's because of who you are—who your friends are, your family. There aren't many of us who have the assistant director of the FBI on speed dial. My guess is she's searching for your breaking point."

"What does that mean?"

"How far can she push you before you run to Rick Stockton and complain."

"I wouldn't do that."

"No—but others would."

Nate might be right.

Mona Hill was late.

Nate was outside in Sean's Mustang. Lucy always found it humorous that Nate liked to drive Sean's sports car over his own decked-out 4×4, but she didn't mind—she didn't particularly like driving, though she had learned to enjoy the Mustang.

She sat in the far corner of a local diner where she could watch both the front door and the kitchen. She didn't want to be caught off guard, and she was already nervous about this meeting.

Why? Because Sean had kept his association with a known prostitute hidden from her? Because he'd made a deal with Mona? Blackmailed her?

Lucy wasn't upset with Sean, but maybe a bit disappointed. That had been a dark time for her. For both of them. She certainly hadn't been herself, and she could see why Sean hadn't thought that she could handle the truth. Or maybe he just didn't want to burden her with it. She didn't like all these secrets coming back to bite them both in the ass. Even now, Sean's association with Mona Hill—and Lucy meeting with her tonight—could jeopardize everything they'd worked so hard to achieve.

Yet.

Mona might have valuable information about the sex trade in Texas, and if they could find Bella—save her—then it would all be worth it.

And that was the crux of every decision Lucy made that had gotten her on the hot plate with her boss. She'd made difficult choices for the sole purpose of saving an innocent. And she would do it all again. She was so tired of second-guessing herself, of worrying whether she'd be fired, or reprimanded, or whether her decisions were right. So many times she'd had to make a decision in seconds. To shoot or not shoot, to negotiate or play hardball. To cross the border or not cross the border.

But she could stand by each and every one. Recognizing that made dealing with Mona, working to locate Bella Caruso, riding out her job at a desk all year if she had to, easier. Resolved, she felt an invisible weight lift from her shoulders.

This was where she was meant to be; this was what she was meant to do.

Five minutes later when she was thinking of leaving, Nate sent her a text message.

She's here. One guy, one girl standing outside. Both carrying. Watch yourself.

Mona stepped into the diner, looked around, and saw Lucy. The woman had changed. She dressed like a sexy businesswoman in a short, straight skirt, fitted jacket, and lacy camisole. She didn't overdo her makeup, and her hair had been done in professional braids, then wrapped around her elegant head. She looked both hardened and smart, but no one would immediately think *prostitute* if they saw her.

Mona sat down. "Your husband has some balls."

"Point?"

"He didn't give me much of a choice."

"What did he tell you I wanted?"

"First, if I decide to tell you anything, my name stays

out of it. I've built a solid business and I'm not going to be jammed by the fucking police or anyone else. Second, this is it. I can't risk it. As far as the world is concerned, Mona Hill is dead. Odette is alive and well and I want her to stay that way."

"If you give me something actionable, I won't need anything else. And I have no desire to jam you up unless you screw with me."

Mona laughed humorlessly. "Screw with *you*? That's rich. Do you know what your husband did to me?"

"Let you off easy."

"Destroyed my entire *business*."

Lucy stared at her pointedly. "You look like you're doing all right."

"Because I was forced to rebuild."

"Maybe he did you a favor. I wouldn't have."

Mona grinned and leaned forward. "Trouble in paradise?"

"What do you have?"

"You didn't know, did you?"

Lucy knew exactly what Mona meant, but she didn't bite. "I don't have time to play games, Mona."

"*Odette*. That's my name."

Lucy stared at her.

Mona said, "Here's what I know about the sex business in San Antonio since I left—it's fucked up. You didn't like me, that's fine, I could give a shit. I never hit my girls. I took fifty percent, but they had a free apartment—a roof over their heads in a decent neighborhood. Better than most of them grew up with. I never forced them to work every night unless they wanted to. My girls were mostly clean, they worked the streets because that's what they did, not because I forced them. I leave, and there's a void. When I rebuilt my business, I tried to get my girls to join me, but most of them were grabbed by pimps who don't give a fuck about giving them money and housing. There's two vying for control—Eli Kinder, a guerrilla pimp who mostly has girls walking the downtown circuit. You can throw him in jail and I would pop a cork. Jugger—I don't know him by any other name—would be most likely to run underage girls. Eli is violent, he's not going to take shit from anyone. Jugger's a businessman, someone gives him an offer, he'll take it. There's a few girls who went out on their own, but they keep a low profile, do mostly an Internet business, Craigslist, shit like that. More power to them. But Eli and Jugger are the two biggest pimps running the streets."

"Two? Only two in a city the size of San Antonio? I don't believe you."

"They're the biggest, I'm telling you, and the ones more apt to branch out. There's a prick named Gutierrez who runs Latinas, but he went underground when the feds shut down his network."

Lucy hadn't heard about that. Could it have been collateral damage from them taking out the Mexican pipeline last year? Small blessings. But that didn't mean he wasn't looking to get back into the business.

"Look—I'm going to give you one more name, but you can't burn her. You burn her, I don't care what your husband threatens me with, I will take you both down."

"Do not threaten me."

"It's not a threat."

Lucy stared at her. She saw Mona Hill for who she was. Last year when Lucy first met her, she'd let her attitude and the jibes get to her. No longer. Lucy may have spooked early in her career, but she'd learned to let the ice flow in her veins and it worked to her advantage here.

Mona assessed her with narrowed eyes, then slid a folded paper over to her. "One of my girls, Victoria, put together her own small network like I did in Houston.

All legal age, no bullshit. Straightforward. Girls who know the score. If there's anyone making a move into Eli or Jugger's networks, she'll know. She'll also know if there's a brand new player working the streets, someone who came after me. You're a good girl, you don't understand what girls like Victoria and I went through to get here, to be in charge. This is her life—you understand, *chica*?"

"I'm looking for a fourteen-year-old who was sold into this life by her stepfather," Lucy said in a quiet voice. "And the people who bought her are moving their business east. They may reach out to you."

"I can promise you, Lucy, I will never cut a deal with anyone. The first time was with that bastard Tobias and look where it got me? The second was with your husband. And I feel like I've made a deal with the devil both times."

Mona stood up.

"Odette," Lucy said sharply. She hadn't realized how angry she was until she spoke.

The woman scowled at her.

"You may not want the deal, but I shouldn't have to tell you sometimes you're not given a choice. I like you a lot less than you like me—but if they come calling, I may be the only one who can save your ass." Lucy rose and handed Mona a napkin on which she had written her cell phone number. Then she walked out.

CHAPTER FIFTEEN

Milo Feliciano's trucking company was closed for the night. The place was dark and deserted and even the security lighting was poor. That wasn't a bad thing, JT thought.

"I should have traded you for Sean," he mumbled when it took Kane an insane amount of time to analyze the security.

"Ouch," Kane said.

When Sean left RCK a year and a half ago, JT hadn't realized how valuable he'd become to the business. His tech skills were second to none. JT'd been more than happy when he convinced Sean to return—though he suspected Jack Kincaid had been the more persuasive partner. Jack had been an asset to RCK from the minute he signed on. He provided an even-tempered, common sense balance among the principals. He was a lot like Kane, without taking undue risks.

"No trucks here."

Kane nodded. "I smell fresh oil and gasoline. They moved out recently." Kane gestured to the semi-hidden security.

"There're two security cameras, one on the main gate and one on the door of the office. Probably one inside."

"We'll have to do this the old-fashioned way," JT

said. He considered first the cameras, then the fencing. "The system appears basic, we shouldn't have a problem."

The chances were that a place like this—since it was most likely owned by a sex trafficker—would have a private security company to handle any alarms. If Sean were here, he could disable the system. JT wasn't an amateur—he'd picked up too much from Sean and the other Rogan brother, Duke. But they didn't have time for JT to try his disarming skills.

The fence wasn't electric. They walked around to the back and cut a hole, then slipped through. Kane immediately located the main fuse box and blew it. They might have ten minutes or they might have an hour depending on the type of response. And sometimes, power outages didn't automatically trigger an alarm.

They didn't hear an alarm, but that might not mean anything.

Kane pointed to JT and gestured to the office; Kane himself went into the garage.

JT picked the lock with ease—it was a standard lock, not an electronic keypad or even a dead bolt. The company was a new acquisition for Hirsch, but JT would have made security his number one priority, especially if this was a front for human trafficking.

They could be wrong—Milo Feliciano may not have any dealings with Hirsch. Sean was running a background on the company, but online sales reports were often delayed. He'd have to go to the county or city business office in the morning to find out if there had been a recent change in ownership.

The office was small and cramped, but not cluttered. There were no chairs for people to wait, and four could stand in the area if they didn't mind getting close. There was a phone, a computer, and notepad on a single desk. Forms were sorted in bins along the wall. An old-fashioned school clock ticked off the seconds, a sound that couldn't be heard except in the deep silence of the night.

A wall of glass, blocked by metal blinds, separated the front office from the back. A short hall led to that office door, a storage room, and a tiny bathroom. The office door was locked, and JT picked that as well.

They'd blown the power so they couldn't check the computer. That might not have been the smartest move. He said into his radio. "Can we get power back?"

"Give me a few minutes."

The filing cabinets were locked. JT popped the lock and looked at the folders. They were all customer records, invoices, truck maintenance reports. Feliciano was extremely organized. Based on the files, the company owned eight moving trucks—two large haul trucks that would require a commercial license, four smaller trucks that were sufficient for most residential moves, and two four-wheel-drive pick-up trucks. He also owned a trucking company in San Antonio. JT took photos of the information on the trucks as well as the name and location of the sister company in San Antonio. He sent it to Lucy.

Possible connection to Hirsch.

JT heard a beep and he immediately had his hand on his gun.

Over the radio, Kane said, "Power restored to the office."

"Roger," JT said. He turned on the computer. Password protected. He hooked up his phone and ran a program that Sean had written, then left it to do its job while he finished searching the file cabinets.

His phone beeped once. That was fast. He scrolled through the files on the computer. Nothing jumped out at him. He then opened the email program.

Bingo.

A copy of a signed contract between Milo Feliciano

and a company, West-East Transport, from two weeks ago. The contract was signed by a lawyer on behalf of the company. Likely a shell corp, but now they had a name, and JT had confidence that Sean could ID the backers.

Better, if they could find solid evidence of a crime, he'd send all of this to Rick Stockton in the FBI, and Rick could open a white collar crimes investigation. Sometimes, the only way to shut down a criminal enterprise was by cutting off their money supply or their ability to launder money.

"Got something," Kane said over the com.

"I'll meet you in the garage."

JT copied the data, then left everything the way he'd found it. The owners might realize there was a breech—they definitely would if they found the hole in the fence—but they might not know when, why, or who.

JT left the office cautiously, made sure the door locked behind him, and crossed the yard to the garage. Kane was in the shadows, emerging only when he saw JT. Kane led him inside.

While there were no trucks stored outside, there were two inside—the two large commercial trucks that JT had identified in the records. The smell of fresh paint coated JT's sinuses.

"Within the last twenty-four hours they painted over the old logo. They're now unmarked, but they can put anything on them," Kane said.

"That's it?"

"No."

JT followed Kane to the far side of the garage. A smaller moving truck was there, this one older and with Arizona tags. Other smells assaulted JT's senses. Feces, urine, and death.

His heart froze.

"There's a body in there." *It's not Bella. It can't be Bella.*

"Young female, dead about forty-eight hours." He showed JT a photo he'd taken on his phone. The girl's face was bloated and barely recognizable, but definitely not his sister. She looked more than forty-eight hours dead, but with the heat and enclosed space, decomp worked faster.

"We need to call Rick."

"I planted a tracker in the cab. They're gonna have to dump the body, Rick's people can catch them in the act."

"We'll leave that up to him. I can't just leave that girl rotting in there. Anything else?"

"Signs that all the trucks had been painted, not just those here. There are slots for ten more."

"There's eight on record in the office—these are two of them."

"I planted trackers on them as well, but these trucks are no good for human trafficking. Too often they have to pull over for weigh stations, they can't go down every road. They'll stick with the small moving trucks like the one the dead girl's in."

Kane was far more compassionate than he sounded, but the brutal truth hit JT hard. Bella had been working for these same people who had killed that girl. Had she known? Was she even alive?

They left the way they came. "How'd she die?" JT asked.

Kane shrugged as he pulled their vehicle out of a hiding spot. "No signs of blood, though from the evidence I suspect there were a dozen or more people transported in the back of that truck. Could be she had heat stroke, they left her there and planned to clean up later. Or she tried to run and they killed her as an example. Any number of things. We'll find them."

He said it with such quiet confidence that JT believed him.

His phone rang. It was Jack. "News?"

"We have eyes on Bella."

"Where?"

"I'll send you the address, but stay clear. Something's going down. Sean and I have cover, but if you come in—"

"Dammit, Jack, I have to talk to her."

"We have a plan."

"Where's Declan?"

"Outside the bar, out of sight. We can't risk having Hirsch or his people spot him. You can come if you want, but stay hidden, okay?"

JT wanted to go—he wanted to see Bella with his own eyes, make sure that she really was okay. But he knew that if he went in, all bets were off.

"Is she safe?"

"For now. I'm not taking my eyes off her, JT."

JT trusted Jack.

"Kane and I will finish up here then head over, contact Declan, and stay out of sight. You need us, we'll be there."

"Roger."

CHAPTER SIXTEEN

For two hours Bella was certain that Martin Hirsch knew she'd been the one who'd helped Christina and Ashley escape. For two hours she plotted how she could slip away. Declan should be in El Paso by now, but it wasn't going to help her if he had no idea where she was. She wished she'd called him instead of Simon; Declan would never try to talk her out of an extraction.

No, you don't. You knew going in that this was going to be dangerous, but it was the only chance of finding Hope. You called Simon because you wanted to be talked out of leaving.

Bella was on edge. She'd been in too deep, too long, and she didn't know if she should trust her instincts. Yet . . . if Simon wasn't bullshitting her, Hope was alive three months ago, and that meant she'd survived whatever ordeal Hirsch and his people put her through. That meant Bella could save her.

Two hours sitting in a sweat-stained bar with Damien watching the door had her realizing that a traitor was the last thing on Hirsch's mind. For all she knew, Hirsch had forgotten the girls even existed.

There weren't many people around—an old couple who looked half-asleep at the bar nursing draft beers and not talking. A Mexican cowboy in his forties with a couple days' growth of beard slouched in the corner. He'd come in thirty minutes ago and ordered tequila and beer. Probably just got off work and spending half his money on alcohol before going home to his wife. He made her a little twitchy because he had hard eyes and his clothes were a little too clean to be a laborer, but everything was making her twitchy these days. A group of men pulled together a couple tables, all working stiffs, drinking beer like water and telling bad jokes and tall tales.

And Damien's men.

It was a dive bar, perfect for a drug deal or clandestine meeting. The bartender and one employee manned the place. Probably had a shotgun under the counter. His employee, practically a kid, came over with two more beers for Damien and Bella. Damien slipped him a twenty and he walked away. She nodded thanks.

Damien hadn't said much to her, but she'd picked up on enough of his earlier conversation with Hirsch to know that Hirsch was antsy about the expansion, that it hadn't been his plan to work this fast, but he had committed. This elusive Z was expecting El Paso to be locked down before they moved on, and El Paso wasn't cooperating.

There was something else going on, something Damien wasn't saying. She tried to get him to talk, but he was more tight-lipped than usual—and he had never had loose lips.

It struck Bella that Hirsch might be shutting down his own cells and turning them over to local pimps in exchange for exclusive transportation of their human product. It would be more profitable for him with less risk because he wouldn't be managing the women day-to-day. Smart business move—if they could bribe or bully the local players into going along with the idea.

The one thing Bella had picked up over the course

of the day simply by being in the right place at the right time was that the El Paso organization, run by a prick named Raul Diaz, wasn't budging. Evidently Hirsch had offended him, and he wanted Hirsch and everyone associated with Hirsch gone.

Hirsch wasn't leaving. Now Bella understood why Damien was worried. Up to this point, everything had been relatively easy for Hirsch—other than losing a few girls. He'd successfully bought up several independent trucking companies, he'd merged his organization seamlessly through Los Angeles and Arizona with other networks, and though she hadn't been to Albuquerque with the group, Damien had told her they'd locked down the players there months ago and already had a base of operation in San Antonio and New Orleans. They were working on a couple of waystations, as he called them, between those two cities, and Z had already secured everything east of Louisiana. Texas was the big deal because recent law enforcement crackdowns had resulted in chaos.

It was a damn lot more than she'd known on Sunday when she helped free Christina and Ashley. Had she realized how deep Hirsch's expansion ran, she really might have gone with the girls—because at this rate, she didn't know how she would find Hope when there were so many places left to look.

"I'm worried," Bella admitted to Damien. "I have a bad feeling." That wasn't a lie. But she wanted Damien to talk, and he might if she acted nervous.

It's not an act. You are nervous.

"We know what we're doing."

"What did you do with the girls?"

He gave her an odd look. "Not important right now."

"It's just you sent them off with Desiree—you know how much I distrust her—and I haven't seen Penny in days."

Damien glared at her. "Shut the fuck up, Doc."

She hit a sore spot with him. Why? She pushed—carefully, but firmly. "Why am I here, D? You know this isn't my expertise."

Damien didn't answer her right away. He was watching the door. Bella recognized his four goons in the room, two at the bar and two near the front door, but Desiree and Bam-Bam weren't here. They'd taken the girls . . . where? East? That had to have been Plan B. The original plan was to leave them in El Paso with the group Hirsch contracted with, but if there was no contract there would be no girls.

And if there was no contract, Hirsch planned on retaliating.

None of this was good.

Damien said, "Reach under the table. I have something for you."

Bella hesitated, on alert.

"Do it," he snapped, his voice low and threatening.

She reached under the table and Damien shoved the butt of a gun in her hand. By the feel of the grip it was likely a .45 semi-auto. She immediately slid it under her thigh. "I don't do guns," she said through clenched teeth.

"You do now."

"I'm a doctor. I can't."

"It's for your own protection. I wanted you to go with the others because I can't protect you here. But Mr. Hirsch wants you at the negotiation."

Nothing could have surprised her more.

"What the hell for?"

"He still doesn't like you, but you're smart. He wants El Paso locked down tonight, and if it doesn't happen, there will be blood."

"I can't be party to that, D."

"You don't have a choice, Doc."

It didn't make sense. She understood that Hirsch

wanted her here because he was suspicious—but then why the hell would Damien give her a gun?

The door opened and a man walked in. Dirty, faded jeans. Worn cowboy boots of the type that held the feet of nine out of ten men in west Texas. Jean jacket, white T-shirt. A little James Dean swagger. Thirties, dark hair that curled at the ends, Texas Rangers ball cap. He looked familiar, but his face was partly shielded.

It was when he crossed the room and sat down at the end of the bar and she caught a good look at his profile that Bella knew exactly who he was.

Kane Rogan's little brother.

She hadn't seen Sean in years. She'd kept up with her brother's business, and heard that Sean had joined RCK, but she'd always thought of him as the computer nerd. He'd never been in the military, he'd never been a cop, he'd graduated from MIT. He was the brains behind the operation. What was he doing in the field? Damn, how things had changed.

If Sean was here, that meant RCK wasn't far behind. Her brother was going to blow everything.

She didn't let on to Damien that she recognized the guy. Damien gave him a cursory, dismissive glance, then refocused on the door.

Maybe Declan had called them in because he knew something that she didn't.

The first book of Samuel. Declan had called JT.

It was as clear as day now, she didn't know why she hadn't seen it before. Declan may have cut ties with Genesis and the Dixons but he and JT were bonded. Declan must have kept in touch with her brother if JT could pull together an operation this fast.

Declan knows Roger is dead. He's worried. And if he called JT, JT would never back down, no matter that she had called off the extraction.

How did he track her down here? To this bar?

"Where's Hirsch?" she asked. The bartender put a bottle of beer in front of Sean. He drank. Who did he come with? Was JT really here?

"Look, Doc, follow my lead. But I can't babysit you. You've shot a gun before, haven't you?"

"It's been awhile."

She was a great shot, but she didn't want Damien to know. It wouldn't fit her cover.

"You have a .45 there. It's clean, but try not to leave it behind. It has a kick. Fourteen round magazine, one bullet in the chamber."

"I'm not going to shoot anyone!"

"Shut. Up. You might not have a choice. We need you, Doc—I don't have to tell you medics are hard to find in our business."

"Then you shouldn't have brought me here."

"Just—"

He didn't finish his sentence. Instead, he picked up his phone and listened. "Okay." He snapped the flip phone shut. He'd looked worried before, now he was both worried and angry.

"Stay," he ordered and walked down the back hall that led to the restrooms and rear exit.

Bella put the gun in her waistband, in the small of her back, then pulled her T-shirt over it. That did little to conceal it.

Hirsch walked in with six men. One stayed with him and the others dispersed around the room. The bartender eyed the men with casual suspicion. So did Sean Rogan.

Bella didn't recognize any of them, but they were clearly taking orders from Hirsch. Where had Damien gone? She knew she was in hot water when she actually wanted the enforcer at her side. At least he was predictable.

Hirsch approached her table and sat down in the seat Damien had vacated.

"What's going on?" she asked through clenched teeth.

"Shut up."

Hirsch called to the bartender. "Double shot of Scotch. Good stuff, not piss water."

Bella would love to shoot Hirsch, right now. Did he know Damien had given her a gun? She couldn't be certain. But if she shot him, six other men would take her out—and even if Sean Rogan had the street smarts to react quickly, it was still two against seven.

JT had to be close behind. If Sean knew where she was, that meant JT did, too.

But if she killed Hirsch, she would never find Hope. Even though it pained her that she couldn't kill him, he was her only connection to the girl.

You're not an assassin. Why are you itching to kill a man?

She'd faced evil many times in her life, including people even more violent and depraved than Hirsch. But he had gotten to her. It wasn't just that he treated women and girls like property, it was the complete and utter disdain he had for anyone he thought was inferior—and that included all women and most men. This was his business, and he would never lose sleep over one dead girl or one lost contract. He would kill whoever was responsible—if it benefitted Hirsch. And usually, showing force—proving he was not to be screwed with—benefitted him.

The bartender brought over the double shot and left. Hirsch drank half, grimaced.

"Fucking cheap swill," he muttered.

Bella had a hundred questions but kept her mouth shut. The one concern was why Damien had left. He'd gotten a call—from who? Hirsch? Likely. Hirsch had entered not five minutes later. Why had Damien left after the call? Why were there so many men? Half of them Bella didn't even recognize. Hirsch didn't usually travel with so many. How trustworthy? Who were they? Locals?

Three men entered through the main door. One tipped his hat to Hirsch, but he sat at a table near the door with Hirsch's men. Damn, Hirsch had at least nine people in here, all watching his back.

Her eyelid twitched.

Now the bartender was looking nervous. The old, half-asleep couple shuffled out. No one else moved. The drunk working guys kept up the mindless chatter, an occasional barking laugh telling everyone they were completely clueless to the tension in the dive.

Hirsch smiled. If his slimy, half-upturned lips could be called a smile. He had a plan and he hadn't told anyone, except Damien. Of that Bella was damn certain.

They waited. Country music chattered through bass-heavy speakers. Not the popular stuff that everyone and his brother listened to, but tunes with a country twang that Bella had never heard before. Kane's little brother ordered another beer. Bella caught him glancing over at the Mexican in the corner more than once. Subtle, but she was trained to watch for subtle.

Was that guy with RCK? At third glance he didn't look exactly Mexican, but he had a darker-hued skin than a Caucasian, black hair and dark eyes. The beard was short but thick, which gave him a darker look.

Jack Kincaid.

She'd only met him a couple times. He'd put the "K" in Rogan-Caruso-Kincaid. Cuban, she thought. Former Army, mercenary, joined RCK when he married . . . snap! Megan Elliott, the fed who was one of JT's friends, whose brother Matt had also been a Navy SEAL.

Small fucking world.

"Calm down, Dr. Carter," Hirsch said. "You're jumpy and nervous and that's not going to serve us well."

"I would be calmer if I knew what the fuck was going on. I'm getting a bad vibe, and I have learned over the years to trust my instincts. Where's Damien? He should be here to watch your ass. I'm not trained for this, I didn't sign on—"

"Shut. Up. Shit, woman. Damien knows what he needs to do. You need to keep your mouth shut until I tell you to open it."

"Don't talk to me like I'm one of your whores."

He leaned over. The expression on his face was pure hatred. "Don't think for a minute that you're not expendable. I survived without a doctor on staff before, I will survive again. Do you understand?"

She made sure he saw the disgust on her face. Through clenched teeth she said, "Yes, *sir*."

He narrowed his eyes and she feared she went too far. Then the door opened and he diverted his attention to the new customers.

A short Hispanic male entered. He was surrounded by four burly goons who all carried weapons. This had to be Raul Diaz.

The bartender didn't comment about the obvious show of guns, just continued wiping down the bar. But he'd been wiping the same section for the last five minutes. Whose side was he on? Hirsch or Diaz? Who had picked this venue in the first place? Had he called the cops? Would he?

Hirsch was too calm. Bella couldn't imagine a scenario where they would all get out of this bar alive.

Hirsch waited until Diaz had started toward him before standing up to greet the man.

"Raul," Hirsch said. "Please sit."

Raul Diaz was a hard man and his voice a low rasp. "I told you last night that I wasn't joining your operation, and nothing has changed."

"I was hoping after you received my gift last night you would have a change of heart."

"Sending me two cheap whores to suck my dick means shit. I have plenty of my own. *Mine.* This town is mine, *gringo*, and you're not wanted here. It's after sunset. You were supposed to be gone. Color me surprised when I got the call that you were here."

Nothing about this exchange was planned—at least on Diaz's part.

Now Bella knew why Damien gave her the gun. He knew that this was going to end in bloodshed. That he was giving her a fighting chance was almost endearing if she wasn't so damn terrified she'd end up dead.

"Sit, Raul," Hirsch said, all humor gone from his voice.

"No."

"We have a lot to discuss. It wasn't the girls—I have plenty of them, and they're all expendable. I could care less what you do with them. But my plan, my vision, I'd hoped that after a good night's sleep you would see and understand how the future could play out."

Raul put both hands on the table and said, "I see you get the bulk of the profit and I take the bulk of the risk, and that's fucking bullshit. I'm not paying you no protection money to keep what's mine, it's *mine.* My network is solid. I don't need what you're selling, and definitely not at the price you're asking. So get the *fuck* out of my town *now* or you're a dead man."

Hirsch sighed. "You're not the only organization in El Paso. And in your arrogance you forgot to keep your enemies closer than your friends."

Noise in the back of the bar had all heads turning. In swaggered three men. They looked so much alike they had to be brothers. They were young—dear Lord, Bella thought, they were in their twenties, if that. One of them didn't even look old enough to shave.

Raul started to laugh. "Oh, you have got to be fucking *joking*. The Moores are *idiots*."

"Are they?" Hirsch said, his voice low.

"You've started a war, *gringo*. A war." He jerked his finger toward his men and walked to the front door.

The door opened and Damien stood there.

His presence surprised Raul only briefly, but brief was long enough.

Damien stepped across the threshold, raised his gun, and fired a bullet into Raul's forehead so fast that at first no one reacted. Bella froze, uncertain what was going to happen next. The boisterous men in the center of the bar were completely silent. Everyone else was either part of Hirsch's group or Diaz's group.

No one reacted, that is, except Jack Kincaid in the corner. He had his gun out and table turned over as a shield so fast Bella wondered if he'd begun his defensive stance as soon as the door opened. His movement snapped Bella out of her trance and she pulled her gun out and crouched behind the table.

Hirsch's men had stood as soon as the door opened, and now surrounded Diaz's men. None of them had the chance to draw. The Moore brothers stared in shock. Hirsch stood, walked over to the brothers, and said, "You made the right decision. Don't make me regret it, or you all will end up with a bullet in your heads, do you understand?"

The shortest of the three, who was clearly the oldest, nodded even though he was visibly shaking. "Yes, boss."

Hirsch crossed the room to Diaz's men. "Will you work for me?" he asked the group.

No one said anything, eyeing each other for answers that none of them had because their leader had been murdered in cold blood. Hirsch sighed, took out a gun, and shot one of them in the gut.

The other men all drew. How the hell did they think they would survive this? It was a dozen to four. But Hirsch was in the line of fire—he was going to get himself killed. What the hell was *he* thinking?

Bella needed to get out of here. One of the men along the periphery jumped up. When had he come in? Right. He was one of two guys who'd come in earlier, but he wasn't with Hirsch. Diaz had stacked the room as well. The men in the center all had guns. They were not part of Hirsch's operation. Had he really thought they were neutral?

Hirsch had started this blood bath.

The man on the periphery grabbed Bella as she started for the exit in the back. He held a gun to her head. "Drop it, you fucking bastard!" he screamed at Hirsch. "You'll pay for this!"

Hirsch stared at him. "Do you think I care what you do to her?" Then he looked Bella in the eye and nodded. What the hell? What did he expect of her? Was this some sort of fucking test? With her *life?*

Bella could see Sean Rogan shift in his seat. But Jack Kincaid remained in the corner, watching.

Jack had experience. He'd been a mercenary. He had a sense of the room and situation, and if he thought she was in immediate danger he would have acted. Right?

Right?

She didn't know what to think at this point.

Do something, Bella!

She went boneless. The guy holding her was startled, let her drop, and she rolled, pulled her gun, and shot him in the neck. She'd been aiming center mass, but the gun had a bigger kick than she expected and it jerked up.

Just like Damien had told her.

He went down. She'd hit an artery in his neck and blood sprayed everywhere.

Fuck fuck fuck!

Behind her more guns went off. She crawled under a table and shielded her head as glass and wood shattered all around her. One of the Moore brothers collapsed. The young kid. She crawled over to him. His brothers looked panicked. What did they expect when they got into bed with a fucking psycho nutjob like Martin Hirsch?

"Help me!" he cried. The oldest brother dragged his wounded brother to a corner, partly behind the bar.

"Can you save him? Please?" Moore begged, clearly worried and agitated.

He'd been shot in the upper shoulder. She pulled out her pocket knife and cut open his shirt. She felt the wound behind him. The bullet had gone straight through. It was too high to have hit any major organs. "It's a through and through," she said. "He's going to be okay, but you need to get him—"

What was she saying? They wouldn't take him to a hospital.

"We gotta get out of here," Moore said. "The cops are going to be here any minute."

The gunfire ended.

She heard Hirsch shout, "Doc, we're leaving. Now."

She didn't understand what Hirsch's game was. To force her to kill a man? In a twisted sense of ensuring her appreciation and loyalty? She understood everything he'd done tonight to gain power—except for putting her in the middle of danger.

She turned to the oldest Moore brother. "Get him on antibiotics. Something strong. Clean the wound with alcohol. Stitch him up, bandage him, make sure the bleeding stops. If the bleeding doesn't stop you have to take him to the hospital. But if you can get the bleeding to stop, and keep the bandage dry and clean, he should be okay."

The two brothers were helping their fallen brother get up. Damn, they were going to get away, but there was nothing Bella could do about it now.

"Now, Doc!" she heard Damien shout.

She jumped up. She looked at the bodies on the floor, then the man at the bar. *Sean*. He'd been shot in the arm. "Oh God, are you okay?"

He gave her a brief nod, started toward the back of the bar, bumping into her.

"Come with me," he said in a low voice, not looking at her.

"I can't," she whispered.

He slipped something into her back pocket and ran out the back. She prayed no one noticed, or they'd shoot him in the back and search her.

Instead, Damien came over and grabbed her by the arm and half dragged her out. Sirens shrilled in the distance.

One of Hirsch's men had a car already running. The three of them—Hirsch, Damien, and Bella—climbed in and it sped away.

For the first time in her life, Bella felt like a real criminal.

She didn't like it.

CHAPTER SEVENTEEN

Sean pursued the three men who'd left the bar. Though he'd gotten the phone to Bella, he couldn't be certain she would call, and these men were affiliated with Hirsch. They could very well know their plan, or at a minimum where Hirsch's next stop would be.

After tonight, Sean didn't see Hirsch sticking around El Paso.

As soon as Sean stepped out of the bar he heard a gunshot. Wood splintered only inches from his shoulder. He pulled his gun and stayed flush in the rear doorway of the bar. At first he couldn't tell where the gunfire came from because the lighting was non-existent out here—in fact, Sean was in the single worst place because the only light was one lone bulb outside the rear door.

Declan Cross was supposed to be watching the back. They couldn't risk Damien or Hirsch possibly recognizing him from Phoenix, so they kept him out of sight. Where the hell was he?

About forty feet away a truck dome light came on, followed by swearing.

"No hospitals!" he heard, then a grunt of pain.

Sean bolted from his hiding spot to the Dumpster ten feet away—and ten feet closer to the vehicle. It was a beat-up pickup truck and all three men were in the lone front bench seat.

"I saw someone!"

"Just go, Wally!"

The door closed.

Another gunshot rang out but it wasn't coming from the truck.

Someone emerged from the scrub grass. The headlamps grazed over him and Sean recognized Declan.

"Police!" Declan shouted. "Out of the truck!"

Instead of stopping, the passenger in the truck fired multiple shots in Declan's direction. He went down. The truck picked up speed and turned out of the gravel lot and into the field behind the bar.

Sean didn't know if Declan was hit, but he couldn't let these guys get away. He aimed and fired at the truck, trying to get the tires, but the distance and the poor lighting hindered him. He hit the truck multiple times but it kept going. Damn!

Sean ran over to where he'd last seen Declan.

"Declan! It's Rogan. Where are you?"

He heard a groan, then, "Fuck, fuck!"

Sean pulled out a small flashlight and searched the area. He found Declan lying in the weeds.

"You hit?" Stupid question. As soon as the words came out Sean saw blood. His leg and shoulder.

"Fuck me," Declan said through clenched teeth.

"What were you thinking shouting 'cop'?"

"Instincts. I didn't want them to get away. Did you get them?"

"No. But I have a name and the local police can track them down." Sean pulled out his phone and called Kane. "Declan's down, about thirty feet outside the back door. Need an ambulance."

* * *

Bella ran out of the bar with two men.

"It's Bella," JT said to Kane. His hand was on the door handle. Kane was talking to the 911 operator.

"Don't," Kane said in a low voice.

"Shit, she's in trouble!"

"Jack said she left of her own free will. We pull her now someone is going to get dead. We have a man down in the back." To the operator he said, "Gunshot wound, Triple D Bar on Main and Tejas. Man down behind the bar, multiple injuries inside."

"Did Sean get her the phone? Can we reach her?"

"Sean will have done what he was supposed to." To the operator, Kane said, "I can't stay on the phone. Send as many buses as you can spare." He hung up.

"But you don't know!"

"JT, we have to let her go. We have a tracker on the car, we'll get her, but right now we need to assess what the hell went on in there."

Kane was right, but it was hard to let her go, especially when they were so close.

Sirens were getting closer when JT and Kane drove the rental toward the back of the bar. They passed several men running from the bar, some of them injured, none wanting to be here when the police arrived. Kane stopped, turned off the lights, and got out of the car. JT heard a whistle that sounded exactly like Kane's, and would have been impressed at Sean's training under his brother's tutelage if he wasn't so worried about his sister.

They approached Sean and Declan. Kane immediately took a towel from his bag and wrapped it around Declan's thigh. "Shoulder wound is a scratch," he said.

"Doesn't feel like a scratch."

"This leg is serious. Ambulance is on its way."

"Did you get Bella the phone?" JT asked.

"Yes," Sean said. "I asked her if she wanted to leave

with me. She didn't. I could have got her out, she knows I could have. She chose to go with them."

Kane said, "JT, call Rick, we all need some cover."

"What the hell is she doing?" JT asked. He itched to go after Bella now. "Sean, I need the tracker."

"Wait," Kane said. "Look, JT, I get it—but you need to focus on getting us some fucking cover because it's a bloodbath in there."

Jack approached them. "Listen to Kane," he told JT. "I'll give a statement, I was in the best position to see everything. But we're all going to be jammed up if we don't cover our asses."

JT hadn't even noticed Jack, and that bothered him. First, because he was worried about Bella, he wasn't focused on the situation around him. And second, it reminded him that until last year, he hadn't been in the field for a long, long time. He'd left that to Kane and Jack. Even Little Rogan had more street smarts than JT did at this point.

"You get Sean's tracker planted?" Jack asked.

"Yes."

"Good. Kane and Sean will follow." Jack looked closer at Sean. "You're hit."

"Scratch."

Kane turned from Declan and assessed his brother. "Through and through, but you need stitches."

"I'm fine," Sean repeated.

Kane pulled out a first aid kit. "You need stitches," he repeated, "but this will work for now." He quickly cleaned the wound.

"Damn, that hurts more than the bullet."

"Shut up, wimp." Kane put a thick pad on both sides of Sean's arm, then wrapped several layers of gauze around it and taped it. By the time he was done, they could hear the police and ambulances in the front.

"JT, call Rick now," Kane said. "Jack and I will track

Bella. Jack will write out his statement and be available for questioning later, but we'll all be arrested if we don't have Rick cover our ass." Kane stared at him. "You have to deal with the cops. I can't do that."

JT had always been the voice for RCK. Kane was perfectly capable of doing it, but he had been in the field for a long time. There could be people with a grudge against him, and sometimes he said and did things that got him in trouble with law enforcement. It was better that he keep a low profile.

"Go," JT said. It was damn hard for him to let someone else go after his sister.

Jack and Kane disappeared into the night.

"I'm going to alert the ambulance that we're back here," Sean said. "Stay with him, JT."

After Sean left, JT called Rick. Though it was well after midnight in DC, his old friend answered on the first ring. "We have a situation," JT said.

An hour later, Sean had given his statement to the police—it was vague and detailed at the same time. The only other person willing or able to give a statement was the bartender, and he was more focused on Hirsch and the thug than on the girl. Jack had sent a statement through JT, though that wasn't going over as well with the local police.

As far as the bartender was concerned, the girl hadn't caused the problems, and he wanted a police report so he could file with his insurance company. JT wasn't certain he believed the act, but he hadn't singled out Bella and that was a plus.

Everyone who was able to walk had disappeared before the cops showed up. There were seven men dead or seriously injured. Diaz, his four thugs, and one man that might be working for Hirsch were all dead. The lone survivor was definitely Hirsch's man according to Sean, and JT made sure when Gianna Murphy came on site that she knew he was to be kept separate and under protective custody.

When JT got Sean alone, he said, "You okay?"

"Barely a scratch."

JT knew it was more than a scratch, but the bullet had gone straight through and Kane's field dressing had held.

"They weren't shooting at me," Sean said.

"What the hell happened?" He put his hand on Sean's forearm. "I'm not mad at you, buddy. I just—hell, I don't know. And then Declan?"

"They got him stabilized, and Murphy said she'd check on him for us."

"Have you heard from Kane?"

"The tracker's working. They're heading east, haven't stopped yet. Have you ID'd the guy Bella was sitting with?"

"Damien Drake, Hirsch's enforcer according to Declan."

Sean nodded. "They came in together and sat nearly two hours. I came in much later. Though it's been awhile, she recognized me."

"You look like a younger version of Kane." So much so that Sean was going to have to watch his back more carefully because, especially in border towns, Kane was persona non grata because of his mercenary work.

"She has the phone, she'll call."

"How do you know?"

"Because she didn't dump the phone."

"Do you have GPS on it?"

"It's a burner, no GPS. But she would have dumped it immediately if she wasn't planning to call. I pre-programmed my burner number, so if she wants to reach out she can."

JT ran through everything he'd heard Sean tell the police and something was off.

"What are you not telling me?"

Sean glanced around, kept his voice low. "One of Diaz's guys grabbed her, had a gun on her. She disarmed and shot him. He's one of the dead."

"Shit."

"Clear self defense."

"You have to write up all of this for Rick."

Sean was about to say something when Gianna Murphy approached. "You sure know how to make an entrance, Mr. Caruso." She assessed Sean.

"This is my partner, Sean Rogan."

"Aw—family business?"

"He and another partner, Jack Kincaid, tracked Hirsch and his people here, but before they could determine whether the undercover subject was in jeopardy, war broke out. We didn't have anything to do with it."

"I believe you, Caruso. The bartender's an ex-con. I know him, he knows everyone. Keeps his ear to the ground for me. Says Diaz was killed in cold blood. Says your boy here was just passing through having a couple beers. Doesn't know who he is from Adam."

"Thank you," JT said. "You have Hirsch's man under guard?"

"If he makes it out of surgery, he'll be protected. They're saying 50/50 now."

"And Declan Cross?"

"He's likely to survive, but they haven't gone in yet. So I got a call from the assistant director of the FBI not ten minutes ago."

Rick worked fast.

"Are we cool?"

"In a manner of speaking. He said you found a body, he's putting together a task force, but isn't going to let that poor girl rot for God knows how long. His words, not mine. So I'm sending a SWAT unit in on an anonymous tip from another business that something suspicious was going on and guns were visible. Something like that, hell, I'll make it up as I go along. But we're going to get her out tonight, ID her if we can, track down Milo Feliciano and find out what the fuck is going on."

"Good," JT said. "I told Rick it was his call. I didn't feel right leaving her there, but we found her under questionable circumstances."

"You must have saved his life, because he's bending over backward to protect your ass. I expected some grey areas after talking to you, not breaking and entering."

Breaking and entering was the grey area, JT thought, but didn't say it out loud.

She glanced around. "Where's the other Rogan?"

"Not here."

Gianna narrowed her eyes. "I'm willing to play your game up to a point, Caruso, but when six bodies drop, I start to get twitchy."

"No games, Agent Murphy," Sean said. "Moore brothers. Know them?"

"Yep. Two-bit, low-level drug dealers. Stupid fucks, but the younger kid, Bobby Moore, has some brains. Unfortunately he uses them to improve on the stupid ideas of his older nitwit brothers."

"The younger brother got himself shot tonight," Sean said. "The other two dragged him out. They left in a pick-up, Texas plates, first three digits 22F. The rest was dirty. Might have been another F or P but then I couldn't read the rest."

"That'll help, but I can probably track them through DMV. Not smart, like I said."

"They cut a deal with Hirsch." He glanced at JT, and JT nodded. They needed to spill what they knew, especially since Rick's involvement meant FBI involvement.

"From our intel-gathering, we suspect that Hirsch is consolidating networks along the I-10 corridor, and now—based on what happened here—when people don't agree to Hirsch's terms, they kill the opposition and promote another faction. It's only going to get worse as they move deeper into Texas where there are dozens of people vying for control after Rollins and her network were taken out."

"But you're talking sex trafficking, not drugs."

"Correct. But I don't have to explain to you that once a pipeline is established they can transport anything they want—people, drugs, guns."

"Nope, I certainly understand that angle. We're in this together. I get that. But you're not cops. Be honest with me—did you discharge your weapon?"

"Not in the bar. I had it out, but no one was paying attention to me, and I dove behind the bar. That's how I got this nick. I shot at the Moores' truck, hoping to disable it. Jack fired, however, in self-defense. He gave me his weapon for ballistics."

JT hadn't known that, but was relieved that Sean was playing by the rules.

"We'll bag and tag it. Is it going to pop up in any other crimes?"

"No, ma'am."

"Then we should be good here." Gianna turned to JT. "How long are you going to be in El Paso?"

"Not long."

"Call me before you leave."

JT drove back to the motel where they were staying. It was a dive, but the lack of anything that resembled luxury meant anonymity and discretion. Sean called Lucy.

"Hey," he said. "Did I wake you?"

"No. Nate and I are sitting outside the trucking

company. JT sent me a name, and on our way back from Austin we decided to check it out, see if there's any activity."

"And?"

"People are working late, but no trucks have come in yet."

Sean didn't like the idea of Lucy doing an all-night stake-out. But he wouldn't say anything, considering he'd been shot. He considered how to tell her so she wouldn't worry.

"What happened with Mona?"

"I got a couple of names, one good lead. Tia Mancini is going to set up a meet tomorrow with one of Mona's former hookers who's taken over the business here."

Sean didn't want to tell Lucy what happened because he didn't want her to worry, but he couldn't keep it a secret. He told her almost everything, glossing over some of the details.

"The paramedics stitched me up. It was a through and through, it doesn't even hurt."

"I know it hurts, Sean. I wish I were there."

"We'll be back tomorrow, Saturday at the latest."

JT said, "Can I talk to Lucy?"

Sean put the phone on speaker. "Lucy, you're on speaker with JT."

"Did I hear that you're outside the trucking company?"

"Yes. Nothing so far, but people are inside."

"Rick's putting together a task force. He wants you on it. Well, I want you on it and Rick agrees. Call him and find out if he wants to raid it if the girls come in tonight. Force Hirsch to do something drastic."

"You want me to call Rick?"

"Of course. You have his number, right? I can send you his private cell if you don't."

She didn't say anything.

"Is something wrong?"

"No," she said.

"Is it Rachel?" Sean asked.

"I'll handle it."

"Don't call Rick," Sean said. "He'll call you. I gotta go. Tell Nate to be careful, and you do the same."

"I will. I love you."

"Ditto."

Sean ended the call. "What was that about?" JT asked.

"You need to call Rick and have him lay down the law on the task force. Lucy is on thin ice with her boss, who has made it her personal mission to fuck with her."

"Why didn't you tell me?"

"Because this is more important than office politics."

"Lucy *is* important."

Sean was pleased that JT recognized that, but he said, "Yes, but she would have helped whether she was sanctioned or not. Let's just cover her now so we don't have to do it on the back end."

Bella had made a tactical error.

She hadn't recognized Hirsch's end game until now.

She should have walked with Sean Rogan tonight. Hadn't she, not twenty-four hours ago, asked for an extraction? Only to be talked out of it? When Simon explained things everything seemed so . . . *just.* The right was obvious, to find Hope or proof that she was dead then take all evidence to the authorities.

But now, she'd killed a man and was very possibly a wanted fugitive, running with a group of vicious sex traffickers who could and would kill anyone who tried to stop them.

Hirsch didn't want a simple expansion. His plan

wasn't only to be the east-west pipeline, but to be protection. That had been perfectly clear in the way he handled Diaz in front of his new recruits.

Do as I say or you die.

Ruthless? Sure, a psychopathic form of ruthlessness.

She had to follow through. At this point, running would be almost as dangerous as staying. If she could just find proof that Hope was dead or alive, she could disappear. But she was fast believing there would be no proof, that the girl was long dead, her body buried in the middle of nowhere. The lingering doubt would destroy her grandparents. They would never know what happened to her.

Had we done enough? Could we have done more? Do you need more money?

Bella knew that Simon had only taken a token fee from the family to locate Hope. They didn't have the money, and Simon wouldn't let them mortgage their house to pay his otherwise steep costs. He didn't need the money—though he was fast burning through his dotcom payout. But Simon was brilliant, he'd always find the way to earn more.

On the one hand, she admired Simon. He was generous, almost to a fault. He was compassionate. He cared about the fate of these girls, and he wanted to punish those who hurt them.

But.

But.

Bella had begun to realize over this year-long undercover operation that she might be expendable. That the ends—finding Hope, destroying Hirsch—justified any means. That Bella was a tool to that end, but there were other tools at Simon's disposal. She had been loyal because they shared a common goal, but was he loyal to her? Did he care if she lived or died if, in the end, they got justice for Hope?

Contrary to her brother's belief, Bella had no death wish. She took risks—that had never bothered her. Risks were a part of life, and risks for a greater good were justified. But she wanted to live because she was making a difference, one girl at a time. She was saving lives, she was stopping men like Hirsch.

Maybe Simon was right. She had let her fear and anger over Penny's death cloud her judgment.

For the first time in a long time, Bella didn't know what to do. She rarely second-guessed herself, but now? She felt helpless and indecisive.

They had turned off the highway long ago, bumping over rough roads. Hirsch seemed unusually happy with the massacre that just happened. Damien, on the other hand, was distant and quiet. Okay, he was usually quiet, but this was different. He was thinking—and he'd been thinking a lot over the last few days. What was going on with him?

CHAPTER EIGHTEEN

Lucy filled Nate in on her conversation with Sean. A few moments later, her cell phone rang. It was a 703 area code. Northern Virginia.

"Agent Kincaid," she answered.

"Lucy, it's Rick Stockton."

"Hello, sir."

"I just got off the phone with JT Caruso. I need you on the task force I'm putting together. Because of a few missteps tonight, DEA Agent Gianna Murphy is going to be taking the lead on the ground in El Paso, but you'll have as much autonomy as you need. JT said you were already surveilling a trucking company possibly owned by Martin Hirsch or a shell corp suspected to be under his control?"

"Correct. It's midnight and people are inside the office. No trucks have come in or out in the ninety minutes we've been here."

"Unless you see someone in immediate danger, do not engage. Take pictures, notes and report back to me and Murphy. I'm sending you her contact information."

"All right."

"I already spoke to Abigail Durant, she's on board."

"I need to clear this with my supervisor," Lucy said, her heart racing.

"Consider it done. JT said you've reached out to Suzanne Madeaux in the New York office?"

"Yes. Hirsch was in prison twice in New York. She's looking at known associates, details on his arrest."

"Good. Follow up if you haven't heard back from Madeaux tomorrow. We need to jump on this. Consider Bella Caruso an FBI asset and we'll protect her accordingly."

"Of course."

"Almost forgot—I'm bringing Kate Donovan up to speed tomorrow morning; if you need anything from headquarters, contact Kate directly. She'll be my liaison when I'm not available."

Kate Donovan was her sister-in-law and closest friend. They hadn't worked together often, but Lucy trusted her explicitly.

She ended the call with Rick. "Promising," Nate said.

"Rachel is going to hate me."

"What's that motivational saying? Ignore the things you can't control or something?"

"I don't like not being in control," Lucy said.

"We have movement."

Lucy picked up her camera and adjusted the lens. They were parked in a used car lot across from the trucking company, one among many cars, blending in.

The lights from two trucks were heading toward them. The street dead-ended at the trucking company. They were large moving trucks, about half the size of eighteen wheelers.

They passed Lucy and Nate's hiding place. She shot photos of the side and rear, trying to zoom in on the plates. She'd have to download the pictures and see if she could bring out the numbers, but they looked like Texas plates. There were no markings on the trucks—they were painted white, no logos, no indication of where they were coming from or where they were going.

They stopped at the chain-link gate. A minute later, the gate slid open. The trucks rolled in. The gate closed.

They parked on the far side of the lot, out of sight of Lucy and Nate.

"We need to see what they're unloading," Lucy said.

"There's no way we can get closer without being seen," Nate said. "Let's wait."

Lucy usually had patience, but tonight she was antsy.

Fortunately, they didn't have to wait long. Fifteen minutes later, three windowless black vans left the property. They weren't the vehicles that had entered. The chain-link gate slid closed behind them. They all had a small logo on the doors to advertise the moving company. She took pictures, then they disappeared from view.

"If the moving trucks were full of people, they couldn't fit them in three vans."

"It might not be just to move people, but to bring the trucks here from El Paso."

"To move people from here to somewhere else?" Lucy asked, though she wasn't expecting an answer. It made sense. Buy up small companies, move the trucks around, there may be girls in them, maybe not. But either way, they would have a way to transport anyone at any time without suspicion.

But three vans leaving?

She started the car and followed.

"What are you doing?" Nate asked.

"I'll lose them if I think they notice me," she said. "But we need information. We can't break into the moving company because this is now an official FBI investigation. We need a warrant. I'll come back tomorrow with a cover story."

"*We* will come back tomorrow. You need backup."

"Are you sure? I don't want you on Rachel's bad side."

"I can't believe you'd even ask me that."

She kept her lights off and followed the vans from a discreet distance. The vans turned right. She waited to see if they were turning left up ahead, which would lead to the southern onramp toward San Antonio. If they went straight they'd be on the frontage road that led to onramp going toward New Braunfels and then Austin.

They turned left.

She pursued. By the time she reached the ramp, they were already on the freeway and far ahead of her.

She turned on her lights and merged. The vans drove in a caravan. It was after one in the morning, traffic was thin. She couldn't follow as closely as she would like, but Nate kept the vans in sight.

Ten minutes later he said, "They're getting off at Pine."

"How can you tell?"

"They all moved over to the right and that's the next exit."

"I have an idea."

She went all the way over to the right and barely got off the freeway before she missed the ramp. She was on the I-10 frontage road and she flew through a yellow light and headed toward the next major street, one mile down, where the vans would be exiting if Nate was right.

Lucy hated driving, but she'd gotten much better over the last two years. Sean had taught her both offensive and defensive skills, even better than her driving class at Quantico.

Her idea paid off. She saw the vans go through the intersection ahead of her heading north on Hackleberry. She was still one light back. By the time she reached the intersection and turned right, she had to speed up to catch up with them.

And they disappeared.

"Where did they go?"

She made a U-turn and slowly drove down the street. She looked down one side, Nate looked down the other. Neither of them saw the vans. Hackleberry was a popular thoroughfare and could take them nearly anywhere in the downtown area, or they could take it north all the way to another freeway.

"Dammit!"

"We have a limited area to search," Nate said. "We can't do it now—but in the morning with more people and time? We'll find them. Let's get some sleep."

He was right, but Lucy didn't like it.

"You did everything I would have done."

"You don't think they saw me, do you?"

"No. They didn't act like they were being followed. If they thought they were, they would have split off in different directions."

He had a point.

Lucy wanted to keep looking—and she drove slowly down several streets between where she lost them and the logical furthest distance they could have gone in the time it took for her to reach the intersection. If they were here, they were now in a garage. Most everything on the main street was businesses, apartments, a church, a school. Off the main street were residences and a few businesses. There were alleyways, garages, carports. There was one light industrial street that she drove down twice, but there didn't appear to be any activity.

"Lucy," Nate said quietly.

"I know."

She left the area and drove back to her house. It was late, she needed to sleep, but she feared she'd missed something.

CHAPTER NINETEEN

Friday

Lucy got out of the shower and noticed a missed call from Suzanne on her cell phone. She hit redial and Suzanne answered immediately.

"I got some info for you. Ouch!"

"What?"

"Okay, fine, *Joe* got most of the info. His ego demands credit." Suzanne laughed at whatever Joe said to her, then said, "I'm sending you sheets on two guys. Over the stints Hirsch did in prison, two guys stand out. One was his first bunkmate, a real jewel. Anton Meyer. Armed robbery, assault, attempted murder, yada yada. In and out of the pen most of his life, active warrant for his arrest on an attempted murder charge three years ago in Jersey. Hey, I'm putting you on speaker with Joe."

"Lucy?" It was Suzanne's boyfriend, NYPD Detective Joe DeLucca.

"Hi, Joe. Thanks for your help."

"No problem. I talked to the detective in charge of the case. We go way back. Meyer's hired muscle. Dumb as an ox, which is why he got sent up so many times, but this last time they think he had someone bankrolling him. Beat a guy to a pulp, he survived, isn't talking. Some territory dispute at the ports."

"Drugs?"

"Here's the thing—they thought it was drugs, but when they dug into the *victim's* life, he was pimping girls. Pimps don't talk to cops, but they also don't just walk away from someone muscling in on their territory. Anyway, Meyer has family in Las Vegas, they thought he went there. Sent the file to the locals. Followed up. Meyer was spotted once or twice, but they never nabbed him. Word has it he's in L.A., but the intel is old."

"Hirsch was in L.A. up until a month ago," Lucy said. "Meyer's wanted—can your Jersey friend send an updated BOLO on him? Something to the effect that he was spotted in Phoenix and may be heading east on I-10. Law enforcement in Arizona, New Mexico and Texas—if we find him, we might be able to sweat him."

"Was he spotted?"

"Not to my knowledge."

"I'll mention a CI. That'll get it out. Dougie will do it for me. Any specific cities you want to hit?"

"El Paso," she said. "That's where we think they are now. But hit all cities that I-10 goes through."

"We'll get it done."

"What about the second guy?" Lucy asked.

Suzanne said, "Damien Drake. He's a few years younger than Hirsch, served far more time. Arrested at eighteen for second-degree murder. Ten years on a ten to twenty sentence."

"Good behavior?"

"That and his age—word is that he was quiet and kept to himself. No problems. Released and walked—on no one's radar for years. No current address, no arrests, nothing."

"Family?"

"None. He was raised in foster care, neither Joe nor I could get any of his records—if they exist. It's a clusterfuck over there, and files that old? Forget it. No active warrants, arrests, clean slate."

"Photo?"

"I sent you his mug shot from his arrest, and that's as current as we've got. It's twenty years old."

"Why flag Drake at all?"

"I should have led with that—it's his psych profile. You can thank Joe—again—for nabbing it."

"Thanks, Joe. What does it say?"

Joe said, "He's a nutjob."

Lucy almost laughed. "Okay. But he hasn't been back in prison."

"He was diagnosed with Borderline Personality Disorder. So, yes, nutjob."

Lucy was surprised by that. She would have suspected something more sociopathic, like Antisocial Personality Disorder, which had a high incidence of violence, drug use, rape, and a complete disregard for rules and societal norms. BPD might manifest itself in loyalty to someone, but when that person disappointed them, they could become unpredictable. Both APD and BPD could lead to violence, however, and Lucy wished she knew more about Damien Drake's background to better figure out how the disorder manifested in him.

There were many levels within every personality disorder, and it was one of the most misdiagnosed mental illnesses—and the most difficult to treat.

"Earth to Lucy," Suzanne said.

"I'm thinking. Can you send me those files?"

"Already in your inbox," Suzanne said.

"Thanks, Suz. This helps."

"Are you sure? Because it's not much. I can't confirm

either of them has been in contact with Hirsch since prison."

"I'll pass their names and faces along. We have some intel from last night, we have a task force and will be comparing notes later this morning. Anything else on Hirsch and his arrest?"

"That one's harder," Joe said.

Suzanne added, "It was a joint operation, and no one seems to have all the details. I'm meeting a friend of mine in the DEA for drinks tonight who's bringing along the operational leader who's retired and in private security for a bank or something. I'll see what I can learn."

"I appreciate it, both of you. Stockton is putting together a task force, he knows we're talking, so you'll probably get a call."

"Sweet. Anytime I can do a favor for the AD, count me in."

Lucy hung up. It had gotten late while she was talking to Suzanne. She quickly dressed, pulled her thick damp hair back into a ponytail, and ran out of the house without eating. While on the one hand she was still angry about Rachel pulling her cold case from her, she didn't want to be late and give her boss yet another excuse to give her crap assignments.

On her way to the office, San Antonio Detective Tia Mancini called her. Lucy was surprised she had information so soon.

"I had it last night," Tia said, "but I didn't want to wake you up."

"I didn't get in until late. What do you have?"

"I pushed Victoria, she'll meet with us this afternoon. Three o'clock. She'll call with the location fifteen minutes before we meet."

"Paranoid?"

"She doesn't like cops, though we have a cordial relationship."

"I'll make it happen. Thanks, Tia."

Lucy pulled into FBI headquarters at quarter to eight.

Only Zach Charles, the squad analyst, was there. She chatted with him for a minute, then poured coffee. The office coffee was barely drinkable—stereotypical bad cop coffee—but Lucy hadn't had time for more than one cup at home and she needed the jolt. She went to her desk and pulled out an energy bar.

She first used her personal phone to send the names, mugshots, and basic information she'd received from Joe and Suzanne on Meyer and Drake along to Sean and JT. She added her own notes about how none of this meant that they were with Hirsch, but Meyer was known to be in L.A. at the same time as Hirsch, and Drake's psych profile made her suspicious.

Lucy's best guess was that Hirsch already had a player in San Antonio. He wouldn't come here without an in or at least a meeting set up, and the best person to know who was new or who had made a deal would be someone involved for a long time. She was putting her money on Victoria, and hoped she could get her to talk. Otherwise, they'd have to go after the pimps Mona Hill had fingered, and that would take more manpower and time—time Lucy didn't think Bella had at this point.

Lucy pulled up the psych profile on Damien Drake to read more carefully, then heard her name.

"Kincaid."

It was Rachel, standing at the end of the aisle that led to the eight cubicles that housed the agents in their squad.

When Lucy caught her eye, Rachel said, "My office."

What had she done this time? Was this about Rick's task force?

She followed Rachel into her office. Without asking, she shut the door.

"Sit," Rachel said.

Lucy sat.

"Why did you go to Austin last night?"

Lucy couldn't keep the shock from her face. "How did you know I was in Austin?"

"Just answer the question."

"It was personal."

"I want to know why."

"I don't have to tell you what I do on my personal time."

Lucy had been so careful last night. She was concerned that she hadn't caught onto Jason's tail the other day—that he was so good that he could avoid her sixth sense of being watched—that she'd been hypervigilant. And she had Nate with her to make sure she wasn't losing her edge.

Except they were followed. That meant tag team, at least two people, to avoid either her or Nate noticing anything suspicious.

"You're a sworn agent of the Federal Bureau of Investigation, you need to answer for your conduct on and off duty."

"What is it you think I did?"

"I want the truth."

It had been Nate's idea to stop by and see Ryan. Lucy didn't know whether it was because he thought she'd be questioned about her whereabouts, or if it was sincerely a spontaneous idea.

"Nate and I went to visit Ryan Quiroz."

She raised an eyebrow, then picked up her phone. She dialed a number and put the phone on speaker.

Nate answered.

"Dunning here."

"This is Rachel Vaughn. What were you and Agent Kincaid doing in Austin last night?"

There was a long pause.

"Agent Dunning?" Rachel repeated.

"We went to see Ryan's new digs, had dinner. Is there a problem, ma'am?"

"Thank you." She ended the call and stared at Lucy. "I think you went to Austin because of a Rogan-Caruso-Kincaid investigation, not an FBI investigation and not to visit Ryan. I think you either convinced Agent Dunning to lie for you, or didn't tell him why you were there. My guess? He went along with it because he's former military and he has an odd sense of loyalty to your family."

Lucy was so angry her fists tightened, and it was all she could do to remain seated. "Do not call Nate a liar."

"Two days ago I asked you to send me what you had related to the Roger Beck homicide. You claimed that you had information and were following up; I specifically told you to stand down and send me everything. I've received nothing. So I followed up with my former office and there is no active FBI investigation into Beck's murder in *any* jurisdiction. It's being handled by Phoenix PD and the Maricopa County Sheriff's Department. So I asked questions. I have a lot of friends in Phoenix, Agent Kincaid. And I learned that Beck rescued two girls from a sex trafficking organization before he disappeared and was executed. So I started to wonder, why is my agent here in San Antonio interested in the murder of a Phoenix cop a thousand miles away—a cop who she doesn't even know? It must connect to her husband's business. Which means you're using federal resources for private purposes."

Rachel stared at her. "You don't have an answer?"

"You didn't ask a question," Lucy said through

clenched teeth. Apparently Rick hadn't called her, and she wasn't going to say a word. Not like this.

"Are you using FBI resources to investigate *anything* related to Roger Beck's murder or this Martin Hirsch you ran without permission the other day?"

Lucy took a deep breath. She honestly said, "After I spoke to you on Wednesday, I have not used any government resources to investigate *anything*. Because you haven't assigned me anything *to* investigate."

"Is that what this attitude is? Because I tasked another agent to follow up on the fake address?"

"I don't have an attitude, other than the fact that you've called me on the carpet for nothing. I listened to everything you said Wednesday. I thought I understood you, that you would at least give me a chance to prove myself. I spent two months going through every cold case, updating every number and name and status, and the one case that has holes, you give to someone else. I could have—and would have—worked it hard and to the best of my ability, but you're not even giving me a chance."

Rachel stared at her for a long minute. So long, that Lucy almost squirmed. And here *she* thought she was good under pressure. Rachel had colder ice running through her veins than Lucy.

Rachel reached into her top desk drawer and pulled out three folders. She was about to hand them to Lucy when there was a knock on her door.

"Come in," she said.

Abigail Durant, the ASAC who oversaw three squads, including Violent Crime, entered. "Oh good, you're here, Lucy. Rachel, have you touched base with AD Stockton yet?"

It was clear from Rachel's expression that she knew exactly what was coming next.

"No," Rachel said.

"I talked to him late last night, told him to read you in this morning. No use interrupting your sleep—I needed a triple espresso to get going this morning. Stockton created a task force headed by SSA Kate Donovan at Quantico, and on the ground headed by DEA SSA Gianna Murphy in El Paso. The FBI has an asset inside a multistate sex-trafficking organization, but the situation is extremely delicate, especially after the shooting in El Paso. Stockton wants Lucy as the point person, and I agree—her knowledge of human trafficking in San Antonio and the surrounding area will be invaluable." Abigail looked at her watch. "Damn, I have a meeting with the chief of police and I'm running late. If you have any questions, talk to me when I get back, or call Stockton directly. I'll shoot you all his numbers and Donovan's number from the road."

She left as quickly as she entered.

Rachel didn't say a word.

Lucy had to try to fix this. "Rachel, I didn't make this happen. I'm sorry, I thought Rick was going to call you before I even got in."

"You knew," she said.

"He called me last night. After he talked to Abigail," she added quickly.

"You went over my head. You couldn't sit tight and let me do my job, you went right to the top and blew me out of the water."

"I didn't—"

Rachel didn't believe her. "You have completely undermined me with my squad. My word means nothing because all anyone has to do is ask someone else for permission."

Lucy kept her mouth shut because nothing she could say would fix this situation. It wasn't her fault Rachel didn't believe her, and if she didn't believe the truth, what more did Lucy have to give?

"You're on this task force? Fine. I apparently have no authority over you. At least for now. But mark my words—as soon as this is over, I will deal with your insubordination. Because I will not have anyone on my squad who doesn't respect me or my position."

Lucy got up and went to the door.

"For what it's worth," she said, surprised that she wasn't shaking head to toe, "I do respect you and the position. I'm sorry this happened like this, it wasn't my intention."

Rachel stared at her. "I don't believe you."

"It's the truth."

"Unless I am ordered otherwise, you're on your own. Our squad is spread too thin to run around doing the bidding for your husband and his company. That means no Nate, no Jason, no Kenzie, no Ryan—because even though Ryan is in Austin, he still answers to *this* office. Understood?"

"Yes, ma'am," Lucy said and got out of there as quickly as possible.

"Suzanne came through," Sean told JT after he read the information Lucy sent. They were sitting in the motel drinking coffee and eating tasteless energy bars. But they couldn't go out, couldn't risk being seen by Hirsch if he was still in town.

Sean showed JT the photo of Damien Drake. "This is the guy who sat with Bella for two hours last night, the one who killed Diaz. I didn't see the other guy. Meyer."

"Why hasn't she called?" JT mumbled, pacing the small room. It was beginning to get to Sean, and very little got to him.

"Maybe she can't," Sean said. "Give her time."

"I've given her hours."

Sean handed JT his tablet to read more about Damien, hoping to distract him from his pacing. JT stopped, read.

"He's a fucking psychopath," JT said, tapping the tablet. "He trusts Bella? Really? It's right here in his psych eval. Personality disorder." JT glanced at Sean. "What'd Lucy say?"

"Clinically, yes, he has a personality disorder, but Lucy warned us not to read anything into it until she can dig in deeper. Based on his record, he has a strong sense of loyalty to those who are loyal to him."

Sean wasn't so certain that loyalty would extend to any sort of protection or help if Damien found out that Bella had infiltrated the organization with the purpose of rescuing trafficked minors.

"And when he finds out the truth about Bella?" JT said. "That she helped a cop extract two girls in Phoenix? What is he going to think then?"

"We don't have confirmation that Meyer is in play, but the FBI has put out a BOLO on him, and if anyone sees him, they'll pick him up for questioning."

"So we don't know if he works for Hirsch."

"We don't know a lot of things," Sean said, "but we *do* know that Bella is safe right now. Breathe."

It's the advice Kane had given him when Lucy was in danger last year, and while it didn't take away the very real fear, it helped him control his emotions, and he suspected it would do the same for JT.

The phone in Sean's back pocket vibrated. He pulled it out. "It's Declan's phone." Declan had given it to him last night before he went to the hospital in case Bella called his number for help or information.

Caller ID read *Simon Egan.*

He handed it to JT.

JT scowled. "Hello, Simon."

He listened for a short while. Sean heard a few words. *Blow her cover.*

Put Bella in danger.

Who the fuck do you think you are?

JT said, "I told you if you lied to me, that was it. I'm taking care of this my way."

Your way! . . . fucking FBI . . . screw you.

Simon Egan apparently knew JT very well.

"Bella wanted to be extracted and you thwarted us every step of the way."

"Bullshit!"

Everyone in the motel must have heard that.

"We're done," JT said. "Declan was shot twice last night and is in serious condition in the hospital. Bella is in grave danger and you damn well know it, but your ego won't let you admit it. You knew where she was, didn't you?"

Sean didn't hear what Simon said, but JT's next threat was clear. "You threaten me and mine, I'll bring the weight of RCK down on your head. Mutually assured destruction, Simon, but at this point, I don't give a fuck. Bella is my family. I will find her and I will get her out of this life if it's the last thing I do."

He ended the call, breathing heavy. Then he took a long, deep breath and calmed down. He was almost back to his old self—the calm, cool, collected JT Caruso. The diplomat.

"What's next?" he asked Sean.

"I'm calling Lucy. No secrets—she needs this information about Damien Drake."

"Agreed. I'm going to touch base with Kane." He walked out of the motel.

Sean had always be slightly in awe of JT Caruso. He'd known him his entire life, and while JT used to treat him like a kid brother—even more so at times than Kane—he'd always been the smart one. Everyone liked JT. He was the mediator, the RCK spokesperson, the negotiator when they had a prospective new client. He managed the money and ensured RCK was fiscally solvent, when Sean's brother Kane didn't give a thought about it.

Seeing JT on edge because of the danger Bella was in had unnerved Sean on the one hand; on the other, it showed that JT was as human as the rest of them. But Sean was glad he was regaining his footing, because they needed a diplomat in this volatile situation.

Sean called Lucy. She picked up immediately. He said, "We confirmed the information Suzanne found. Damien Drake is Hirsch's right hand—I saw him last night with Bella at the bar, and it matches with what Declan told us earlier. We have no intel on Meyer."

"Another city, running things?"

"Maybe, or maybe he's not involved. Jack and Kane are staking out a place an hour east of El Paso where Bella is now, we're assessing the danger level then will decide whether we need to pull her or follow her."

"Rick Stockton called me last night about the task force."

"Everything okay?"

"I don't know that it ever will be. I went in this morning assuming that Rachel knew—she didn't. Not until Abigail walked in and told her. Rachel is livid, and actually, this time I don't blame her."

"That's not on you." Lucy hated making waves. Sean used to live for stirring the pot, and sometimes still enjoyed it—especially when he was right. But Lucy respected people who did what they said they would do; she appreciated experience and hard work and she worked as hard as anyone in the FBI office. He hated that she had been so stressed and frustrated over the last two months. He tried to make their home life as easy and comfortable as possible so that at least she had a peace to relax.

"Well—you have to take it in context," Lucy said. Of

course—trying to look at it from Rachel's point of view when that woman had been a thorn in Lucy's side for months. "This was after she asked why I went to Austin."

Sean froze. "How the hell did she know you were in Austin? Did she send that agent to follow you again?"

"I don't know. Nate was driving the Mustang, we were careful. Not because we were doing anything wrong, but because if someone is following me and I can't tell? Where have my instincts gone?"

"Nowhere." Then it hit him, and he wanted to confront Rachel Vaughn himself. "She put a tracker on the car."

"But it's your car."

"You've been driving the Mustang since we've been back from our honeymoon."

She still called the Mustang Sean's car, but he'd recently bought a Jeep Wrangler and was having a lot of fun with it. Lucy enjoyed the Mustang, and it was a far better and more reliable vehicle than her too-sensible, older, foreign sedan.

"What can I do? Confront her? I don't want to do that—not now, after this whole thing with the task force. She was blindsided."

"So?" He didn't have any sympathy. "If there's a tracker on one of our cars, I want it off."

"Then she'll know I know."

"I've had it up to here with this bullshit." He took a deep breath. "I'm sorry. I don't mean to take it out on you."

"You're not. I just—shit. You're right."

Sean laughed, trying to take the edge off. "You never swear."

"It's been one of those weeks. I'll take care of it."

"Check the car when you can, you'll figure out something. I know this is eating at you—you'll do the right thing, and whatever you decide I'll back you one hundred percent."

"Thank you."

"I love you, princess. It's going to work out—we'll make it work."

CHAPTER TWENTY

When Lucy got off the phone with Sean, she left the office. Nate followed her.

"What's going on?" he asked as they approached her car.

"Rachel forbade me from using you or anyone else while I'm on this task force. She's so angry—and I don't blame her. She thinks I'm undermining her authority."

"She asked for it."

"Don't—I know you mean well, but this whole situation has been screwed up from the beginning. It wasn't just me lying to her about going to San Diego in January. It's everything else. It's the office—what people have told her about me. What happened to Barry—I think his attack impacted everyone more than I thought, and they blame me."

"That was not on you."

"I know that, but sometimes, people can't help but feeling the way they do. I'll be okay—really."

"But you still need backup."

"I'm going to call in a favor with Brad."

"Yeah, that would work."

"But first I need to find the tracker on my car."

"What tracker?"

"I think Rachel put a tracker on the Mustang. That's how she knew we were in Austin. It's how she knew we were at the restaurant with Kane."

"That's really fucked."

"I'm going home to check it out, then figure out how to get rid of it. Sean's . . . well, upset is not really the word I would use."

"I wouldn't put Sean and Rachel in the same room anytime soon."

She smiled—otherwise she'd be worried all over again.

Nate took her hands. He wasn't an affectionate person, but they'd gone through so much together over the last year that she had a warm kinship with him and felt as close to him as a brother.

"I get it, Luce. You do what you need to do, but if you need anything, call. I don't care if Rachel says I can't work with you. On my own time I can do whatever I want, and backing you up is number one, okay?"

"I'll call."

"When's Sean getting back?"

"Probably tonight. He didn't say, but there's no reason for them to stay in El Paso."

Lucy thanked Nate then left. She called Brad Donnelly on her drive home.

"Kincaid, or is it Rogan now?" Brad answered.

"Both. Technically, I'm Lucy Kincaid Rogan, but it makes life easier to go by Agent Kincaid."

"What can I do for you?"

"Gianna Murphy."

"She's solid—don't worry about her."

"Not that—I trust your assessment. She was put in charge of a joint task force that I'm also on."

"In El Paso?"

"Multijurisdictional. I need your help."

Lucy knew that she had a problem asking for help,

but no longer. She needed it, especially since Rachel had cut her off from FBI Human Resources.

"Anything."

"Can your office run the staff of North Tonio Trucking? They were recently sold to West-East Transport, which is owned by a known human trafficker—at least, that's our educated guess, we don't have proof yet. I sent a message to Kate Donovan at the FBI to ask White Collar Crimes to look into the shell corp history. Nate and I were on a stakeout last night when two trucks came in that we believe came from El Paso and likely carried sex slaves. We didn't have probable cause, and Rick Stockton said only breech if a life was in immediate danger. We didn't even see the girls, it's just our guess based on information from El Paso that there were girls being moved to San Antonio. Nate and I tracked three vans that left the facility, but lost them off Hackleberry Street."

"Sure, I'll do it. But Zach is the king of information. Is he on vacation?"

What did she say? The truth. "I'm on my own."

"You're going rogue?"

"No, I'm on the task force, but I can't use anyone in my office."

Silence.

"You still there?"

"That's fucked."

"It is what it is. Like you said, two strong-willed women don't always get along."

"But this is different. Crap assignments are one thing, but this is an active investigation."

"It's a DC operation run by Stockton. Kate is his right hand on the task force. But you have more immediate access to local records. And sex trafficking and drugs go hand in hand, so we're really helping each other."

"That's not the issue, you don't need to hard sell me.

We don't have someone with the skill and experience of Zach on our team, but I have a new recruit who's a whiz kid. You've got to meet her. Fresh out of the academy, green behind the ears, but give her a year and she'll run circles around your husband when it comes to computers."

She laughed. It felt good to relax. "Sounds like a competition."

"Sean's ego can take it. I'll reach out to Gianna, tell her I'm on board. We've worked together before, known each other a long time. Her husband and I were tight."

"Were?"

"John was killed in action three years ago. Army. We went to school together."

"So you go way back."

"I introduced them and I'm their daughter's godfather. Trix is ten now. I go out and visit at least once a month."

"I'm running home for a few minutes and then need to check out the trucking company."

"Need backup?"

She considered it, but declined. "I'm going in as a potential customer."

"Can I give you some advice?"

"Of course."

"Lose your standard uniform."

"Uniform?"

"Slacks, blouse, blazer. Good for an FBI agent, but totally pegs you as a cop. Jeans and a tank top. It's what all the twenty-somethings wear."

Maybe, but Lucy was a bit more conservative in her dress. Still, Brad had a point. "I'll dress down."

"I have a desk for you if you need it."

"Thanks."

She ended the call and pulled into her garage. She turned on all the lights and brought out a heavy duty flashlight. She searched the undercarriage of the Mustang and found the tracker attached to the metal frame near the front. She removed it and stared.

Lucy had hoped Sean was wrong, but he wasn't often wrong about these things.

She brought the tracker inside. She knew how they operated in general, but she wasn't familiar with this model. She took a picture of it and sent it to Sean.

Bandit came to greet her. She gave him a dog treat and let him out back. He did his business and bounced back in, wagging his tail.

The golden retriever had been clingy ever since Sean didn't come home last night. In the few months that they'd had the dog, he'd become a fixture in their lives and Lucy couldn't ever imagine living without him. More, Sean was happier than she'd ever seen him—and not only because they were now married. If she'd known how good a dog was for them, she would have adopted one a long time ago.

"I miss him too, Bandit," she said and scratched his ears. "But you still can't sleep in the bed. Sean would never forgive me."

Sean had established firm rules for Bandit and made Lucy promise not to break them when he wasn't there. The number one rule was no sleeping on the bed or furniture. To that end, Sean had bought a half dozen dog beds and scattered them through the house.

Sean responded to her text message.

That's a sophisticated tracker. It sends data to a server that can be downloaded and viewed in real time. It also makes you vulnerable to a long-distance tail. Send me the serial number and I'll see if I can figure out when it was activated.

She did as he requested, then made herself a sandwich though she wasn't hungry. Her stomach was tight and she needed to unwind and decompress after the conversation with Rachel and finding the tracking device. She would stick this out because she wasn't a quitter. She wasn't going to let Rachel chase her out of the office. Lucy loved being an FBI agent and she was damn good at it—so she gave herself a deadline. If things didn't get better before the end of the year, she'd ask for a transfer. She'd have put her two rookie years in and many agents transferred after that. She might not get the squad she wanted, but she'd rather be working in cyberterrorism where she had something to do than be on the squad she wanted but sitting at a desk.

She didn't want to leave San Antonio. It was now her home—her home with Sean. They really loved it here. She would try to make it work with Rachel, but she could only do so much. In the end, it would be up to Rachel Vaughn whether Lucy stayed or left.

Not for the first time, she considered joining Brad in the DEA office. It would be a lateral move. There was a special course at Quantico for FBI agents transferring to the DEA or another federal law enforcement agency like the ATF. Brad had mentioned it casually to her more than once.

But she didn't want to be in the DEA. While she admired Brad and supported their mission, she wanted to work against violent crime. She had a strong drive to right wrongs—to find predators who preyed on the innocent and gain justice for victims. Was that drive stronger than her desire to stay in San Antonio?

She'd figure that out when she was forced to make a decision.

Sean called her just as she was about to leave.

"The tracker went live the week after we returned from San Diego," Sean said. "I've downloaded the report—she has checked it daily, and sometimes more often."

Sean was angry, and Lucy didn't blame him. *She* was angry, but she didn't know what to do about it—yet.

"I'm going to leave it in the house for now," she said. "I don't know how I'm going to talk to her. She's already angry about the task force."

"I would put it on her desk and tell her GPS trackers are illegal without a warrant."

"I'm a federal agent."

"Doesn't matter—she can put a GPS on a government car, or require that you drive a government car when on duty—but she cannot put a GPS tracker on a private car without a warrant. Besides, it's *my* car and it's in *my* name, and I don't work for the fucking government."

"You don't think there's an investigation into either of us, do you?"

Sean hesitated, just long enough to make Lucy nervous. "No," he said slowly, "and if there is we're in deep shit, because that means two of the highest ranking FBI agents in DC don't know about it."

He was referring to AD Rick Stockton and AD Hans Vigo, who was Lucy's mentor. Sean was right—if they knew anything, word would have gotten to Sean and Lucy if there was an investigation.

"Don't say anything."

"I'm sweeping the house and my plane as soon as I can. I won't say anything—yet. But I'm going to find out if there's an investigation, and you're not going to like how I do it."

He didn't say more; he wouldn't over a phone. Some might assume he'd call Rick directly, but Lucy knew Sean. He planned to hack into a government database.

Yes, it was better that she didn't know that for a fact.

Lucy heeded Brad's advice and changed into jeans, heeled boots, and a tank top. She was uncomfortable walking around in the form-fitting shirt, so she found a worn plaid shirt she'd had for years and put it on, rolled up the sleeves, and instead of buttoning it she tied the ends under her breasts. Had the same effect but at least didn't make her feel as awkward. She brushed out her hair, and used her curling iron to add a few soft curls. Her naturally wavy hair took curls well. She then put it back into a loose and sloppy pony tail, added more make-up than she usually wore, and exchanged her small post earrings for gold hoops.

She drove the Mustang—sans tracker—back to the moving company. The gate was closed, but there were two cars parked by the office. She stopped at the gate and got out of the car.

Time to play dumb.

She frowned, looked around, tried the gate, then went to her phone and searched the Internet for the trucking company. Most times, archived websites were still up for businesses and individuals. This company had just been sold, and its website was still there—bonus for her.

Before she could call the number, however, a tall lanky Hispanic male came out of the office and walked over to her.

"What can I help you with, sweet thing?" he asked. He looked at the Mustang with almost the same lecherous gaze as he had her body.

"Are you open? Your website says you're open. I need a moving truck?" She frowned, kept her voice both confused and stressed. "My boyfriend is going to shoot me because I kept postponing getting the truck and now we're moving *tomorrow* and I really, *really* need one. You just *can't* be closed."

"We're in the middle of some changes," he said, and actually sounded like he felt bad about it.

"Changes? What? Can't I just rent one little truck? You have one . . . two . . . four." She counted those she could see through the gate with her finger. "Anything, please, will work. We can make two trips if you only have a small one."

"They're reserved," he said.

She frowned and forced tears to her eyes. "*Everything* is reserved. *Everywhere.*" She spoke rapidly in Spanish, criticizing her "boyfriend" for making her do this in the first place, and tossing in a few choice swear words. "I . . . I don't know what to do. I just need it for *one day*—I can pick it up tomorrow morning and return it tomorrow night?"

He unlocked the gate. "Come in, I'll see if I can find you something. No promises."

"Thank you thank you thank you!" she squealed.

She opened her car door and he said, "Leave it there."

She was really winging it because she didn't plan on renting anything—she had no fake identity, and if anyone ran her name that would be a serious problem. She slipped her wallet under the seat, grabbed her purse, and shut the door.

"What's your name?" she asked as she followed him to the office.

"Oliver."

"I'm Lucia."

"That's a pretty name for a pretty girl."

She giggled. It felt so odd coming out of her throat that she almost laughed.

"If your boyfriend gives you shit, he's not a good boyfriend, you know?"

"He is, really. He's in construction. Works for his uncle. Puts in long hours and I just have a little part-time job. I'm a cocktail waitress over at Enrique's—been there?" It was a real place, but a bit more upscale than where she figured this guy would get his booze.

"Nice joint, I haven't been in."

"Tips are good. Anyways, it's our first place *together*, you know? And I messed *everything* up."

He entered the office. "We'll see what we can do."

A shiver went down her spine as if someone was watching her. She glanced around but didn't see any security cameras.

"Ollie?" a tall man who looked like an older version of Oliver came out of the back. "We're closed."

Lucy smiled nervously and looked at Oliver.

"She just needs a truck for tomorrow, Frank. We need to change the website."

"We don't have any trucks right now. Sorry."

"Well, we have the two seventeen-foot trucks that were ours from the beginning—"

"They're not ours," Frank cut him off. "We can't be renting them, the new owner wants an inventory."

"I just need it for *one day,*" Lucy said.

"We don't have anything," Frank said firmly.

"Hold on, Lucia," Oliver said and he and his brother went into an adjoining office and closed the door. But not before Lucy saw someone else was sitting inside.

This appeared to be a small, family-owned business—Frank and Oliver were likely brothers. It was crowded but clean with pictures of family and the first dollar they made on the walls. How had they gotten into business with Hirsch?

If they had.

The late night trucks and three vans tell you they are in bed with the trafficking. Just because they don't appear to be criminals doesn't mean they aren't.

She heard them talking in muffled voices. She leaned over the desk and saw a desk calendar. Last night had been circled with "11–12" written in the box. Sunday was circled with the same green marker and "3 a.m."

The door opened and she turned and smiled. She got

a clear image of the guy sitting at the desk, his feet up. She had her phone out. "I need to text my boyfriend and tell him the good news?" she asked hopefully. She took several pictures of the guy in the office.

"I'm sorry, Lucia," Oliver said. "We just sold the company and I didn't realize that we couldn't rent anything because of insurance issues. But we'll be back in business full-time next weekend, and I'll give you a twenty-five percent discount."

Frank rolled his eyes, but didn't contradict him. He went back in the office and slammed the door.

"My brother is kind of a jerk sometimes," Oliver said quietly. "He didn't want to sell, but times have been tough, you know? He has three kids and is worried about things like college. None of our brothers and sisters went to college, and he wants his kids to go."

"I *completely* understand," she said. She picked up a business card. "Is this you? Oliver Martinez?"

"Yes. Call next week and I'll set you up really good."

"I hope we can postpone the move for a week," she said. "My boyfriend says we should always shop local businesses, so he didn't want me going to one of those chains. You're not going to be a chain, are you?"

"No, nothing like that. Just another small business, just not as small as ours. They have a couple places, all in Texas."

"Oh, that's good! Does one of those other places have a truck for me?"

"There're not that local. One's in El Paso, and I think the other is in Port Arthur."

"Too far for us," she said and pouted. "But, thanks anyway, I'll be back if I can, you're really nice for trying to help me."

"If your boyfriend gives you shit, dump him and I'll treat you right." He winked. "Pretty *chica* like you shouldn't have to take any nonsense."

He walked her back to the gate and let her out. She waved at him as she drove away.

Now that was all very, very interesting.

Lucy was almost late to her meeting with Tia Mancini and the prostitute Victoria Smith. Victoria had insisted they meet at a bar in a downtown hotel, and three p.m. Friday traffic was ridiculous.

She was still dressed in her jeans and tank top, and Tia grinned at her when she walked in. "Good cover. I wouldn't peg you as a cop."

"I'll remember that. You feeling good?" Tia had been shot and nearly killed last year right in front of Lucy. The fact that she received immediate emergency care had saved her life.

Victoria didn't look amused. "I don't have time for you two to play catch up," she said, swirling her drink around her in glass. Ice clinked against the sides. "Tell me what you want."

Tia raised her eyebrows. "It's your show, Kincaid."

Lucy said, "I understand that you don't work with underage girls."

"It's bad business," she said simply.

"I don't have to explain your business to you, but you're aware that there are two types of underage prostitutes. Those who, more or less, go into the business willingly, and those who are manipulated and threatened into commercial sex."

"Agreed."

"I'm tracking a sex trafficker who makes his business by threatening young girls—many under the age of fourteen—often kidnapping them or grabbing runaways."

"Guerrilla tactics," Victoria said. She seemed honestly disgusted. "It is, unfortunately, a profitable business. If you're looking for proof that I'm not involved, I can offer you nothing. I'm not going to put my employees on your radar. You have my word, that is all."

"I'm not looking to jam you up or any of your employees," Lucy said. "But you need to know that this man is ruthless. Last night in El Paso, he attempted to make a deal with the head local pimp. Raul Diaz."

"Don't know him."

"He ran the majority of the working women in El Paso. He didn't want to go into business with Martin Hirsch, so Hirsch killed him and his inner circle. Shot Diaz in cold blood, and when his detail didn't immediately change loyalties, had them killed. It was brutal and effective and Hirsch lost only one man in the process." Lucy didn't want to let on that Hirsch's man survived. It could put him in danger, and if he made it through the next twenty-four hours, they had a source of information. He might not talk—or they might be able to roll him.

"And?"

"Hirsch is expanding his operation east. We don't know his end game, but he has systematically gone through several major cities along the I-10 corridor uniting factions and incorporating his business. And his business is providing underage girls in this market. We need to stop him."

"I do not know this man."

"If he hasn't reached out to you yet, he may."

"And I will turn him down."

"Did you not hear what I said? You have one of the largest and most successful prostitution organizations in San Antonio. He'll want to tap into that."

"But you have shown in this conversation that you don't know the business. I have an escort service. I don't run streetwalkers. All my girls are professionals. Some have day jobs and work only weekends for me to make extra money. They are escorts, provide a girlfriend experience, companionship, and yes, sex. But sex is part of the service, not the only service. There is no reason for this Hirsch to contact me because we have completely different business models."

"If not you, who?"

"I don't see how I can help you."

"I shouldn't have to spell it out for you."

Victoria began to look slightly uncomfortable. Her perfect manicured fingers tapped the side of her now-empty glass. She put it down on the table.

Lucy pushed. "I tracked three vans last night. They were likely bringing in new girls to San Antonio permanently. That impacts your business."

"On the contrary, it doesn't even touch it."

Maybe Lucy really didn't understand the sex trade. She understood human trafficking. She understood sex slaves and criminal organizations and drug networks. But the so-called "high-end" hookers? The escorts and thousand-dollar-a-night dates? That was out of her bailiwick.

"I lost them off Hackleberry. That neighborhood borders downtown, the riverwalk, all the convention centers. I'm pretty certain businessmen, especially conventions, are your bread and butter."

Victoria didn't say anything.

"You know who *is* in the underage business. Who a violent predator might reach out to in order to expand his business."

Again, nothing, but she was thinking.

"I have two names. Jugger and Eli Kinder. Who do I go after?"

Victoria glanced at Tia. She then said, "The person you want is Ginger. Ginger Hodge. She used to work for me, but we had a . . . well, we'll call it a disagreement. She started her own business, it caters to what I will call special requests."

"Why her?"

"Because she's run circles around both Eli and Jugger. They run the streets, no doubt, but they're street pimps, they don't know my business. Why do you think Mona Hill was so successful for so long? She gave options to working girls. *Real* options, and she held up her end and protected them. She left and the system fell apart. I took the high-end trade because I have no desire to work the streets. It's dangerous and disgusting and the clients are unpredictable. Eli and Jugger battle among each other and a few other scumbags."

"Those are the kind of battles that Hirsch likes to exploit."

"But they're ineffective. Ginger is smart—and she's also a bitch. She doesn't care who or why. She does a reasonable job protecting her business, but she uses intimidation to keep her people in line. Men, women, girls, boys, she doesn't care as long as she gets paid. And she's always looking to expand. Everyone knows that."

Lucy pushed a bit. "It sounds like she's your rival and you're siccing me on her."

"I don't like the exploitation of women," Victoria said simply. "In my personal business, everyone is empowered. They don't want to work, they don't. They want to leave, they leave. They don't want to work for a week, they don't work. Ginger is old school. You give her what she wants or you're screwed. One of her clients wants a kid, she gets them a kid." Victoria hesitated, then said, "She has a house in the neighborhood where you lost your vans." She turned over her coaster, pulled out a pen, and wrote something down. She held onto it.

"I give you this, you can't let anyone know it came from me. While I have a good business, there are always people wanting to screw me over. If they find out I've snitched on one of my colleagues, no matter what a bitch she is or how much she deserves it, I am toast. I don't want to have to disappear like Mona."

"I promise," Lucy said.

Still, Victoria hesitated.

Tia said, "You have my word, Victoria. You keep your nose clean, I'm not going to give you trouble. You go down the same path as Mona Hill? No promises."

"These are the names Ginger uses and her closest associates. I don't know where she lives." Victoria handed the coaster to Lucy. Now she had to figure out how to use the information to locate Ginger and the girls.

Tia took the names from Lucy. "I'll verify the information and find an address."

"Thanks, Tia."

CHAPTER TWENTY-ONE

There was a knock on Bella's door, followed by, "Are you sleeping?"

She sat up in bed and glared at Damien. "It's the middle of the afternoon, of course not."

"We're leaving in an hour."

"What's going on, D? Really, what's happening now?

"Keep your head down and do the job."

"I don't want to be a fugitive."

She wasn't sure, even at this point, whether Simon—or even her brother with all his contacts—could bail her out after the shooting at the bar. Was that why Hirsch insisted she was there last night? Because he knew she'd do anything to save herself? Give him something to hold over her?

"It's fine. There were no cameras in the bar, and processing the scene will be next to impossible."

He didn't know how far forensics had come since he was behind bars, but she didn't say anything.

"D, I don't know how much more I can do." She was testing him, seeing how far she could go before he became suspicious. Not that she was undercover—she didn't think anyone was close to blowing her cover, especially after last night—but that she might bail on all of them.

He sat on the edge of her bed. It was oddly intimate and wholly uncomfortable. But she didn't flinch.

Would you actually sleep with him to protect your cover?

She didn't know. Dear God, she didn't know how far she would go. She'd already killed a man, why not screw a killer? For her, there was no connection between romance and sex, anyway. Sex had been a job for her in the past; she could treat it as a job now. It wasn't like she was a saint.

But he'd killed Penny—or let her be killed. He deserved the same punishment as Martin Hirsch.

"Look, Doc, I didn't want you there last night. I'm sorry you had to do that. But this business is not for the faint of heart. You need to know *everything* that you've signed onto. Martin is right, you act tough, but you're soft on the inside. At least, I thought so until last night—you did what you had to do to survive, and that's all that matters. So suck it up, Doc. That guy you shot? Not worth one ounce of guilt." He stood, and she was relieved. "What's going on in that smart brain of yours?"

What did she say? She had to think of something—because for a second she wondered if he *was* suspicious. If she'd somehow tipped her hand, just a bit.

"It's my grandmother's birthday today."

"Your grandmother?"

That surprised him.

It was the truth. March 23rd had been her grandmother's birthday.

"I've been thinking about her a lot lately. She had a rough life." Her mother hadn't been a drug addict her entire life, but she hadn't been a good kid. Her grandmother had been widowed early in life—Bella didn't know the details—and tried her best to raise her daughter on next to nothing and working two jobs. She'd once told Bella that she was the daughter she should have had. That she was proud of her, proud of her potential.

And look at her now. She was no longer a cop, not even a PI—she worked for a man with an agenda even Bella didn't completely understand, and she had turned her back on the people who loved her the most. Laura and Adam. Her brother. All because of her search for Hope.

But it was so much more than looking for Hope. So much more. She had only begun to realize that maybe, in some way, she was searching for answers for herself. Who she was, who she could be. She'd done everything for everyone else—even being a cop wasn't her first choice. Now? She didn't know what she would do when—if—she got out of this hole she'd dug.

"Where does she live?" Damien asked. He seemed genuinely interested.

"She's long dead. But she raised me because my mother was a junkie."

"How'd you do medical school? It's expensive."

She almost forgot her cover. She was a fool, talking to Damien about her life.

"I was smart, got scholarships for college, took out loans for medical school. It's how I started gambling—I was in so much debt." She waved her hand. "You don't give a shit."

"I do."

Did he? How could a man like Damien who didn't give a shit about anyone or anything even care about her made-up problems?

"Anyway, it's nothing. Just this time of year I think about my grandma. She loved chocolate—she was funny that way. I can't cook to save my life, but I learned how to bake her a chocolate cake and the last time I saw her before she died, I'd baked her a cake."

Her grandmother had died without ever knowing what happened to Bella. It broke Bella's heart thinking about it.

"We leave in an hour."

Just as she thought he was about to exit, he leaned down and kissed her hard. It was so sudden, so shocking—even though she'd just been thinking about what she would do in this type of situation—that she froze.

"I like you, Doc. I really like you."

Then he walked out.

Shit.

Shit shit shit!

Bella didn't know why she'd shared that about her grandmother with Damien. It had slipped. And unfortunately, he seemed to care. He actually listened to her, seemed to feel . . . something.

Impossible.

One hour. She checked all her supplies and stared at the phone Sean Rogan had slipped into her back pocket. She wouldn't be able to take it with her. They hadn't searched her this time, but she didn't know why—it was standard protocol. They might trust her now after last night . . . no, Martin Hirsch would never trust her. He might be lulling her into a false sense of security.

Now she had this situation with Damien and if she didn't walk, she might be forced to sleep with him.

No.

She hadn't come this far to give away her body again. Since the day her brother and Kane rescued her, she only had sex on *her* terms. When she was first rescued she never thought she'd ever have sex with anyone—it was meaningless. Then she went through a wild phase. She was far too promiscuous, and she knew she'd disappointed Laura. But the idea that she could control men, that they didn't control her, was liberating.

It didn't last long. But in the end, she realized that she might always think of sex as a tool. As a *thing*. There wasn't any romance in her life. Her few boyfriends over the years hadn't lasted because she was difficult and quirky and she really didn't like people very much. They never understood she needed time alone. A lot of time alone. And alone meant without *them* 24/7. They were so damn needy and had their feelings hurt when she said she didn't want to see them over a weekend, that she would just break it off. She wasn't going to coddle someone to make them feel better and damn if she was going to walk on eggshells.

She'd find a way to turn down Damien easy. But he hadn't forced himself on her, and he had walked away. This farce wasn't going to go on forever, she just needed proof, one way or the other, that Hope was dead.

You're not even thinking that she's alive anymore.

After fifteen months? She wasn't even certain she believed Simon about these so-called videos that had recently surfaced. And *if* she was alive, had she broken? Bella had once believed that no one could be broken, that there were always pieces that could be put back together.

That wasn't always true.

She had to believe that Hope was not only alive, but could be saved. For her own sanity.

Not just for her. For Hope's grandparents.

And if she was being honest with herself, it wasn't just because of Hope that she needed to stay. Martin Hirsch was dangerous and volatile and she wanted to stop him. More, she needed to identify and stop the mysterious Z.

Then she could walk away.

If she survived.

One Year Ago

When the police had no leads about Hope and they hadn't been able to compel her stepfather to give them good information about whom he gave Hope to, Hope's grandparents reached out to Simon Egan.

Simon had cultivated relationships with many in law enforcement because so many cops were frustrated by what they could and could not do in the line of duty. They'd pass his name and number to those who were desperate. Some could pay Simon's fees, some couldn't, but Simon didn't take a case based on the ability to pay. Case in point: Hope's grandparents. They were both retired, on a fixed income, and the only thing they owned was their small southern Illinois house.

They'd been willing to mortgage it to find Hope, but Simon wouldn't let them. He asked for a thousand dollar retainer—because he'd done a background check, he knew they had a savings account with three thousand dollars in it.

But first Simon and Bella flew to Chicago to listen to their story. They couldn't take the case without knowing everything there was to know about the victim and the family. That was a year ago February.

Hope had been named after her grandparents, Frank and Ellie Hopewell. Their only daughter Theresa had married Greg Anderson, a lieutenant in the U.S. Army.

"She was young, only nineteen, and Greg was a bit older, but we liked him so much. He was good to her, and he doted on Hope," Ellie said, nostalgic. She had pictures of the happy family out on display, as if to prove not only to Simon and Bella but to themselves that there had once been happier times.

For ten years Theresa and Greg had a good marriage, and they visited Frank and Ellie often. Theresa and Hope lived with her parents when Greg was deployed overseas, first for eight months then for fourteen months. They seemed a perfect, average middle-class family.

When Hope was eight, Greg was killed in action and Theresa went into a deep bout of depression. She was prescribed antidepressants, but they had unpredictable side effects. The doctors changed her medication and she found herself in an up-and-down cycle of depression and extreme joy. One doctor diagnosed her as bipolar and changed her meds again. That started her down a spiral of self-medicating. No one in the medical world seemed to know how to treat her, and soon Theresa stopped seeing anyone.

"In the middle of all this, she met Ron," Ellie said. "We didn't like him from the beginning."

"Theresa changed. At first we tried to understand because we all loved Greg so much, we missed him as well. And Hope—she didn't know what was going on. We took them both in of course," Frank said. "We wanted to help anyway we could. We love that little girl."

"We knew something was wrong," Ellie said. "Hope was twelve, almost thirteen, at this time, living with us more than her mother because Theresa was drinking so much . . . binges, they call it. And Ron didn't do anything to help her."

"He pushed her," Frank said, bitter. "Didn't care that she was killing herself with booze and drugs."

Ellie paled. "It was—a difficult time. We didn't know they had married. They never told us, Hope did. And I was certain it was to get ahold of Greg's benefits. Frank and I went to talk to Theresa at her apartment in the city—we had never been there. It was awful. No place for a child. She wasn't herself. She said we could never see Hope again. We went to a lawyer, he said we had no rights. We went to another lawyer, and he said he might be able to help."

Frank said, "We were on Hope's emergency card at school, Theresa never took us off. I picked Hope up at lunch one day and asked her about Ron and her mother. I didn't want to do anything Hope didn't want us to do, but then she broke down and said Ron had . . . he had . . ." Frank couldn't say it.

"He touched her," Ellie whispered, as if saying it too loudly would make it more real. "We took her to a doctor and he confirmed it, reported it, but by law we couldn't do anything more. We trusted the system, that those in charge could get Hope out of that home."

Bella's heart broke. Sometimes, the system worked.

Many times, it didn't.

"We kept waiting to hear something, anything—we just wanted Hope with us. After a week we went to our lawyer and he said there was nothing we could do except wait. CPS was involved, and Theresa had rights and claimed that we had made the whole thing up. Theresa—" Frank's voice broke.

Ellie took his hand. "Finally, there was a court hearing, about whether Hope should be removed from Theresa's care. We went, because our lawyer said as her only other living relatives that the judge may grant us temporary custody instead of sending Hope to foster care. They didn't show up. And that's when we found out that Theresa was in the hospital from a drug overdose and Ron said Hope had run away. But she didn't. If she had, she would have come to us. The police investigated and they couldn't prove that Ron did anything to her. They, too, said she must have run away. Nearly thirteen years old, problems in the home, no sign of foul play. She just disappeared."

"No one just disappears," Frank said.

Unfortunately, people did.

"We thought she was dead, that Ron had killed her for reporting him," Ellie continued, "and we wanted him to go to prison. Then Theresa got worse and Ron had them . . . had them not resuscitate. We couldn't even see her, talk to her, before she died. We don't even know if she could have been saved! He shut us out. We had no rights. We are her parents, but we had no rights."

Frank patted her hand and murmured something Bella couldn't hear. They were so close. They'd suffered so much, yet they loved each other beyond it all. Unconditionally.

Like Laura and Adam.

Bella was one of the many who would never have that. She accepted it because if she dreamed of someone who loved her just the way she was, and it didn't come true, then what did that make her? Damaged? Broken? It was easier to recognize that some people could have it, some people couldn't, and she *chose* not to have it.

Besides, her life was dangerous. It was *her* life, and there was no room for anyone else.

"We need to know the truth," Frank said. "If Hope is—if she's dead, we just want to bury her. But if she's alive, if he's done something to her, hid her someplace, we want to find her. We hired a private investigator and he wasn't any help."

It sounded as if they'd spent a lot of money on lawyers and private investigators and no one gave them squat.

"We'll take the job," Simon said without even consulting with Bella. "We have a few questions, then we'll get started."

Two weeks later, Simon and his people found Ron Dumfries. He was shacked up with a bimbo who like

Theresa had not only a drug addiction, but a child. In this case two girls, aged ten and seven.

Simon and Bella watched Ron for several days before they had Declan Cross and an associate grab him on his way home from a bar on Friday night. He didn't put up much of a fight because he was intoxicated, and they tied him up in an abandoned warehouse until he was sufficiently sober and scared.

They had enough on him to turn over to the police, but they had gotten none of it legally. Proving he'd sold Hope would be next to impossible.

And they had no idea where she was or who he'd sold her to.

"Who the fuck are you?" Ron sobbed. He'd been tied up for eight hours. He'd puked and peed himself, and had started crying not long ago. Real tears. Bella watched. She had been skeptical of this tactic, but it worked—and she wondered how often Simon had employed borderline torture to get his information.

She decided she didn't want to know. Sometimes, the ends had to justify the means. If they found Hope, did it matter what they did to this scumbag? And what about the two little girls he was living with now? Was he molesting them like he had Hope? Would he sell them too?

She hardened her heart and found it wasn't difficult to do.

"That's not the question you should be asking," Simon said.

He was dressed impeccably in khakis and a crisp white Oxford shirt. No tie. His attire varied only slightly day to day.

"What do you want?"

"Again, not the question."

"I don't know you, I don't have shit for you. I don't know what you fucking want."

"Ask me why."

"Why? Why what?"

"Why you are tied to that chair."

Ron blinked. It took him a minute to comprehend, but he still didn't get it. "Because you tied me here?"

"Technically, my associate Mr. Cross tied you to the chair. But why did I order him to do so?"

"I don't know. Why?"

"Because you are a child rapist and a kidnapper and the lowest form of scum on earth."

Ron stared at him as if Simon was crazy.

"What?" He sounded confused. "I don't rape kids."

Simon slapped him. "You raped Hope Anderson. I have the proof."

"Hope? Theresa's kid? Hell, she's not a kid. She was practically all grown up. She hit on me."

Simon slapped him again. And again. Bella felt sick. Partly from Ron's head being violently assaulted and partly from the idea that he thought a twelve-year-old was "practically all grown up." He was sick, he had no remorse. He would do it again if he had a chance.

"Where. Is. Hope."

"I don't know!" Ron screamed. "I don't know!"

Simon hit him so hard the chair fell over and Declan struggled to straighten it up. Blood flowed from Ron's nose and mouth and he was blubbering. "I don't know, I don't know!"

Before Simon could hit him again, Bella stepped forward.

"Let me," she said quietly.

She got close to Ron and squatted in front of him. "We know you gave or sold Hope to a sexual predator. Don't argue semantics. Who did you give her to?"

He didn't want to talk, but Simon stepped forward and raised his hand.

"Martin Hirsch. Fuck, he's going to kill me!"

"And you think I'm not?" Simon said, the fury in his voice making it shake.

Bella turned to him. She saw the truth in his eyes. He fully intended to kill Ron Dumfries. She shook her head. "Simon, no."

But he wasn't listening to her. "Who is Martin Hirsch? Tell me everything or I will make you suffer."

Ron spilled his guts. Martin Hirsch was in L.A., but Ron heard through the grapevine that Hirsch was looking for blonde girls under fourteen who had no family to care what happened to them. Ron, apparently, had turned over a couple runaways to Hirsch over the years—girls who he'd picked up off the street, had sex with in exchange for a place to sleep and food, and when they got too "clingy" according to Ron, he turned them over to one of Hirsch's people for a thousand bucks a pop.

A thousand dollars.

There was no remorse in Ron, only fear of his own pain and suffering. Bella wanted him to suffer.

"Do you know what they do to child molesters in prison?" she said quietly.

"No fucking way. You beat me up! No way you can prove any of this shit. No—"

A gunshot went off and Ron's head exploded, his brains and skull splattered on the corrugated metal wall behind him. Some of his blood hit Bella's shirt. A drop on her neck.

Bella turned and stared at Simon, unbelieving. He couldn't have . . .

He pocketed the gun. "He would disappear before the police put him behind bars. *If* we could prove that he sold Hope. Which we can't do, and you know it."

He shook his head. "Don't feel guilty. He would have

raped those two little girls he's living with now and sold them when they became trouble. You know it as well as I do. You've been there, Bella. Don't tell me it won't happen again."

He walked away.

Declan said, "Go with him. I'll take care of this.

Bella should have walked away then. She was in too deep with a man she obviously didn't know.

But there was no turning back now. Not when Hope Anderson was still out there, waiting for someone to care enough to find her.

Bella cared.

She had to find her. Or all of this would be for nothing.

Present Day

Bella realized that she was a killer long before last night at the bar.

She'd killed a man when she was fifteen to save her life.

She'd killed in the line of duty to save her partner.

And she'd killed last night, when Diaz's bastard held a gun to her head.

But last year, while she may not have pulled the trigger, she'd been party to a cold-blooded murder. Ron Dumfries was a rapist and sex trafficker and thief who had no remorse. She didn't care that he was dead. She did, however, care about who she had become since that day. What she had to justify in order to find Hope.

It has to be worth it.

If Hope was dead, it was all for nothing, and she was finding it harder and harder to live with herself.

Hope had to be alive.

She *had* to be alive, or Bella realized she had nothing left. No soul, no future. Because how did you come back from a deep darkness that grew bigger every day?

She stared at the phone Sean Rogan had given her. A lifeline.

But she couldn't hold on.

CHAPTER TWENTY-TWO

Sean and JT had just arrived at the small El Paso airport when Sean's untraceable burner phone rang.

JT grabbed the phone off the charger before Sean could.

"Be calm," Sean told him.

JT answered. "You could have gotten yourself killed last night."

"JT?" the surprise was evident in her voice. "You shouldn't be following me."

"Simon lied to me, he lied to you."

"No. Well, he probably lied to you, but he knows you don't approve of what I'm doing."

"You cannot possibly believe Hope is still alive."

"I have two minutes, and you want to argue with me?"

She was right. They needed intel. "We're working on shutting down Hirsch's operation on our end."

"You're bringing in the feds?"

"Rick put together a task force, only people we explicitly trust."

"If they jump too soon, I'll never find Hope."

She was still so focused on the girl who was missing, a girl who was most likely dead, a girl Bella might never be able to find.

"JT—I know you don't approve of my work, but I am damn good at it. And someone has to do it. If not me, who?"

"I never disapproved of your work, Bella. I've always been proud of you."

"Really."

The sarcasm wasn't lost on him.

"I don't approve of Simon Egan's tactics. But that's not you—I hate that we haven't talked in nearly three years. Hate it. I can't lose you, sis. Not again."

"You're not," she said quietly. "JT, I'm okay. I know you're working with Declan. I know you and Dec have been talking on and off over the years, and I'm glad. I never wanted to come between you and your team. When I asked Dec for an extraction, I didn't know what I was facing, right then and there, and I panicked. But now I know what's at stake, and I'm safe for now."

"You can't possibly believe that. Declan is in the hospital. He was shot twice by the Moore brothers outside the bar when he attempted to stop them."

"Dec is hurt?" She was worried, and she should be.

"It could have been you, Bella."

"He's going to be okay, right?"

"Yes. But he can't help you, only I can. You have to let us get you out. We're not far."

"Please trust me. You're going to follow, okay—just keep your distance. Don't spook them. As soon as I have confirmation about Hope—whether she's even alive—I'll call. I promise. But you have to let me do this. I'm losing the phone. I can't risk it—not when I'm so close."

"No!"

"You're obviously not going to give up—I'm just asking that you stand down for a little longer. Trust me. We're leaving El Paso soon, then I'll be meeting Hirsch's partner. This is so important. It will change everything—and gives me my best chance of finding Hope."

"Where?"

"I can't tell you what I don't know." She paused and JT thought he'd lost her. Then she said quietly, "Hirsch sent all the girls who came with us from Phoenix off with Desiree Jones and her thug Thad. Three of the girls are underage—well, four are underage, but do not trust the girl named Sara. I can't say for certain, but I think they're headed for San Antonio—and they might already be there."

"Is that where you're going?"

"No. I don't know where I'm going, but it's not San Antonio. I know how to get out of a jam, and I memorized this number. I'll call you. Okay? I'll call you when I have what I need. Trust me. Please trust me. I love you, Jimmy."

She hung up.

"Fuck!" JT exclaimed.

JT was relieved when Sean didn't say anything. Bella was in so deep, she didn't even realize she was in danger.

"I have an idea, and we need everyone to help," he said.

"Anything."

"We need to find this girl Hope. Dead or alive, we need to know exactly what happened to her before she dropped off the face of the earth. Her social media profiles, her family, how she was hooked up with Hirsch—I don't trust anything Simon Egan said, so we verify it all."

"Declan will know," Sean said. "He said she was sold by her stepfather."

"So did Simon."

"Still, we need to talk to him, get everything we can on Hope Anderson."

"You're right. Get word to the hospital that as soon as he's able to use a phone to call in."

JT called Laura Dixon. He told her he spoke with Bella, and what he and Sean planned to do.

She said, "Adam and I will begin the groundwork."

"If you need anything, call me."

"How did she sound?"

"Determined."

"That's Bella. Is she okay?" Laura sounded worried, and JT didn't blame her. Bella had never gone this deep, and there was an edge to her voice that worried JT as well—as if she didn't care what happened to her, as long as she took Hirsch and his operation down. That kind of thinking got people killed, and JT couldn't lose anyone else.

"For now," he said. "We could have got her last night—we were right there! But she didn't want to go. I should have forced her."

"She would never have forgiven you."

"Not if she believes Hope is still alive."

"We have friends in Simon's organization. I can find out exactly what he knows."

"Be careful."

"Simon would never come after me or Adam."

"Not physically."

"Not any way."

"I'm sending you contact information for Lucy Kincaid. She's an FBI agent in San Antonio, and my partner Jack's sister. I trust her—and she has the knowledge and resources to help on this. Send her what you know as well, okay?"

"A federal agent can certainly expedite some things, I'll reach out."

"There's four underage girls on their way to San Antonio now. Bella doesn't know their fate."

"I can't leave now—I just arrived back in Seattle with

Christina and Ashley, and they are having a difficult time."

"We'll take care of it on our end, but do you have room for them?"

"I will always have room."

JT hung up and closed his eyes. "She's desperate," he said. "Desperate people do stupid and dangerous things."

"She's also smart," Sean said.

"Let's go, Sean—if we can find these girls, maybe that'll give us the information we need to find out what happened to Hope and bring Bella home."

Bella held onto the phone. She needed to dump it—but it was now her only lifeline. She may have bought herself some loyalty with Damien. She hadn't slapped him when he kissed her, after all. She could easily lie, say she picked it up in the bar, picked it up in the other house, that it belonged to Desiree.

She slipped the small flip-phone in her bra, under her breasts. One benefit of having decent-sized boobs was the ability to conceal small objects. She almost laughed at the thought.

She really was on edge.

She walked out of the house, half expecting Damien to have heard her end of the conversation, but he was on the phone talking to who knew, and Hirsch was sitting in the passenger seat of the limo. Their driver was checking something in the engine.

Oh shit, if JT put a tracker on their car and they found it, she was in deep shit.

Damien was angry. He closed his phone, leaned into the window, and said something to Hirsch. She walked over casually, tossed her bag in the backseat, and caught Hirsch's response.

"Fucking rat. Send someone to deliver a message. I

want Milo's head on a platter. If he didn't rat us out directly, he flapped his gums."

Damien glanced at Bella, his expression unreadable, and got back on his phone.

"D said we're leaving."

"Shut up."

She sat in the back of the car. It was the middle of the day, early spring, and the heat level was rising, but it wasn't unbearable.

The driver closed the hood. "I didn't see anything, boss."

"Get in. Damien! We're leaving!"

Damien climbed into the backseat with Bella. Was he sitting closer than usual? She couldn't tell. Maybe an inch or so. She stared out the window.

He was still on the phone, listening. "You sure?" She couldn't hear whoever was on the other end. "Take care of it," he said after a minute, "and call me when it's done. No excuses."

He ended the call and pocketed his phone. "Jerry said Milo has disappeared. No one has seen him in two days. It's looking like he called the cops."

"I want him dead."

"Jerry's on it."

"And the girl?"

"They haven't ID'd her, and there's nothing to connect to us."

Bella slipped on her sunglasses and pretended to relax. It was damn hard to appear relaxed when she was so tense a coin could bounce off her nerves.

Hirsch got back on the phone. Bella didn't understand most of the conversation, but at the end she nearly jumped through the roof. That she didn't was a testament to her training and instincts.

And she could be wrong.

She *had* to be wrong.

Hirsch spoke, his voice dripping with anger and sarcasm. "What would you have liked me to do, Tommy? She was made an example like you insisted, it was handled. Milo was your contact, your guy. Don't fucking tell me he didn't squeal, he's nowhere to be found."

Tommy was such a common name. There was no way it was the Tommy who had tormented her for thirteen months. The Tommy that worked for Sergio. He was dead, wasn't he?

"Sergio will never hurt anyone again."

That's what JT had told her that night eighteen years ago when he saved her life. He didn't know about Tommy; no one did. Bella had never asked what happened that night because at the time she didn't want to know. The girls—they'd been freed, but likely most went back to the streets. At the time, Bella didn't know how to help anyone, she could barely help herself. She'd been a child. But the guilt ate at her. What if those others had had the same chances she had? What if those others had been taken to Ruth's House to heal? To go to school? Maybe even college? To become someone . . . someone more, someone better than they thought they could be?

She was in a daze, she realized, because she suddenly became aware that they had stopped. They were in the middle of nowhere, where a small, private airstrip had been maintained. Perfect for drug runners and other criminals.

"Are you waiting for an engraved invitation?" Hirsch scowled.

She got out of the car. Damien handed her her black bag. He intentionally rubbed his hand against hers.

He may be the only reason she was alive right now.

She was going to be sick.

She swallowed the bile that rose to her throat and

smiled. "Hey, do you have a bottle of water? I'm really thirsty."

He half smiled and handed her one from the backseat. She drained the water. He seemed pleased that she'd asked him for something.

She had no idea what she was going to do, but there was no turning back now.

CHAPTER TWENTY-THREE

Lucy was happy to see Brad when she walked into his office, especially after getting off the phone with Sean and JT. She needed answers. More, she wanted to figure out where Bella was going, especially if she *wasn't* heading to San Antonio.

But at this point, finding those young girls had become her number one priority. And that included finding Hope.

"If you find out what happened to Hope—if she's dead or alive—Bella will leave," JT had said. "That's the only thing driving her right now."

Lucy hoped and prayed she found Hope alive. While she didn't know Bella, she had begun to put together a profile as she learned more about her past and what she had done over the last eighteen years. Going undercover for so long had to be soul-destroying, but more, she'd personally justified it because of the greater good: saving a young girl from the same fate she had suffered. In some ways, Lucy suspected Bella was saving herself. If Hope was dead, Bella might snap. There were some things you couldn't come back from.

"You took my advice, I see," Brad said.

"I didn't have time to go home and change."

He waved away her casual attire. "Learn anything?"

"They won't rent to me because they're under new ownership. Frank and Oliver Martinez. Brothers. Frank sold the business, Oliver went along with it. He doesn't know what's going on, but Frank suspects it's something illegal. That was my gut. He's sketchy. Not a criminal per se, he seems to be of the don't ask, don't tell variety."

"Think we can lean on them?"

"Yes. Not yet, though. I saw their desk calendar. They had '11–12' circled on Thursday—the time the trucks came in from El Paso—and '3 a.m.' circled on Sunday. Something is going on then—we need to be there. My guess? The girls were brought in from El Paso last night, and are being shipped out on Sunday. The same girls, or a different group. But if we catch them with *any* underage girls, we can nail them."

"Excellent—we'll put together a tactical team."

"I took some photos, can you run them? I don't know that they'll help, but I want to ID his boss. At least, I think he's in charge—he stayed in the office and made the other guy do the talking. He made my instincts twitch but I didn't get a really good look at him. The pictures are from an odd angle because I was pretending to text and didn't want to be obvious."

"Send them to me. I still think Rachel's wrong not to let you use your office with this case. I'll talk to her."

Lucy's stomach tensed. "Don't. Please. The situation is already volatile, and I don't want to make it worse."

"Are you sure?"

He doubted her request, and she didn't blame him for wanting to intervene. If she thought that he could fix everything that ailed her and Rachel, she'd let him. But it would only make things even more treacherous. She wasn't lying to Nate that she would have to leave at the end of the year if things didn't improve. She didn't *want* to leave. But having Brad or Nate or anyone else interfere? It would be the kiss of death.

A young woman in a narrow skirt and crisp white blouse knocked on Brad's open door and said, "The conference call is starting. SSA Murphy is already on and Assistant Director Stockton of the FBI has requested to join."

"Get him on. What about Donovan?"

"They're bringing her in now."

Brad and Lucy walked down the hall to the conference room where a state-of-the-art telecommunications system enabled them to video conference with four different locations. The large screen was split between El Paso and DC. A young girl—she couldn't be *that* young, Lucy thought, considering she wore a badge and gun on her hip—was working the equipment with ease. This must be the whiz kid Brad was talking about. She was in her early to mid twenties with long white-blonde hair pulled into a sloppy bun and wore no makeup, making her look younger.

"I'm Agent Lucy Kincaid," Lucy said by way of introduction. "FBI." She extended her hand.

The girl slapped her hand side to side instead of shaking it. "Hey," she said. "Aggie Jensen." She went back to typing. "Director, you there?"

Rick's voice, then his face appeared. "Yes. I have Kate Donovan with me as well. Kate—how do I make this wider?"

On the DC end Kate typed a few buttons and the camera on the computer zoomed out. She sat next to Rick with a cup of steaming coffee. Kate drank coffee like water.

"And we have Murphy in El Paso," Aggie said informally. "Here we have Kincaid and head honcho Donnelly. Everyone sound off?"

When it was clear that the communication was acceptable, Rick began.

"I brought this team together because we don't have the luxury of time. You should all be up to speed regarding the shooting in El Paso. If, not, talk to Agent Murphy, who was debriefed by civilian consultants yesterday and understands the situation. To summarize, Bella Caruso is a private contractor working for an organization that rescues sex slaves in the US. She has been undercover for the last year as Doctor Isabella Carter. She is not a doctor, I don't have the information as to how she was able to establish such a cover, but we don't want to blow it because it would put her in greater danger than she already is.

"I should also state that Bella is a friend of mine, so I have a personal stake in this. Her brother and I were Navy SEALs together. Extracting her—even against her will—might be our only option, but I'm relying on this task force to give us actionable and accurate information.

"Our goal is to protect Bella while secondarily building a case against Martin Hirsch and the unsub he is partnering with. The unsub goes by the name of Z. He is meeting with Hirsch in an unknown location. All we know is that they left El Paso within the last hour and are heading east. I need to brief the director on this and other cases, so I am turning the com over to SSA Kate Donovan. She's recently been promoted to assistant director at Quantico and she's in charge of cybercrime instruction. She is my point person on this matter. When Agent Donovan speaks, consider it coming directly from me."

Rick nodded and walked away, leaving Kate at his desk. Kate adjusted the camera on her end so it showed mostly just her.

"I want to add," Kate said, "that we don't have any direct evidence of human trafficking at this point. Everything is circumstantial, which is why intercepting them this early could blow a conviction. We have an agent working closely with two girls who were rescued in Phoenix, but as of now, it's a delicate situation. We have confirmed that there are three, possibly four, underage girls in jeopardy and they may be in San Antonio or en route to San Antonio. They have now become our focus. Where is everyone? I see Kincaid, Donnelly, Agent Murphy?"

"This is it," Brad said.

Gianna said, "I'm working closely with the El Paso Chief of Police, but he's still dealing with the fallout from the shooting last night, which dropped six bodies. I'll fully brief him."

"Two people in El Paso and two in San Antonio? We need more—and we can't rely on the civilian consultants, not for the active investigation."

Gianna said, "Perhaps you can give us an understanding of exactly how we're going to be working with RCK? I've worked with consultants before, but not in such an in-depth capacity."

"This is now an FBI investigation into Martin Hirsch, West-East Transport, and the unsub known as Z, but we're relying on information from RCK because of the time-sensitive nature. If those girls are shipped out of the country, we lose all jurisdiction and likely any chance of getting them back. RCK was instrumental in the joint FBI/DEA op taking down the Flores Cartel, and they were hired to vet DEA and FBI in San Antonio after Nicole Rollins was uncovered as a traitor. They have the expertise and resources to assist.

"But this is still a joint FBI/DEA op. We're going to build a case against Hirsch and his associate Damien Drake in the shooting last night and work from there to tie them to sex trafficking. We hope that when we extract Bella Caruso, she'll have hard evidence that we can use. Agent Murphy? Status?"

"Thank you, Kate. Call me Gianna. I was informed early yesterday by JT Caruso and Kane Rogan about Hirsch in El Paso. It's my understanding that Bella Caruso is a former cop and now a private investigator? Either way, according to them, she works for a private organization and while I understand this is a gray area in the justice system, I'm not looking to jam her up. But she has answers.

"Last night there was a shooting at a bar outside of El Paso. Based on witness statements, which included Mr. Sean Rogan and Mr. Jack Kincaid, a meeting occurred between Hirsch and a local criminal named Diaz, and when Hirsch didn't get the answer he wanted from Diaz—who runs most of the girls in town—Damien Drake shot and killed him in cold blood. Raul Diaz has a rap sheet a mile long, but his murder sets into motion a chain of events that I don't know that Hirsch is really prepared for. Or maybe he is and intended to start a war.

"According to witnesses, Hirsch offered Diaz's men a position on his team, they didn't answer favorably, and Hirsch himself shot one of the men. A fire fight began. Six dead, one man remains in critical condition—the one in critical is one of Hirsch's men and we have him under lock and key. He survived surgery but hasn't regained consciousness. The police chief has some information about the Moore Brothers—they are the individuals who made a deal with Hirsch. He's working on tracking them down and expects to have one or all of them in custody by the end of today."

"Excellent," Kate said.

Gianna continued. "From the information and evidence we've gathered, it seems that Hirsch wanted

Diaz to use Hirsch as the exclusive provider of sex workers. Not quite sure how that works."

"It's transportation," Lucy said. "He wants to turn over his operation to locals, and then be responsible for moving humans to and from their key locations throughout the I-10 corridor, coast to coast."

"Any transportation pipeline is lucrative, especially of this magnitude," Brad said. "Control transportation, control the drug trade. It would be the same with human trafficking."

Lucy said, "Once they have the network in place they can use it for anything—people, drugs, guns. Hirsch owns multiple trucking companies throughout the southwest, and we've located a possible new acquisition here in San Antonio."

Kate said, "White Collar has opened an investigation into the finances behind the trucking companies and are building a timeline and financial profile. I hope to have a preliminary report tonight. But this is secondary—we'll use the information to track them, and ultimately build our case, but we need to find those girls before they disappear."

Gianna said, "We raided a trucking company this morning. RCK found a body in a truck and reported it last night. The place has been cleared out. The only truck that remained was the one with the body. According to our witnesses, there were two other trucks the night before which means someone retrieved them."

Lucy wondered if Sean had planted tracking devices on any of the trucks, but she didn't ask. Instead she said, "Two trucks came in last night at the San Antonio company we suspect Hirsch bought. Do we have photos from the El Paso company?"

"Yes. We put out an arrest warrant for the registered owner of the truck, Milo Feliciano, but he's in the wind."

Kate said, "If Hirsch and his people hear about the raid, they're going to know we're onto them, which could make them both reckless and more dangerous. Lucy—did you have a report from San Antonio? You checked the moving company."

"Last night, Nate Dunning and I staked out the place. Two large single-trailer commercial trucks came in just after midnight. Three black vans left fifteen minutes later. We followed, but didn't want to tip our hand. We lost them in a downtown neighborhood.

"Since, I've learned that a woman who runs a group of prostitutes—including underage girls—has a house in that neighborhood. My contact in SAPD is working on getting the exact location. We have a tip from Bella Caruso that three or four underage girls that traveled with her from Phoenix to El Paso were brought to San Antonio. We have no photos, but if we see anyone who fits the bill, I think we should extract them."

"We could be putting the investigation in danger," Kate said. "There's no evidence that Hirsch moved them. In fact, he was still in El Paso as of last night."

"If they're sent across the border, we may never get them back," Lucy said.

"Point taken. Use your best judgment."

Lucy continued. "Detective Tia Mancini is willing to work with us on whatever we need. We met today and considered, if we get eyes on the girls, putting together a raid. Between Tia's office and Brad's office, we should have enough people."

"And your office," Kate said.

"My squad is spread thin right now. Ryan is in Austin, we have two new agents including another rookie."

"It's a two-, three-hour operation tops," Brad said.

Lucy didn't say anything. She knew they needed help, but she didn't want to make the call.

"Do you have a SWAT team in place?" Kate asked Brad.

"Partly—I'm the SWAT team leader but work with Leo Proctor all the time."

"I know of Leo—he's one of the best in the business," Kate said. "I want him and his team backing your plan."

"I concur," Brad said. "I'll call him, give him the heads-up in case it comes to pass. We have an MOI with FBI SWAT, there's no red tape to cut through."

"Who's staking out the house?" Kate asked.

"We're still trying to locate it," Lucy said. "We know the neighborhood, not the exact address. Tia is working on it, when we get eyes on it we'll get out there."

"You, Dunning, and who?"

"Me. And Brad."

"Is Nate on a time-critical case?"

"Like I said, he has a heavy work load right now." This was getting ridiculous, Lucy thought.

Kate seemed to read between the lines. "Brad, you good with this?"

"Yes, ma'am, I have Kincaid's back. And I can call in a couple agents for the weekend if we need them."

"Sean and JT are on their way back from El Paso," Lucy said.

"They're focused on the undercover asset; we're focused on these girls," Kate said. "It's hard to separate the two at this point, but we need to. If the asset is on site in San Antonio, we need to protect her cover. Arrest her, take her to FBI headquarters, sit on her until we decide whether to put her back into play or extract her. Agreed?"

They all concurred.

"I've emailed you all my cell phone number and email," Kate said. "Call or text me with any questions. I'm available 24/7 for the duration of this task force. I'm hoping for a speedy resolution. Remember: priority for

El Paso is to build a case in the bar shooting against Hirsch and Damien Drake, locate the Moore brothers and interrogate them, and interrogate the survivor when he regains consciousness. San Antonio, our priorities are to determine if Hirsch is local, if so track him, identify this 'Z' he's working with, and locate the underage girls our asset identified. Photos and names have been distributed to everyone. Anything else? Questions?"

Lucy said, "I reached out to my contact at the National Center for Missing and Exploited Children. JT had an idea and I think he's right—if we find Hope Anderson, or at least learn what happened to her, we can extract Bella Caruso without trouble. This all started because Hope's stepfather sold her to Martin Hirsch for a thousand dollars."

There was silence. Brad tensed next to her, and Kate shook her head in disgust.

Lucy continued. "The two girls rescued in Phoenix can't testify to the murder of Officer Beck, but they have information about Martin Hirsch and his organization. They are currently in protective custody. According to JT, they are unwilling or unable to talk at this point but are being treated for injuries and with counseling will likely open up. One definitely wants to help, but she's scared."

"No one can blame her," Kate said. "I don't mean to sound callous, but the sooner the better."

"I've been communicating via email with Laura Dixon, who runs Genesis Road with her husband. They work with trafficked minors. She's helping us gather all the background information on Hope Anderson. I've asked her if I can talk to Christina Garrett, one of the girls who was rescued. She's going to try to make that happen."

"You don't sound confident."

"We're emailing, it's hard to discern tone in email,

but she's protective. They've been through hell and back, I don't blame her."

"We've all been through hell, Luce—push. I know you don't want to, but more information is to our advantage."

"Understood."

There were no further questions, and Aggie terminated the call and started packing up the equipment. Before Lucy could talk to Brad about their plans, Kate called her directly.

"Hi, Kate."

"What the hell is going on there?"

"It's complicated."

"It's fucking with my task force. Is Brad there? Put me on speaker."

Lucy did. "Kate," she said, "please don't flex your muscle. My situation with my new boss is difficult, and if you jump in you're going to make it worse."

"I don't care. Brad—what's going on?"

"Rachel Vaughn is a good cop, but she has a distinctly different style than Lucy."

"I lied to her, Kate—about San Diego. I shouldn't have to explain to you how that caused problems."

She didn't go into more details. There was no reason to.

"You need backup. You can't go in blind."

"I have Brad."

"I'll make the call," Brad said. "I don't agree with this bullshit, but I understand it. Anything I can do to smooth things over I will—but I'm not going to make a move without SWAT, and FBI SWAT is the best we have locally. Leo's not only a personal friend, but my SWAT team trains under him because he is the single best trainer in the state of Texas. And it's a damn big state."

Kate didn't say anything for a minute. "Luce? You good?"

"Yes. I'll make it work."

"I'll do it your way, but if I think you need a partner on this, I will make the call, understood?"

"Yes."

"I'll tell Dillon you said hi." She hung up.

"I told you it was fucked," Brad said.

"Tia will call me when she has a location on this house."

"Get some rest—best time for a raid is the middle of the night. They're always the most fun."

"What the hell happened?" JT demanded.

The four of them—Sean, Kane, Jack and JT—were standing at a small airstrip where Kane and Jack had lost Bella. They stood around the car that they'd been tracking.

Kane stared at JT, and Sean feared they were about to come to blows. JT had been up and down all week because of Bella and the danger she was in, but for the first time—especially after talking to her—it seemed that they were making progress.

Then Hirsch dumped the car and jumped into a plane.

"We have to find them now," JT said.

"Could she have said she's not going to San Antonio because that's where she's actually going?" Jack suggested.

"Hell if I know anything at this point!" JT walked away.

Jack almost went after him, but Kane shook his head. "Give him five." To Sean he asked, "Can you track the plane?"

"If I had the equipment and had logged it when it took off. Finding it in the air will be next to impossible, unless I had an airport radar system and unfettered access, which in this day and age is next to impossible."

"Did she dump the phone you gave her?"

"She said she would. Anyway, it doesn't have GPS on it, if that's what you're getting at."

"Do we have any other information?" Jack asked.

Sean said, "Lucy mentioned that the moving company said that they were bought by a semi-local trucking company which owned businesses in El Paso and Port Arthur. I did some research—there're three independent truck companies in Port Arthur. It's not a big place, economically depressed, struggling to rebuild after the floods last year. It's on the Louisiana border and has an active port. If he's heading there they could be trying to get out of the country by boat—especially if they found out their cover was blown at Milo's company."

"We have to assume they know the authorities found the body."

"But they would think Milo did it. He's gone to ground."

"Why?" Jack asked.

"Your guess," Sean said. "Murphy and her people are working on tracking him down."

Right now they had nothing on him except that a dead girl was found on his property. He wasn't even the legal owner of the truck she was found in—the owner was registered as Dell Bend Trucking out of Los Angeles. The FBI was trying to put together all the companies under West-East Transport, but Hirsch wasn't making it easy to track any of them. If they could get to Milo, he might be able to fill in the blanks.

Kane pinched the bridge of his nose, a rare outward sign of frustration.

"Okay," Kane said after a moment, "we need to go to Port Arthur."

"I need to be in San Antonio," Sean said. "Lucy needs backup." It was more than that—working with Laura Dixon, looking for these girls, going through the NC-

MEC database of missing children and trying to identify the girls—it would tear her up. He needed to be there tonight when she slept—or more likely didn't sleep.

Jack nodded. "Can I use your plane to fly us to Port Arthur?"

Sean glanced at his watch. It was three—seven hours to drive home. "Take the plane, I'll drive to San Antonio. If you need me in Port Arthur tomorrow, I can do that." He tossed Jack his keys.

"Just make sure Lucy is covered. There's a fifty-fifty chance this is all a smokescreen and they're en route to San Antonio. And after what went down in El Paso, we know Hirsch and his crew don't give a shit about collateral damage."

CHAPTER TWENTY-FOUR

It was well after six by the time Lucy got home. She was exhausted and thought that a nap would be in order. She didn't expect Sean until very late. Lucy didn't know the details about why he'd given his plane to Jack, but Sean would clue her in when he got home.

As soon as she pulled into her driveway, she saw that her boss Rachel was sitting in her car right in front of Lucy's house.

Lucy shifted gears. Rachel came here because she checked the tracking log and thought that Lucy had stayed home all day. How long had she been waiting for her? Why didn't she call first?

Though she'd given Brad and Kate the photos from the trucking company, she wanted to run them through the RCK facial recognition program, a beta program Sean had been developing for over a year.

But that would have to wait.

She pulled into the garage and shut the door. She went into the house, uncoded the alarm, and fed Bandit. "Sorry I'm so late, buddy," she said. "I'll take you for a walk after my mean old boss leaves."

Lucy walked to the door and looked at the security panel. Rachel was standing on the front stoop. Her expression was both worried and angry. If that was even possible. Lucy waited.

The knock came a minute later.

Lucy opened the door. "Can I do something for you?"

"Ask me in."

Lucy opened the door wider and made a motion with her arm to enter. She closed the door and set the alarm for *home.* External sensors only. Rachel looked at her oddly, then glanced around. Then she said, "We have a problem."

"Yes we do."

Lucy motioned for Rachel to follow her to the living room. The kitchen was off limits, as far as she was concerned—it was her favorite room, for friends and family, of which Rachel was neither.

Lucy loved her house. This was the home she and Sean had made, and it felt almost like a violation to have someone who had it out for her under the roof. Petty, maybe.

Bandit ran in, tail wagging.

"Lie down," Lucy ordered and Bandit looked at her in surprise. She never spoke sternly to him—which is probably why he listened to Sean more than her. "Down," she repeated.

He immediately went to the dog bed in the corner of the living room. His tail was still wagging, but he stayed.

Rachel sat down formally, and Lucy sat across from her. She wasn't going to start this conversation.

"Just because I told you not to use FBI resources didn't give you a license to go home for the day."

Rachel was beginning to look uncomfortable. Was it the house? Lucy's attitude? She didn't care. Maybe Rachel would begin to understand how Lucy had been feeling the last two months.

"You went over my head to work on a non-FBI case.

Worse, the number two in the FBI has put you on a task force, taking you out from under my direction and authority. Undermining me in the process, and essentially telling my entire staff that my decisions mean nothing."

"That is simply not true."

"What about it isn't true? I finally had an opportunity to talk to AD Stockton and explained that his actions put my authority at risk, and yet he dismissed my very valid concern. He should have called me and asked who I could spare."

"This is an area I'm well versed in. But I didn't call Rick."

"You didn't have to. Did you think I don't know that he was at your wedding? It's clear your husband is working this case and he asked for your help, and his good old friend Rick is more than happy to oblige."

"You have it wrong, and I don't need to explain to you what's going on. I'm sure Rick filled you in on the details. Neither Sean nor I called Rick. Nor did I tell Rick that my boss put a tracking device on my car. That's how you know where I've been. That's how you know I was in Austin last night. I am so angry I don't know where to begin."

"You can see my point."

"It was my private vehicle!"

"You disabled the GPS on your government cell phone, which is against regulations."

"So you put a tracker on my car?"

"I don't trust you."

"I've done nothing to deserve that."

"You lied to me."

"This is about San Diego?"

"It's about San Diego, it's about falsified government reports, it's about your belief that anything goes because you have friends in high places. It will all come back to bite you in the ass, Agent Kincaid."

"You believe things about me that simply are not true. I don't deserve this. You don't trust me—fine. I admit I lied about why I went to San Diego, and for that I am sorry—I didn't think I would be given the okay to work the case."

"And therein lies the problem. You knew I would say no, so you didn't tell me until you were forced to."

"It was my nephew who was killed."

"Twenty years ago."

"I had a lead."

"You still lied to me."

They were talking in circles.

"I wanted to start with a clean slate," Lucy said. "And I've tried."

"Yes, you have."

Lucy was surprised at the admission.

Rachel continued. "You've done what I've asked, and your work is competent. But you still have this attitude that you can do whatever you want and damn the consequences."

Lucy took a deep breath. "I'm sorry you think that, but you're correct about one thing. There are times when I accept the consequences because action is better than inaction. When someone is at risk, when there is no one else who can do the job at that moment, I will do it. I will take risks to save a life. I will do what needs to be done for justice. I recognize that could put me on the hot seat, but it's better than letting someone get hurt, or worse."

"You're not the only FBI agent in San Antonio. The rules are there for a reason. And you just flip off the rules you don't like."

Ironically, Lucy had always believed in the rules. The rules had saved her time and time again. To focus on what was expected and do a good job.

But over the last two years, she realized that sometimes the rules needed to be bent. Had she not gone to

Mexico to rescue Brad Donnelly, he would have been tortured and killed. And while Kane might have been able to save him, without her and Sean they wouldn't have located the boys who had been kidnapped from the foster care system and forced to work as drug mules for the cartels.

"Do not ever put a tracker on my car again without telling me first. If you have a valid reason, I'll understand. But that level of privacy intrusion is unacceptable."

"What are you trying to hide?"

"What are you trying to find?"

This conversation was getting them nowhere. Lucy got up and retrieved the tracker from where she'd put in in Sean's desk. She handed it to Rachel. "You probably want this."

Rachel stood and took it from her. "I hope you recognize that this is the final straw."

"I didn't call Rick, I didn't ask him to put me on this task force. I didn't go over your head. I was working on it on my own time."

"Against my orders."

"A woman's life is in danger. Young girls have been forced into prostitution and they need help. You read my cases, you know why I am the most qualified in our office to work on a human trafficking case. I know the players who are left or who to talk to in order to find them. If I can do something to help, how can I stand aside and do nothing? If you were in my position, you would do the same thing. I have done everything to earn your trust."

"It's not enough." Rachel walked to the door. Lucy followed her, disengaged the alarm, and let her out.

Lucy had no more ideas. If she hadn't earned Rachel's trust by this point, there was no way she could do it.

* * *

Lucy returned at seven-thirty from walking Bandit—too short a trek for either of them, but she was antsy to get back to work. As soon as she returned, she had an email from her friend Grant Mara, the assistant director at NCMEC.

Lucy:
I know Adam and Laura Dixon personally. They are good people who have made remarkable inroads in helping the victims of sex trafficking. I'm glad you're working with them.

Hope Anderson has been in our database for fifteen months. We added her immediately upon contact with her family who reported her missing. As you know, our resources are tight and running the tens of thousands of missing children through our facial recognition system is a laborious process. I personally ran her as soon as I received your message—giving me the time window greatly helped. I found several videos with her over the last fifteen months. Per your request, I've pulled out the most recent—there were four uploaded to the dark net three weeks ago. I'm sending you a link to access them on our private server—you have the password. I know you've been through this drill, so I'll cut to the chase.

Focus on the third of the four videos. It provides the most visual setting detail and there is clearly an audio soundtrack dubbed in, possibly to mask external noise like a train or airplane. Each video has an embedded time stamp when it was created—all between four and six weeks ago. They were uploaded together three weeks ago. Location data has been masked in the videos, and the upload location is anonymous, though we have developed some new tools to help us crack some of the coding.

I've sent all four to our tech experts now that this is an active FBI investigation and if we get any other details that might help you find her, I'll call you immediately.

I've flagged her image so if any video or photo with her comes up, I'll be notified.

Take care of yourself. I don't have to remind you that analyzing these videos is difficult and gut-wrenching work. Next time you're in DC, call me and we'll have dinner or a drink. You can bring your husband too, haha.

Best,
Grant

Grant was right, the videos would be disturbing, not only because of the content but because she'd lived through this once. But she had to do it—if not her, who?

She watched all four videos all the way through, but with no audio. She would have to build up to that. It seemed that Hope was drugged—it was in her eyes. But would the average person know?

They would know she was underage—she didn't look eighteen. They would know what they were watching was exploitative—but they didn't care. These had been posted on the dark web, where the most vile porn videos were readily available. The legitimate porn sites—and Lucy used "legitimate" very loosely—wouldn't show these, or would take them down as soon as one of their users uploaded them. In one of her email exchanges with Laura Dixon that afternoon, Laura had passed along the information that Bella and her partner, Simon Egan, had uncovered videos of Hope on a popular and legal porn site twelve months ago. But nothing since.

Nothing, Lucy realized, because they'd sent Hope down a darker, more destructive path.

Immediately, she realized that one of the men in the

videos with Hope was Anton Meyer. To double check, she brought up the most recent photo of him—taken three years ago before he fled on the attempted murder charge.

It was Meyer.

She immediately sent a message to everyone in the task force.

I have positively ID'd Anton Meyer as one of the men who raped Hope in a pornographic video uploaded to the dark net. I obtained four such videos from AD Grant Mara at NCMEC. I do not recognize the other man in videos one and four and briefly in video three. I've screen captured the best image and am attaching it here. These videos were uploaded three weeks ago and Hope was clearly alive.

She sent the message and watched the videos in real time. By the time she was done, she had tears on her face. She needed a break. She showered in a failed attempt to feel clean. She hugged Bandit because the dog was following her everywhere, as if sensing her anxiety. She made a fresh pot of coffee because she would be up late. Thirty minutes later, she sat back down with her coffee, just as depressed, but determined to analyze the third video that Grant had flagged. She'd just begun when her phone rang. It was a Seattle area code.

"Kincaid," she answered.

"This is Laura Dixon, with Genesis Road."

"Hi, Laura. This is Lucy. Do you have something?"

"I'm responding to your last email. I thought a call would be best."

Lucy had to think—she'd sent off an email after she received the videos from Grant. She'd wanted to let Laura know that they had proof that Hope was alive at least three weeks ago, and that she was analyzing the videos. She'd also asked if she could speak to Christina Garrett.

I know she's still recovering, but she has information we need. I will be gentle with her.

Which part of her message was she responding to?

Laura said, "You're working with Grant Mara at NC-MEC?"

"Yes. He said he knows you and your husband."

"We've met a few times. Genesis has a small office in DC. We share information. He does good work, though it's heartbreaking. And you're analyzing the data?"

"Yes. I have experience."

"I'm so sorry. I know it's difficult."

"I've learned to compartmentalize. It's sometimes the only way we can do the job."

"Still."

There was more, Lucy was certain.

"How are the girls?" Lucy asked.

"Ashley is in the hospital. She has a serious medical issue and needs a second surgery, but she's too weak right now. She has been abused since she was a young child. And she's only thirteen."

Laura's compassion transcended her calm voice.

"Christina is at Ruth's House and I'm working with her. Physically, she is healthy. Malnourished, but she seems to have latched onto the exercise routine I developed for her. I told her not to rush it—but some girls find strength in it. Emotionally, she's angry. Bitter. Depressed. She reminds me in many ways of a young Bella." She paused. "I shouldn't have said that."

"I know Bella's history," Lucy said, though she wanted to know more. But the more might never come, and that was okay. Lucy was a private person as well, and talking about the tragedies of her past was difficult for her.

"Christina is blaming herself that she didn't get Ashley out sooner, and that's fueling her need to push herself."

"That's to be expected," Lucy said.

"Yes, but it makes it difficult to talk to her right now. Her mother is here as well—and that situation isn't going as I'd hoped, either."

"I've had extensive experience working with victims. From what JT said you are the best. I'm sure you'd agree solving their problems in less than a week would be a miracle."

"JT is too kind. He said you married Kane's younger brother. I've never had the pleasure of meeting Sean, he's much younger than Kane, but JT speaks highly of both of you as well. He doesn't praise lightly."

"I understand if you don't want to push Christina—she needs to trust you. But I'd like to talk to her. Do you think she would Skype with me?"

"What do you plan to ask?"

"I'm going to be blunt with her. You can be in the room, of course, and she might fall apart after she talks with me. Either out of anger or pain. She'll need you. But I'd like you to let me talk to her on my terms."

Laura didn't say anything for a long minute.

"Mrs. Dixon?"

"Call me Laura. It sounds like you want to interrogate her."

"Tough love. Everyone has a skill. I need information, and I know she has it."

"You don't know that."

"Hope was in L.A. a year ago, at about the time Christina was brought into Hirsch's organization. I want to ask her about Hope, about Anton Meyer, and about sex videos she was forced to do."

"She hasn't said anything about that—"

"Hope wasn't the only one. I need to know why Hope

wasn't working the streets but Christina was. And she's not going to want to tell me."

"Sometimes, these girls do what they need to do to survive."

"I know that as well as anyone, and I'm not going to make her feel guilty or cast blame on anything she did or didn't do. As far as I'm concerned, she's a survivor. But as a survivor, she needs to help. Anton Meyer was in Los Angeles at one point, and so was Hope. A month ago, he made a sex tape with Hope. My guess is she saw one or both of them."

"I don't feel comfortable putting that pressure on her right now."

Laura sounded torn, and Lucy had pushed her. Laura was the gatekeeper, if Lucy didn't get through her, she would never find the information she needed.

"At least, ask her if she'll talk to me."

Laura let out a sigh. "I'll ask. No promises. And if Christina wants my opinion? I'm going to tell her I don't think she should do it, not right now."

"Why? The lives of other girls are at stake. Not just Hope, but three underage girls we believe were with Christina in Phoenix and are now somewhere in San Antonio."

"Because my job is to help Christina heal. Sometimes, talking works. And sometimes, it makes everything worse. I haven't figured out yet what it will do to her, and there is nothing more important to me than protecting this child from any further suffering."

CHAPTER TWENTY-FIVE

Sean arrived home after eleven Friday night. Bandit greeted him as if he'd been gone for a month instead of two days. "Hey, Buddy, I missed you too."

Sean started upstairs, anxious to see Lucy, but Bandit ran down the hall.

"What is it?" he asked.

Bandit turned into his den. Sean followed. Lucy was sitting at his desk. She looked up at him, tears in her eyes. His chest tightened.

"What's wrong?" He was immediately at her side, touching her. She was shaking.

He looked at the computer. She'd turned off the volume, but one of the screens was his custom-designed geo-tracker program and the other screen was a pornography video.

"It's Hope," she said. "Grant found a recent video. It's only three weeks old. Bella was right—she's alive."

"You should have called me—I could have been here sooner." He would have driven a hundred and twenty miles an hour to be here for her.

He averted her face from the screen.

She stood up and hugged him. "I'm so glad you're home."

He hated that she'd taken on this depressing task

herself. There was a group of volunteers, mostly law enforcement or former law enforcement, at the National Center for Missing and Exploited Children who painstakingly went through videos like the one of Hope to find a location or any other identifying feature of the perpetrator or the victim. If they believed the individual was underage or being held against their will, they would first run the video against geo-tracking software to see if there were any identifiable tags. If the predator was smart enough to remove the markers, they would look at details in the video to narrow it down by city or neighborhood. Sean had read about one case where a unique window face had led to the exact street where a young boy had been repeatedly molested. The police found him and arrested his rapist.

Sean didn't have the resources that NCMEC had, but he had a custom computer program that did much of the same thing, on a smaller scale.

"I would have done this for you, Lucy."

"I'm okay."

He kissed her. "You're shaking." He hugged her tightly to him. He would do anything to protect his wife, but he also knew that she would never turn her back on someone in need, no matter how much it hurt her. As a teenager, Lucy had been kidnapped, repeatedly raped, and her rapes shown on the Internet. Anytime another young woman was exploited, Lucy faced her own fears. She was strong—the strongest woman he had ever known. But it got to her, each and every time.

"Do you mind?" he asked and gestured to the computer.

She shook her head and stepped aside. She sat on his sofa and Bandit was immediately at her side, as if sensing her sorrow.

Sean sat at the computer and brought up the log that

was generated while Lucy worked on locating the video. She'd been methodical, but one thing Sean understood better than most was computer technology. While there were no location tags on the video, it was uploaded from a unique IP. That IP address was masked—they couldn't trace it to any one computer—but Sean could run a search on that unique address and hopefully find a pattern of usage. If he could narrow it down to a city, then a provider, he could give the FBI detailed information that would help them get a warrant. Though computer companies rarely, if ever, gave law enforcement information, if it was a child pornography case they would assist.

And if they didn't? Sean would hack in and get exactly what he needed. He was trying to avoid breaking the law now that he was married to a federal agent, but he wouldn't hesitate if it would save Hope.

He sent the video into the background—Lucy had another program running that would identify visual features. He ran the IP search. It would take time, especially running both programs simultaneously. He turned off the screen.

"Okay—the computer will work while we sleep."

"I should have waited for you."

"Yes, you should have, but I know why you didn't."

"I couldn't do nothing. As soon as Grant sent me the video and said it was only three weeks old, I realized we didn't have time to waste. I compared it to the video Bella saw and it's clearly a different location—the other videos he's processing are all in different locations. There were four at the same location, but the one I'm analyzing has the most unique features."

"Did you eat?"

"I'm not hungry, Sean. Don't push it."

"Then come to bed."

He took her hand, turned off his office light, the hum

of his hard drive telling him his computer was doing its job.

"Is JT here?"

"He went with Jack and Kane."

"To Port Arthur?"

"Yes. We don't have to talk about this now," he said as they walked upstairs.

"I want to know."

"I told you Bella called. She said they're not coming to San Antonio, but JT isn't positive she's not misdirecting us."

"She told you the girls were here."

"Yes—and my gut tells me that's exactly what she wanted JT to do, come and rescue these girls. But the information you found at the moving company, coupled with what Bella told JT, we think they're going to Port Arthur even though the girls were moved to San Antonio. Until, like you said, they're moved out Sunday morning."

He kissed her. "It's nearly midnight, Lucy. Let's sleep. We'll be up early."

Lucy had barely drifted off to sleep when her cell phone rang. She immediately reached for it.

It was Laura Dixon.

"Laura," she said.

"Um, no, this is Christina."

Lucy sat up. It was two in the morning—midnight on the west coast.

"Did Laura give you my number? Did she tell you I wanted to talk to you?"

Sean was now up, and he turned on the light next to his side of the bed.

"She told me. She doesn't want me to talk to you. So I waited until she was asleep."

"It's okay. You don't have to talk to me, Christina. But I have some questions and I think you can help."

Every victim was different, but Lucy had always done better with the direct approach. After her kidnapping and rape her family walked on eggshells. Except Jack. Jack had told her, basically, to suck it up and move forward and stop feeling sorry for herself. She needed Dillon's quiet counsel to deal with her grief and humiliation, but she also needed the push to stop feeling like a victim and start acting like a victor.

It was too early to push Christina with that approach, but she would not treat her like a victim. Her mother, her family, even Laura Dixon with her quiet Dillon-esque approach, could be the shoulder and loving arms she needed. Lucy would be the rock.

It was all she knew how to do.

"Do you want to Skype with me? Or just talk?"

"Talk. Laura said you're an FBI agent."

"Yes."

"She also told me that the doc who helped us escape isn't really one of them, that she's trying to find another missing girl. Like me."

"That is true."

"And you think I can help find her."

"I do."

"I don't remember Hope. I don't know that name."

"That's okay. There are other things that you do remember."

Sean reached for her. She kissed his hand, then swung her feet over the edge of the bed. She didn't want to shut him out, but his presence would distract her. She opened the doors to the sitting room off the master bedroom where she often sat to read and relax. She closed the doors and sat in her comfy chair.

"Laura wanted me to sleep on it, she said. I think I

hurt her feelings when I told her I wanted to talk to you alone."

"She understands."

"That's what she said, but she was hurt. She's really nice. So I told her I would sleep on it."

"But you can't sleep." Lucy understood sleepless nights.

"No."

"She understands what you're going through. So do I."

"Why do you people always say things like that?" Christina said, her voice suddenly bitter. "No one understands. I just want people to stop talking about it. I want my mom to stop crying, but she can't look at me without crying."

"I know. My mom couldn't either."

Christina said suspiciously, "Are you lying so you can make me think you know?"

"No," Lucy said. "And if we were on Skype, you would see that I'm being truthful. I don't know what you went through. It's different for everyone. For me? I was kidnapped and taken a thousand miles from my family and raped by different men while chained to the floor. The man who kidnapped me made a video and people paid money to watch. But it was only two days. Two days of hell, but not a year. So no, I don't know what you went through."

"I wasn't raped."

"You were, Christina."

"I only fought back once."

"That doesn't matter. You were coerced, manipulated, threatened, I don't care what you believe, but it's not on you, and I know Laura has told you the same thing. But guilt—guilt is powerful. It's one of the most powerful emotions we have working on us. Sometimes it helps. Mostly, it traps us into blaming ourselves for something that is totally out of our control."

"I ran away from home."

"And I met the man who kidnapped me online. I talked to him, agreed to meet with him because I thought he was a nineteen-year-old college student from Georgetown University. I was going to Georgetown, and he was cute. But the photos he sent weren't of him, they were of someone else. I felt so stupid. But my mistake did not justify what he did to me. Your mistake doesn't justify what happened to you. I'm sure Laura has told you that it's going to take time, that you need to forgive yourself. That's all true. I'm going to tell you something she hasn't told you. You won. You got away. You have your life back. It's not the life you imagined, it's not the life you expected or even wanted, but it's yours, all yours."

"The cop who helped us? He's dead. Laura didn't want to tell me, but I overheard her talking. He's dead because he helped us. It's not fair!"

"It's not fair, but it's real. He helped you because he wanted to help you. He died a hero's death, and I believe in my heart that heroes go directly to heaven."

"Laura is a God person. I'm not."

"You don't have to be. Just believe that he died doing exactly what he wanted to do. You know what? My brother was in a coma for nearly two years because he walked into a trap meant to kill him while he was trying to save me. He gets migraines to this day because of what happened. He'll never be without pain and I blamed myself for a long time. Roger Beck did what he did because he wanted to. It was his choice. Just like it's my choice to be an FBI agent and go out and find predators and put them in jail. And it's your choice to live. I didn't know Roger, but I know people like him. You two weren't the only people he's helped. He's been doing this for a long time. I'm truly sorry he died, but that's solely on the person who killed him."

Christina was listening.

Lucy reflected on how young she was. Lucy herself had been eighteen when she'd been raped. Her high school graduation day. It had been horrific, but had she been younger? Would it have been worse? In some ways, yes; in other ways, no. Sexual exploitation was cruel no matter what, and just because Christina had—at the time—convinced herself she had to go along with it, didn't make her any less a victim.

"You told Laura that you didn't know Hope. Yet, we know that she was in Los Angeles at the same time you were."

"So?"

She was defensive. "It may not mean anything. You may not have known her name. But anything you can tell me will help us find her. She was thirteen at the time, blonde, blue eyes, petite. She has a mole on her neck—about the size of an M&M."

"I know who you're talking about," Christina said. "I never met her, but I knew about her. I saw pictures of her . . . they called her Pixie. Because she was like Tinkerbell, small and feisty, they said. I didn't know Pixie was Hope until Laura showed me her picture, and I didn't want to believe it."

"Believe what?"

"That she was alive. I mean how?"

"We're survivors. You. Me. Hope. Do you know how Hirsch or the people in charge of you decided who was going to work the streets and who was going to do movies?"

"Everyone worked the streets—it's what we did. Parties, conventions, hotels, streets, it all became a blur. If we tried to get away—it just got worse. I just did what they told me to do and it was okay."

"But Hope was in Los Angeles."

"Ashley knew Pixie. Hope. They came at the same time, but Hope ran. Ashley said she was punished, and then she never came back. Ashley thought she was dead. They didn't say anything about her, and we didn't ask. Others heard that she had the good life, that those picked to do movies had hotel suites and good food and pretty clothes and for awhile . . . sometimes . . . I thought why not me? What did I have to do to have the good life, too? Not sleep on crappy mattresses and let disgusting, smelly men fuck me?"

The anger seeped through, and Lucy let her continue. It was hard to listen to, but it had been harder to live through.

"I didn't believe it. I thought it was just a lie to keep us in the game, you know? I just started blocking everything out. I did what they told me and after awhile . . . it just all blended together, one day after another."

"Anton Meyer. He was in Los Angeles."

"Laura showed me his picture, too. He's mean."

"Did he hurt you?"

"I don't want to talk about it."

"You don't have to, but it would help me if I knew what he did."

"He—he told us he was responsible for breaking us in."

Lucy's stomach flipped. She didn't want to hear anymore. She knew exactly what Christina meant.

"Okay. I don't need details now—"

Christina continued. "Sometimes, he would come in drunk and said that the boss gave him the pick of the litter, like we were dogs. That's what he called us. Bitches in heat."

It was all Lucy could do not to start shaking, out of rage and suppressed memories. She didn't want to go back to the time she was held captive, when she was told there was one thing she was good for and that was giving paying customers a show.

While Lucy had worked with victims, mostly to pull out details to help with an arrest or conviction, counseling took a special skill that she didn't have.

"And Damien Drake?" Lucy's voice cracked and she hoped Christina didn't pick up on it.

"The only time I ever saw him was with Mr. Hirsch. He was like, I don't know, his bodyguard. Oh—and sometimes with the doc."

"You're doing great." Better than Lucy, she realized. "I have proof that Hope is alive, that she's with Anton Meyer. I'm working to find her, to rescue her like Roger rescued you."

"Don't let them kill you, too."

Lucy realized that was really bothering Christina. That Roger died for her and she had a warped sense that she didn't deserve to be rescued. Christina might not have shared that with Laura, and if she did, Laura might not have picked up on that nuance.

"They won't. Because I'm not going anywhere without backup. I promise you."

"Okay."

Christina had confirmed so much, but there was little new. Lucy had one more person to identify. "Do you know a man named Z?"

"Tommy Z?"

"If he goes by Z, yes."

"I don't know him, never saw him, but I know his name. Tommy Zimmerman."

"How do you know that?"

"Because we're invisible. If they're not fucking us or we're not sucking them off, they don't even notice us. Like I can tell you that Mr. Hirsch never once fucked any of us, it was as if we were disgusting to him. Damien did sometimes, but he never hurt anyone, unless they ran—then he had to."

"He hurt the girls who ran."

"He had to."

"Didn't *have* to. It was his choice."

The shrug was in her voice. "I ran once. I went to solitary for three days. He got me out and said he was sorry, but he had orders. He's . . . he's creepy but not in the same way that Anton was creepy. I don't know why. He never yelled, he never smiled—well, except with the doc."

Odd for her to recollect that. What did it mean? That they were friendly? More?

"Do you know where Tommy Zimmerman is? A city, town, state—anything that can help us track him down?"

"No. Just not L.A. He called often, like every week or two, talked to Mr. Hirsch."

"You've done great."

"I haven't done anything."

"You have. We know that Z is Hirsch's partner, but we don't know anything about him—now that you've given me his name, we can find him." She hoped sooner rather than later.

"You really think so?"

"Yes."

"Will you let me know? If you find her? No matter what? Even if she's, you know, dead?"

"Yes, I promise."

"Laura promised she would never lie to me, and she hasn't. So I'm going to tell her I called you."

"Good."

Christina was quiet for a long minute.

"Christina?"

"Did it get better with your mom?"

What did she say to that? "My mom is older—I'm the

youngest of seven kids. I never talked about it with her. Ever. But what made all the difference was that she was there for me. Just . . . there. And eventually, she stopped looking at me like I was about to shatter." She didn't add that partly that was because she'd moved in with Dillon. Christina didn't need to know all of the details, but she wasn't going to lie.

"Like how long? Weeks? Years?"

"Somewhere in between. I had someone else to talk to."

"A counselor?"

"Well, I shouldn't tell you this. I was forced to go to a counselor, but I quit after a couple of sessions. I had a hard time talking to a stranger. The person who helped me the most? There were two—my brother Dillon listened. He was calm and centered. A lot like Laura. And my brother Jack. Jack taught me not to feel sorry for myself. He taught me self-defense, that I was stronger than I thought, and he never once, for a minute, showed me pity."

"Really? You talked to men about what happened?"

"I didn't talk to Jack about it—he knew, I didn't have to say anything. And Dillon is . . . well . . . he's special. And it's not a man thing. For me anyway. You talk to who helps you. If it's Laura, great. If it's someone else, that's okay too. The important thing is that you find a way to put everything that happened in the past and get beyond the guilt, the regrets, the what-ifs. You can't live like that. Trust me."

It was too late for Lucy to act on the new information. She sent the name "Tommy Zimmerman" to Kate and copied in the rest of the task force, as well as the facts about Hope's alias as "Pixie."

Lucy had felt a kinship with Bella as soon as she found out why she'd gone undercover. While intellectually, and as a cop, she had understood Bella's need to rescue the innocent, it wasn't until Kane shared her story that Lucy realized they were a lot alike.

Except Lucy didn't know if she could have done the same thing. She was so antsy and nervous discussing casual sex, she often cringed at public displays of affection, sexual comments had her blushing and embarrassed. She could talk about it as a cop, she could listen to rape victims, but that was because she could separate her job from herself when she needed to. But every moment of her life? Not anymore. She'd done it for a long time, put up that icy barrier so nothing—not the good or the bad—could get inside.

Sean changed all that. She had survived because she was a survivor; Sean had given her a new life.

Lucy admired Bella's ability to separate what happened in her past with who she was today, while using the experience to save others who had found themselves in the same situation. Lucy was quickly losing it. Could she do this? She'd held it together when Christina was on the phone, but now her composure was melting. The feelings of being a victim, the pain and anger and humiliation, washed over her.

She put her head in her arms and took a deep breath. Then another. She had to regain her center.

Sean opened the door. "Luce? You've been quiet."

She looked up and saw Sean in the light. Relief and love replaced the pain and anger. "I'm okay."

Sean took her hand and helped her up. He held her close, kissed her forehead. She put her hand on his chest and felt his heart beating. Fast, too fast. As they held each other, his heart calmed and so did hers.

"You need to sleep, Princess," he whispered.

She let him pick her up and carry her back to bed. She touched his face, brought his lips down to hers.

"I love you so much," she whispered. And she kissed him. She never wanted to let him go.

Sean was exactly what she needed.

CHAPTER TWENTY-SIX

Saturday

Bella woke up as soon as her door opened.

"Sorry to wake you," Damien mumbled.

She sat up in her bed. She always slept fully dressed—usually sweat pants and a tank top. But she still felt uncomfortable.

"We have a situation," he said. "One of the whores was beaten pretty bad last night. We need you to take a look at her."

And so it began. Back to the business of keeping Hirsch's girls healthy and breathing.

Until he decided to sell them or kill them.

"Five minutes," she mumbled.

"I made coffee."

"Thanks."

She waited until he shut the door then changed into her jeans, bra, and a grey T-shirt. Grey like her mood. She couldn't even crack a smile.

They were on a large piece of land off Highway 82, right before it turned into the TB Ellison Parkway heading into Louisiana. The property went deep, from the road to the bay. There were two boats docked and when they first arrived last night she thought for certain they were leaving the country.

Someone owned the house. She didn't know if it was Tommy Z—who could *not* be the Tommy she knew eighteen years ago—or Hirsch himself. It wouldn't be under either of their names. Hell, they could be renting, or their shell corp could have bought it.

The trucking company Hirsch had bought was practically walking distance from the house—if you liked to trek a mile in humidity so thick you couldn't walk outside without feeling like you were drowning. Even now, in March, it was sticky. A shipping company that might not even be open and an oil refinery that was certainly closed or working at a fraction of its capacity were also nearby. The town was depressed, worse because of last year's flooding, but there were some signs of economic activity.

The house itself was a real house, far cleaner than anything they'd lived in up until now. Old—at least from the forties—and showing its wear, but it was well-maintained for the most part. Except that it smelled rotten. Like mold and dead things, probably because it hadn't been properly cleaned out after last year's horrific flooding throughout southeast Texas. The furniture and carpets were new, but Bella suspected the mold and dry rot had been painted over.

Still, it was big enough for all of them and none of the girls stayed here. Four bedrooms, two bathrooms, and Hirsch gave her her own space. She was stunned.

You're one of them now. He trusts you.

He didn't trust her. He just wasn't *as* suspicious.

But she had to remain cautious. Very, very careful.

She pulled her hair back into a ponytail and washed her face and brushed her teeth. Took a deep breath, grabbed her black bag, and went out to the kitchen. "Where is she?" she asked Damien as he handed her a to-go cup of coffee. She was nervous—she always poured her own coffee.

"Two sugars, just how you like it," he said.

"Thanks." She shouldn't be surprised he knew how she drank her coffee—they had been associating for the last year. Living in the same house much of the time.

He smiled.

Two smiles in two days from a man who rarely turned his lips up.

"I'll take you to the house."

She didn't see Hirsch or his goon anywhere. Maybe they were gone. Or sleeping. On one of the boats perhaps.

Damien drove into town. Oil tanks populated the landscape. Bella didn't know much about the business of oil refineries, but it seemed to be the primary source of income in the community—that and the port.

He drove past the port, then into a mixed neighborhood—small, single family homes and duplexes on the corner that didn't look much bigger than the single-family homes. Some houses were completely boarded up. Some had been reduced to rubble, untouched since the hurricane. Others, the residents were in the middle of rebuilding what they had, putting back lawns and flowers and painting their homes. Land was cheap in Texas, so she wasn't surprised that all the homes—occupied or not—were on large lots. Most didn't have fences; some were framed by chain link.

He stopped at a small house across from a refinery that appeared to be abandoned, though she saw a lone car inside the tall, barbed-wire topped fences.

She already felt greasy just walking around Port Arthur. But that might have more to do with the humidity. She couldn't imagine living here when it was ninety degrees and ninety percent humidity.

"What happened?" she asked before getting out.

"Our operation here is large—our guy runs most of the whores. It's a quiet town, no one bothers us. One of the regulars was drunk, apparently had a bad day, took it out on one of the girls."

"And what did your guy do with the drunk?"

"Took him home, told him he was cut off for a couple weeks. He didn't even know what he'd done."

Bella bit back her anger.

"She has a cut that needs stitches. Do a good job, she's a pretty one, always surpasses her quota."

This was the time when she could blow it. Even after nearly a year, she could blow it because she wanted to pound Damien, then pound the john who hurt the prostitute. She didn't care if the girls were legitimately in the business, she had no tolerance for such brutality.

"You know, D, if you don't tell your pimps to keep the johns in line they'll really cut into your profits."

"Doc, don't."

"I can't help it, D. These are working girls. They're just trying to survive, do the job, have a life, you know? Just like you and me."

"I'll talk to Gino, if you want."

He sounded like he would do it as a favor to her, and she was already in too deep. "Don't do anything on account of me. I'm just stating the obvious."

They got out and Damien glanced around. The neighborhood was depressed, quiet. A dog barked in the distance. It was early Saturday morning, not even six a.m. No kids were out playing. No elderly people were out walking. It was a ghost town. Maybe more of these houses were vacant than she'd originally thought. People permanently relocated after the flood. Maybe that's why Hirsch wanted it—fewer people, more opportunities to move his product under the radar.

Damien knocked and a woman opened the door. She

was in her thirties. She had a black eye and didn't say anything as Damien and Bella walked in.

The black eye looked fresh.

Had she bitched and someone hit her? Damien?

Bella looked at his hands. He had old cuts, nothing recent. But one well-aimed punch might not leave a mark.

Damien led the way to the back. The house was clean but cramped with furniture and that faint moldy scent that seemed to permeate the entire town. A huge television was mounted on the wall. A woman—not a young girl—was watching cartoons. She was in her thirties and had recently come off work, it seemed—she was still dressed in a short skirt and her makeup hadn't been washed off. The old mascara left her with raccoon eyes, and the bright blue eyeshadow didn't do her complexion any favors. She completely ignored them.

As Bella walked through she determined that six women lived in the two-bedroom, one-bath house. They were in their twenties and thirties. How many of these places did Hirsch operate?

Damien opened the bedroom door on the left without knocking.

Three twin beds were in the room. One had a woman sleeping, snoring quietly. The other was empty and unmade. The third had the victim.

"The doctor's here," Damien said. He stood in the doorway.

Bella wanted him to leave, but he didn't, and she wasn't going to ask him. She had a feeling that he would leave and consider it another favor, and she didn't want him to think she needed to repay him.

She assessed the girl. She was younger than the others, but over eighteen. Probably twenty, twenty-two. Bella didn't know why she was relieved.

Her hair was wet and it was clear that she'd showered when she got off work. She was under a thick blanket even though the room was uncomfortably warm.

"What's your name?" she asked. She spoke crisply. She wasn't here to coddle the women, and if she started to do that, Damien would be suspicious.

"Sue-Ann," she rasped in a thick southern accent.

"I need some light—I can't see anything, D."

Damien turned on the lights. They weren't bright, but they would suffice. The sleeping woman didn't budge.

Bella frowned at the visible damage on Sue-Ann's petite body. Her neck was bruised. There was a deep cut on her cheek that she had washed, but it was still bleeding. She also had a black eye, and she winced when the lights came on.

Bella wasn't a real doctor, which made all this that much more difficult. What if she had internal bleeding? What if there was something more serious that she couldn't diagnose?

She opened her bag and took out a pen light. She checked Sue-Ann's pupils. They reacted slowly, and one pupil was distinctly larger than the other.

"Follow my finger," she said.

Bella had had a concussion in the past and knew exactly what the symptoms were. She went through the protocol checklist.

"She has a concussion," she told Damien.

"She can take a couple days off. I'll tell Gino not to dock her. Just stitch up that cut."

"She was beaten up, D. I think the cut is the least of our worries right now."

"What worries?"

She didn't respond. "Sue-Ann, tell me what happened."

"That's not necessary," Damien said.

Bella got up and left the room. Damien followed. How did she play this? Professional.

"Damien," she said firmly, "the girl was beaten severely. She has a serious concussion and could have internal bleeding. I need to know exactly where she's hurting. If she has a broken rib, I can't fix it with my medical bag. We'll have to get her to a clinic or someplace where I have access to equipment and supplies. If they're just cracked, I need to tape them up. If they're broken and I don't know? She can puncture a lung. I won't know anything until I check her out, understand?"

"You're testy today."

"I'm tired." She took a deep breath. "Look—you want me to do my job, this is how I do it. Remember the skinny black girl I patched up in L.A.? I still had my medical truck back then. I had what I needed. I think Sue-Ann has the same sort of injuries."

"Think he got off strangling her? He was drunk. He didn't mean it, it wasn't like last time."

"I don't give a shit if he meant it, I just care about getting her healthy so she can do her fucking job, and if I miss something . . . well, I won't." She knew what would happen. If Sue-Ann was seriously injured and needed major medical attention, they would kill her.

"I get it. We might have someone in town who can help—I'll make a call."

"Thank you," she said, calmer.

She went back into the room. Damien didn't follow her. She didn't dare shut the door, because that would make him suspicious.

She sat on the edge of the bed. The movement made Sue-Ann wince.

"Tell me what happened."

"I just need to sleep, sugar," she said. Whispered was more like it.

"Well, you can't," Bella said. "You have a concussion. Someone has to wake you up every hour on the hour to make sure you're okay for the next day or two, okay?"

"I'm fine, really."

"Tell me what happened."

"I don't want to make trouble."

Bella wanted to throttle her on the one hand, and grab her and run her to the hospital on the other.

"You have no trouble with me. I'm a doctor. Yeah, I lost my license for some shit that went down, but I can figure out what's wrong with you. I just need to know what happened."

Sue-Ann tried to sit up and grunted.

"Just stay down. Talk."

"Well, Papi is always a little rough, but he's had a tough life, you know?"

And being a hooker wasn't a tough life? But Bella remained silent.

"He had a real rough day. His ex-wife wants full custody of their kids. He didn't get a raise he was expecting. And his truck broke down out on the highway. He started drinking early, and sometimes, you know, when a man drinks too much he can't keep it up. I tried, really I did, because he needed relief, but it wasn't enough. Then I suggested that maybe we watch some sexy movies, get him in the mood. But he didn't take it right, and just got a little out of hand, that's all."

This woman had no self-esteem or self-respect. Unfortunately, in Bella's world—first as a forced prostitute, then as a cop, then as an investigator for Simon—she had met far too many women like Sue-Ann. Most had shitty childhoods. Didn't have support from anyone. Some were abused, some were just left on their own with no direction. Some watched their parents fight, or their mothers take a beating, or their daddies drink or touch them.

It was fucked. The world was fucked. Bella hated people.

"Where did he hurt you?"

"My holes both hurt. More than usual." She wasn't looking at Bella. "I had to shower because there was blood."

"Are you still bleeding?"

She shrugged.

"Where else does it hurt?"

"My throat a bit."

A bit? Probably hurt like hell.

"My titties hurt. He bit them. Harder than usual."

Bella wished she hadn't had any coffee. Her stomach threatened to rebel and she wanted to pummel the bastard who hurt Sue-Ann.

"My stomach hurts," she added.

"Did he hit you in your stomach?"

"No. Not exactly."

"Not exactly." That was enough. "I need to touch you, inspect your injuries. I'd like to remove your shirt."

"I'm fine, sugar. Really."

"You're not fine. Stop saying you're fine." She stopped talking. She was going to get herself in trouble.

Sue-Ann couldn't take off her shirt without help. She was naked underneath. Bella pulled down the blanket.

A puddle of blood pooled between her legs.

"Why didn't you tell me you were still bleeding?"

"I—it's not much."

"It's a fucking river. Shit."

She had no idea what to do.

Bella put on latex gloves. She took Sue-Ann's temperature. It was elevated. She inspected her breasts. The bastard had bitten her repeatedly. Her stomach was showing signs of bruising like her neck. He hadn't hit her, she said, but he must have done something.

"I need to look between your legs. You've had exams before, right?"

"Sure, we have them twice a year, like the dentist. I'm clean, too. No diseases, always use a condom. It's a rule. Well, Papi didn't this time, but he meant to. He was just really angry."

STDs were the least of Sue-Ann's concerns right now.

When Simon's doctor friend trained her, he focused on reproductive exams because any medic for prostitutes would be doing hundreds of them a year. They had become routine for Bella. She didn't really mind it. She couldn't send off Pap smears or test much of anything, but at least she could make sure everything appeared healthy, and there were some cheats to detect common STDs.

Sue-Ann was anything but healthy. She was bleeding from both her vagina and her anus and there was extensive tearing of both. Would they heal on their own? Bella had no idea.

She changed the sheets and put a towel down and then wrapped a pad and gauze around her in an effort to stop the bleeding. Sue-Ann cringed, but she didn't cry.

"Tell me if I'm hurting you."

"I'm fine."

She wasn't fine. She was far from *fine.* Bella said, "I need to stitch up your cheek. It's going to hurt. I'm going to give you a shot to dull the pain, but you'll still feel it."

"Okay."

Bella glued the corners of the cut, but it was too deep for her to glue the entire wound. Sue-Ann yelped at the first needle, but then she restrained herself.

Bella had enough experience with stitches that she did a decent job. There would be a scar, but nothing that couldn't be hidden by makeup.

If she survived. Because at this point, Bella thought there was something far more serious wrong with her.

"Sue-Ann, I'm going to have your people wake you up periodically. I don't want you getting up and walking around for the rest of the day, okay? Stay in bed. Rest. Drink water. Broth. Orange juice. Fresh, not the fake crap. If you throw up or have any sharp pains anywhere, you need to tell someone. I'm going to tell these people the exact same thing, okay? And no sex at all no matter what for at least a week. I'll come back and check on you tomorrow."

Tomorrow. Would she even be here tomorrow?

"I'll be fine. Thank you."

Sue-Ann smiled, but her eyes were unfocused.

"No smiling, you'll pull at the stitches."

Bella gathered her supplies and walked out. She found the woman with the black eye in the kitchen drinking what looked like tomato juice but smelled like a bloody Mary.

She slammed a small bottle of antibiotics on the table. "Do you know if Sue-Ann is allergic to penicillin?"

The woman shrugged.

"She needs these three times a day. One pill with a small light meal. Someone needs to wake her up every hour or two to make sure she's coherent. She has a concussion. She's bleeding. The john beat her, strangled her, and fucked her with something other than his dick. She's torn up bad, and there will be no sex for at least a week, probably longer."

"What the fuck do you think this is? A charity?"

"You want her to make money? She takes a ten-day vacation, starting now."

Damien walked in as she spoke.

"Do what Doc says," Damien said.

The woman scowled but nodded. "You tell Gino. Last time I gave him bad news he whopped me."

Damien turned and walked out. Bella followed him. In the car she said, "He tore her up. She's bleeding. I don't think anything I did is going to help. She needs a hospital."

"No hospitals. You know that."

"I could give a shit about most of the crap in this business, but that john—Papi, she called him—strangled her, cut her, fucked her with something sharp, her asshole is cut and while I *think* I got the bleeding stopped, I don't know how the hell she's going to take a shit or pee without tearing again. She's a nitwit, doesn't even recognize how badly she's hurt, and she apologized for him. Oh, boo hoo hoo. Poor old Papi has a bad day and takes it out on his whore. Lot of good it's going to do if she dies."

"Is she going to die?"

Bella wasn't expecting the question. She hadn't even expected to rant, but she was furious. She needed the anger to keep her from calling the cops. If the cops here could even be trusted.

"Honestly, if she keeps bleeding? Yes. She'll die. I need to come back and check on her tomorrow." She needed to call an ambulance. The authorities. Someone to rescue that girl who didn't even know she was being abused.

Damien didn't say anything else. He didn't drive back to the house. Now Bella was worried.

"I didn't meant to take it out on you," she said quietly.

He reached out and took her hand. Held it. Comforting her? Shit, what was she doing?

He still didn't say anything and Bella became worried for other reasons.

He drove to a house in what passed as middle class in this town. Children's toys were in the yard.

"What are we doing here?" she asked.

"Wait."

Damien went up to the house and for a minute Bella thought this was Papi's place and Damien was going to kill him. A chill ran down her spine.

The door opened and a short, greasy-looking man stepped out. He and Damien argued. Damien didn't raise his voice or his arms, but the man was causing a scene. Bella caught a few words, but not everything. It was clear Damien wanted information.

But at least he hadn't killed the man in broad daylight.

Five minutes later, he got back in the car. They drove clear across town, to a trailer park. He parked down the street.

"Come with me," he said. It wasn't a question.

Again Bella was worried.

They walked in through the back, unseen by anyone. Damien found the trailer he was looking for. He opened the door, entered, and motioned for Bella to follow him.

He wore gloves. Bella didn't. She didn't touch anything.

The place stunk to high hell from booze and puke. Snoring came from the bedroom.

Damien walked down the short hall, but Bella stayed where she was. There was a scuffle, and swearing—none of which came from Damien.

He hauled a huge, naked man out of the bedroom as if he weighed nothing. Bella knew Damien was strong, but she hadn't really thought about how strong until now.

"On your knees," Damien ordered.

The man tried to hit him and missed. Damien pushed him down.

Papi.

His hands had open wounds from his pounding on Sue-Ann, but she apparently didn't inflict any damage on his doughy body.

"Tell the Doc that you're sorry you hurt the whore last night."

"What? What the hell you talking about?"

"You are Papi Chavez. You picked up a whore from Gino last night."

"So?"

"You beat her up, strangled her."

"She liked it."

"You fucked her in her asshole," Bella said. "You ripped her open. She like that, too?"

"She wanted it! She asked for it, so I shoved a bottle up her ass."

Bella hadn't meant to open her mouth. She had no idea what Damien planned to do. Scare the living hell out of this prick? Beat him up? He wouldn't care. He wouldn't remember, or if he did he'd twist it around, take it out on the next hooker he picked up.

Damien pushed Papi down on the filthy floor, grabbed a cushion from the couch, and put it over his head. Before Bella could tell him *no*, Damien fired his gun twice through the cushion into Papi's head.

Bella stared. The carpet was so dark she couldn't see any blood, but she smelled it. Blood and gunpowder and death.

"Let's go."

She was frozen. Every instinct in her told her to run, that Damien was out of control, but she was rooted to the spot.

"*Now.*" Damien grabbed her by the arm and pulled her out of the trailer.

In the car, Damien seized her and held her hair tight in his hands. She thought for a second that he was going to hit her—punishment for not coming when he said, for questioning him with her eyes, for making him kill Papi. She didn't make him, but he might think that.

You're glad he's dead.

No. She wasn't. Not happy or sad. Shocked.

"She's just a whore," Damien said, "but she doesn't deserve to suffer. People think I don't care about anything. Maybe I don't. Except you."

He kissed her hard. Either he didn't notice she wasn't kissing back or he didn't care. He touched her breasts. His hands were shaking. Bella's head was spinning. First Sue-Ann. Then Papi. Now . . . *this.*

He kissed her neck, sucking her so hard she was certain she'd have a hickey. "Not here," she said.

Not here. Not anywhere.

She had to get out of this mess. Now.

"I've never felt this way about anyone, Doc."

"I know," she said, because she didn't know what else to say.

"Monday I'm going back to L.A. I have a few things to take care of. I'm going to ask Hirsch if you can come with me."

He looked at her, hopeful, like a little boy.

Like a sick, psychopathic little boy.

But it was her out. She'd go with him, then run. She had many friends in L.A. and could easily disappear.

"That sounds like a much needed vacation for both of us," she said and smiled.

Inside, her heart was as hard as steel.

CHAPTER TWENTY-SEVEN

Lucy didn't want to go into FBI headquarters, but she did anyway. Nate wasn't around, and no one else spoke to her. She sat at her computer and sent a follow-up email to the task force summarizing everything they'd learned in the last twenty-four hours, putting the information all in one place. She added the details she'd received from Christina Garrett, without naming the young victim. She made a point of including her boss Rachel on the CC, as well as Abigail Durant. While normally she wouldn't copy in the ASAC on anything that wasn't specifically requested, she didn't want to rely on Rachel to convey the information correctly.

Basically, Lucy planned on covering her ass every step of the way.

Next she sent the information about "Pixie" to her contact at NCMEC and then called Tia Mancini.

"Have you tracked down Ginger?" Lucy asked.

"Hello to you too."

She rubbed her eyes. "I'm sorry. Late night."

"I'm playing with you, Lucy. No, I haven't, but I'm working on it. I had a couple bites from her girls, but the places they gave up are nowhere near the neighborhood you lost the vans."

"Sean's sitting on the trucking company to see if he

can get eyes on any of the people we have flagged. So far, nothing is happening. There's an active warrant for Anton Meyer—attempted murder, fleeing to avoid prosecution out of New Jersey, and we're working on a federal warrant because I ID'd him in a porn video with a minor. Every PD in Texas was sent a sheet on him yesterday—can you push it through? Get his face on everyone's mind?"

"Consider it done. Be careful, Kincaid."

"Ditto."

Lucy hung up. If Rachel was in the office, she was sitting behind her closed door.

Lucy was gone an hour after she came in, making sure Zach knew where she was in case anyone asked. She drove over to DEA headquarters and updated the timeline she'd created yesterday.

"Can I help ya, Agent Kincaid?"

She jumped, then turned to face Aggie Jensen. "Don't sneak up on people," she said.

"Sorry." She didn't sound sorry. "The boss told me to make sure you had everything you needed."

"I'm good, thanks."

"Hey, you asked us to run those pictures you took from the trucking company?"

Lucy had almost forgot. She'd planned on enhancing them at home, but when she got the videos of Hope, she shifted gears.

"Yes, are you done?"

"Easy-peasy. I can confirm that the two seventeen-foot trucks that came in two nights ago were the same two trucks RCK photographed at the trucking company in Texas."

Lucy had thought they were, but confirming the evidence would be key in a future prosecution.

"I wrote up the report already. And the guy in the office? The one sitting down half hidden?"

"Yes?"

"I merged the photos you took, adjusted for lighting, and got a positive ID. Guy's name is Anton Meyer, there's an active warrant for him out of New Jersey. My grandma lives in New Jersey."

It took Lucy a second to process that the last sentence was just small talk. She was focused on Meyer.

"You're one hundred percent certain it's Anton Meyer?"

"Yep. I'll swear to it in court."

"Can I see the picture?"

Aggie sat at the computer and typed rapidly. "You can access all this, Donnelly gave you full clearance. I made you a login and password. It's your FBI login, and your password is taskforce1, all one word, with the numeral '1.' You'll have to change it, but it'll get you in. Here you go."

Aggie talked as fast as she typed.

Lucy stared at the picture. It was definitely Anton Meyer. The picture looked almost three dimensional. She hadn't recognized him yesterday because he now had a scruffy beard, and he'd been wearing a ball cap. But Aggie had removed the ball cap and it was clearly him. She pulled up his mug shot and shifted it so it was at the same angle as the fuzzy picture from yesterday.

"See?"

"You're right."

"Of course I am."

She was arrogant, but not in a snotty way. Sean would definitely like her.

"Thank you."

Aggie beamed.

Lucy sent a message to everyone on the task force that Anton Meyer was still in San Antonio and she was alerting SAPD. She then called Sean and filled him in.

"So far, all is quiet," Sean said. "I just got off the

phone with Kane. They're in Port Arthur. Kane has an old Marine buddy there who's hosting them, so they can keep a low profile."

"Do they know where Bella is?"

"No. They tracked down Hirsch's plane and confirmed he landed yesterday at five-thirty p.m. They paid a mechanic to call if anyone came for the plane. But discretion is important. They don't want to tip their hand, put Bella in more danger. We're confident this is where they are. It's not a large city. They'll find her. Hold on."

Sean went silent. A minute later he said, "Anton Meyer just drove into West-East Transport."

"Watch him. Follow him if he leaves. I'll talk to Brad and see if he wants to grab him now or wait."

"Wait," Sean said. "He's not living at this place, he'll lead us somewhere—and maybe to Hope Anderson."

Sean was right.

"Okay," she said.

"I'm not going to let him out of my sight. I wouldn't mind a tag team if Brad has anyone to spare. I shouldn't even have to ask—you should be able to send Nate."

"Sean—now's not the time to go to war with my boss."

"Your call. I can tail him, not a problem. But I much prefer a dual tail, and someone I trust. And not you—you have far too much on your plate to play stake out with me. However much I would love to spend today with you."

Lucy said, "I'll let you know when Brad has someone in place."

"You said anything weird, and this is weird."

JT stood with the Chief of Police outside a sagging trailer in a run-down trailer park on the fringes of Port Arthur. A field next to the hodge-podge collection of trailers was filled with debris from last year's flood. Couches, collapsed trailers, refrigerators, and garbage. A temporary fence had been put up to keep people out. An oil refining plant with dozens of large white tanks separated the "park" from the main town. It was high noon and the humidity was cloying.

He'd reached out to the Chief of Police last night after Sean ran a background on him and said he was on the straight and narrow. Kate Donovan concurred, and said the chief had gone through two National Academies with the FBI and served on a joint terrorism task force with the Houston field office. Kate vouched for JT, and Chief Garcia had called him as soon as he verified there was a dead body.

"It's not that a dead body is all that unusual—the greater Port Arthur area, which includes Beaumont, ranks fifth in the most dangerous cities in Texas. We have our share of crime. But it's been on the decrease, and I aim to keep working on increasing my budget and reducing violent crime. But this body—this body is definitely out of the norm."

The coroner was there and Garcia was waiting for him to give the all-clear. When he did, Garcia said to JT, "You can take a gander, just don't touch anything."

JT stepped into the trailer behind Garcia. The coroner had moved the body, but the chief showed him photos that he'd taken on his cell phone. First thing JT noted was the guy was naked. Second thing was that he had been executed. The pillow over the back of his head was more effective in preventing blowback than silencing the gun, though it would have some suppression effect.

The place reeked, and JT had seen enough. He stepped outside again.

"Do you have an ID?"

"Peter Chavez, friends call him Papi. Had a steady job for years, laid off, his wife left him and took the kids into Beaumont where she could work as a hairdresser. He's been working for the last year at one of the refineries. Drinks too much—I'm sure ya'll smelled that stink—and has been arrested a half dozen times for assault. Drunk bar fights. Spent six months in jail last time—nearly killed the guy with a broken beer bottle." Garcia shook his head. "He sure pissed someone off."

"He was executed," JT said.

"That he was."

"Did someone call in the gun shot?"

"Nope. His wife called it in at ten this morning—she was dropping off the kids for the weekend."

In that disgusting pit?

Well, JT could imagine. There were times his mother hadn't lived much better. When all you cared about was your next fix, you really didn't care if your house was clean or stunk of your last regurgitated meal.

"The kids didn't see that—did they?"

"She said no, I think she's lying. But don't matter, she gave her statement and I let her go before you got here." Garcia had a calm, too calm and slow, way of talking. He sounded like a bumpkin cop, but that was either an act or just his personality. JT knew from Sean's background on the guy that he'd graduated summa cum laude from Texas State University in Houston with a dual degree in criminal justice and biology. He'd served in the Army as an officer for ten years before leaving the military and becoming a cop.

"She has an alibi?"

"She didn't kill him—she's a hundred pounds soaking wet. I tested her hands for gunpowder residue, came up negative. Her alibi will be verified, no doubt, but I'll follow through. Always do." He paused, assessed the surroundings with sharp eyes. "We canvassed the neighbors, no one claimed to see anything. Might be lying, but it'll be mighty hard to turn any of them. They don't like us folks very much, though it's gotten a bit better since my men and women have been helping rebuild. Disasters have that effect of bringing out the best and worst in people. Anyway, coroner said he's been dead two to four hours. Hard to figure more exact since the humidity and heat messes with TOD, and our coroner is just a bit too cautious with his estimates. My guess? Smack dab in the middle and we'll call it three hours."

"Nine this morning?"

"Nope, that's two to four when the coroner got here pretty close to the call, about eleven. So I'll call it eight a.m., take or leave. I know where he likes to drink, one of the few bars that didn't cut him off. Wanna come along for the ride?"

JT almost said no. But an execution in the small town of Port Arthur less than twenty-four hours after Hirsch shows up? Could be a coincidence. JT didn't believe in coincidences.

He followed Garcia's government-issue police Bronco. Before they entered the bar—which had opened at six a.m. and already had several cars in the lot—he asked, "You said Chavez has been in prison for assault. Any chance he could be involved in something more serious?"

"Like?"

"Sex trafficking."

Garcia rubbed his mustache. "Can't say. Wouldn't think he was smart enough to pull something like that off, but he's been known to frequent prostitutes."

"Underage?"

Garcia's expression shifted slightly. "These questions are mighty specific."

"It's why I'm here, Chief. My security company is helping the FBI track a sex trafficking ring and word is one of their principals is here in Port Arthur."

"Well, let's find out what Papi Chavez has been up to, shall we?"

The bartender didn't want to talk to the police, but Garcia was persuasive and the man eventually gave up Gino Dominguez, a local pimp.

"Well, shit," Garcia said in his southern drawl when they were back in the parking lot.

"Problem?"

"Gino is a tough nut to crack. Sure, I know he's running girls, but he doesn't run the young 'uns. I would know. I keep an eye on him a bit, but we have far more serious crimes here than a few hookers looking to make a buck. I ran him up for beating on one of his girls, told him if it happened again I'd be all in his business, and he's been quiet."

"So?"

"Well, I'll tell ya, I'll back your play, Mr. Caruso, but I have an idea, if you'll trust me with it."

JT's patience was wearing thin, but Garcia had been more than helpful in including him this far along.

"Tell me the plan."

CHAPTER TWENTY-EIGHT

It was shortly after noon when Sean called Lucy.

"Meyer's on the move. Same black van he drove in with. I have no idea what he's been doing for the last two hours, but he came in alone and he's leaving alone. Unless someone is in back."

"Brad posted an unmarked pick-up truck, an undercover car that looks like shit—his words, not mine—down the street. Rusty green and the back gate is missing. He'll follow, you frog-leap him."

Sean laughed. "I love you. It's leapfrog."

"Right. That's what I meant. I gotta go, but keep me in the loop."

She hung up. "Meyer is on the move," she said to Brad.

"I know—my guy checked in. I sent him Sean's make, model, and cell phone. Proctor is standing by."

"He may not go to the house."

"Wherever he goes, if it's a private location, we're taking him down," Brad said. "Orders from Donovan."

Lucy understood Kate's reasoning, but it might not help them find the girls.

Still, Lucy was itching to interrogate him. She'd read his file, had a solid sense of his personality and how to make him flip.

Lucy was usually good at waiting, but now she was antsy.

They were so close to finding Hope.

Or not. You don't know how long Meyer has been in San Antonio. He could have her anyplace in Texas. Anywhere in the south. He might have dumped her or sold her or have her working the streets in another city.

But he knew where she was three weeks ago. Lucy had to believe she could make him talk.

Her phone rang. Sean. She put him on speaker.

"You're here with Brad, me, and his team."

"Meyer pulled into a house right off Hackleberry. Smack dab in the middle of the neighborhood where you lost him."

"It was three vans."

"There's a long driveway, garage is behind the house. I almost missed him, but I saw the garage door go down. The property is deep enough to conceal three vans."

Brad told Sean, "Circle the block and stake out the north end. I'll have my guy sit on the south. If he leaves, I want to know. I'm bringing in SWAT.

They staged the SWAT team one block over, out of line of sight of the house.

Nate was there—which pleased Lucy. Jason Lopez was also there, which made her nervous. What was he going to report to Rachel?

Do your job, Lucy, and stop thinking about office politics.

Leo Proctor and Brad were in charge, which made Lucy breathe easier.

"We have two men on the rear, and two men in an unmarked van in the front. We have civilians in houses surrounding Meyer. No good intel inside, but based on one Good Samaritan who was very chatty with Agent

Kincaid earlier, six to eight women live on-site. The neighbor thought they were college girls. Came in all hours of the day and night."

"Ginger?" Tia Mancini asked. She was there representing SAPD.

"No visual."

Lucy said, "The house is owned by a company and managed by a local property management firm. We're sending the names to the white collar agent on the task force hoping to get intel before we sweep them up into the net."

Proctor said, "Donnelly and I assessed all entrances. There are three on the main house, two on the garage. I have two men on each entrance, no exceptions. There are both hostiles and innocents inside, and I don't want to see any blood. Kincaid, your plan."

"Detective Mancini and I will approach the house with a warrant for Ginger's arrest. We'll be on open coms. The goal is to extract all residents from the home before engaging Meyer."

Jason said, "What if he's just sitting in the living room? Takes a hostage."

"He'll hide," Lucy said. "As soon as we identify ourselves as law enforcement, he'll bail. He will either hide in the house—if he thinks we're just looking for Ginger—or if he's suspicious, he'll go out the back."

"And we'll nab him there," Proctor said. "Vests, everyone, including you Kincaid, Mancini."

"You don't have to tell me twice," Lucy said.

"Wait," Jason said.

Everyone looked at him.

"This is happening quickly. What if our intel is wrong?"

"It's not wrong," Brad said, irritated.

"It just seems we're rushing when maybe a stealth approach is warranted."

Brad looked at Lucy. "Kincaid? This is your op."

Why was Brad putting her on the spot?

Or maybe it wasn't that. Maybe he was shifting his weight to her, showing Jason and everyone else that he trusted her judgment.

"I've read his psych profile and analyzed his crimes," Lucy said. "He'll hide or bolt. This is our best lead to find Hope Anderson, and we need to act now. She very well could be inside that house—if not her, then the four other underage prostitutes our asset identified."

Proctor nodded, then spoke into his com to his team. "Wait for my signal." Then to Lucy and Tia, "You two are on. Be safe."

Lucy and Tia approached the house on foot. In a low voice, Lucy said, "Are you really okay?" She was a bit worried because Tia had nearly died right in front of her only nine months ago.

"Honey, don't you worry about me. I'm good."

Tia knocked on the door loudly. There was no answer, but they heard a television in the front room.

Tia rang the bell and knocked again. "SAPD! We have an arrest warrant for Ginger Foxx, open the door now or we will come in."

There was some scrambling, then a tall black woman opened the door. It wasn't Ginger, but she also wasn't one of the underage prostitutes.

"Badges," she said. She didn't have a southern accent. She eyed both of them suspiciously. Calculating.

Tia and Lucy both showed their badges and ID. She took her time looking at them. Buying time, certainly.

"Ginger Foxx," Tia repeated.

"Ain't here," the woman said.

"We have a warrant to search the premises."

"Well, this ain't my house, I think I'll be calling the landlord. Come back in an hour."

"What's your name?" Lucy asked.

"Desiree, not that it's your business. I ain't Ginger."

Desiree was one of Hirsch's people. Lucy hoped Brad had picked up on it through the open com.

"Well, Desiree, the warrant gives us the right to enter these premises. Stand aside or you will be arrested for obstruction of justice."

The woman scowled, then opened the door wider.

"Are there any guns on the premises?"

"Don't know, I don't live here, like I said. Just visiting."

In her earpiece, Lucy heard, "Have a runner!"

"How many people are in the house?" Lucy asked. There were two girls—neither obviously underage—sitting on the couch staring at the television. Either terrified of Desiree or terrified of the police. Maybe both.

Desiree shrugged.

She had a bad feeling. She said, "Agent Proctor, I need two female officers to frisk and cuff as we clear the house, and two officers as backup."

"Ten-four," he replied.

In less than a minute two SWAT officers and two SAPD cops approached, only one was female.

"I'll back them up, you clear the house," Tia said. "This way, you three."

"We ain't done nothing!" Desiree said. "You can't frisk us."

"We can. It's for our protection as well as yours."

"Fucking cops."

Donnelly, who was geared up but not wearing full SWAT tactical gear, entered after the three women were removed by SAPD to be identified and detained while they cleared the house.

"Place is a fucking pigsty," he said.

Partially empty takeout cartons, pizza boxes, and a

plethora of beer, wine, and hard liquor bottles were stacked precariously high on the dining room table. It had once been a nice house—it had a solid foundation and structure—but the carpets were old and stained and the hardwood floors warped. An unclean smell of body odor and an abundance of conflicting perfumes wafted through Lucy's nostrils.

"Dunning and Lopez grabbed Meyer leaving through the back door. You were right, he bolted."

"It's how he hasn't been caught—he'll rabbit over confrontation." He acted the big tough guy with those who couldn't defend themselves, but when push came to shove he was a scared thug who didn't want to go back to prison.

"Let's clear this place."

Donnelly and one SWAT officer cleared the ground floor and basement. Lucy went upstairs with the other officer. Proctor moved in with another team as backup. It was a clean, precision operation. Lucy found fourteen girls upstairs, several of whom were clearly underage, plus a few she suspected might be as well. She asked each one for their name and age. They gave their first name only and all said eighteen or older. She had to eyeball it, make an educated guess. Six she separated as underage. They would be taken to a hospital instead of the jail.

"You can't arrest us!" one of the younger girls said.

"What's your name?" Lucy asked.

"Sara," she said defiantly.

Sara. Word had come down from Bella Caruso that there was an underage prostitute named Sara who was a problem and might turn on her fellow hookers.

"Most recently from Phoenix," Lucy said bluntly. The surprise on Sara's face told Lucy she was right.

She turned to her backup. "Separate Sara from the

others. Under no circumstances is she allowed to talk with any of the other girls."

"You'll be sorry," Sara said. "I'll be out in a day, and you know it. You have nothing on me."

Lucy ignored her. She was staring at the bedroom Sara and three of the other girls had been hiding in.

She'd seen this room before.

The walls were painted pink. The queen-sized bed was made with a simple green and white comforter. A couple generic pictures had been mounted, but that wasn't what caught her eye. It was the unicorn lamp on the nightstand.

It was so ugly and cute at the same time that Lucy couldn't forget it. It had been in the most recent videos of Hope.

Hope had been here a month ago. In this room. In San Antonio.

Was she still here? If not, where could she have gone?

She turned and jumped when someone moved behind her.

Brad.

"ERT is on their way to process."

"Hope was in this room a month ago."

"I didn't see her. We have sixteen women in custody, six flagged as underage, one you isolated. Meyer was caught fleeing, and we found another guy in the basement. Wouldn't give us his name, but he had ID on him—it says he's Thaddeus Brown from Los Angeles."

"I need to talk to the girls right now."

"You know my office shares the FBI ERT, right?"

Lucy nodded, but she couldn't be concerned about office politics right now. She realized the problem she and Rachel had wasn't going to be resolved anytime soon, but the FBI had the best forensic processing unit in the area. San Antonio PD was good, but because there was clearly evidence of child pornography on-site, jurisdiction naturally fell to the FBI. She wanted it that way, she just didn't like that she was using this task force to go around Rachel. She wished her boss was on her side. They could do so much good if they worked together.

She recognized, not for the first time, that she'd been spoiled the last six months with Noah in charge of her squad. He'd been her training officer in DC, he'd been a mentor and a friend. The mutual trust they'd fostered was instrumental in solving multiple complex cases. Without it? They wouldn't have stopped the black market baby ring. They wouldn't have put an end to the Flores Cartel and their human trafficking organization. People would have died.

Trust was crucial in this business, especially when you were a field agent. Lucy trusted Brad, and that's why they'd worked so well together from the beginning.

But they'd worked together to earn that mutual trust. Rachel wasn't even giving her a chance.

At this point, finding Hope was Lucy's priority, and all other problems in her life had to be put aside until she knew exactly what happened to that poor girl.

Lucy went back downstairs. The girls had been ordered to sit on the driveway. There were SWAT officers guarding them. She looked each one over carefully. None of them was Hope. The house and garage had been cleared, no one else was inside. Drugs and weapons were confiscated. Lucy pulled out her phone and showed Hope's picture to each and every one of the girls and asked if they had seen her. "This is Hope Anderson. She's also known as Pixie."

Some of the girls clearly didn't know who she was. But several of them reacted. She had Brad write down their names. She would separate the two groups and have them interrogated separately.

"Ginger Foxx isn't here," Lucy said to Tia when she got to the end of the row.

"Nope, but we have a lead on her. It's all about timing—she was returning from the store, saw our trucks, slipped away before anyone recognized her. My department will track her down."

"When you do, let me know, but you take the lead on interrogating her. We want Hope—Ginger would know exactly who she is because she was in this house three weeks ago."

"On it," Tia said and walked off to coordinate with SAPD.

Brad approached. "What are we doing?"

"The five girls I flagged to the hospital, the sixth—Sara—to a solitary cell at juvie."

"You sure?"

"Yes. The others to jail unless any of them claims to be under eighteen now that they're going to lockup. But I need to interrogate Anton Meyer as soon as possible."

She was relieved she didn't have to explain or justify herself. She told Leo Proctor to alert ERT when they arrived that the girl they were looking for had been in the pink room. They had Hope's DNA on file from the missing persons report her grandparents had filed, and if they could tie Ginger or Meyer to Hope, they could pile on charges until one of them broke.

Everyone had a breaking point. It was just a matter of psychology—figuring out what they feared the most. If it was Hirsch—or the mysterious Z—then Lucy would play it a different way. She could lie and manipulate and tell them anything to get them to cooperate. And she would, because as soon as Hirsch realized they were onto him, he might cut his losses and disappear.

But right now he didn't know this chase was all because of one girl. He might think it was because of the shooting in El Paso, or the body found at the trucking company. He would most likely go under for awhile, then pop back up when the heat died down. If that were the case, Hope might be safe awhile longer.

But if he suspected that Hope Anderson was the reason for federal and local investigations, he would have her killed without hesitation. Lucy couldn't let that happen.

Brad drove and Lucy called Kate. Her sister-in-law sounded rushed.

"I heard about the raid. No shots fired, everyone in custody. Win-win."

"Partly. Ginger Foxx is in the wind and SAPD is taking lead in tracking her down. I have proof that Hope was here a month ago. The same room that was in the NCMEC videos is in that house. I alerted ERT about the room, it was recent enough that there is likely DNA evidence. But I need some leeway in interrogating Anton Meyer."

"Anything you need. What do you have on him now?"

"I expect Meyer to lawyer up, but he's not the sharpest tack and I can play with that. The problem is these girls are scared and I don't know if I can get any of them to talk right away. The others are old-timers, and they're not going to talk to a cop. I'll talk to Tia Mancini about putting a ringer in jail with them, see what we can shake out when they don't think anyone is paying attention. Anyway, I want to push on the Hope angle. She's fourteen so she's covered by local and federal special circumstances laws. There were drugs found in the house, but not enough to argue distribution and sale unless ERT digs up more. I need time with the girls and leverage with the suspects."

"Meyer isn't going anywhere—there's an active warrant for him out of Jersey, and with the video you found of him with Hope, we can hold him on child porn charges. Do what you have to do."

"Thanks."

She hung up and took a deep breath, then called Tia Mancini. "Tia, it's Lucy."

"We still haven't found Ginger."

"Can you get to the hospital and work on the five girls?"

"Sure, is that the priority at this point?"

"You have everyone in SAPD looking for Ginger, but you're one of the few who can weed through the bullshit from the prostitutes."

"True."

Tia had a huge amount of compassion for girls in this situation, but after last year when one such girl used and twisted that compassion, ending up with Tia on the operating table, Tia had become more cautious.

"I need just one who will agree to talk," Lucy said. "The sooner the better. I'm going at the suspect hard."

"I'll work on it."

"And would you ask each of them if they recognize Hope? No one admitted it at the house, but one on one they might. I know she was in that house a month ago, and she was also in Los Angeles a year ago. According to our undercover asset, two dozen girls were moved from El Paso to San Antonio, and most of them came from Phoenix or Los Angeles. Don't give them any hint that we have someone on the inside. If they make bail and go back to the business, I don't want to risk our asset."

"I'll call you when I have something."

Brad drove to the jail where by now their suspects would be processed and held until their arraignment—or in Meyer's case, his extradition to New Jersey, if the feds allowed it. Lucy would rather keep him here in Texas because Texas had much broader laws, and after so many years would the witnesses in his original Jersey case be reliable? He might get sentenced for fleeing to avoid prosecution, which would mean much less jail time than manslaughter or human trafficking or child rape.

"Who do you want to go at first?" Brad asked Lucy. "We have Desiree, too. Her prints were in the system—Desiree Jones, resident of Los Angeles, California. Multiple arrests for prostitution in L.A., no real jail time. Thaddeus Brown has an active warrant for assault from six months ago. Missed his court date."

L.A. They definitely knew who Hope was. Had they come with the girls from El Paso? It made sense. Hirsch pulls them in, relocates them to a place where they know no one. Keeps them on edge, under his thumb.

"I can see pros and cons with each." Meyer was definitely going in for more jail time, but he would have more information on Hirsch than even Desiree might have. It would be easier to negotiate for a reduced sentence with Desiree. Even let her walk in exchange for her testimony. Lucy had no doubt that they could build a solid case against her, but it would take a lot of time and resources and the charges were minor compared to Hirsch. She had a record, but all misdemeanors. A good lawyer would get her off with time served. She might know that. Unless Lucy could convince her they had more on her than they actually did.

Prostitution—even when you ran the organization—wouldn't get her more than a slap on the wrist. Tia Mancini's experience with Mona Hill over the years had proved that. There was no evidence that Desiree was privy to the underage sex tapes, because she hadn't been in Texas three weeks ago. Ginger? She would have known. It was her house, her girls, and she let Hirsch in.

But Tia's people were still looking for her. And putting her in the house at the time the tape was made would be difficult.

"Brad—remind ERT that it's a child pornography case and we need any and all tapes, cameras, photos. Especially print that room—if I can place Desiree or Ginger or Meyer in that room three weeks ago, I can jam them so hard they'll never get out of prison."

"I'll send them a message, but they know what they're doing."

Of course they did, but Lucy learned that reiterating what was important helped focus the team.

Lucy had one ace in the hole with Meyer, and she was going to play that card. It might be her only chance.

"Meyer," she said.

Brad seemed surprised. "Are you sure? He's a convicted felon, has a long rap sheet, wanted for attempted murder. He has no reason to flip, because you can't cut him a deal."

"I know."

Lucy didn't know if she was making the right call. "I need ten minutes to set up something," she said when they arrived at the jail.

"I'll talk to the warden and take care of the paperwork."

"Thanks for trusting me with this."

"Luce—I've trusted you from the beginning. Remember last year when I played bad cop with the Sanchez family in order to get George to turn? It was your idea that George was the weak link, but it was my idea on how to work the situation. You trusted me even when I berated you in public. You knew it was part of the game, and you went with it even when others on the team didn't see the play for what it was. That shit is hard to explain to people, but I've never doubted you. That you risked your life and your career to save mine is icing on the cake."

Lucy didn't know why Brad's words affected her so deeply. Maybe because of the problems in her own office; maybe because she was doubting her own reasoning with Anton Meyer. But she needed it.

"Thanks, Brad."

Anton Meyer was the same age as Martin Hirsch but had a much longer rap sheet. Lucy had talked to Joe DeLucca, Suzanne's boyfriend, and asked for more background on Meyer, over and above what was on his rap sheet. Joe passed along one tidbit that Lucy might be able to use to her advantage.

She sat at the table. Meyer was handcuffed, but otherwise not restrained, directly across from her. Brad stood in the corner, arms crossed, observing, playing the role of big tough cop.

"I'll be out by the end of the day," Meyer said.

Lucy looked at her watch. "It's five p.m. It is the end of the day as far as the jail is concerned, but you won't be getting out today or any day in the future."

He laughed. "I can post bail."

"You won't get bail."

"You must be new," Anton said, leaning forward, trying to intimidate her. "Fresh meat." He licked his lips.

This was a man who was naturally intimidating, in size and attitude, and he expected men and women—but especially women—to cower. She didn't flinch—showing fear would be the end of the interrogation and she would never get anything out of him.

He said, "Let me explain something to you, *chica*. There's a thing called an *arraignment*. That means that the *po-lice* need to state the charges in front of a judge. The state—that would be *you*—will ask for a ridiculous bail. My lawyer will counter. The judge will set it somewhere in between. And I will pay it and walk the street and *you'll* be looking over your shoulder for the rest of your life."

"It's a felony to threaten a federal officer."

He laughed. He had no fear of her or her office.

"They sent in a little rookie to talk to me? They know they have no case." He looked over at Brad. "You her trainer? Training her proper?" He winked and laughed.

Brad glared at him but didn't open his mouth. Lucy had asked him to refrain from getting involved in the conversation unless she gave him a signal. She knew it was difficult for him to stand back, but she had to play this delicately.

Anton Meyer didn't respect women. He'd likely faced female cops in the past and treated them like objects. Used foul language, gross flirting, insults. The men he expected to rise to defend them, reiterating his belief that female cops were weak. But with the male cops, he understood the game—he could pound his chest with the best of them. If Brad stepped in to defend her, nothing she said or did would matter to Meyer. They'd still put him in prison, he'd still go away for a long time, but she wouldn't get the information she needed.

Brad, unknowingly, had given her the final piece of her interrogation puzzle when he reminded her of how they'd played George Sanchez. Interrogation was as much a game of chess as it was an interview.

Lucy, however, couldn't lose her temper either. She had to remain calm no matter how loud or belligerent Meyer became. No matter what he said about her, about women, about Hope.

And above all, she could show no fear.

"First, Mr. Meyer, there's an active arrest warrant out of New Jersey. So at a minimum, you'd be extradited back to that state."

He showed no concern about the warrant. What had Joe said? The witness may have recanted. Meyer didn't fear the warrant because he was familiar with the system. He could claim he didn't know, he could plead to a lesser charge, or go to trial. If the statute of limitations was up they wouldn't even have a case.

"However, my colleagues in New Jersey have given me broad discretion. We have numerous federal charges we can make against you, and the state of Texas has numerous charges as well. All of these will have to be dealt with before you can even consider being released on bail. Even if your attorney expedited on Monday in federal court, I would ask my SAPD counterpart to immediately arrest you again and you'll go through the same process in another court. Then, if you were granted bail there, I would arrest you and extradite you to Arizona where you would go through the process in their court. And if you were granted bail again—and still had the money to pay—I would extradite you to California where we would go through this yet again. Then in Illinois—don't you remember that rape charge you bailed on in Chicago? Statute of limitations is five years, it's only been three, so I can let you see the inside of their prison system. And then, finally, New Jersey. Between now and then I would have far more charges and more states to move you to. So trust me when I say even if you had the best attorney on the planet and unlimited resources, you won't be getting out of jail for at least a year, just going through this process.

"Couple that with the fact that one of the charges against you is pedophilia, and the fact that we're in Texas which is not only a death penalty state but has some of the toughest laws against child pedophilia in the country, I don't see you making it out of Texas alive. I take some comfort in that."

Meyer glowered at her. "I'm not a fucking pedophile. You have nothing because that's a *fucking* lie."

"Agent Donnelly, what is the legal definition of pedophilia?"

"Sex with a child under the age of fourteen."

"How old was Hope Anderson when she was kidnapped?"

"Twelve."

"How old is she now?"

"She was fourteen last week."

"So last month she was thirteen?"

"Correct."

"So anyone who is convicted of having sex with Hope Anderson last month would be a pedophile, correct?"

"Yes, ma'am," Brad said.

Lucy turned on her tablet and showed a screen shot of the video of Meyer raping Hope. "Cybercrime experts at Quantico and the National Center for Missing and Exploited Children have verified that this video was uploaded twenty-three days ago. Hope was thirteen."

"So? No one will believe she's a kid. Look at her—she's a total woman."

"How she looks is irrelevant. She's a child, and the burden of proof is much lower. She could have a fake ID that says she's twenty-one, and it will not matter. She will not have to testify. She will not have to face you in court. This isn't the only video I have. We've found numerous videos of Hope and you, as well as other men, and we're in the process of using advanced facial recognition programs the military has developed in order to identify said individuals and issue warrants for their arrest. We have already ID'd two men and issued warrants."

She was making it all up. While it was true that they were working on identifying the men in every video, it took far more time and resources than either Quantico or NCMEC had.

Meyer didn't know that.

"I'm not a pedophile!"

"That won't matter when I inform the warden that you are."

"You can't do that!"

"I can do it, I will do it, I will enjoy doing it. Sex with a child under fourteen is the legal definition of pedophile, and do you think the men in prison are going to argue semantics with you? You can whine, 'oh I thought she was eighteen' but when I get done spreading the word, no one will believe you. They will do to you what you did to Hope, but far, far worse."

He lunged for her and she didn't budge. She'd been waiting for it because she'd intentionally baited him, and had willed herself not to move. Brad flinched and took a step forward, but he didn't interfere.

Meyer slammed his handcuffed fists on the table. "You fucking bitch, you can't do any of that! I'll tell my lawyer! I'll fucking skewer you. And when I get out, I'll make you suck my dick, you two-bit whore cop!"

His spittle sprayed everywhere, but Lucy didn't move a muscle. "In addition to pedophilia," she said, using the word far more often than she needed to because it seemed to set Meyer off more than anything, "we have you on sex trafficking across state lines. That is a federal crime. However, I would much prefer to send you to state prison in Texas where they really, really, *really* don't like child rapists."

He slammed his fists down again. "Bitch!"

"As I said, we have two men identified from the videos, and as soon as we locate them we'll offer them the same as I'm about to offer you. A deal, for information leading to the arrest and conviction of Martin Hirsch and Thomas Zimmerman."

At the name of Zimmerman, Meyer blinked. He leaned back in his seat and stared at her. "I don't know who you're talking about."

Oh, he knew. He knew exactly who Lucy was talking about.

"Plus, the exact location of Hope Anderson."

"I don't know any Hope."

"You called her Pixie."

That she knew the name surprised him, but it was clear that either he didn't put Hope and Pixie together until that moment, or that he had forgotten until now.

"You were with her here, in San Antonio, last month. Maybe even more recently. She wasn't at the house this afternoon. Where is she?"

He was thinking. Was he thinking of lying? Or trying to figure out a way out of this?

"So what you're saying, if I tell you where this girl is, I walk?"

"No."

"Then I'm not going to say shit."

"What I'm saying is, if you don't tell me where this girl is, I will make sure that every prisoner on your cell block knows that you're a pedophile who likes raping little girls."

"You can't do that."

She smiled, a mere upturn of her lips, and waited.

"What do I get? Time off? Time served? What?"

"You get to live," she said so quietly that no recording could hear her.

"Agent Donnelly," Lucy said, "what federal judge is on call this weekend for arraignments?" Lucy asked while Meyer considered whether she was serious.

"Hodgins."

"Hmm. And Monday?"

"Perez, I believe, will be handling all arraignments on Monday."

Lucy glanced at Brad. They were making this all up, and that Brad realized what she was doing thrilled her to no end. "Legally, we can keep him until Monday, right?"

"Absolutely. We don't have to charge and arraign him for seventy-two hours."

"We'll wait for Perez. She's good, she'll send him where I want."

"Wait. Wait!" Meyer ran both hands through his short hair. "I need to talk to my lawyer. He'll negotiate a better deal."

"First, I can't make a deal because I'm not a lawyer."

"But you said!"

"I said that if you didn't cooperate that every prisoner on your cell block will know you're a pedophile. If you cooperate, they won't hear that from me."

"I'm not a pedophile!"

She turned the tablet to face him.

"She's a prostitute! I didn't know how young she was! We were just making a sex tape. Nothing more, it was just sex. Consensual! That's it, consensual sex!"

It was all Lucy could do to control her rage. Her rage wasn't going to help, not now. The calmer she was, the more unhinged Meyer became.

"Do you think this is the only video I found? I know that Martin Hirsch traffics underage girls. The two girls rescued in Phoenix? Yes, I see you know about them. One is still under fourteen, and the laws are bulletproof when a victim is fourteen and younger. She knows exactly who you are. They are both in protective custody far, far away where Hirsch will never get to them. If you give me Hope Anderson, I'll get you in solitary. Now. Not tonight, not tomorrow. Right. This. Minute."

"I don't know!"

"Explain."

"Look, I don't know. I don't know! Damien called Monday and said there was some heat in Phoenix and he wanted to move some of the girls. Told me anyone who was a problem to ship out to Z."

"And Hope was a problem?"

"No, Pixie was cool. She was totally with the program. But one of the other girls had a fucking cow and got in my business, and then Pixie got in my face. That girl is insane when she's off her meds."

"Meds? What medication?"

"Just a figure of speech."

Lucy didn't think so. It was the way he was talking. And from the videos she watched, it was clear that Hope had been drugged. Drugging the girls kept them under better control.

"Monday? How many girls left with Hope?"

"Six. We were getting twice as many by the end of the week, so it wasn't, like, that big of a hardship."

He talked about the girls like they were goods, products to be moved around at his convenience. She wanted to hit him. She wanted to scream at him, pound him with her fists, force him to recognize that he was a bastard who didn't deserve to breathe.

He might have seen something in her eyes, but it didn't have the effect Lucy thought. He shifted uncomfortably, as if he was the one who was scared.

"Who picked them up."

"Jorge. That's all I know—he's a driver for Mr. Hirsch. Jorge picked them up late Monday night."

"Where did he take them."

"I don't know. I'm serious, I really don't know. I really don't know!"

She believed him.

"You know the locations of Mr. Hirsch's other houses."

"Yes, but—"

Lucy slipped him a pad of paper and pen. "Write them down. All of them. If you don't know the address, write down the fucking cross street and the color of the paint. Every single detail of every house. Write down Jorge's cell phone number. The make and model of the truck that picked up the girls. Their names, when you turned them out, everything. Now."

"Look—you don't understand."

"Do I look understanding? Write."

They locked eyes and Lucy didn't budge. She became her old icy self, but with far more confidence than she had two years ago.

Meyer took the pen and started writing.

Twenty minutes later he put the pen down. "So, uh, what happens now?"

"We'll keep you in solitary until Monday when it's up to the courts to decide which jurisdiction you fall under. I will work to keep it federal, not Texas." Criminals had a partly accurate impression that federal prisons were easier time than state prisons. But for a pedophile? A sex trafficker? Lucy didn't think he would have an easy time anywhere.

And the federal government had tougher laws across the board about sex trafficking across state lines. No way was the AUSA going to give up someone like Meyer.

"Okay. Thanks."

Thanks? He had thanked her? She didn't think that had ever happened in the year plus she'd been a federal agent, and she'd interrogated a lot of criminals. Meyer was a brute in that he was big and acted tough, but he certainly wasn't the brains of the operation.

She walked out, told the guard that Meyer needed to be in solitary until his arraignment, and she and Brad left.

As soon as they were out of the private meeting hall, she stopped and leaned against the wall.

"That was fucking amazing," Brad said. "You flipped him in thirty-three minutes. It was like a Jedi mind trick."

She had to smile at the comment. Smile or she was going to scream.

"And he thanked you. Thanked you for putting him in solitary. I've never seen it before. They're going to show that recording to every interrogation class at Quantico for the next decade. Shit, Lucy, it was truly amazing."

"Thanking me was unexpected," she said, because she needed to lighten her mood. She won, but she felt disgusting, like Meyer's filth had rubbed off on her. "We need to check out all these addresses, prioritized by distance. We start here and move out along the I-10 corridor."

Most of the houses didn't have specific addresses, but they had street names.

"I'll map these out, that might give us more information."

"Good idea, and pull property records where you have the exact address. Hope is in one of those houses."

"Did you notice the look on his face when you mentioned Zimmerman?"

"He didn't know that we had his name."

"It was more than that. He didn't pull the 'I'm more scared of them than you' card."

"I don't think he's that bright." Unlike Damien Drake, though Lucy didn't say that.

"Maybe. Or maybe this Zimmerman isn't who we—or Meyer—thinks he is."

CHAPTER TWENTY-NINE

JT had to hand it to Chief Garcia. While it took a bit of patience to get the information out of one of Garcia's informants, they learned that Papi Chavez had been with one of Gino's hookers last night, Sue-Ann Bowers, and she had been knocked around.

"My CI said Sue-Ann had to call Gino for a pick-up at the motel, something none of them ever do, and he carried her out. I asked around the motel, but they shut up tighter than a—" he hesitated. "Well, let's just say no one is talking. However, I know where Sue-Ann lives. Gino owns a couple houses, for his girls, bunks them three, four to a room. But they keep to themselves, don't cause no trouble."

This time, JT drove with Chief Garcia from the police station to a house in the middle of a borderline neighborhood. Definitely a far cry better than where Papi Chavez lived, but that wasn't saying much.

Garcia was in full uniform and JT wondered if the occupants would ignore him. They didn't. A woman sporting a black eye opened the door. "We're not causing any trouble, officer."

Garcia took off his hat. "I'm Reg Garcia, the chief of police, ma'am. I need to speak with Sue-Ann Bowers, if I may."

"Why?"

"Well, ma'am, that's between Sue-Ann and me."

"She's sleeping. She works nights."

"I had a report that there was an assault last night, and I need to talk to Ms. Bowers and get her side of the story."

"Assault? There was no assault."

"Well, I beg to differ, especially when there's a dead body I need to account for."

"What? Dead who?"

"Peter Chavez, ma'am. Murdered this morning. And Sue-Ann was the last known person to see him alive."

The woman's face paled and she said, "Wait here."

"That's fine, ma'am, but leave the door open."

She reluctantly complied.

"Would Gino kill a john to protect one of his hookers?" JT asked.

"Honestly, I wouldn't think he'd care much, he's not all that nice of a person, but stranger things have happened. Heat of the moment? He didn't pay?" Garcia shrugged. "What do I know? I'm fifty years old and been married to the same woman for thirty-two years. Have never wanted to wander off that reservation. I leave the vice crimes to my head of vice."

"Then why are you investigating this?"

"Because, Mr. Caruso, this had gone beyond vice to murder, and I have a hand in all murder investigations. Way to keep my department on the clean side."

A short scream echoed from inside the house. Garcia had his gun drawn faster than JT and ran in. JT followed.

They found the woman who'd answered the door shaking an unconscious blonde girl. "She won't wake up!"

"Back away," Garcia said, all business. He checked her pulse, then pulled out his radio. "This is Chief Garcia. I need an ambulance dispatched to my location

STAT. One female, twenties, unconscious. I have a pulse, but it's weak."

"Chief, there's blood," JT said.

The chief looked to where JT pointed. Her blanket was soaked with blood. The chief pulled it down and saw a towel and gauze wrapped around her bottom, all soaked red.

The chief said, "She's lost a lot of blood, appears to be hemorrhaging. She's covered in bruises and—sweet Mother Mary—bite marks. There's been an attempt at medical care."

He listened, then said, "ETA five minutes. The hospital isn't far."

He turned to the woman and said firmly, "If Sue-Ann dies, I will arrest you for accessory to murder after the fact for not bringing her to the hospital."

"I didn't have to! We brought in a doctor!"

JT's stomach sank.

"A doctor came here and did this?"

"Yes. Yes! Early this morning, before six!"

"What's his name."

"I—I don't know. It's a girl doc. She just went by Doc. She was blonde, I don't know! I don't know!"

"Who brought this doctor."

"I—I—"

Now the woman was scared. Terrified. She wouldn't say a word, not if Hirsch was behind this.

"You will be telling me everything," Garcia said. "Turn around. You are under arrest."

JT looked at the unconscious girl. Bella had been here, had tried to help, but this girl needed emergency medical attention. And Bella had just walked away.

Walked away knowing she would likely die.

Before six.

Papi Chavez had died around eight this morning.

Bella—what have you done?

* * *

Bella stayed in her room most of the day. She exercised in the small space. And paced. And drank water. She couldn't keep down any food. Damien didn't seem to think anything was odd, which was good because she didn't know how long she could hold it together. Not anymore.

Damien had killed a man *for her.* Because she had been justifiably angry at how poor Sue-Ann had been brutalized by that drunk bastard. She had no remorse that Papi Chavez was dead, what did that say about her? Yet . . . she would never have killed him. Damien did it as a sense of . . . what? A noble gesture? Did he think he was a white knight?

Bella had done a lot of things she hadn't wanted to do while undercover, but she'd never—not once—slept with anyone she didn't want to sleep with. She made out, flirted, teased, but she never screwed anyone unless it was on her terms.

She could not—would not—sleep with Damien Drake. The thought made her physically ill. She knew who he was and what he had done, and that he'd fixated on her somehow, thought of her differently than other people in his life, disturbed her.

What happened if he found out who she was? If he found out she was undercover? That she had been a cop?

He wouldn't. He *couldn't* learn the truth before she got away.

Contrary to what she'd told her brother, she hadn't abandoned the phone Sean Rogan slipped in her pocket. Simon was too far away to help, and she was beginning to wonder if he would actually come and extract her.

But JT would. Her brother had never let her down. For years she'd used his guilt against him. She hated that about herself, but JT had felt so guilty that he'd been overseas when their dad gave her to Sergio. It wasn't JT's fault—none of it was his fault—but she never told him that. She never told him she didn't blame him. Did that mean in the back of her mind she did? A little bit? Or that she just wanted him to feel as guilty as she felt? Because of the things she'd been forced to do. And things she hadn't been forced to do. Like escaping.

And costing Julie her life.

Bella reached under the mattress for where she'd hidden the phone, then there was a knock on the door. She froze.

"Yeah?" she called.

"You sleeping?" Damien.

"Trying."

"Mr. Hirsch is here. We need to talk."

Talk? About what?

"Coming."

She left the phone where it was. How long would it take JT to get from San Antonio to Port Arthur? That was, if he went to San Antonio. Four, five hours? She didn't know. Kane could fly a plane—she'd text JT tonight, ask him to get her out. Call in the cavalry and arrest Hirsch and Damien.

She had failed. She hadn't found Hope.

But Bella didn't want to die, and everything had already gotten out of hand. She had enough evidence against Hirsch to stop him, and everything else was icing on the cake. And maybe, just maybe, they could flip Damien into telling them where Hope had been sent—or confirming that she was dead. To give her grandparents closure. A small thing, but still important.

She opened the door. Damien was standing right there. Too close. He ran his hand up and down her arm. She didn't flinch.

"Z is coming. Let me do the talking."

"Is this about this morning?"

"It's gotten complicated."

Damien led the way to the dining room. Hirsch was sitting at the head of the table. Not eating, not talking on the phone, just staring straight ahead. As soon as Damien and Bella walked in, Hirsch scowled. "You should have talked to me first," Hirsch said. "What the fuck got into you, Damien?" He turned to Bella. "Did you tell him to kill the john? That girl was just a whore! Now the heat is coming down at the worst possible time."

The cops found Papi's body. That was the only explanation for Hirsch's anger. No—Hirsch wouldn't care about that, unless it led back to him.

It wasn't Papi. The police had traced Papi to Sue-Ann. *That* was why Hirsch was furious.

"For *two fucking years* Port Arthur has been safe. Under the radar. A perfect spot to coordinate our operation. And the cops arrested Gino on suspicion of murder. But we all know Gino didn't kill that prick, don't we?"

"The cops don't know that, sir."

"But you do!"

Damien didn't budge. "They'll have enough evidence if they're halfway decent cops. The gun's in his car."

Damien must have planted the evidence after he brought her back here this morning.

"Don't be an idiot."

For the first time, Damien directed his anger at Hirsch. The tension in the room increased ten-fold.

"Let me spell this out for you, Damien," Hirsch said. "The cops traced the john to Gino and Gino to Sue-Ann and found the whore unconscious. She's in the hospital having surgery as we sit here arguing about whether I should shoot you in the head."

Damien glared at him. "Do not threaten me."

"Carter's now a liability," Hirsch continued as if Damien hadn't spoken. Did Hirsch not realize that Damien was a greater threat? "The whores in the house gave her description to the police. Not yours, which is good because I don't want to lose you. We've been through too much together. But this is fucked, and Carter is a problem."

Bella froze. No fucking way. Her cover hadn't been blown, but she was going to be executed anyway.

"I'll take her back to L.A. with me."

"Too risky."

"Don't talk about me like I'm not here," Bella said.

"You don't have a say in this."

"I went to that house because *you* ordered me to!"

"I didn't order you to kill the john!"

"I *didn't*. But if you let your merchandise be abused like Sue-Ann, then you won't have much of a business left, will you?"

"Watch your mouth, Dr. Carter. Never forget that you're as expendable as any of the other whores."

Damien tensed. He was going to do something rash. When had he become an emotional juggernaut? This was going to get them nowhere. Bella had to buy time.

She put her hand on his arm. Gently squeezed. "D, Hirsch is right. I'm sure he has a plan."

"You're not a whore," Damien said.

Hirsch grunted. "All women are whores, Damien. Just because she has a brain between her ears doesn't mean she doesn't use the hole between her legs to lead you around by your dick."

Every muscle in Damien's body rippled. She could see it—she could feel it—why didn't Hirsch realize that he'd created this monster and his monster was going to turn on him?

"Let's go, D," she said. "I don't want to go to jail, I

don't want you to go to jail, either." She lied so smoothly now she wondered if she'd ever learn how to tell the truth.

"Z is here, no one is going to do anything until we figure this out. Too much is at stake."

The door opened and a squat, broad shouldered man in his forties walked in. He had a thick head of brown hair and cold blue eyes and walked with the swagger of a man who resented his lack of height.

Tommy.

"It's been one fucking screw up after another," Tommy said. "Phoenix, El Paso, this mess—I told you to take care of the whore, and by *take care* I meant if she can't work, she needs to be at the bottom of the fucking ocean. And now San Antonio is in jeopardy. And it's your people, Martin. Your people are screwing it up.

Tommy looked from Hirsch to Damien to Bella then back to Hirsch.

He didn't remember her. It had been eighteen years, she'd been a young teenager then, he didn't remember her.

She almost breathed easier.

"My people are not the problem," Hirsch said. "I told you expanding too fast was going to raise flags."

"Because you put the wrong people in charge. It's that Desiree bitch. I told you that black whore was a liability, that she didn't want to get with the program. She's now in jail, and she'll flap her gums."

"She doesn't know anything about Port Arthur."

"But she knows about *you.*"

Tommy turned to look at Bella again, frowned. He recognized her, but he hadn't placed her.

She had to disappear before he remembered.

"What happened in San Antonio?" Hirsch asked.

Tommy turned back to him. "Really, you don't know? I found out fifteen minutes ago when my bitch Ginger called and said her house had been raided. She'd left Desiree there to watch the girls and wham-bam, the feds show up! FBI, DEA, SAPD, SWAT, everyone and their brother came to the party. They have fourteen of my girls. They weren't even supposed to be there, until you fucked up El Paso. They were supposed to be on a fucking *ship* by now. But El Paso was a clusterfuck and now you don't even know that the police raided San Antonio. I don't fucking believe this. How long have we known each other, Martin? *Eighteen years.* But you saving my ass once doesn't buy you a free card for lifelong stupidity."

Martin Hirsch saved Tommy? Eighteen years ago? When Bella escaped and Sergio had been killed? How? Hirsch had barely been out of prison then.

Small world. She almost laughed, except she was so terrified right at that moment that she didn't dare open her mouth.

"You forget that it's my contacts, my associations, that built our network," Hirsch said. "My network thrived on maintaining small organizations throughout the country where any one that is taken out, they can never rat on anyone else. Everything was self-contained until you wanted to expand overseas. You're the one who insisted we bring Desiree out from Los Angeles, not me. So don't put all this on my feet. We can and should go back to the small cells. Regroup and continue the expansion on the original timeline. For every trucking company the cops find, I have three more they know nothing about. You've always been the brawn, Z. I have always been the brains."

Tommy did not like being ridiculed or made to feel stupid. Bella could have told Hirsch that. It was why Tommy liked to bully Sergio's prostitutes, because Sergio would belittle him, and Tommy couldn't stand it.

"Why is there a whore here?"

"This is Dr. Carter."

"From the mobile clinic?"

Hirsch nodded.

Tommy stared at her. He was thinking.

Thinking would get her in trouble.

Hirsch's driver came in and handed Hirsch a note.

"What the hell does that say?" Tommy demanded. "No secrets, Martin."

"We had a situation this morning, but it has been resolved."

"What situation?"

"Local pimp made a mistake. He paid for it with his life." Hirsch turned to his driver. "Confirm all this, get back to me, and be ready to leave if we need to."

Hirsch was protecting Damien and, de facto, protecting Bella by not telling Tommy everything that had happened between last night and this morning. She didn't read more into it—Hirsch would throw her under the bus if it would save him or his business. But she'd take anything she could get right now.

The driver left and Tommy sat down at the table with Hirsch. He turned to Damien. "Take your bimbo to bed, the big boys have business to discuss."

Damien gave Tommy the evil eye and both Tommy and Hirsch straightened their spines. Then he turned and ushered Bella out the back door. They walked down to the small private pier that extended forty feet into the bay. The water wasn't blue—it was a slimy green along the rocky shore. But Bella breathed in relief.

"I'm sorry you had to be treated like that."

Damien hadn't cared what Hirsch said to her in the past. Or maybe he had, he just hid it well.

"Look, I knew what I was signing on for, okay? I needed money, Hirsch was paying. I'm no saint."

"I won't let them hurt you, Doc. I promise."

"You said you had business in L.A.—why don't we go now? With the heat coming down on Gino, it might be best."

"I have to be here tomorrow."

"Why?"

"No questions. Just trust me."

Trust him. Right.

"Okay," she said.

She wouldn't be here tomorrow, anyway. If everything worked according to plan, JT would bring RCK in to raid this place and she would be safe.

They sat outside for nearly an hour, not talking, and Bella finally felt slightly less apprehension than earlier. Damien looked at his phone. "They're done. Let's go back."

Suddenly, she didn't want to go back. What if Tommy was still there? The longer she was around him, the more he might remember.

"D—"

He stopped, faced her. His face was unreadable, like always.

Like always except when he told you he loved you. Except when he kissed you.

"It's nothing," she said. "Let's go."

She followed him back into the house. As soon as they stepped inside, Damien was grabbed by two men and Bella was grabbed by Tommy.

"Bella," he said, spittle flying from his mouth. "As soon as Martin said your name, I knew I recognized you. Just took me a few minutes to figure out from where."

He slapped her so hard she fell to her knees.

Damien fought the two men. He elbowed one in the nose, breaking it, then slammed the head of the other into the wall, cracking the plaster.

"Enough!" Hirsch yelled. He had a gun on Damien. "Did you know?"

Damien's nostrils were flaring. "You'll be sorry."

Tommy said to Damien, "Did you know that her

name is not Isabella Carter and she isn't a doctor? Her name is Bella Caruso. She was a whore for Sergio until he was killed by a team of mercenaries. It took me a long time to figure out exactly what happened that night, but it was you, all along. Your brother was in the Navy and then it all made sense. You betrayed us."

She didn't bother denying it. He wouldn't believe her anyway.

Damien froze.

"Want proof? Look at her tattoo. On her right shoulder."

Damien hesitated, then pulled the back of her shirt down, partly revealing her falcon tattoo.

"There're letters there somewhere. I know, I put them there. She might try to hide them, but she can't. SXC."

Damien must have seen them. Bella closed her eyes and waited for the bullet to end her life.

Tommy said, "Martin said she saved your life, Damien, so I'm giving you a chance. Are you with us?"

"Yes," Damien said. His voice was back to the cold, emotionless robot he'd been for the last year. Before he decided that he had feelings for Bella—feelings he'd never had before.

They were now gone.

And Bella was as good as dead.

"Restrain her. I need to know why she's here and how much she knows. I'll bet you she's the one who has jeopardized our entire expansion, and she will pay for it. Slowly." Tommy leaned over and whispered in her ear. "And very, very painfully. I will enjoy torturing the truth out of you, Bella Caruso, and then I'll leave your bloody, broken body on your brother's doorstep."

CHAPTER THIRTY

Sean got off the phone with Kane. The situation in Port Arthur had gone from bad to worse.

He was at DEA headquarters, but he let Lucy do what she did best. She was running the task force with cool precision, had tasked Brad's tech guru Aggie with mapping out all the locations Meyer had given them, and they were creating a plan of attack. Sean could have helped, but his help wasn't needed. Brad let him sit in his office, so he closed the door and used the privacy it offered.

He dialed an unlisted number. Mona Hill picked up after four rings.

"Yes."

"It's Rogan."

"Of course it is."

"The Port Arthur police had a warrant for murder for a pimp named Gino. His body just turned up. We think Hirsch ordered his execution to protect his operation."

"And why would I care?"

"I need information."

"I gave your cop wife everything I know."

"Something big is going down in Port Arthur. One prostitute is already in the hospital. I need to know what their plan is."

"I'm not in business with these people. I told you that."

"Mona—"

"Odette. Call me that name again and I will never answer your calls."

"Odette, you have always been the queen of information. You know what's going on. Or you have a good idea. There are lives at stake, including a fourteen-year-old girl."

Silence.

He waited.

"There's one rumor related to Port Arthur. If I tell you will you leave me alone?"

"For a while."

"You're a bastard, Rogan."

"Tell me what you know."

Brad walked into his office, planning on making a private call, and was surprised to find Sean still in there. He was on the phone. Brad didn't feel he needed to afford him privacy considering this was *his* office and Sean wasn't even a cop, but he made a motion to leave and Sean shook his head and put up his finger.

"How certain are you of this information?" Sean listened, then said, "I appreciate it. . . . No, it doesn't mean I won't call you again." He hung up.

"News?" Brad said.

Sean got up and closed the door.

Brad frowned. "Your office vetted my office, I thought you of all people trusted everyone here."

"I do. But I have information, and I can't tell people where I got it."

"Okay." Brad was getting used to this. He worked with Criminal Informants all the time. Sean was hardly a CI, but if there was ever a grey area, it was RCK.

"Based on what Bella said and what we've been able to ascertain with Hirsch and company moving east, we thought he was shipping girls out of the country. On the contrary, word is he's *expecting* a shipment. All these little moves here and there along I-10? To solidify his network and expand his market."

"How many are we talking?"

"Don't know. But it seems dozens of pimps from Florida to California are *all* expecting six to eight new girls tomorrow."

"Sunday."

"And they're coming in through Port Arthur."

"Your brother is there, right?"

Sean nodded. "They know Hirsch landed, but they haven't found him. The one potential witness is dead—a local pimp suspected of killing a john. My guess is Hirsch had him whacked to keep him from talking. The girls in the house they raided aren't talking, and the one girl who might talk, she's still in critical condition."

"What do you think we should do?"

"Send a team to Port Arthur."

"Wouldn't a big federal splash put Bella at risk?"

"Maybe. But the feds will lose track of these girls as soon as they are moved along Hirsch's pipeline."

"Four of the houses on Meyer's list are in Port Arthur and Beaumont. I'll bring this up to the task force, but ultimately, it's Donovan's call." Brad opened the door, glanced back at Sean. "You know what Donovan will do, don't you?"

"Pretty much. My bag is already packed, and I have Kane's plane fueled because he took mine."

"Military transport would be faster."

"Your call, as long as I can hitch a ride."

Brad nodded, and left Sean to do who knew what. Sometimes, Brad was amazed at how he got his information.

He found Lucy in the conference room directing his staff. It burned him that Rachel was being stubborn about this task force. Not because Brad had to use his staff—he and the FBI shared frequently—but because she hadn't come by at all. Brad had reached out after the interrogation and asked her to observe. She hadn't shown up.

But Jason Lopez was here, and he was watching closely. Too closely. It was like he was Rachel's spy, and that didn't sit well with Brad.

Brad approached Lucy and gave her the information Sean had uncovered. She walked immediately over to the map she and Aggie had created and added flags to the pins already there. "Brad—you understand smuggling using shipping routes far better than I do. How can they get people in here? This isn't a deep sea channel, is it?"

"They have a small port authority, but they can handle major vessels. However, they wouldn't go through any legitimate facility—not one that's so small. It's easier through a large busy port because they can't check every single container. My guess is that they'll bring in a ship to the middle of the gulf, then unload their cargo to several smaller ships that will skirt under the radar, so to speak. It's still risky, but human trafficking is a two-way street—criminals in the U.S. import people as well as export them."

"They would need a house or . . ." Lucy snapped her fingers. "Trucking company on this waterway."

"Trucking company, my guess. A house taking in a few dozen—or hundreds—of people? Don't see it happening, even in the middle of the night. But a business, maybe. If there was one that fit their needs."

Aggie said, "Agent Murphy is calling, says it's urgent."

"Speaker," Lucy said.

Aggie transferred the call in the conference room.

"Gianna, it's Lucy and Brad. What do you have?"

"My cop found the Moore brothers holed up in one of their flops. We tag-teamed them. They were scared shitless, excuse my language. What went down in the bar was unexpected, and they squealed, begged us to protect them. I'm sending you everything we got, but there are two takeaways. First is when they made the agreement with Hirsch they were told that they would be in control of the sex trade in El Paso in exchange for a percentage and access to Hirsch's transportation network. The network was primarily for prostitutes, but they would take guns, drugs, documents, whatever was needed for an extra fee. They'd be given a liaison to work with to make everything run smooth."

"Sounds like a protection racket," Brad said.

"It is, but everything's sugarcoated. The Moores were idiots not to see it, nor to realize that if they were in charge of the sex trade, that means Diaz is dead. Diaz wouldn't play ball with Hirsch, Hirsch had him killed. They really did not see that coming."

"Which is why our jails are full," Brad added.

Gianna laughed. "Second tidbit? They were expecting a brothel with thirty girls, all trained, all ready to work, of all shapes, sizes, and races. They'd be delivered next weekend with their liaison."

"Hirsch was delivering a brothel," Lucy said flatly.

"Staffing a brothel, I should say. The Moores were to find a minimum three locations to house them and move in their own girls as well. They planned on reopening their uncle's run-down bar and working the girls out of there."

"Do they know where Hirsch is now?" Lucy asked.

"I thought we knew he was in Port Arthur?"

"We do, but we need an exact location."

"Truly, they don't. Hirsch told them he was solidifying

agreements across Texas, and they didn't ask for specifics."

"Good work, Gianna," Brad said.

"I have something else—we found Milo Feliciano. He's dead. He'd been hiding out with his mother, but left because he'd heard the heat had died down a bit. He was shot in the head while he sat at a stop light in broad daylight this afternoon."

"Who?" Brad asked.

"My guess? Hirsch still has people here, and they think Milo sold them out after the raid on the trucking company. His mother knows nothing, as far as she's concerned he was just under the weather."

"Okay, thanks," Lucy said. "Be ready to work on a simultaneous raid."

Brad raised an eyebrow. "Simultaneous?" he said.

"I'm working out the kinks with Kate, but I think we can make this work."

"I'm yours when you call, Kincaid. Out."

Brad looked to Lucy for more info. "Define."

"We have thirty-two addresses from Meyer. If we take down only those in the area, the others have time to move. If we can coordinate with all the FBI offices and local police, and raid them at the exact same time from Los Angeles to Shreveport, we have a chance of taking them all out—and finding out who might be on Hirsch's payroll."

"That takes a lot of time and organization."

"Kate's doing it—don't underestimate her."

"Or you."

"Or Aggie," Lucy said. She glanced around and then lowered her voice. "That girl drives me a little crazy, but she's smart and anticipates what I'm going to ask for next. It's kind of . . . disconcerting, but I'm not complaining."

Brad smiled. He glanced up and saw a familiar profile walk by the open door. "I'm glad I got her. She was an Army brat, I'd give her a break on the quirkiness. Let me know when we roll."

"Go take a nap—it'll be late tonight or early tomorrow morning. I'm thinking early on a Sunday morning would be a fine time to raid thirty-two houses."

He didn't disagree, but he'd wait until Donovan put the next-to-impossible task together. He'd organized Operation Heatwave and while it had been substantially larger in scope, it was focused in San Antonio, he had two months to put it together and an entire squad of support staff.

"Can I get you coffee?"

"Actually, Aggie has kept me properly caffeinated," she said and smiled. The only sign that Lucy was tired was the circles under her eyes, but Brad knew she wouldn't rest until they had a plan in place.

He stepped out and found Rachel standing at the one-way mirror looking into the conference room. "I'm glad you came."

Rachel didn't look like her old self. She looked tired and overworked and she'd only been in San Antonio for five months.

"I don't know why you had me come here, other than to rub my nose in the fact that I have no control over my agents."

"I asked you to come so you could see your agents in action."

"What did she tell you?"

"Nothing. She went out of her way to tell me nothing, so it was pretty clear there is friction between you."

Rachel turned to face Brad. "Why are you so loyal to a rookie? Did you date her or something?"

Brad decided not to be insulted. First, because Lucy was hot and she was exactly the type of girl he'd date. Second, because Rachel didn't mean it. "Lucy was assigned to Operation Heatwave when she first arrived in San Antonio. I didn't want her because I don't trust rookies. They make mistakes and screw up and we all pay for that. She didn't. Her instincts are better than almost every agent I've ever worked with. She flipped Anton Meyer so fast I thought he would tell her where Jimmy Hoffa was buried. You need to watch the tape. And she saved my life, Rachel. But that's not the only reason I trust her. I would take her onto my team in a heartbeat, no questions, she is that good—but I know she doesn't want to work in the DEA."

"Do you know her files are all sealed? I can't even access them. Half her colleagues think like you do—she's the next Eliot Ness solving cases right and left and being a damn hero. The other half of her colleagues are scared to death of her."

"I don't think so—"

"Barry Crawford hasn't made it a secret that he blames her and her husband for his kidnapping and torture. Yet neither she nor Rogan was brought up on charges, and there wasn't even an investigation. Some agent out of Sacramento—where RCK is headquartered—rubber stamped everything they did. Even I don't understand it, it had to do with asset forfeiture and money laundering. Other agents think that your boss was killed specifically as a way to get to Kincaid."

That pissed Brad off. "Stop right there. Samantha was a friend of mine, a good friend, and my boss. She was killed to get to *me.* If it weren't for Kincaid, I would have gone off half-cocked and ended up dead, just like Sam."

"Be that as it may, controversy surrounds her, and if her colleagues can't trust her, how can they work with her? Nate Dunning is the exception, not the rule. And I suspect it's because he has loyalty to her family. Special Forces tend to stick together. Then *this.* She worked this case—on her own time—when I ordered her not to.

I get called by the Assistant Director of the FBI and told to put her on a task force—over my objection. I told her she couldn't use FBI resources and then got another call from the AD of Quantico telling me they need my office. And then *you* call Leo and pull him into a SWAT operation without going through me."

"SWAT works directly under Abigail Durant, and you know that."

"But it was for *this* op! You don't see it." Rachel stared through the one-way glass. Brad tried to see Lucy as Rachel saw her, and he couldn't. Aggie was half in love with Lucy, thought she was brilliant, and people listened to her. At least, his staff listened to her because he had given her his stamp of approval *and* she had proven herself during Operation Heatwave. Now, Lucy was directing traffic, it appeared, and everyone paid attention and did their job.

"Are you not impressed?" he finally asked.

"I am. I think she's the best agent I've ever worked with."

Brad did a double take. "Then what's the problem?"

"Everything. My authority means nothing. Partly it's my fault—I came in here thinking I had a clean slate, when it's clear that there are huge problems."

"Maybe you should try to start again," Brad said.

"And then next time I give Kincaid an assignment she doesn't like, will she again call Rick Stockton? Come crying to you?"

"Kincaid doesn't go crying to anyone," Brad said, "and she didn't call Rick. JT Caruso and Rick were SEALs together. It's as simple as that."

"But my office should have been brought in."

"I agree."

She looked at him, eyebrow raised.

"I think Lucy would agree, too. This all happened above her. RCK is Rogan Caruso Kincaid. They made the calls to Rick, they worked the case before they even called Lucy for help."

"You can see why I find that hard to believe."

"But why do you have to question it? Maybe Lucy did know from the beginning. But she wasn't intentionally undermining you. I know her, I know how she works, and this conflict in the office is tearing her apart."

Rachel nodded toward the window. "She doesn't look torn apart. She's in her element, that is clear. She also looks like she won and I lost."

"This is not a competition. There are no winners or losers. You're not listening to me."

"I am." Rachel rubbed her eyes. "I get it, I do, but it remains that if I tell her no, I'll never know if that will be the last decision I make."

Brad could understand that, he supposed. It was intimidating to know that Lucy had connections to some of the highest people in the FBI. But it was also a benefit. "I guess it comes down to trust. And until you get that, you're right."

Brad walked away. He'd done everything he could to help Lucy and Rachel. He liked Rachel, he always had, but in the end, Lucy was not only a colleague but a friend. He would always be on her side.

Lucy found Sean in Brad's office. She shut the door and wrapped her arms around his neck.

"What's wrong?"

"Nothing. Everything. I just wanted to see you for five minutes. Kate's busting her butt getting thirty-two simultaneous raids together. I told her I wanted Port Arthur."

"Kane's plane is ready, but Brad promised military transport and they go much faster."

He kissed her and smiled, then his smile disappeared. She must really look like crap.

"What is it?"

"The vastness of this network. What's going to happen in two months? Someone will fill the void. It's heartbreaking."

"And what have you told me time and time again? That it's all worth it if you can save one. And you've already saved more than one."

"I want to find her, Sean."

She didn't have to tell him she was talking about Hope.

"Tia is talking to one of the girls who has been in the house for months. She knows Hope, she's being reticent right now. Tia thinks she knows more than she's saying."

"Do you want to go to the hospital and talk to her yourself?"

She shook her head. "Tia knows what she's doing."

There was a knock on the door, then Aggie popped her head in. "I've got Kate Donovan on Skype and she needs you now."

Lucy motioned for Sean to join her. It was nearly dark. Brad had ordered in sandwiches from a local deli, but she'd just picked at hers. She was surprised that Jason Lopez was still in the conference room—she thought for certain that he would bail as soon as the SWAT operation was over. Maybe Rachel wanted him to spy on her, report back.

She didn't trust what he would say, but she couldn't worry about that now.

Kate was on the phone with someone and had muted her end of Skype. When she saw Lucy she said something, then hung up the phone and typed on her computer.

"You got it, Luce," Kate said with a grin.

"Because you worked your ass off."

"Me? No. I tapped into the resources of every agent-in-training on campus this weekend to help me. It was a valuable training tool, so I should be thanking you for coming up with this insanely wonderful plan. Eight a.m. Eastern Time simultaneous raids in seven cities and thirty-two locations. Half the police chiefs and sheriffs think I'm crazy, the other half are whooping it up to have something fun to do. Damn, I love this job."

Eight a.m. was seven a.m. in San Antonio.

"To make it as easy as possible—ha ha—the local FBI office is coordinating in most of the locations. I have far more control over them then I do the locals. But so far, no police department has refused to help. With Murphy's help, DEA is taking lead in the cities where I got pushback from the SAC. I wasn't going to get into any departmental bullshit on this, and honestly, we're asking a lot. We have thirty-two teams of eight. We reached out to Genesis Road and the Dixons are sending counselors to every city to work with rescued victims. I have a federal warrant just waiting to be signed that will cover every jurisdiction, and I've been promised by the Assistant AG herself that I'd have it in my hot little hands—and all your inboxes—before midnight. All communications are going through me from the local teams, and I have enough people here to help me. Donnelly—you there?"

"Yes, ma'am."

"Ma'am? Really?"

Brad grinned.

"You're taking point in San Antonio. There are three locations there. That means twenty-four people. I've reached out to the FBI office and they will have twelve agents available, but you're in charge. You pick the team leaders and insure they have been fully briefed. However, I'm going to speak to every office simultaneously at six a.m. ET in order to fill them in on the mission and purpose before we send the teams out. Stockton thinks that having someone from on high give the big rah-rah speech will get everyone psyched. He'll be on my end, too. Questions."

"Port Arthur," Lucy said.

"It's yours. Grab a flight out ASAP, the team leader is SSA Bing Hamilton. Yes, that's his real name. Bing. He's the SSA out of Beaumont. He's expecting you. He's already put together a team—there are four locations in the Port Arthur/Beaumont area. He understands you have some autonomy in this, so you won't be assigned to a specific location, but you need to back him if he needs it. He's pulling in extras because I gave him the heads-up that the head honcho may be there and that we're also dealing with possible trafficked women from other countries coming in through their waterways."

"Do we have anything on Tommy Zimmerman yet?" Sean asked. "I've run him, but without more details I can't narrow him down. I have a hundred plus possibles."

"I've narrowed it some based on a profile from Dr. Vigo—he won't be married, he's between the ages of thirty-five and fifty-five, he's shorter than average, and has likely never filed taxes. But he does have a record—a man like him wouldn't have been able to stay clean. I have three men, two of whom have sexual assaults on their record. One in California, one in Massachusetts, and one in Virginia."

"Send them to me," Sean said. "You're amazing."

"I know. Better than you, Rogan."

"Dream on."

Lucy usually enjoyed Sean and Kate's friendly competition, but she was getting a headache and she wanted to get to Port Arthur as quickly as possible.

"Anything else, Kate?" she asked.

"Be careful, Luce. Everyone. And no one goes off the grid, got it?"

"Got it," Brad said.

Aggie disconnected the Skype call and Brad said, "Nate, I need you here, buddy, okay?"

Nate looked over at Sean, and Sean nodded.

"I'll go to Port Arthur," Jason Lopez said. Lucy had almost forgotten he was there.

"Because Rachel wants you to keep an eye on me?"

Jason was surprised by her bluntness; even Lucy herself was surprised.

"Yes," he said.

"Thanks for being honest."

Sean wasn't happy about it, it was clear, but Lucy was tired of walking on eggshells. She would earn this position on her own, or not. But she was done battling with her boss. It was exhausting.

Besides, she'd gotten a scoop on Jason from Suzanne in New York, who'd texted her earlier.

> Luce—I talked to some of the old-timers in VCMO and they remember Lopez. He was considered over-cautious but smart on his feet. A kiss-ass, but likeable and friendly. Wish I could give you more. Love ya, Suz

It wasn't much, but it rang true. He wanted to please Rachel and he felt guilty that he was following Lucy. But he had no balls when it came to standing up to Rachel. A people pleaser, her mother would have said. And add in that Rachel was his superior. Yes, Lucy liked him—he was a likable person. People naturally wanted to talk to him, which would make him good in the field.

But trust . . . that was something he was going to have to earn.

Brad said, "Lopez, you go with Lucy and Sean. Do you need anyone else?"

"I might take Nate back," Lucy mumbled. She really was hungry and snippy; normally she'd never say something like that.

"It's fine," Sean said, putting his arm around Lucy. He squeezed her shoulders, then dropped his arm. "You said you had a military plane."

"I'll call my contact, get you up out of Lackland in two hours?"

"Good. Nate—can you stay at the house tonight and feed Bandit in the morning?"

"Sure thing."

"And don't let him sleep on the bed again. Don't tell me you didn't—I found dog hair on the comforter."

"Busted," Nate grinned.

"And I thought Lucy would be the worst sucker for those sad brown eyes," Sean said. "Let's pack a bag. Lopez, I'll pick you up on the way to Lackland."

"I'll write down my address."

Sean winked. "I know where you live." He steered Lucy out. "You are going to sleep the entire flight, Princess. You're a zombie. And testy."

"It's been a long couple of days."

"That it has."

CHAPTER THIRTY-ONE

Anticipation of dying had to be worse than actually dying, Bella thought, as she sat strapped to a chair on a boat docked at the end of the haphazard pier.

Tommy had hit her only once, then had Damien restrain her. They left her here. Too far from people for her screams to carry, so she decided to save her energy.

But all she could think about was that Tommy would come back and finish the job. After he attempted to torture her for information that she didn't have.

She'd fucked up. She should have walked with Christina and Ashley. Hell, she shouldn't have even gotten in this deep in the first place. What had she been thinking?

You wanted to give the Hopewells peace of mind. The peace of mind that your grandma never had.

She didn't even know what time it was. Nearly midnight? Long dark, certainly.

She tried to get out of the binds, but they were tight. The chair was bolted to the deck so she couldn't scoot it over to a sharp edge to work on the ropes. She was trussed up like an animal, and her circulation was next to nothing.

The boat creaked. She held her breath.

Someone was on the deck above.

She couldn't see anyone in the dark, but the hull door opened and the frame of a large, fit man stepped through.

Damien.

He didn't turn on any lights—there might not even be lights on the boat—but he sat down on the other chair in the belly of the boat. He had a small flashlight, which he shined on her. She blinked from the sudden brightness, then her eyes adjusted. Damien was a dark shadow now.

"I told Z and Hirsch I would get answers from you. I don't want to hurt you, Doc, but I will."

He would. It didn't matter that he thought for five minutes that he loved her, that she made the sociopath *feel* something. Because he would hurt her and have no remorse in the morning.

"What do you want to know?'

"Are you a cop?"

"No."

"Z says you are."

"I was a cop. I didn't like their rules."

"Were you one of his whores?"

"You want the truth?"

"Yes."

"Yes, then. My father gave me to Sergio. Tommy worked for Sergio. So de facto I was one of *his*. Against my will. Like Christina and Ashley and so many others."

"Would it be better for them to give sick pleasure to their fathers or stepfathers or their mother's pimps than to learn to make a living on their own?"

He asked the question so matter-of-factly that Bella didn't have the opportunity to be disgusted. She tried to keep her voice as even as Damien.

"They deserve a choice. And no woman would choose to be held captive and beaten and forced to have sex with disgusting animals."

"None of us have choices, really."

"You do."

He shrugged, sighed. "You lied to me, Bella."

"Sometimes."

"You're not a doctor."

"No."

"You were a cop."

"Yes."

"Why did you work for us?"

"To find a missing girl."

"Who?"

And that was the crux of it. Tommy wanted to know who she was after so that he could find her and kill her. To punish Bella. Because Tommy was a sadistic bastard.

"I can't tell you."

"You have to."

"If I tell you, Tommy will kill her. He'll torture her and kill her right here, in front of me, to make me suffer."

"Why?"

How did she explain to someone who had no understanding of empathy?

"Why did you kill Papi Chavez?"

"Because you wanted me to."

"I didn't ask you to."

He seemed to consider that. "Do you regret he's dead?"

"No." Her voice cracked. She was telling him the truth. She didn't care one whit about Papi Chavez. Sue-Ann would likely die from her injuries. He deserved worse.

"Then why are you angry that I killed him?"

She didn't know how to explain. "Because it's murder."

"You killed the man in the bar."

It was like talking to a child. "He had a gun. He would have killed me."

"Papi damaged Sue-Ann and she can't work for a long time. You said it yourself. It's bad for business if we let the johns hurt our merchandise."

"They're people, Damien. Not merchandise. *People. Girls.*"

"Most of them would be dead anyway by now."

No remorse. No idea of what he was doing to these girls.

"Damien, you don't want to die."

"No."

So damn matter of fact she wanted to scream.

"Let me go, because I swear, my brother and his friends will hunt you down to the ends of the earth if anything happens to me."

"You're trying to scare me but it won't work."

"Dammit! My brother is a Navy SEAL. They don't give up. Tommy was right, JT came in and saved me from Sergio and Tommy eighteen years ago. Where was Tommy? He didn't die with Sergio. Because he's a weak bastard. He ran. He slipped away. He didn't stay and fight, did he? He ran and left his partner to die. And that's what he's going to do to you and Hirsch. My brother will come, mark my words. He knows where I am."

"I think you're lying to me."

"I'm not. He doesn't know exactly where, but he's here, in town. He was in El Paso. I saw him. He's not going to let this go."

Damien didn't budge.

"Dammit, if you ever cared about me, let me go. Please."

He stood up. "I thought I cared, but you taught me one important lesson, Doc. I really don't care about anyone."

He left, taking the light with him.

Bella screamed in frustration. What was Tommy

going to do now? Because he had a plan, and nothing that Tommy did would be good.

Damien Drake walked back to the house, an odd sensation in the back of his head. He really tried to understand what Doc was saying.

Stop calling her Doc.

But he couldn't understand.

He'd always been different from other people. He didn't remember his parents. He'd been told by one of his foster families that his father was in prison for murdering his mother, but he didn't remember any of that.

Yes you do. You saw everything.

He'd been three at the time. Or so he was told.

He'd been called names growing up, and that didn't bother him. What did it matter what someone called him? He took jobs in high school. Good jobs. Bad jobs. Got paid well for getting money out of shop owners. Went to prison because he was told to kill someone and he did. He was paid well for it, didn't rat, and got out in ten years.

Martin had looked out for him in prison just like Damien looked out for Martin. People liked to beat up Martin because he talked too much and thought he was smarter than everyone else. And he was smarter than everyone.

Except the doc.

So Damien protected him and no one messed with Damien. He didn't feel pain—he'd once bled so much that he passed out and he only felt an odd floating sensation. Two days later he woke up in the infirmary.

When he got out of the joint, Martin offered him a job. Protect him. Punish those who didn't do what they were supposed to. Collect money from deadbeats. He got to screw women who didn't say no, which was fine, but other than that brief release, he didn't much care for sex. He got the same release with his hand in the shower.

It would have been different with Doc.

When he kissed her that first time he'd felt something different. Something deep inside. For the first time he was really looking forward to sex. He thought about it all the time these last few weeks when he saw her. A slow, low ache. And the kiss ignited it.

But she was a liar. A cop. Maybe not anymore, but she had lied to him, to Martin, to everyone.

He walked inside.

"Well?" Hirsch demanded.

"She wouldn't tell me who. She came to rescue a girl, but she wouldn't say who."

"Did you punish her?"

Damien shrugged. "She's still tied up."

"So you got shit. Did you fuck her? You want to. I can see it."

"I wanted to. I don't anymore."

Z looked at him like so many people looked at him, like he was both crazy and weird. Everyone except Martin who trusted him. Damien wasn't going to let Martin down.

Doc didn't. She didn't look at you the same way as everyone else.

But she was off the table.

"She said something odd, though. Her brother was in El Paso. She saw him there."

"What?!?" Hirsch said. "Impossible."

"I figured it had to be at the bar. She claims he knows she's in Port Arthur, that she somehow communicated with him."

"She didn't know until—" Hirsch shook his head. "Either she's lying, or she has a phone hidden. Find it, Damien."

Damien searched the doc's room. There was nothing

suspicious—until he turned the mattress over and found the phone. He brought it to Hirsch.

Z took it out of Hirsch's hand. "This is it. This is how I destroy her." He opened it up. "One number programmed in here. Her brother."

"Why the fuck do you care about destroying her?" Hirsch said. "Kill her and dump her in the Louisiana swamp. Don't play games. We have a huge shipment we've promised to distribute this week, I don't have time to screw around with some former cop who feels all noble trying to get women to stop being whores."

Z said, "We have two problems. The first is that I don't trust Bella or anything that she's said. She could still be a cop. Or some fucking rogue cop wanting to go down in a blaze of glory. I don't plan on being a part of that blaze. The second is if she's right and her brother knows she's in town, he will fuck with our shipment. We have *one* trucking company here, and if they track it down, we're screwed. We do this the smart way." He smiled. "I have the perfect idea. That bitch will die, and if all goes well so will anyone who tries to rescue her."

CHAPTER THIRTY-TWO

Sunday

Lucy slept and Sean wrapped his arm around her, letting her head rest against his shoulder. They were in a C-27J, a small cargo plane that was also perfect for surveillance missions. Though it was loud inside the plane, it wasn't as bad as most of the military craft Sean had been in before. He loved planes, he loved the history of flight and the ingenuity of the Wright brothers and everyone who dreamed of the seemingly impossible.

But tonight, instead of talking or bribing the pilot to sit in the cockpit, Sean stayed with Lucy because she was exhausted and needed an hour of downtime.

He stared at Jason Lopez, one of the reasons for Lucy's sleepless nights this week.

"Just say it," Lopez said.

"Never follow my wife again without her permission," Sean said.

"Orders," Lopez mumbled.

"Hitler's men were just taking orders."

"Okay, that's enough. Shit, Rogan, do you think I wanted to do it? I feel like crap. I didn't know that Rachel had put a tracker on Lucy's car until Wednesday when she told me what restaurant she was eating at. Then it all clicked together. For what it's worth, Lucy won. Rachel knows she can't touch her. Doesn't make her happy, but that's that."

"That's not what this is about. There are no winners in this bullshit, only losers. Do you think Lucy hasn't been sleeping just because of the case? She understands Rachel, and she's far more forgiving than I am."

"What do you want from me, Rogan? I didn't want to be in this position. I like Lucy. She's smart. I don't like the gossip in the office, or the tension, or the fact that when Nate looks at me I think he wants to break my neck—and I know that he could. Everyone knows there's this . . . this *thing* between Rachel and Lucy, and people take sides or just try to ignore it."

"What do I want from you? Refuse to play the game, because that's exactly what this is. It's an intimidation tactic. I know them well."

"Why didn't you just kick me off the team?"

"Lucy wanted you on. Which pisses me off because she thinks she has something to prove to you and Rachel."

"At least you admit that you would have kicked me off if you had a chance."

"Because I don't think you have Lucy's back. I don't know what you would do if push came to shove. I've never seen you on the gun range. I've never seen you in active shooter scenarios. I've never seen you stand up for her or, frankly, anyone in the office. Your record is solid—but I don't know you and I've never worked with you. You already have two strikes against you."

"Do you think it was easy doing this? It's not. I didn't want to come. I'm walking into the lion's den, and I don't mean because Lucy knows Rachel ordered me to stick with her. I know RCK is in Port Arthur, and by sticking to Lucy that means facing people who already don't like me. I wasn't supposed to even be in San Antonio this weekend. I haven't seen my wife and kids in four weeks."

That surprised Sean.

Jason continued. "Bobbie didn't want to move them from school in the middle of the year. Andy is ten and plays baseball and I've missed every game this year. He's angry I took this position because he was going into travel ball next year, he's that good, and now he has to prove himself again. And Grace is six. She's putting on a brave front, and every night I've been gone I've called her after dinner to read to her. Except tonight. Because I have a case. I called her on the phone and said I was out catching the bad guys and would call as soon as I could. She said what Bobbie always tells me when she knows I'm working a dangerous case. 'Come home in one piece.' "

His voice cracked. Sean didn't have anything to say—it was easier to dislike someone when you really didn't know them.

"There is nothing on this planet more important to me than my family, Rogan. Nothing. I only took this position because Bobbie said it was the right thing to do, to help rebuild a struggling office. She's a nurse and loves her job, but she has to start over, too. Her parents live in Scottsdale and help with the kids when Bobbie and I are both at work. I don't know what we're going to do when we don't have family in town. My baby sister even talked about relocating here if she could find a job—she's in Colorado—because she knows none of this has been easy. I haven't even found time to look for a house, and Bobbie has to sell the house on her own because I can't help being here, which adds more stress and worry on all of us. So back off."

Sean did. He looked at Jason differently now—he hadn't wholly forgiven him for what he'd been complicit in, but he considered that maybe he had been stuck between a rock and a hard place, and he had other people in the mix to consider.

Sean closed his eyes, but he didn't sleep. Unlike his brother Kane—who could catnap anywhere, anytime—he'd never learned how to turn it off, just like that.

Family *was* important. Sean hadn't realized how important until recently. And the most important person in his family was right here, sleeping with her head on his shoulder.

At five a.m., Lucy and the rest of her group—RCK and Jason Lopez—arrived at the FBI RA office in Beaumont. It was a small, two-room office with a tiny SSA office in the back, housed in a government building downtown, and the assembled group was spilling out the door, everyone decked out in full gear. Sean, Jack, and Kane stayed back, letting JT be the point person for RCK.

Lucy introduced herself to SSA Bing Hamilton—a large, older black commander who had clearly served in the military and had the obvious respect of everyone in the room who knew him. Immediately, Lucy was at ease.

"My partner Agent Lopez, and JT Caruso."

"We talked on the phone yesterday," Hamilton said to JT. "Good to meet you all. AD Stockton is going to address the group first, then AD Donovan will give the tactical briefing." He motioned for them to follow. To one of the men in the room he said, "Torres, get the damn donuts and coffee in the hallway, that's why this place is so crowded. Didn't I tell someone to set up in the hall?"

"Yes, sir."

"You should fill up while you can, the way these men and women eat it won't be here long."

JT introduced Lucy to Port Arthur Police Chief

Garcia, who was standing with another of his officers next to a wall map. Four flag pins stood out. "We surveilled the four sites last night," Garcia said. "The blue flag is an apartment building, twelve units. It's going to be the most difficult to hit because we don't know if one or all of the units are potential targets. It makes it difficult for me to raid the place—there could be innocent civilians inside, with no confirmation of illegal activity. Are you sure your intel is solid?"

"It came from a suspect in custody," Lucy said. "Do you have police reports from that building?"

"Here's the sketchy thing—there have been several calls from neighbors into dispatch for domestic situations in several apartments—never from the apartment building itself. But every call has been cleared by the responding officer."

"Same officer each time?"

"Yes, and he's been relieved of duty."

"He doesn't know about this op, does he?"

"I don't know—not from me, but when you get this many cops in one place, word gets out. However, I pulled him last night based on a report from a recent arrest. It's bullshit, I made it up, but told him to go home and sleep for the weekend and we'd investigate the complaint. He was ticked off, but no more than any other cop who has a prisoner file a complaint."

Hamilton said, "Because the apartment is going to need more support, I've pulled pairs off all the other teams, and brought in every agent in my office, even those not on call. There's only eight of us in the Beaumont RA, but we're all here and accounted for. The DEA sent two extra agents as well, so we should be covered. But it means you'll be going to one of these three houses with a team of six."

"What are the situations in these three?" JT asked.

Garcia pointed to a red flag not far from where they'd

found Sue-Ann unconscious yesterday. "This house is run just like the place we shut down yesterday. Three bedrooms, one bath, only women live there, not a family. It's owned by the same company that owns the other house. Based on the setup and our drive-bys, I'm guessing six to eight women currently live there. We don't expect trouble taking it down." He pointed to the green flag. It was further out and appeared to be in an industrial area. "This one makes me itch. I personally staked out the place for two hours last night and there was a lot of activity. I didn't see any women—on the contrary, I saw four men, all carrying. The neighborhood is mixed use, and the house is falling apart. One of the men I identified as Brian Acosta, a lowlife who has been in and out of prison, but there are no active warrants against him."

"What was he in for?" Lucy asked.

"Assault, attempted rape, robbery, car theft. He's been out for the past year."

"And the yellow flag?"

"Small place on the river, no activity, though someone lives there—two cars were in the carport as of midnight last night—it's owned by Walter Grayson, but there's nothing on the guy—no record, no Texas driver's license, nothing. Could be an alias, or out of state owner. I couldn't get anything else over the weekend. There's a dock with two boats, though most of the places on that road have boats."

Lucy looked at the surveillance photos of each place.

"I want to be on the team with the green flag," Lucy said. "JT—if Hope is here, she's either green or yellow."

"How can you be so sure?" Lopez asked.

"Location. They're not going to make sex tapes with an unwilling, drugged teenager in an apartment building where there is even a chance that someone will become suspicious. And this building has neighbors on all sides. Like the chief said, there's been repeated calls into dispatch, so someone is watching the place. My guess these are all working girls, more or less willing.

"The green flag—the house with armed thugs, in a borderline industrial area—no one is going to call the cops. They're either too scared or part of the problem. It's also a large lot, no one too close. There's a basement—see these windows?—clearly boarded up. Multiple points of egress. The yellow flag—boats. Remember, word is they're bringing women *into* Texas, not shipping them out. Donnelly said they'd transfer them from a larger vessel to small vessels somewhere in the gulf, thus attempting to avoid scrutiny. Any residence with a dock on our list is suspect."

JT asked, "Are there any trucking companies in Port Arthur with dock access?"

Hamilton nodded. "We ran that after we got the preliminary report from Donovan last night. Two companies—one a major chain affiliated with the port, and one a small independent."

"The independent," Lucy and JT said simultaneously.

"The problem is that we're tight on people with the apartment building."

"RCK was cleared by the FBI to work this case. All of us have tactical training," JT said. "There's four of us here—but Stockton requested that we work with an established team, not on our own."

It sounded to Lucy like that was a sore point with JT, but she understood why. There would be a lot of attention on an op this size and if RCK acted on their own, a lot of people would know. And if anything went south, it would create far more problems.

Hamilton and Garcia conferred, then Garcia put a black flag where the trucking company was. "Eight minimum on the trucking company—because of the size and scope. But it's close enough to the yellow flag that if they get in trouble, yellow team can be there in less than five minutes."

"Thank you, sir," Lucy said.

"Let me rearrange the team," Hamilton said. "You and Lopez have green, we'll put two of RCK on yellow and two on black."

JT said to Lucy, "Where do you think Bella is?"

He was really putting her on the spot. She hesitated. "I don't know. Anyplace, really. It just depends what they need her for, in her capacity as a doctor. If the shipment of women already came in, my guess is that she's with them. If it hasn't, then . . ." She looked at the map. "The yellow flag."

"Why?" Jason asked.

"Because it's not owned by anyone we know to be affiliated with Hirsch. He's going to keep a low profile. He's on edge. Either Walter Grayson is an alias or it's an absentee owner or one of Hirsch's associates. There's line of sight out of all sides—tactically important. The waterway. I think Hirsch is there, or was there, and where Hirsch is, that's where Bella is."

Lucy's phone pinged, and so did JT's. Lucy looked down—Sean had sent a message to them, and copied in the entire Task Force.

With Kate's help, I've identified Tommy Zimmerman, aka "Z," the alleged partner of Martin Hirsch. Zimmerman, 41, was born in Bakersfield, California, and was in and out of juvenile lockup. Kate's working on getting his juvie files unsealed. He ran away from a group home for teenage sex offenders when he was sixteen. I ran a search on the address and there have been numerous public protests over this group home from neighbors, until it was shut down ten years ago. There's no active warrant for his arrest as the statute of limitations ran out on that charge when he was eighteen.

Zimmerman was in San Francisco where he was ar-

rested at the age of 21 for rape, but the victim was deemed unreliable and the charges dropped. He owns no property, has never paid taxes as an individual, and lives off the grid except for one key fact: he is on the banking records of West-East Transport, which is headquartered in Louisiana. The records are being further examined by the White Collar division. Kate is putting a white collar prodigy in charge of finding a physical address for Zimmerman using all the information we collected.

I couldn't find a recent photo of him, but downloaded his mugshot from twenty years ago and used age enhancing software to give you an approximate likeness.

"No," JT whispered.

"What's wrong?" Lucy asked, glancing around to see who was paying attention to them. Only Jason. Garcia and Hamilton were getting the Skype call ready for Rick and Kate.

"Tommy Zimmerman—he knows Bella. He *knows* her."

"I don't understand."

"San Francisco. That's where Kane and I found Bella eighteen years ago. He was there the same time she was. She told me about him—only knew him as Tommy. He was about twenty, she said, and he wasn't in the house when we raided the place. We figured he skipped town to avoid the heat, but never seriously looked for him because we had Bella, and she was safe. If he's here, he's going to know she's not a doctor."

"People change a lot in eighteen years. Especially a teenager."

But Lucy could see the danger, and she was just as worried as JT.

Before they could discuss it, Hamilton ordered everyone to quiet down. A minute later, Assistant Director Rick Stockton came on-screen.

"Thank you all for being here today at this historic moment. At no time in FBI history have we coordinated such a large multistate, simultaneous takedown—and never this fast. I don't have to tell you all that the FBI never acts this quickly." He paused, probably because he knew there would be some laughter. "But when the lives of innocent women and children are in danger, we can't wait to act. Kate Donovan, the new Assistant Director at Quantico, has moved heaven and earth along with all of you to coordinate this strike in less than twenty-four hours.

"AD Donovan will brief you on the overall tactical plan, but I want to give you a brief background. We're here today because one person refused to let an innocent child be exploited through child pornography. A civilian—former Seattle PD Detective Bella Caruso—learned that twelve-year-old Hope Anderson had been sold by her stepfather into a life of sex slavery. Hope turned fourteen last week. For fifteen months, she's been raped, abused, and moved from state to state in a blatant and cruel act of sexual exploitation.

"Caruso has been undercover for nearly a year trying to ascertain where Hope had been taken. In the process, she has directly helped rescue from forced prostitution a minimum of nine underage girls, the youngest twelve years old, and indirectly saved dozens from continued exploitation.

"The FBI became aware of this private investigation when Phoenix police officer Roger Beck, who helped Caruso bring two girls to safety, was shot and killed in the course of his heroic efforts.

"While we can debate vigilante justice any other time, today is not that day. Bella Caruso is one of our assets, and finding and extracting her safely is one of our primary goals.

"To restate: Our goals are first to locate and extract

the minor victim Hope Anderson. Locate and extract the FBI asset Bella Caruso. Arrest the known criminals involved in the multistate sex trade, and anyone else we determine through our raids is involved in their operation. Give an opportunity to those women who are willingly and unwillingly working for these people. In this order: all girls who you believe are under the age of eighteen or who tell you they are under eighteen will be admitted to a local hospital, put into protective custody until we can ascertain their name, medical and psychiatric condition, find their family, and determine if their home life is safe enough to return to. Any girl who is over the age of eighteen who gives you any indication that they want out of this business will be taken to a halfway house. Laura Dixon, with Genesis Road, an organization who works with and rescues sex slaves, is coordinating safe places for women who want to get out of the business regardless of their age. And women over the age of eighteen who do not want our help or who put your life in danger will be arrested and processed by the local police.

"Make no mistake: the work we do today will have a far-reaching effect on the sex trade all along the I-10 corridor. We are making a stand. We are standing with the victims and protecting them with the full weight and power of the Federal Bureau of Investigation united with multiple federal, state, and local authorities. You will not know what you are facing. I expect you to be cautious, but compassionate. I want no blue blood spilled today. I want no innocent blood spilled today. You are all well trained by your respective agencies, and I trust that you all will get the job done. Be safe out there."

Rick turned over the tactical end of the briefing to Kate, but it was clear that Rick's speech had both quieted and motivated the men and women who heard it.

"Damn," Lucy heard from a voice behind her, "why can't that guy run for President?"

She smiled at the thought as she imagined Rick hearing that comment. He would run far, far away. She glanced at JT, knowing he'd heard it too, but JT was frozen, fear locked on his face.

She whispered, "JT, we will find Bella. She isn't going down without a fight. She's a Caruso, don't forget that."

He nodded but didn't look assured. Lucy had nothing else to say that might make him feel better.

At exactly seven a.m. local time, Lucy followed her Green Team leader, the Port Arthur SWAT assistant commander Gordon Fall, into action.

They had a team of eight, and Fall assigned everyone clear responsibilities. Early was clearly a smart move, because no one was awake. They announced themselves and their warrant, used a battering ram simultaneously on the front and back doors, and cleared the decrepit, two-story house room by room. A dozen girls were there, all underage, all dazed and confused.

Two men were caught in bed with girls. Neither made a move for a weapon, and no shots were fired. The men were separated from the girls.

Lucy and Jason were tasked with clearing the basement. She motioned toward the staircase—the only way in and out of the underground floor. She led the way, gun drawn. She'd clipped a tactical flashlight to her gun because the lighting was so poor.

The basement was damp and reeked of mold. There was a studio down here, and when she found a light switch, bright lights lit the room. An empty bed. Two stationary cameras. Film lighting on the ceiling.

Her stomach twisted and she still pushed forward.

There were several rooms in the basement. One door had a lock on it. She broke it. Cautiously opened the door, flashlight covering the room in a wide sweep.

A blonde girl slept in a twin bed. She didn't move when the light hit her body.

Lucy found a light switch—on the outside of the room. There were no windows in the room, just the bed and a toilet and sink. Those who held her captive could lock her in the dark whenever they wanted. They controlled everything in her life.

Lucy quickly searched the room. Only the girl was there. She went to her side, looked at her face.

Hope.

She said to Jason, "It's Hope Anderson. Clear the rest of the basement."

Jason complied, and Lucy holstered her gun. She gently shook the girl.

"Hope, my name is Lucy Kincaid. I'm with the FBI. You're safe now."

"I don't wanna," Hope said, drowsy—or drugged. "Not now. I'm sick."

"Hope, I'm going to take you to the hospital."

Hope opened her eyes. They were unfocused. "Don't make me. I'm sore. Not today." Her words were slurred.

Lucy inspected her eyes. She was clearly under the influence of something that hadn't worn off. She was thin, far too skinny, and had bruises all over her body. Small bruises, from the fingers of men holding her.

"No one will ever make you do anything you don't want to. Never again."

Hope tried to focus on Lucy. "Who are you?"

"Lucy. My name is Lucy."

"Lucy."

Jason stepped in. He stared at Hope. "You found her," he said, almost as if he hadn't believed they would.

"She needs a hospital. Can you carry her outside?

Right to the ambulance. Don't let her out of your sight, Jason. Not for a minute."

Lucy's voice was tight.

"I won't. I promise."

Lucy turned to Hope. "Hope, this is Jason. He's my friend and partner. He's going to stay with you. He's a policeman too, just like me, and he won't let anyone hurt you. Okay?"

"A policeman," she said dreamily.

"I got her," Jason said. His voice was as tight as Lucy's, but he spoke to Hope with warmth and security. "Hope? I'm Jason. I'm going to take care of you now. I'm going to wrap you in this blanket and carry you outside."

"I can't go outside, I'm not allowed to go outside."

"You are now," Jason said. "You're going to be fine. I promise. You're safe."

Whispering to her, Jason carried Hope upstairs and outside to the waiting ambulance.

Lucy stared at the eight-foot-by-eight-foot room Hope had been in since she was moved from San Antonio on Monday. One week in this dungeon after more than a year of being exploited. Was this the worst she'd been in? The best?

Lucy breathed in deeply, forced herself not to scream at the injustice of what Hope had suffered. Of the memories that flooded through her of being chained to the floor and raped.

And the reminder that she did what she did because she could save girls like Hope.

Lucy walked upstairs and said to Gordon Fall, "We need to process the entire house. There's a studio downstairs with equipment—tapes, computers, the works. It goes to the FBI ChildSafe project. All of it."

"We've got it, Agent Kincaid."

The two men who had been arrested were kneeling

on the lawn, handcuffed, a cop standing watch. She wanted to hurt them like they hurt Hope. It overwhelmed her, this physical need to do violence. And it shocked her, because it came on so suddenly, so powerful.

She felt an odd kinship with Bella Caruso at that moment, and she hadn't even met the woman. Because Lucy could see herself doing the exact same thing, if it meant saving young girls like Hope Anderson.

She approached the officer guarding the two men. "Make sure the warden knows that they're pedophiles."

"Yes, ma'am."

And she walked away before she did something she would regret.

The lone female SWAT commander in Texas, Sally Chandler, led the small six-person Yellow Team. JT trusted Lucy's assessment, which is why he attached himself to Chandler, but he was having doubts. This was an ordinary house in an ordinary neighborhood that had mostly been reconstructed. The houses were set far apart, but nothing was so bad off that it looked suspicious.

Of course, looks were deceiving.

"And it's oh-seven-hundred," Chandler said. "Deputies, you two inspect the boat at the dock. Be alert, you have little cover on the approach. Park, Rogan—take the back. Caruso, you're with me." They started moving, and Chandler held JT back for a moment. "You're looking for your sister, and I'm not too happy you're part of my team because when family gets involved we make stupid mistakes." She stared him hard in the eye. "Are you good?"

"Yes, ma'am, I'm good."

"Follow my lead, Caruso."

He nodded, and they approached the house from the front.

There were two cars in the carport, the same two that had been reported from surveillance the day before. JT felt the hoods. Cold. He followed Chandler to the front door, keeping an eye on the nearby windows.

"On my mark," Chandler said over the com system, "three, two, one." She pounded on the door. "This is Commander Chandler with the FBI. We are here to serve a federal warrant and are coming in."

She nodded to JT and he used a small battering pole to force open the door.

Sally entered first and JT followed. He heard Sean and his partner break in through the back. Movement to the right had JT spinning around, gun aimed and read to fire.

An unknown man jumped up from where he'd been sleeping on the couch.

"Get down, put your hands on your head," Sally said.

The man put his hands up just as a new person came into the room. JT recognized him as Damien Drake.

"Keep your hands where I can see them," Chandler said to Drake.

Drake slowly put his hands behind his head. He didn't take his eyes from JT.

"You're her brother. You have the same eyes. She didn't lie to me."

As Chandler cuffed the first man, JT kept his gun on Drake.

"Where is Bella?" he asked.

"I don't know."

"I don't believe you!"

At that moment a gunshot went off in the back of the house.

"Armed suspect coming your way!" Park said over the com.

A man rushed into the room, seemed startled to find JT and Chandler in the living room. It was Martin

Hirsch, JT recognized him from the recent photos, and he had a gun.

"Drop it!" Chandler ordered.

Hirsch aimed at JT, his eyes wild. Drake moved at the same time, and JT thought he was reaching for a gun. But he rushed JT, knocking him to the ground as Hirsch fired his weapon. Chandler fired three times in rapid succession, hitting Hirsch in the chest twice and the head once. He was dead before he hit the ground.

Drake was on top of JT. JT pulled himself out from under his body and turned him over. He'd been shot in the gut.

Chandler had the first man handcuffed, and then approached Hirsch, gun drawn, and kicked his fallen weapon out of reach of any of the three suspects. She felt for his vitals.

"He's dead."

JT knelt next to Drake, putting pressure on his wound. "Call an ambulance!" JT said. Why had Drake jumped in front of him? Why would a bastard like him want to save JT?

"Where's my sister? She was here, right?"

"She didn't lie to me."

"What?" That's what he said before and it made no sense. "Do you know who I am?"

"Doc." Drake smiled. JT couldn't stop the bleeding. There was some serious fire power in the .45 Hirsch used. Drake's innards were leaking out of JT's fingers as he tried to hold them in, but Drake was smiling as if he didn't feel anything. "Doc's brother."

"Yes. The doctor. Where is she?"

"She said her brother was in town. I didn't believe her, but I wanted to."

"What are you talking about? Where is she?"

"Z knew her. Took her."

"Tommy Zimmerman has her?" JT didn't want to

think about what was happening with Bella. He must have known who Bella was when he saw her. He would kill her, if she wasn't dead already. "Where did he take her? Dammit, Drake, tell me!"

"He'll call you. It's a trap. He'll call because he's twisted that way. She said he was twisted and I didn't understand. Why hurt someone to hurt someone else? But now I know. I understand."

"You're not making sense. Where did Tommy take Bella?"

"Tell Doc for the first time in my life, I'm sorry. I never knew what feeling sorry was like—but I understand. I'm sorry. I'm sorry I didn't let her go when I had the chance. I wish . . . I wish I'd . . ."

Drake lost consciousness.

JT shook him. "Wake up!"

Chandler said, "An ambulance is on its way. There's no one else in the house or the boat."

Sean came in from the back of the house. "The surveillance photos from last night show two boats at the dock. One's missing."

Chandler said, "Park, secure this guy." She gestured to the man who had been sleeping on the couch. He looked confused and hungover.

JT left Drake and walked over to the man. "Where is Bella?"

"Who? What's going on?"

"The doctor! Where is she!"

JT hit him. He couldn't control himself.

"Caruso!" Chandler shouted.

Agent Park pulled the man up. JT took a step back, worked on his temper. "Where is the doctor," he said slowly. Methodically.

"I don't know. Really, I don't know! I just drive, see? I drive Mr. Hirsch where he wants. Z took the doc last night, out on the boat. I . . . I don't know why or what for, I'm just a driver."

Chandler said, "Park, get him out of here. I'll put an APB out on the boat. Rogan—which boat is it?"

Sean took his phone from his pocket, showed Chandler the surveillance photos he downloaded from the FBI server. "This one," he tapped.

"Keep an eye on your partner," she said and stepped out of the house, her phone already to her ear.

JT stared at Hirsch's dead body and felt nothing—not for Hirsch. But the panic was building inside. "She was here, Sean. She was here."

"We'll find her, JT. Zimmerman took her on the boat, he hasn't killed her yet."

"Drake said he'd call, that he was setting a trap."

"We have the advantage here," Sean said calmly.

"What advantage?" JT snapped. "A psychopath who tortured and raped my sister has her on a boat God knows where! What if it was Lucy? What would you do?"

Sean's jaw tightened. JT shouldn't have said that. "I didn't mean—"

"If it was Lucy I would find her. And we will find Bella, JT."

"We're so close, but she's not here." JT looked around the house, but didn't see much of anything. An ambulance shrilled in the distance. Hirsch was dead—no remorse there. But Damien Drake. He knew something. What the hell had he been talking about?

"Lucy just sent me a message. They found Hope."

"Is Bella with her?"

"No. Hope's on her way to the hospital, drugged, lethargic, malnourished, but alive. No sign of Bella or Tommy Z. That doesn't mean anything, JT, and you know it."

"Did someone tip him off?"

"Who? This op was tightly sealed. And neither Hirsch nor Drake was expecting us."

"I know." JT took a deep breath. He had to regain his edge. His training. He stepped outside, needing a clear head. Sean followed.

"JT?"

"I'm okay." And he was. Bella wasn't here, but she wasn't dead. Drake had made that clear—she would be part of a trap. A decoy, perhaps, to give Zimmerman time to slip away. "We're close."

Chandler walked over. "Okay, Coast Guard is up and out and has a photo of the boat. They are aware of the situation, they know Bella Caruso is an FBI asset and that Tommy Zimmerman is armed and dangerous."

"Thank you. I'm sorry I lost it in there."

"You didn't," Chandler said. "The suspect, Drake, saved your life."

"I don't know why."

"Seemed pretty happy that your sister didn't lie to him, for what it's worth. Maybe he had a change of heart at the end. Wouldn't be the first time a bad guy wanted redemption."

JT wasn't certain that was the situation, but he couldn't focus on Damien Drake right now.

"Sean, do you have any way—*any way*—to track that boat?"

"Maybe. I need my plane and some equipment."

"Do it. Whatever it takes."

Sean got on his phone and JT heard him say *Jack*. Interesting that he called Jack instead of Kane.

But JT forgot about Sean when his cell phone rang. He reached into his breast pocket, but no one was calling him.

The phone kept ringing. In his pocket. Sean's extra phone, and Bella was the only one who had that number.

"Bella," he answered.

"Bella can't come to the phone right now, but you will obey my instructions and do exactly what I say or I will torture your sister until she begs me to kill her."

CHAPTER THIRTY-THREE

Bella was tied to the railing of the boat as the sun continued to crawl up the sky.

Today could be the day she died.

But so far, it had been a glorious day. If she did die today, she would die knowing that something she'd done had made a difference. Somehow, someway, the FBI had swooped in and destroyed Martin Hirsch's entire operation.

She didn't know the details. But before dawn, Tommy had received a call from someone in Los Angeles. She'd overhead the conversation—at least Tommy's part of it. Multiple brothels had been raided and there were dozens of arrests.

Tommy started calling people, trying to find out more information, but few people could or would talk to him. It seemed that the raids were in multiple cities, not just in Los Angeles, and they'd all happened at roughly the same time.

She didn't know *how* they did it, but *damn* was she happy about it. She closed her eyes and tilted her face to the sun.

Maybe there really was a God out there, commanding an army of good people who battled evil. Maybe Laura and Adam were right. Faith could move mountains.

If only she'd found Hope. Maybe that failure was her punishment for every evil act she'd turned her back on over the last year. That she would die without knowing what happened to Hope.

Maybe she deserved it.

Tommy slapped her. She shook it off, looked up at him. His nostrils were flaring, his face red with anger.

"What did you do?" he said through clenched teeth. Before she could answer, he hit her, knocking her to the side. Her binds tightened and she grimaced, but she couldn't help but be pleased that Tommy had lost his entire business. And maybe she hadn't been directly responsible, but she'd gotten the ball in motion, hadn't she? She owed Declan a huge thanks—if she got out of this alive. He'd called the cavalry, and the cavalry was winning.

She spat blood onto the deck, the coppery taste reminding her that she was still alive. And Tommy was angry. Because she'd won.

If she died today, she'd die a winner.

"Get that fucking smirk off your face."

She braced herself for another blow, but his phone rang and he walked away from her. He listened for a moment, then said, "What? Anton is in prison? When? And no one told me? No one fucking told me? That idiot knows too much. Fuck!"

She opened her eyes when he stopped talking. He was staring out at the coastline. She pegged them being in Louisiana waters now, they'd moved east quite a ways before Tommy dropped anchor.

He looked down at his phone again, just staring. Then he pocketed it and pulled out Bella's burner phone.

Her heart skipped a beat as he pressed redial and waited.

Then he said, "Bella can't come to the phone right now, but you will obey my instructions and do exactly what I say or I will torture your sister until she begs me to kill her. Then I'll send you the video so you can enjoy it as much as me."

"He won't come," she said.

Tommy put a finger up, made it like a gun, and mock shot her. "We're on a boat in the Gulf," he told JT. "The Gulf is a big fucking place. Your dear little sister is tied up right now, and I don't think she'll get undone before the boat sinks to the bottom. One hour, give or take. I want one million in bitcoins deposited into my account immediately. And by immediately, I mean before the boat goes down. When I see the money there, I'll tell you where she is. If I don't, well, I'm not really sorry. You fucked with my business, and I'll fuck with yours."

He hung up.

"You'll never tell him where I am," Bella said.

"Of course I will. You both deserve to die." He pulled out his gun and shot her in the calf. She screamed with the sudden, burning pain.

"What the hell!"

"In case you get free. There's sharks in the gulf. Lots of them. You won't get far in the water." He leaned over her. "Just so you know? The boat isn't rigged to slowly sink. It's rigged to explode. As soon as your brother gets here."

He slapped her again and left the boat for the small dingy strapped to its side.

They weren't too far off the coast, she could just make out the shoreline, but he'd dropped anchor and they weren't close enough for anyone to see her let alone for her to scream for help.

"JT, don't do it," she whispered. Prayed. She shifted, wincing at the throbbing pain in her leg.

Of course JT would come for her. He always did.

She didn't want him to die.

She worked on getting out of her binds. Maybe, just maybe, she could find the bomb and disable it.

What are you thinking? You don't know how to disable a bomb.

But maybe she could teach herself how to pull up anchor and get the boat closer to shore, then swim to safety.

One thing Tommy was right about was the sharks in the gulf. But the closer she got to shore, the better chance she had of swimming in before they smelled her blood.

She hoped. Because she was way out of her league right now.

First things first. She began working on the ropes that bound her.

"It's done," Sean said.

"How—don't tell me." JT didn't want to know how many laws Sean broke to obtain a million in bitcoins and transfer them to Tommy Zimmerman.

"I just borrowed them. I'll get them back," Sean said. "Besides, the guy is an idiot—I've already traced his phone."

"He called me from the phone you gave Bella—you said there was no GPS on that."

"True. But before he called you, he was very active calling people. Kate Donovan has received multiple calls from local law that one phone number was calling phones that had been confiscated in the raid. My guess—someone called him about one of the raids, and he started calling around trying to figure out what was going on. He made those calls from a smart phone and, really, that's just not smart."

JT didn't understand how Sean was so . . . *humored* . . . in the face of Bella's captivity. He'd been smiling and cracking jokes as soon as JT got off the phone.

"Just knock it off, Sean. I'm not in the mood."

"We'll get her."

"He's going to kill her. He's never going to tell me where she is. He's never going to let her go. She's probably already dead."

"She's not dead. You heard her on the other end of the phone.

"Please, don't placate me."

They were still at Hirsch's house. Damien Drake had been transported to the hospital, but the prognosis was dire. Kane had called in with a report from Team Red: the trucking company raid had been a huge success. They'd found two hundred and thirty young women between the ages of sixteen and twenty from Chiapas and Campeche who had been promised jobs in the U.S. None of them spoke English, and all of them were scared. They'd been transported across the gulf in the middle of the night, arriving at three a.m. and locked into trucks.

Everyone had their hands full processing the dozens of arrests and hundreds of victims. And yet Bella was still out there, in danger.

"I'm not. Bella is off the coast of Louisiana, and I'm tracking Zimmerman's phone. He's moving from the boat Bella is on toward the coast."

"How the hell do you know where Bella is?"

"I hacked into a satellite. Don't be mad, I know I promised I wouldn't, but at least it's not a government satellite."

Sometimes JT didn't know whether to kiss Sean or hit him. "I don't want to know how."

"Good, because it would take too long to explain. We need to go—Kane and Jack are already on their way to Holly Beach."

"Where?"

"It's on the coast and highway 82, near the most direct way for him to get from the Gulf to shore."

"I'll drive."

"We're not going there. Kane and Jack are going to intercept Zimmerman. They're bringing a couple SWAT guys with them. You, Lucy, and I are going to get Bella off the boat. I did tell you I was getting my helicopter license, right?"

"But you don't have it."

"Semantics. I've put in the hours, I just haven't taken the test." He glanced at his watch. "But we really need to go now. Lucy is on her way to the helipad."

"You don't need to bring her into this, Sean—it's dangerous. I'm a SEAL, I can get Bella."

"Yeah, but Lucy is trained in underwater search and rescue, and one thing Jack has been beating into my head is to always have backup."

"I don't see him," Kane said as he peered through his binoculars. "Are we too late?"

Jack looked down at the phone app that Sean had installed. It showed a dot approaching the coast. "Look . . . five degrees east."

Kane adjusted. "Well, I'll be damned."

"Don't tell him he nailed it, your brother's ego is already big enough. A helicopter? Really?" Jack shook his head.

"We still have to get him. Do they have Bella yet?"

"Negative." Kane spoke through his com to the two officers who were assisting them. "Plan B."

"Roger."

If Sean and JT had already grabbed Bella when Zimmerman reached shore, they would have arrested him as he docked. As it was, they needed to confirm that she was on the boat—Sean had tapped into a real-time satellite feed, though there was a one-minute delay to view the data. So far, the boat was where it was supposed to be.

They wanted to grab Zimmerman quietly without giving him the opportunity to do anything foolish, like blow the boat or take a hostage. Though it was early Sunday morning, there were joggers running along the beach, children building castles in the damp, rocky sand, young lovers walking hand in hand in the cool morning breeze.

Kane adjusted the binoculars. "Zimmerman is getting in a black Chevy four-by-four."

"We have him in sight," SWAT said.

"Don't lose him. We'll meet up with you."

Kane and Jack left their hiding place and jogged over to the parking lot where they slipped into the back of the unmarked SUV. Zimmerman was just sitting in his truck. What was he doing?

"I don't have a good feeling about this," Jack said.

"Word from Sean?"

"Negative. But he's flying a helicopter solo for the first time in his friggin' life and a two-hundred-pound Navy SEAL is rappelling down a rope over a sinking boat and the Coast Guard is still ten minutes out. I'm going to cut him some slack."

"Why?" Kane said with a smile. "Let's take this bastard down, because I don't have a good feeling about this, either.

Bella had broken free of the ropes. It had taken her a ridiculous amount of time, and her wrists and fingers were raw. Her leg throbbed, but she'd taken off her shirt and tied it around her calf to stop the blood. A helicopter was flying toward her. She had to hope and pray that it was a rescue helicopter—but what if they got too close? What if she couldn't get off before the boat exploded? Was it timed or did Tommy have a detonator?

Too many what-ifs. She couldn't count on anyone but herself.

She might have to jump in the water and take her chance against the sharks. At this point, they seemed less likely a threat than the freaking *bomb* on the boat. At least she had a chance to make it to shore before they smelled blood.

She hoped.

She'd already tried to turn on the boat, but it was dead in the water. She had many talents; mechanics was not one of them. She didn't know how to hotwire or fix anything.

She searched the boat for anything she could use as a weapon, in case Tommy came back. Or a flare to signal for help. Nothing. No first aid kit, no flare gun, no phone, no working radio.

Well, shit.

But the helicopter could signal a lifeguard or something. She pulled herself up and balanced on her good leg and waved her arms.

The helicopter was descending. Were they in trouble? God, she hoped not.

A man climbed out of the chopper and balanced on the edge. What the hell was he doing? Rappelling down? The helicopter came closer to her—the man was only fifty feet away. Getting closer. And closer.

JT.

"Jimmy!" she screamed. She almost laughed. He hated to be called Jimmy. He'd been named James Terrence Caruso Jr. and he hated being named for their bastard of a father.

But Jimmy . . . that's how she knew him when she was a little girl. Her Jimmy. Her brother.

Her savior.

He dropped to the deck of the boat and Bella hugged him.

"Isabella."

She winced. "You know how much I hate that name."

He smiled. "Don't call me Jimmy."

Then he hugged her tightly, again, and wrapped a harness around her waist. "This is a makeshift rescue harness, we didn't have a lot of time to prepare. But it doesn't look like the boat is sinking."

"It will. There's a bomb."

JT's good humor faded. "Did you hear that, Rogan?"

"Kane's up there?"

"Sean. He's new at this. He heard, he wants to go now. Hold on."

She wrapped her arms around JT, and he had one arm around her waist and the other on a handle that was attached to the pulley. Suddenly her feet were off the boat and they were being pulled toward the helicopter slowly. Very slowly.

The helicopter swooped past the boat and headed toward shore.

Not a minute later, an explosion pushed hot air toward them, making them rock in the wake of the blast.

But they didn't fall, the helicopter didn't crash, and Bella smiled.

She was alive.

CHAPTER THIRTY-FOUR

JT had his head in his hands, taking ten by himself. He'd almost lost his sister.

His sister and everyone else he cared about.

No one had hesitated to help when he called on them. He expected it from Kane—Kane had been there with him from the time his father first went to prison, when they were kids. Kane had never questioned him, never said no when JT wanted to act. And this time, when JT's judgment was clouded by the threat to Bella, Kane had stood by him with sound advice and definitive action.

Kane was a rock, and JT realized so was everyone else. Jack, Sean, Lucy, Rick—no one backed down. They risked their lives and their careers to find Bella, and JT would never forget it.

His phone rang, and he almost ignored it. But he glanced at the number. Rick Stockton. He'd hoped he'd get a day before he had to deal with the fallout from this last week. Because even though they'd done a whole lotta good, they still had some things to answer for. Bella had things to answer for.

"Hey."

"How are you?" Rick asked.

"Alive. Good."

"Bella?"

"With the doctors. Zimmerman shot her in the leg. Not fatal, but they needed to go in and remove bullet fragments. She's recovering now, then I can go see her."

"This was a close one."

"Rick, be honest with me—how much trouble is she in?"

"I don't know, to be honest. But considering the success of this operation—and I mean it, it was a huge win for us—I think she'll be okay. I'll do everything in my power to ensure that. I'm sending Kate Donovan and Noah Armstrong out to take statements and interview everyone involved, including Bella."

"Armstrong? He's back?"

"It's not official, but he and I have been talking, worked through a few things. He's considering a couple assignments right now, but he's still on the federal payroll and is one of the few people I trust to wrap this case up. He and Kate make a good team. They'll be out there in the morning."

"Thank you." His voice cracked.

"Buddy, get off your ass and celebrate the win. Self pity doesn't become you."

JT smiled. "Roger that."

Lucy Kincaid walked into Bella's hospital room. She was awake, a bit pale, a nasty bruise on her jaw, but clearly she didn't want to be lying down.

Lucy understood exactly how she felt.

"We didn't really get much chance to talk in the helicopter," Lucy said. She sat down on the chair next to her bed.

"Lucy Rogan. Sean's wife." Bella smiled, tried to sit up, then winced. "Shit, I hate being immobilized."

"The doctor said the surgery was quick and easy, you'll be out of here tomorrow."

"I haven't seen Sean and Kane in years. Everything's changed."

"Some things," Lucy said. "We found Hope."

The surprise on Bella's face was immediately replaced with fear. "She's dead."

"No, she's alive. My team found her here, in Port Arthur, locked in a room. I'm not going to lie to you—she's in bad shape. She's been heavily drugged for quite some time, forced to create porn movies. The withdrawals are going to be bad, but they took her to a top facility in Houston where they're going to monitor her for a few days, stabilize her, and wean her off through controlled doses. I don't know all the details. Then she'll be placed into the custody of Laura and Adam Dixon. Who you know."

"Yes—how do you?"

"Through JT. We'll have plenty of time to compare notes, but Laura will be in Houston tomorrow to help Hope. And then maybe you can visit her as well."

"You found her. I—I've been looking for so long, I'd begun to believe she was long dead."

"I found her because you didn't give up. Once I had the information that you'd been working with, I contacted a friend of mine in NCMEC who sent me recent videos that we confirmed were of Hope Anderson. I analyzed them and located an address in San Antonio where one of the videos had been made. We raided a brothel, arrested Anton Meyer, I interrogated him and he gave up dozens of addresses."

"Anton? How'd you get him to talk?"

"Psychology. I'll see if I can get the FBI to let you watch the tape. You might enjoy it."

"I think I would."

Lucy had so many questions for Bella, and she wanted to get to know her better, but now wasn't the time. "My sister-in-law, SSA Kate Donovan, will be here tomorrow.

You can't leave until she debriefs you. She's working closely with Rick in DC. But I've already worked it out, and because you'll need to be available for more questions, you can stay with Sean and me in San Antonio for a few days, if that's okay with you."

"Yeah, sure, thanks."

She looked uncomfortable with the hospitality, but Lucy figured that was more her personality than anything. For the longest time after Lucy's rape she couldn't accept the genuine help of others. She always thought it was because they felt sorry for her.

She got up and said, "I'm really glad that we finally met. I know you and JT have been strained over the years, and I hope you can let that go. He moved heaven and earth to find you."

"It sounds like a lot of people did," Bella said.

"Yes. And he might not say it—because he's your brother, and I know my brothers get worried when I take on a dangerous case—but he's proud of you."

"I don't know if that's the word I would use."

"It's the word I did use."

"Do you know if Declan's okay? JT told me he was shot in El Paso."

"He's fine, going to be released tomorrow, he'll be interviewed by the FBI as well. So will your boss, Egan. But that's way over my pay grade."

"He's not my boss anymore."

From the doorway, JT said, "I'm glad to hear that."

Lucy looked from Bella to JT, then said, "I'll see you both later."

JT gave her a spontaneous hug as she walked out. "Thank you for everything, Lucy."

The door swung closed, and Bella surveyed her brother. He didn't look like he'd gotten any more sleep than she had.

"I'm sorry."

He shook his head, sat down, and took her hand. "Don't."

"I am. I caused a lot of problems."

"Well, I can't say I was happy to hear that you went undercover with a sex trafficking organization and put your life on the line, but now that it's over, you did good."

"Good?"

"Well—shit, Bella, what am I supposed to say? You risked your life over and over but in the process saved dozens of girls—hundreds if we count the girls rescued in this morning's operation. They're still weeding through all the reports and it's going to take a few days to have real numbers, but right now it's being floated that over three hundred fifty girls and women are being processed, and of those more than eighty are underage. The boat that came in yesterday? It had over two hundred women and children from Cuba, brought in ostensibly to work off their transport. They were told they would be doing domestic and agricultural work for one year. They didn't know they'd be working in the sex industry."

"I had no idea Hirsch reached that far." She caught his eyes, as always, surprised that she seemed to be looking into her own. They were so different . . . and yet they were blood. And maybe not that different. "What happened to Tommy?"

"He's not dead."

"You wish he was."

"Kane and Jack wanted to take him out, but they were working with SWAT, and Tommy tossed his weapons out. He didn't want to die. We believe the bomb was actually on a timer, not a detonator—SWAT didn't find a switch on him. He's not going to get out anytime soon, but Rick will need all your evidence and your testimony. We have to dig deep into him, but right now you're the only one who can actually identify him as part of the Hirsch operation. We're rounding up everyone else, but from what we can gather, everyone knows his name—at least by 'Z'—but so far no one can put a face to his name. Except Damien Drake."

"Damien?" She hadn't thought about him since Tommy took her from the house. "What happened? Where is he?"

"Sean and I were part of the team that raided the house where we found Hirsch and Drake. Hirsch had a gun on me. Drake took the bullet. Two bullets."

"He what? Why?"

"He somehow knew I was your brother, and when Hirsch realized he wasn't getting out, he wanted to take me with him, I guess. Drake he saved my life, but he's now in critical condition. If he makes it, he might be the only other person who we have to make a solid case against Tommy Zimmerman."

"He knows everything. He's smarter than Hirsch ever gave him credit for."

"Bella, be honest with me. Was there something else between you and Drake?"

"No." She sighed. "I manipulated him, I used him, and I didn't realize that he had developed—I won't call them feelings, because he's incapable of real emotions, but I'll call it, well, he was a bit softer around me than others. I heard through Hirsch that the police found the body of the john who had beaten up one of his prostitutes. She was really bad off, I did the best I could, but she's probably dead." That had been so hard for Bella—leaving, not calling help. It made her feel more like a monster than a good guy. "I was furious, pushed his buttons, and Damien drove over there and executed him. He told me he did it for me, because I was upset."

"That explains a lot."

"I had no idea he was going to do it. I have the address for the prostitute, maybe you can send someone to check on her."

"We found her. She's on life support in this hospital. It was touch and go, and she's not out of the woods, but you gave her a chance."

"What?"

"You slowed the bleeding so when we found her—in the course of investigating the murder of the john—we had the time to get her to the hospital."

"She didn't deserve any of it, but I was stuck—I didn't know what to do."

"I know."

"I don't. I don't know if I can live with myself."

JT squeezed her hand. "Bella. Don't. We all have to make tough decisions sometimes. Sometimes, there is no right or wrong."

"I don't know anymore."

She closed her eyes and considered her life. Whether she had a future. How she could live with herself after the choices she'd made.

"Focus on the successes."

"I don't know if I can."

"Work for me."

She opened her eyes, surprised. "What?"

"Don't look so stunned. I made a mistake three years ago when I let you go off with Simon Egan."

"*Let* me?"

"You know what I mean."

"Not really."

JT sighed. "Declan told me I was an idiot, that if I had offered you a partnership in RCK that you would never have worked for Simon."

"I don't know if that's true. You never gave me the opportunity."

"Because you're my sister, and I didn't know how to work with you, especially since we don't always see things eye to eye."

"I don't want your charity."

"It's not charity. I'm stubborn, you're stubborn. I realized, though, that Kane and Sean are better together. That having family makes the team stronger, not weaker. Even after everything that Lucy has been through, Jack always goes to her, trusts her."

"What about Lucy? I don't understand."

"It's not my story to tell, but she had her own crucible, things that happened to her that you would understand. And yet, Jack doesn't coddle her. And I think I tried to protect you from things you'd already faced. I didn't see it. I was blind with rage, with deep sorrow, with an overwhelming sense of failure. It was so much easier to leave you with Adam and Laura because they only saw the future, not the past. I'm sorry I failed you."

Bella didn't want to cry, but her eyes burned. "JT, you have never failed me."

"I want you back, Bella."

"I am. Forgive me?"

"Nothing to forgive."

She almost laughed. "I don't know if working for you is the answer, but I'll think about it."

"Jack and Lucy have another brother, Patrick. He runs RCK East, in DC, along with two other consultants. You don't have to work directly for me. But you can still be part of the family business."

"DC?"

"I'm outnumbered. There's three Rogans and two Kincaids at RCK. I wouldn't mind having you in the mix."

"Provided I'm not in jail for what I've done."

"We'll cross that bridge later."

"Okay." She took a deep breath. "I promise, I'll think about it."

JT leaned over and kissed her on the forehead. "I love you, Bella."

CHAPTER THIRTY-FIVE

Tuesday

Lucy took a deep breath and knocked on Rachel's door.

"Come in."

Lucy entered, closed the door behind her. She didn't know what to expect. At one point last week she thought that the next time Rachel asked her into her office she would be suspended pending review from the Office of Professional Responsibility. After everything that had happened since Wednesday? While Lucy wasn't expecting praise, she certainly hoped she wasn't being reprimanded.

"One minute," Rachel said as she typed on her computer. Lucy sat down.

Of course, she *had* emailed a request for three days off. That was almost exactly the number of vacation days she'd accrued in the last twelve weeks. This could be Rachel's way of telling her no.

Bella was flying to Seattle in the morning. Kate had already debriefed her, and she was debriefing all the non-government employees, while Noah was debriefing the government employees. Lucy had already talked to him. It had been bittersweet. She missed him, and was reminded how different it was working with someone like Noah—who trusted her explicitly, and whom she trusted with her life—and someone like Rachel Vaughn, who seemed to second-guess every decision that Lucy made.

Lucy really wanted to go to Seattle and talk to Hope after everything that had happened. Hope, too, was heading out there to heal at Ruth's House with Laura Dixon. Lucy had made a connection with Hope in Port Arthur, and she'd visited her again on Monday, before she returned to San Antonio. Hope needed all the support she could get right now, and Lucy knew, at least in part, what Hope had gone through.

Though Lucy wanted the time off, she realized she was asking for a lot, and already told Sean if Rachel denied it that she would finish out the week and they could fly to Seattle Friday night for the weekend. Not ideal, but she would be willing to compromise.

She wanted to make this work. She didn't want to leave the San Antonio field office—her friends, her house, her career. This case more than anything showed her who her friends were and that she had a network that she could tap into at any time. Brad had been solid. Nate had had her back, as always. Tia Mancini had come up with key information and was willing to both help and share intel. She'd made a new ally in Gianna Murphy in El Paso, and Jason Lopez had surprisingly let her take the lead when it mattered.

But in the end, Lucy refused to be a doormat. Yes, she was a rookie and she would swallow her pride and take any assignment Rachel gave her. But she wouldn't let Rachel diminish her accomplishments or make her feel inferior or like she had to walk on eggshells all the time. So if Rachel didn't give her a real chance, she would put in her request for a new assignment at the end of the year.

Rachel pushed her keyboard up under her monitor

and said, "Sorry about that, I had to get that message out."

"No problem."

"I received your request for time off. You put in extensive hours this weekend for the task force, and while we don't specifically have comp time, Abigail informed me that there's an unofficial use of comp time after cases that have required, by necessity, overtime hours."

"I have the vacation days," she said.

"Barely." Rachel looked at her for a few seconds. To make her uncomfortable? To expect her to talk? Lucy wasn't fazed. "What are your plans?"

"Excuse me?"

"I'm interesting in your plans for your three days off. I'm assuming time away with your husband. You're not on call on the weekend so you could take five days. Go back to that cabin of yours in Colorado."

Lucy considered saying that's exactly what she planned on doing, but why lie? Lying to her boss had gotten her into hot water earlier this year. While she might not get what she wanted, she wasn't going to lie again.

"I'm going to Seattle. Hope Anderson will be discharged from the hospital in the morning, and my brother is flying her and Bella Caruso to Seattle. Hope's grandparents are coming this weekend, and after talking to Hope I think I can help her before she sees them. She's not going to heal in a week, but . . . well, I have some experience in this type of counseling."

That was the truth . . . and a bit of a fib. She helped victims in the heat of the moment—at the hospital, after a crime, when they were emotionally on edge. Their extreme emotions helped Lucy maintain her calm edge so she could listen and know exactly what to say and when.

Long-term counseling brought her past too close to

the surface. And while she understood what Hope had endured, fifteen months of forced prostitution was far beyond what Lucy had experience with.

Yet she'd felt a kinship with Hope, and Hope sensed it too. She knew she could help. Not only with Hope, but with Bella, but she didn't say that to Rachel. Lucy might want to extend the olive branch to her boss, but she recognized that RCK, and JT Caruso in particular, was a sore point right now.

"I appreciate you being honest about this."

Lucy nodded. She knew she had to come clean, get everything out on the table. It couldn't be easy having Kate and Noah around, interviewing staff, asking questions. But if she didn't face the repercussions now, she'd regret it. Living like this, waiting for the proverbial other shoe to drop, was no solution.

"I am sorry I lied about San Diego," Lucy said. "I didn't know you and I suppose it's difficult for me to trust a new boss, just like it was difficult for you to trust me. Noah and I had worked together on many cases, even before I was an agent, and he was my trainer. We had a . . . well, a symbiotic relationship, I guess you could say. When I returned from my honeymoon I felt uncomfortable, like I'd missed something. I tried too hard to make you like me. And everything I did failed. So yeah—when I went to San Diego, I didn't feel like the truth was an option. I am sorry."

Rachel nodded, but didn't say anything. Lucy continued. "I want to go to Seattle to talk to Hope, to make sure Bella is okay, to wrap up some of the details for the prosecutors. These girls aren't going to talk to just anyone, and while Laura at Ruth's House has experience with this, we may need the girls to testify. I can help them with that. They'll know that I'll be there when the time comes, and I can only make that promise face to face."

"You're right. There's no need to take any vacation time. I'll approve your trip to Seattle as official business. All I want in return is a status report on the case by Monday morning."

Lucy must have had a surprised look on her face. "Thank you," she managed to get out.

"I had a heart-to-heart with the assistant director last night. He called me to apologize—I was stunned, to say the least. I didn't expect it."

Lucy had no idea that Rick was going to call Rachel.

"He apologized for undermining my authority and authorizing you to work for the task force without going through me. He explained that you and he had a personal as well as professional relationship and he trusts you explicitly. He told me about his relationship with JT Caruso, that they go way back to Navy boot camp, and that because RCK has high security clearance and has worked for the government from time to time, that he sometimes bends the rules when they ask for help. I was—well, I guess there is no better word than stunned. I knew most of what he said, but I appreciated his honesty."

"I'm glad."

"He told me you sent him an email."

Lucy froze. Why would Rick mention that?

"That you asked that he not put you in this position again, that any requests for your official assistance should come through your direct supervisor. He didn't go so far as to say he would always do so, but he did acknowledge that he should have looped me in earlier. I appreciate you standing up for me."

"You said something earlier that resonated. It was about trust. You don't trust me, and I reflected that I didn't trust you—not because of anything specific that you did, but because you never gave me an opportunity. I don't trust easily, and I realized that I didn't give you any opportunity to earn my trust. We both made mistakes." Lucy wasn't going to take all the blame in this, but she certainly had her fair share. "And I want to fix it."

"Consider it fixed. When you return on Monday, clean slate."

Lucy didn't want to look a gift horse in the mouth. "I appreciate it."

"Can I ask you something off the record?"

Lucy didn't know if she could trust her—yet didn't they just have the conversation that they needed to work on that? "Yes."

"Did you go to Mexico to rescue Baby Joshua last year?"

"I'll answer that question honestly, but first I want to know why it's so important to you."

"Because all the official reports said you weren't down there, but you were missing for two days. No one knew where you were—and everything about that rescue has been classified. When you surfaced, you were in the hospital in McAllen overnight for undisclosed injuries. At the same hospital that Baby Joshua was taken to."

What should she say? She couldn't lie—not when they were so close to having a good working relationship. But she couldn't tell her the entire truth.

"Off the record," Lucy said, and waited for her nod. "I didn't go to Mexico to rescue Baby Joshua. However, I was there for an unrelated reason. The reason the files are redacted is to protect innocent people." As well as others, but Lucy would never talk about what happened in the Rogan family. "I ended up on the same military transport out of Guadalajara as Baby Joshua. That's probably more than I should say, but it is the truth."

Rachel nodded. "Thank you."

"I appreciate you understanding why I need to go to

Seattle. When I return, I'll have the report and be ready to get back to work."

"I'm sure there'll be plenty to do." She handed Lucy a folder.

Lucy took it, but didn't open it.

"I read over all your reports again," Rachel said. "You're not a part of the Hostage Rescue Team, yet you have worked several hostage negotiations over the last year—and even two prior to your assignment in San Antonio. Perhaps more than two—that's all that was in your file."

If she was waiting for Lucy to expand, she would be disappointed.

"Yes, ma'am."

"I talked to Leo Proctor. In addition to being a decorated SWAT captain, he's the head of our local HRT. He recommended you for a spot on his team. To be honest, I planned on recommending another agent. So I requested the transcript of the hostage negotiation in San Diego. It was flawless, but you had a personal connection because of the victims, so I wanted another case to analyze. So I pulled your other files. You, Brad Donnelly, and three civilians were held hostage in a private residence. That included two children who were in immediate danger. You were calm enough to manipulate the suspect into walking into the sniper's line of sight. It's a rare skill set that you have. So I ended up passing your name up the ladder. The next four-week training program is at Quantico starting May fifteenth. If you pass, you'll be certified and can be called out or loaned out as needed. There's a small stipend, but I sense you wouldn't care about that."

"No, ma'am."

"Will you do it?"

"Yes." She didn't even have to think about it. She'd been considering asking for a spot on the ERT—Evidence

Response Team—because she had experience with processing crime scenes. But hostage negotiation was something she found herself not only good at, but she felt like she really could make a difference.

"Good. Go home and get ready for your trip."

"Thank you, ma'am. I appreciate you giving me another chance to earn your trust and respect." She got up and had her hand on the doorknob.

"Lucy?"

She turned and faced her boss.

"You earned it."

Though Sean detested flying commercial, it would have taken far too long to get to Seattle in his Cessna and they'd have had to stop to refuel. Nate was staying at the house with Bandit. Sean wanted to bring the dog, but the sole direct flight they could get out of San Antonio that afternoon would have insisted he be crated in the cargo hold. Sean didn't want to do that to his dog.

The benefit of commercial flying, however, was the opportunity to relax. Sean bought first-class tickets, and Lucy didn't complain. She leaned back and closed her eyes.

"So Rachel finally came to her senses."

"Sean." She took his hand.

"I know, I know, we talked about it. But you can't expect me to get over how she treated you."

"What doesn't kill us makes us stronger."

He leaned over and kissed her. "You're strong enough for two."

"It was really sweet of you to let Jason and his family stay at the house this weekend. I didn't know he was in a studio apartment."

"Well, I was hard on him."

"We both were."

"I talked to my realtor and she's going to find him a few places to look at, take some of the stress off. I know what it's like being separated from the love of my life, I can't imagine living without you for four months."

"What are you going to do with yourself when I'm at Quantico for a month?"

"Annoy the hell out of Patrick." Sean grinned and leaned back in the wide, comfortable first-class seat. "Seriously, though, now that I'm back with RCK I have plenty to do, though I'm going to be traveling a bit more than I like."

"Because there's no one else who can do what you do."

One of Sean's key talents was breaking into secure buildings. RCK often was hired by businesses and governments to test their security. Sean worked with his brother Duke and Lucy's brother Patrick to develop better security protocols. Sean often admitted to Lucy that he loved that part of his job. Unfortunately, it required him to be gone for days, sometimes a week, at a time.

"I'll double up the jobs while you're gone so I don't pine away," Sean teased. "It'll be good for you to reconnect with Patrick and Elle."

Lucy glared at him. "Stop."

"She's not that bad. And Patrick loves her."

"I don't get it."

"I do."

Lucy looked at him. "Why?"

"Elle keeps Patrick on his toes. She's both smart and physical. She never stops moving. And she has a huge heart."

"Too big sometimes. And the jury is still out on the smarts."

"Ouch."

"She's book smart, but she has no common sense. And Patrick is constantly cleaning up her messes."

"Maybe he likes to do it."

Lucy hadn't really thought about it that way. "As long as he's happy," she relented.

"That's what we all want." He rubbed his finger on her palm. "I'm happy, Lucy. We've been married for five months, we have a dog, a house, jobs we love, and each other."

"Please don't jinx it."

"I'm not. I'm going to be grateful every day I wake up with you, and thankful every night when I go to sleep."

"You're lucky you mentioned you're happy with me before you mentioned Bandit. I swear, I'm going to get jealous over an animal."

"There's room in my heart for both of you." He laughed and kissed her.

She swatted him, then leaned over and put her head on his shoulder. "How's JT? I didn't see him after we left the hospital yesterday morning."

"He's going to stay in Seattle with Bella for a while. Taking time off from RCK. I don't think he's had a vacation in—well, ever."

"Family is complicated. But they need each other."

They sat in silence for a long time, and Lucy thought Sean had fallen asleep. She wished she could, but she had a difficult time sleeping on planes, or anywhere in public.

"Luce?" Sean said quietly.

"I'm awake."

"Are you really okay?"

She sat up. He was looking at her with the love and affection she'd grown to cherish, and with a hint of worry she always feared.

"I am."

"This case hit much closer to, well, everything you've been through. And yet you're going to Seattle to talk to Hope and the other girls."

"Because I can help them. And by helping I feel . . . free. Empowered. I can't explain it, not really, but I know I can do some good there. I am so impressed with the work that Laura and Adam Dixon have done, they're the real heroes in this."

"Well, for what it's worth, you're going to give Wonder Woman a run for her money in the heroism department."

CHAPTER THIRTY-SIX

Friday

Bella had missed Washington. She'd missed the peace of Bainbridge Island, she'd missed the salt air, the green trees and cool breeze and morning fog.

She sat on the deck of Ruth's House, her hands wrapped around a mug of hot coffee. Morning was her favorite time. A new day, new opportunities, a fresh start. The hint of dawn creeped over the Cascades.

But she may have blown all her new beginnings. She'd had to confess to everything she'd done over the last year, and it wasn't easy. She felt both pride and shame and she didn't know how she was going to get through it.

She'd been independent her entire life. Even before her father gave her to Sergio, she'd run the house. Her mother was hardly capable of taking care of herself, let alone a child. JT was so much older. She didn't blame him for leaving—he thought she was in good hands with their grandmother.

And for a time, it had been bliss. Her grandmother was funny and wise and a great cook.

She was sad that she'd raised a drug addict for a daughter who had married a brute of a man. She'd died not knowing if Bella was dead or alive, and that had haunted Bella for two decades. That, more than anything, had driven her to search for Hope. When she looked at Hope's grandparents and saw the love and fear on their old faces, she didn't want them to die not knowing the truth.

Adam came out onto the deck. He still walked with a cane—he always would. He'd been shot multiple times five years ago overseas and barely survived. But it was the bullet that shattered his knee that had caused the permanent limp. He didn't work overseas anymore, though he raised money and managed Genesis stateside. He'd been such a tough Navy SEAL. Like her brother, Bella couldn't imagine anything could hurt Adam. They were soldiers, they were strong, they were tough as nails.

But she'd seen the soft side, the deep need to right wrongs. And the love. Love she'd turned her back on because, deep down, she didn't think she deserved it.

Adam sat down on the chair next to her, looked out at the lake.

"I'm sorry," she said. Apologizing was hard for her. She didn't say the words lightly. She didn't give fake promises or capitulations. She was sincerely, deeply sorry that she had hurt Adam and Laura. They had loved her unconditionally, but she had imagined conditions that weren't there and built up her walls. Because she didn't know how to give love back.

"All is forgiven."

Her eyes watered. She didn't cry—she hated crying. Tears were for the weak. Tears solved nothing.

But still, her eyes were damp. Adam and Laura were quietly religious people. It sometimes bothered her growing up, and she didn't know why. Now she did. She'd never felt herself worthy of any sort of unconditional love, and that's what they had. They loved without reservation. They loved without barriers. They loved each other and they loved her and they loved everything that God created.

Bella had said many hurtful things to them over the years about a distant and unloving God. She'd seen evil. She'd faced evil. She'd battled evil. She'd never been able to reconcile their faith with her reality.

Until now.

There was evil, but there was also good. Amazing good that Bella had doubted until now. She didn't know if she'd have their faith, but that was okay. She had a kernel of hope that maybe—just maybe—good would triumph over evil. And with that, she could move on.

A rare peace washed over her. Her past would always be a part of her. But it was her *past*.

She wanted a future.

She sat there with Adam and felt his forgiveness. She hadn't realized how much she needed it.

They finished their coffee in silence and watched the sunrise over Seattle.

An anguished cry came from the house. She started to get up.

"Lucy is with her," Adam said.

Giving up control was hard, but Bella leaned back into the chair. "Fifteen months," she said. "It's going to be so hard for her. They had her on uppers and downers and everything in between."

"She's strong. The withdrawals will pass."

"I'd like to stay for awhile."

"This is your home forever, whether you're here or not."

"I don't know what to do with myself," she admitted. "JT wants me to work at RCK. I love my brother, but I don't know if I can work for him."

"Not for him. With him."

"I don't know if that would work."

"They have a DC office. One of the Kincaids runs it."

Bella nodded. JT said she could work in Sacramento with him, Duke, and Jack Kincaid, in DC with Patrick Kincaid, or in Texas with Sean and Kane. He was giving her options. She just didn't know if that's where she was supposed to be.

"What if it doesn't work out?"

"Then it doesn't."

"I just—I don't know. I don't know what I can do. I can't be a cop again. I thought about it, but even if they'd take me back, I don't want to be there. Not knowing everything that I know."

"You'll find the right path. There is always a place for you with Genesis, but I know it's not right for you."

"Why?"

"Because you will never accept that you can't save everyone."

"I know that."

"No, you don't, and that's okay. It hurts you too much to watch those we can't save slip away."

"How do you do it?" She couldn't believe she'd never asked him that before. It seemed like such an obvious question.

"Faith. It's not the answer you want, but it's the only answer I have. We make a difference. I know that. Laura and I will do this work for the rest of our lives. It's our calling. Before you came here, when I was still in the Navy, I was a proud man. Too proud sometimes. I was a SEAL, I was strong, I relished the idea that my men and I were heroes. That we were the mightiest warriors trained on earth. But even back then I felt that I was there temporarily, that there was something for me just out of my reach.

"When my SEAL team was assigned to extract an operative in Thailand, I saw firsthand the tragedy of human trafficking. The commercial sex trade with underage girls and boys, the forced labor camps, the despair and sorrow it forged. Some people call it a vision. A message from God. Or for people who don't believe, a lightbulb moment. I knew I could save one person. And then one more. And then one more. That God didn't want me to fight for my country, but He wanted me to fight for humanity. I'm a patriot, am proud of my Naval career, but at that moment I knew I had another calling.

"So I do it because of what I always said to you. If not me, who? If not now, when? Every person matters. Each and every one."

From the moment Bella arrived at Ruth's House eighteen years ago, when JT brought her here because he didn't know how to help her, Laura and Adam had told her in their own way that she mattered. That she was loved. She never really believed it until now. With all the mistakes she'd made, with all the heartbreak she'd caused JT, Laura, and Adam, she didn't think she deserved anything good.

But she mattered. She, too, made a difference.

"I love you, Adam."

She'd never told him before. She'd never said *I love you* to anyone, not to her mother, not to JT, not to Laura or Adam. She did—she always had—but she'd never recognized it because she was so angry inside she had no love to share. She kept it buried, she kept it separate from who she thought she was.

No more.

"We love you as if you were our own daughter," Adam said, his voice cracking.

Now the tears fell freely, tears that hadn't fallen in years. She got up and hugged Adam tightly.

She was home. And someday, she would know her true path.

That day wasn't today.

And that was okay.

Read on for an excerpt from

SHATTERED
by Allison Brennan

Available in hardcover from Minotaur Books

PROLOGUE

She sat on the edge of her son's bed, clutching his favorite stuffed toy. A dog. Matthew had wanted a puppy for years. She'd convinced her husband that they should get a puppy for Christmas.

But their son would never see another Christmas.

She didn't know how long she sat there, but it was dark when her husband came into the room.

"Please, honey, come to bed."

She stared at the man she had once loved. The man who had fathered her only child. The face she had admired, the smile that made her heart flutter, now made her physically ill. She hated him. She had never hated anyone more than the man she had sworn to love, honor, and cherish. The man she had promised to be faithful to, the man she had promised to stand by in everything life threw at them.

She could barely speak, but she said, "You should have been here."

"Don't—please don't."

Tears flowed, but they didn't soften her heart. Tears of rage were so very different from tears of grief.

"I can't look at you. I can't live with you. It's your fault our son is gone!"

"You don't mean that. Please, I'm sorry. I'll say it as many times—"

"It'll never be enough! *Sorry* doesn't bring Matthew back!"

"I know you're hurting, honey. I'm hurting, too." His eyes wandered to the wall of photos. Of Matthew growing up. Baby. Toddler. Kindergarten. And the last photo, second grade. His last school picture.

His voice cracked. "Stay with your mom for a few days. Until—"

"I'm not coming back."

He reached for her. "I know you're hurt, but we can survive this together."

She jumped up before he could touch her. She didn't know what she'd do if he put his hands on her . . . if he tried to console her.

She might kill him.

Death would be too good for him. He should suffer for the rest of his life. Suffer because *he wasn't here.* Suffer because he had lied, he had cheated, he was a selfish, disgusting excuse for a human being. How had she loved him? Why hadn't she seen the truth before it was too late?

She ran to the door of Matthew's room. The anger and hate bubbled up and overshadowed the deep, numbing pain.

She had never realized how much it would hurt to lose her only child, but if she dwelled on it, let the pain in, she would drown in her grief. Instead, she focused on the reasons Matthew had died. The anger that would keep her breathing.

"I hope you suffer for the rest of your miserable life. I hope you know that because of *you,* my son is dead."

Through the sobs that shook her husband's body, he said, "He's *our* son. Please—don't. Don't do this to me. To us."

"I hate you." Those three words changed everything. There was no going back.

She walked out without another word, without looking at her husband, leaving him sobbing in the middle of their dead son's room.

She hoped he suffered twice as much as she did.

I hate you.

She should have been speaking to a mirror.

CHAPTER ONE

Wednesday

Maxine Revere, investigative reporter, learned the hard way that insinuating herself into the middle of an active police investigation was a recipe for disaster, which is why she focused primarily on missing persons and cold cases. Law enforcement was usually willing to talk when the case was dead in the water. Unsolved cases grated on the nerves of most cops. If Max used her extensive financial resources and media access to gather actionable information, cops would often work with her.

Worse than shaking things up in the middle of an investigation was showing up right before a trial. The bad guy was behind bars, the powers that be were a 1,000 percent positive they had the right person, and Max's involvement caused the chief of police, district attorney, and prosecutor to lose sleep. She didn't much care—if they were confident with their evidence, there was nothing to lose sleep over.

But Max rarely did anything the easy way, so when her old college friend—okay, old college ex-boyfriend—

called her weeks before his wife was to go on trial for the murder of their only child, desperately believing that she was innocent, Max agreed to fly to Scottsdale, Arizona, to listen to John's theory which—she had to admit—sounded intriguing over the phone.

Still, in Max's experience, while occasionally the wrong person was accused and imprisoned, the prosecution rarely went forward with a costly trial when they didn't have ample evidence for a conviction. Not only because of the cost, but politics. A high-profile case such as a wealthy mother killing her eight-year-old son? Everyone was under a microscope from the beginning. With such scrutiny, the DA wouldn't let it go this far without *something* solid to sway a jury. So even though it was John Caldwell—a man Max respected and even admired—asking for her help, she needed more than his faith in his wife's innocence.

It was the cold cases that had her flying from New York to Phoenix. Three cold cases in the southwest that were eerily similar to the murder of Peter Caldwell.

Max had interviewed many defendants and witnesses during her decade-long career as an investigative journalist. Most of the lawyers she dealt with either wanted nothing to do with her or attempted to manipulate her into printing only information favorable to their client.

She didn't know what to expect from Charles North, the respected criminal defense lawyer who represented Blair Caldwell. But a condition of her interview with Blair was that she would first meet with North, where he would "lay down the rules."

Max always enjoyed these conversations.

Boxer, North, and Associates had the top floor of a high-rise in downtown Phoenix, boasting views of Chase Field. As Max waited for North in the lobby—

decorated in subdued desert hues—she wondered why Blair asked that the interview be conducted in her attorney's office. Blair had expressly said she hadn't wanted Max to come to her house. Originally, she'd planned to meet with the Caldwells yesterday, but instead John came alone to the Biltmore, where Max was staying, and gave her what she considered a lame excuse for Blair's absence. They'd talked for several hours, and the anguish in John's voice was clear.

His son's death had gutted him and John was desperate to protect his wife. She was innocent, the result of a legal system gone awry, according to John.

"Blair couldn't kill anyone, let alone our son. But the police couldn't find a suspect, they twisted everything around, and arrested Blair. They have no evidence. None."

Max had reminded John multiple times—because he didn't seem to absorb her meaning—that she would give him the truth, but that maybe a private investigator would be more appropriate than an investigative reporter.

"Blair's attorney has a private investigator on staff," John had said. "They don't care who *killed Peter. They only want to prove it wasn't Blair."*

John was correct, but Max had explained—twice—that she didn't work active homicide investigations. Cold cases were different because—usually—the crime was more than a year old and the police didn't have a suspect. The only time she stepped into a hot case was for a missing person because a media spotlight could often be helpful.

John was convinced that if Max solved the three cold cases that were similar to Peter's murder, that she would de facto solve Peter's murder. Max thought he was stretching. Yet here she was, waiting to talk to Blair and her attorney. John was one of Max's few close friends.

How could she say no? How could she turn her back on a friend when she didn't have many to spare?

Besides, the three cold cases were more than a little intriguing. Peter Caldwell aside, if her staff had presented her with the cases as a possible investigation for her monthly crime show, *Maximum Exposure*, she would have seriously considered them.

Her phone rang and she almost sent it to voice mail, but it was a call she'd been expecting. She stepped away from the receptionist and answered.

"Counselor," she said, her voice warm and smooth, "I've been expecting your call."

"You threatened me, and I've had enough."

She went from cordial to heated in a heartbeat. "I didn't threaten you, Mr. Stanton. I gave you a courtesy call."

"Courtesy? That's what you call exploiting my son's murder?"

She went from heated to angry in the next heartbeat.

"I said I didn't need your permission, but I want your help." Her voice was even but sharp. "You're the one who has been avoiding my calls."

"Let me explain something to you, Ms. Revere," Stanton said. "Without me, you have nothing. No one will speak to you. You step out of line, you will be arrested. My son is off-limits. Are we clear?"

"Your son's murder is unsolved, and I believe I can solve it." Why did she say that? She'd never solved a murder nearly twenty years cold. It was next to impossible.

But she was angry, so she didn't backtrack—not that she would have. Showing doubt, showing weakness, wouldn't get her what she needed.

"Do you think I haven't used every legal resource at my disposal to solve Justin's murder? He was my son, I'm the district attorney, and I have never forgotten."

Max dialed back her anger. Just a bit. "My track record speaks for itself, Mr. Stanton. I have connected Justin's murder with two, possibly three similar crimes, but I need more information. Meet with me. Please," she added, "I'll explain my theory and share everything I have learned." Which was very little at this point. "If after we meet you are still adamant about not helping, I'll respect that."

"And back down?"

"Of course not," she said. Obviously the San Diego District Attorney didn't know her reputation. "I'll still investigate. I simply won't include you. I'll fly to Idaho and speak with your ex-wife."

"Leave Nelia out of this." She could hear the venom in his voice. Score one for her—she knew how to ensure his cooperation.

"Justin was her son, too."

"Blackmail now?"

"Really, that's what you're going with? Blackmail." Max was trying to give Andrew Stanton some leeway because he had lost his son, but the lawyer was making it difficult for her to play nice.

"Nelia has been through hell, I won't allow you—"

"Stop," Max said. She spotted who she presumed to be North's assistant standing by the reception desk looking at her. "You have my producer's phone number. Call him. He'll answer your questions and you can feel free to browbeat and threaten him over the phone. Ben lives for conflict. But I *will* be in San Diego tomorrow afternoon. Either you work with me or you don't, but you're not going to stop me."

She ended the call and took a long, deep breath. She

needed to regain her composure if she was going to be on her A game with Blair Caldwell.

Max was digging a deep hole for herself. The four cases—Peter Caldwell's murder and the three others—had many similarities, but similarities didn't solve crimes. She'd been pulling together research for the last two weeks, and she still had very little to go on. The police had connected none of the four cases, and proving they were linked would be impossible if she couldn't access police records and forensics reports. The first two homicides were unsolved; in the third the father was in prison; and the last—Peter—was built on circumstantial evidence.

She and her staff were working several threads, but so far nothing she pulled led anywhere. Max could neither prove—nor disprove—a connection. She needed to be in the field, talking to people who had been there, reading the files, analyzing the data, reinterviewing witnesses and suspects. And even then, she had never tackled an assignment of this magnitude.

Yet, you tell Stanton that you can solve his son's murder.

She had put her reputation on the line with one angry comment. That deep hole she saw herself standing next to had just gotten a whole lot wider.

"Ms. Revere?" The young man who had been standing at the reception desk walked over to her. "I'm Ron Lee. Mr. North is ready for you."

"Thank you," she said formally and pulled herself together. She didn't know why this investigation had gotten under her skin. She prided herself on maintaining a level of detachment from the victims, the surviving family, and law enforcement. But lately, she'd found herself more wrapped up in the lives of the people involved in an investigation than she was comfortable with. She couldn't seem to find the personal detachment that had served her well for so long.

Max followed Ron down the wide hallway, which turned before reaching double doors with CHARLES NORTH engraved on a gold plaque. The assistant knocked, waited for permission to enter, then grandly opened both doors.

"Ms. Maxine Revere," Ron announced formally.

North rose from his desk and crossed the large corner office. Blair wasn't in the room.

He took her hand. "Ms. Revere, I'm Charles North. We spoke on the phone." He turned to his assistant. "Ron, please sit with Mrs. Caldwell until I need her."

"Yes, sir." Ron closed the doors on his way out.

North motioned for Max to sit at a conference table that could comfortably sit twelve. He sat at the head. Common tactic. Max smiled and took a seat two down from him. "Thank you for arranging this meeting."

"As I told you last week," North said, "I disapprove of Mr. Caldwell's investigation and his ill-conceived theory. He is a man grasping at straws who doesn't understand the legal system and the primary goal of my team. Our goal is for the jury to return a not guilty verdict. We believe that the State will not be able to prove their case against my client."

As with many lawyers who Max had met over the years, North spoke clearly and formally.

"You indicated during our earlier conversation that the prosecution lacked evidence, but you were not specific."

"I will not outline our legal strategy to the media prior to trial. As I also said over the phone, I would consent to an interview after the trial is concluded. It is my understanding that you will be covering the trial for NET?"

It was worded as a question, because Max hadn't actually said anything about media involvement in Blair's trial.

"NET will be covering the trial."

"But not you?"

"Either myself or Ace Burley, NET's crime reporter." She didn't want to cover the trial, but she was already out here. She might be stuck with it. NET gave her a lot of leeway to run her show and her investigations as she wanted—a condition of her agreeing to host *Maximum Exposure* in the first place. So when they asked for something—like coverage of a trial—she generally agreed. It was her least favorite aspect of her job.

"Then what is your interest in this case? Other than the fact that you're John Caldwell's ex-girlfriend."

Had John or Blair told the lawyer about her relationship with John? She hadn't expected the information to be kept secret, but she certainly hadn't intended to lead with the fact that she'd dated John for a year while they were both at Columbia University.

Max leaned back in the leather chair. "Mr. North, Blair already agreed to talk to me. Please bring her in."

"I advised Mrs. Caldwell not to speak with you. She overruled me, but be aware that she is only doing this for her husband. I ask that you consider that before using anything she says."

Max already suspected that Blair agreed to talk to her because John wanted it. She said, "Over the past decade, I have covered dozens of trials, investigated hundreds of cold cases, and interviewed thousands of witnesses, victims, suspects, and family members."

"Your point, Ms. Revere?"

"You have a job, I have a job. Let me do my job. Because whether or not Blair Caldwell speaks to me is irrelevant. I'm not packing up and going home."

Charles sighed. "I doubted you would, though I had hoped."

"Does the truth scare you?"

"The truth is subjective."

Max laughed, but she wasn't amused. "Truth is *objective*. It's neither good nor bad. It's what we do with the truth that is subjective, because *we* are flawed."

The defense lawyer sat there for a moment. "I think you and the Caldwells are making a huge mistake."

"I'm not making a mistake," Max said. "I can't speak for John or Blair." She leaned forward, kept her voice calm and friendly. She may not be able to sway the lawyer, but she didn't want him to actively oppose her efforts. "Charles, I have one question for you and I promise that I will not quote you, I will not even mention the situation except for what has already been reported in the press."

"I can't promise to answer, but you may ask."

"The local news reported a leak out of the DA's office that they'd offered Blair a plea deal and she declined. I'm not asking for the details," she added quickly, knowing what his primary objection would be, "but did you recommend to your client to accept or decline?"

He stared at her for a long moment. He would make an outstanding poker player—maybe that's why he was so good as a trial lawyer.

"Wait here."

He walked out of the interview room without answering her question.

She liked him.

Charles North was a top criminal defense attorney, and his firm wasn't cheap. He'd made his name after defending a professional athlete charged with killing his mistress. The jury had been hung, and the prosecution retried the case, and then lost—a not guilty verdict. North had made a small fortune on the two trials, but the ballplayer had walked free. Max didn't know if he was guilty or innocent. She'd never looked into the case. But North had been praised by his colleagues, including the prosecution, for his professionalism.

She'd always wondered what motivated lawyers to specialize in criminal defense. Some, perhaps, because of the money. A big defense trial could be extremely lucrative. She'd known enough lawyers in her life to know that most didn't take cases out of some noble cause of righting wrongs, believing that their clients were always innocent and they were champions of a corrupt court system. Most treated their clients as a job. They did due diligence, ensured legal rules were followed, and worked out plea deals to the benefit of their clients. The most *noble*—for lack of a better word—defense lawyers believed in the system just as much as the prosecution. They went into practice because they believed in their hearts and souls that every person, rich or poor, black or white, deserved a fair trial. That the goal wasn't to win or lose per se, but to ensure that the police behaved, that the prosecution played aboveboard, that the accused was treated appropriately. And yes, that the evidence was fair and untainted.

North's goal was clearly to get a not guilty verdict, which didn't mean he thought his client was innocent. That only meant he thought the prosecution had no case.

There was no way in hell the DA or the cops would meet with Max. She'd gone through the motions—if necessary, she could say so-and-so declined to comment. But she wasn't expecting a quote or cooperation. The only way Max could learn about the case was through the defense and it was clear North wouldn't give her anything—except allowing her to talk to his client against his advice.

She was going to have to get everything she could out of Blair Caldwell.

Sometimes what someone said—or didn't say—wasn't as important as how they behaved.